GOING THE WHOLE HOG

Erica Adams

Little Crow Publishing
32 Molyneux Park Road
Tunbridge Wells
Kent TN4 8DY

e-mail: littlecrow@ukf.net

A catalogue record for this book is available from the British Library

Printed and bound in Great Britain
Typesetting by David Brown, Maynards Green, Sussex

Cover: Moffitt Design
www.moffittdesign.co.uk

ISBN 0 9532239 2 2

Other books by the same author

THE PIG AND I

THE PIGNAPPER

You won't be able to read them
in public for fear of letting out
uncontrollable piggy snorts and
squeals of laughter.

I dedicate this book to my husband Maurice's replacement hip which enables him to stand and do the vegetables – and pour drinks.

My special thanks also go to:-

The rest of my husband.

My daughter, **Jan**, for her patient good humour and professional skill in setting up the cover design.

Dick Purdue of SuperiorBooks.com for his expertise, and the generous amount of time he has freely given in the final revision.

Christina Jones for her bubbly, enthusiastic encouragement and good advice.

Rhona Martin and the Tunbridge Wells Novel Group (who are thankfully nothing like the Novel Group in this book). And to **Sheila Alcock** of the same Writers' Circle for urging me on.

Sue Wheeler for passing on her medical knowledge regarding ripped off toes.

Harry Collins, jeweller, for his advice on the amethyst ring.

One

'I'd like a book on how to use a computer,' Maeve Salmon said. And the very words thrilled her.

'You should have gone over there to Enquiries,' the librarian sniped, 'but, as you're here ... She sighed heavily, eyes flicking back and forth along the lengthening queue ... 'what kind of computer is it?'

'Well it's a big rectangular box,' Maeve explained, motioning its size and, in so doing, bumping her hands into her unfettered breasts which hung lower than usual.

'But what *kind* is it. A Mac or a PC?'

'A Mac or a PC,' Maeve repeated, hopeful that Miss Make-the-customer-feel-small would explain the question.

'Well g-won lady, *tell* her.'

Maeve turned sharply, seeing a short dark man with mangy-looking dreadlocks standing behind her. 'Well g-won,' he repeated, 'I don' have all day to wais' standin' here y'know.'

'Is it a Mac or a PC?' the bespectacled woman repeated, her voice now quite shrill.

'I ... I don't know,' Maeve stammered, 'but it's mushroom coloured and ... and there are two slits in the front ...'

'Oh bwoy, now I heard everyting,' the Rasta muttered. 'Don't she fuckin' know nuttin' except how to swing her tits.'

Maeve felt herself flush and inwardly cursed that Charlie Dimmock whose lead she had followed. She would rein in her breasts with a bra the minute she got home. *And* abandon any idea of a water feature.

'Do you have windows?' the woman said, now on a different tack.

'Yeees,' Maeve said slowly.

'Ninety-five or ninety-eight?'

'Not that many, it's only two bedroo...' she stopped as loud guffaws erupted from the gathering crowd.

'Oh bwoy, she don' live in Buckingham Palace den,' chuckled the man, patently enjoying himself now and in no hurry to move.

'You *look* as if you'd have Windows Ninety-five,' Miss Starchy-pants-Prim-and-Proper announced in a way that made Maeve think that having a rampant venereal disease might be more acceptable. 'Wait there,' she abruptly ordered, flying off with fleeting apologies to the muttering book-clutching queue, then whizzing back with a dog-eared volume, barking, 'Try reading this *Windows for Dummies.*'

'But I'm not going in for window dressing,' Maeve protested as the librarian snatched the library card from her hand, swizzed it through a slot, hammered the date in the front of the book, then shoved it and the card back at her.

'Oh bwoy, did yo hear dat,' chortled the man, exposing the pink side of his hand as he motioned attention to her, as if this free entertainment was all his doing.

If he wasn't careful she would clout him Maeve thought fiercely, never ever having wanted to hit anyone as much as she wanted to hit him now.

'Windows is a computer operating system,' the librarian said shrilly.

'She didden even know dat,' crowed the man, beaming round, raising titters from the eager audience.

And that's when Maeve let fly.

A woman screeched loudly as the Rasta's tottering clodhoppers smashed onto her sandal-clad foot. The queue, emitting a collective squeal, staggered backwards as the impact, like a Mexican wave, travelled through it.

'And they reckon school teaching's stressful,' wailed the librarian, clawing her hair.

'Hey man, dat clout wid your handbag was quite funny,' giggled the man goodnaturedly, rubbing the side of his head, well cushioned with matted curls.

'No real harm done,' grunted the woman whose foot had been stamped on, equally magnanimously. Then like a yogi taking up the stork position, she lifted her foot to rub her crushed toes, exposing a grimy slip and God knows what else - Maeve didn't allow her eyes to linger to find out.

The librarian, her mousy brown hair now sticking out at all angles, snatched off her glasses, leant forward across the counter, peered closely at Maeve, straightened herself, shoved her specs back on, grunted, reorganised them to rest on both ears, grabbed up the book and propelled it forward. 'Just *read* it,' she screeched, the neon strip lighting reflecting off her lenses combining ominously with the dangerous glints in her eyes.

Maeve looked down at the tatty book. She hovered, unsure.

'Go! Just pick it up and go!' the petty tyrant yelled, setting one elbow beating up and down as she reached past with the other arm for the Rasta's book.

'That just missed my nose,' Maeve protested, forced to dart back from the flailing funny bone.

'Pity,' the librarian spat, wrestling the book from the tightly clasped hand of the grinning man.

'Bwoy, I wouldn't-a missed dat, mus' come here more offen,' he pronounced as he finally relinquished it.

Maeve tottered out, avoiding eye contact with anyone. She stopped by the notice board outside in the library foyer, vacantly staring at the postcards and ads whilst trying to compose herself. And, as she sightlessly stared, words began to come into focus - meaningful, profound words. She sharpened her gaze, pulse quickening, as she read a badly typed postcard:-

Are you a writer, or do you want to be become one? If so, join the TOOTHING WRITERS' CIRCLE to meet fiendly helpful people with the same interest. Contact Mrs Shakespeare on ...

This Mrs Shakespeare was obviously not much of a typist but her name was encouraging. Galvanised, Maeve dug out a pen and an old receipt from her dented bag, took the number down, and hurried off to the car park.

Back home, even before recradling her breasts in her 36D bra, she punched out the number and waited, a strange hunger building up inside her. It was as if she was starving, yearning for sustenance, though she'd had a good breakfast.

'Hello, who is it?' a woman answered, just as she was on the point of replacing the phone.

'My name is Maeve Salmon,' she replied, feeling strangely nervous.

'Hello Maeve, if you're chasing up your Betterware order I'm afraid you're a little premature. We're still waiting for the electrostatic dusters to come in.'

'No. I am enquiring about the Writers' Circle.'

'Hang on,' the woman said, immediately bellowing, 'Sher -

LEE,' in her ear, then, in answer to a faint responding cry, yelling: 'It's someone called Maeve about your writers' circus.'

Maeve was wondering whether to put the phone down before identifying herself further when a soft voice said:

'Hello. Shirley Shakespeare here. It's Maeve is it?'

'Yes. Maeve Salmon,' she confirmed.

'Sorry about Parsnip. Since my husband Willy left me she's been my flat mate. We're not lessies though,' she hastily added, 'it just helps out with the rent. Are you a writer Maeve?'

'Well, in a way. I'm trying to write a novel.'

'I like your humility,' Shirley purred. 'Trying. Trying. If only some of the others in our circle knew the word.'

'I mean it,' Maeve stressed. 'I'm just a beginner.'

'Just the kind of person we're looking for,' Shirley said, in the voice of a covert sadist on the lookout for someone to torture. 'You've just missed the Circle's monthly meeting but why not give our Novel Group workshop a try - it's held on the first Tuesday each month and we meet at Hugos' house. Just bring what you're writing along and read out the first four pages.'

'Yes, I'd like to come, where does Hugo live?' Maeve asked, her heart giving a little flutter like the wings of a baby bird being pushed from its nest.

Shirley Shakespeare let out a trill of merry laughter. 'He's known as Hugos, Maeve, not Hugo. He was christened Hugo S. Thayre, but was always called Hugos, a witticism thought up by his parents. Apparently they always had it in for him, even as a kid.'

'So where does Hugos Thayre live then?' Maeve asked, only realising the weird humour of his parents after she'd uttered the name.

'Number four Dickens Road, do you know where that is?'

'Yes, quite near me. I could walk it.'

'Excellent Maeve. Quite excellent. We start at eight so I'll see you there then. Any more questions?

'Yes. Did you say your friend was called Parsnip?' she asked, wanting to establish that Shirley Shakespeare's flat-mate's raucous call hadn't affected her ears.

'Yes, she is known as Parsnip.'

'Unusual,' Maeve muttered, wanting to know why but not wishing to get tied up in another Hugos Thayre.

'She claims it's because her pa's snip didn't work,' Shirley kindly offered. 'You know, his vasectomy. She alleges that because of this cock up at the Marie Stopes Clinic she was an unwanted child - always plays on people's sympathies. But I believe she's made the whole thing up because I was at school with her and it was only after she'd reached puberty that we all started calling her Parsnip - and if you could see her putty colour and peculiar shape you'd understand why.'

'Oh,' Maeve said, trying to conjure up a mental picture of her. 'Is she a member of the Writers' Circle too?'

'Parsnip a writer! Good God no,' Shirley burst out as if she'd been talking about a real vegetable. As if a turnip or swede would have stood more chance.

After she'd hung up Maeve went straight to her *Pig 2000 Calendar* to write the date of the next Novel Group meeting down. It would be a reminder, but she wasn't sure if she'd have the courage to go. As she unhitched it off the back of the bathroom door she saw with dismay that it still displayed January, the month that poor Hector had died. She dabbed at her eyes with the end of a towel trying not to look at the actual date, but her eyes were drawn to it like twin searchlights seeking out pain. Printed in light grey across the square representing the traumatic day that transformed her from wife to widow, was the picture of a pig sitting next to a computer screen with the words *Don't hog the computer* printed underneath it. Strange that that was the very day her computer-mad husband had actually stopped hogging it, she thought sadly, hurriedly turning the pages to April, the current month.

But she'd missed the first Tuesday, so she flicked forward to the first one in May seeing *When in doubt follow your snout* was printed across it. And her spirits lifted, displacing her doubt like a burst water main dislodging a manhole cover. She had been in doubt, but this was a clear sign. Across the square, she scribbled down the Novel Group details. She *would* follow her snout to Hugos Thayre's house in Dickens Road. This porcine saying had confirmed it.

Now all she had to do was read the *Windows for Dummies* book, learn how to use Hector's peculiar computer typewriter, then go over and over the first chapter of her novel so that when she read it out they'd marvel that such writing could come from a raw beginner such as herself.

She took up the library book and began to read.

Two hours later, dejected, sore-eyed and headachy, she gave up because in all that gobbledy-gook she'd ploughed through, there was not one word on how to switch the bloody thing on!

Two

Maeve groaned, lay down her pen, flacking her aching hand around. She'd been gripping the biro for over three hours but still the characters in her story clamoured to escape from her capricious mind to the durable safety of paper.

She thumbed through the last few pages, heart sinking as she took in the increasingly illegible scrawl. Why was she bothering? she brooded. No publisher would be able to read it. It was hard enough even for her. She turned her gaze longingly to the typewriter attached to the computer further along the desk. If she couldn't discover how to work it soon she'd have to fork out on an old-fashioned manual one. Galvanised by the thought that she would copy it out into neat type by one means or another, she took up the pen again but, just as she did so, the phone started ringing.

Hoping whoever was on the other end would give up, she began writing. But the telephone kept up its nagging call, ruining her concentration, until at last she banged the pen down and marched out to answer it on her bedside phone next door.

'Maeve Salmon here. Who is it?' she said briskly.

'Hello mother,' her daughter replied in a jolly voice.

'Oh hello, it's you Freda.'

'You sound stressed. You're missing him aren't you. Why *don't* you come and live here with us.'

Freda was on her pet subject again. Ever since Hector had died her kind-hearted daughter had been urging her to move in with them, but Maeve knew they needed their privacy as much as she needed hers. She remembered hearing one of their night-time sessions when she and Hector had stayed there last year.

'Why *don't* you,' Freda wheedled.

Deciding her daughter needed some kind of explanation instead of the usual blunt turn-down, she started: 'If ever I go stone deaf *then* I'll ...'

'What do you *mean*?' Freda cut in. 'What's going stone deaf got to do with it?'

Really, you'd think a daughter who'd passed all her exams and had once been a school teacher would be quicker on the uptake, she thought, glimpsing herself in the wardrobe mirror and seeing that, since that morning's session at the hairdresser's, her crowning glory wasn't just the colour of sun kissed hay, it was also its texture.

'If ... ever ... I ... go ... stone ... deaf,' she slowly enunciated, trying to think up a tactful way of putting it, 'I wouldn't be able to hear you and Bernard ...' She stopped, hoping Freda would do her usual butting-in bit, but, cussed as ever, she didn't. 'If ever I go deaf,' she repeated, 'I wouldn't be able to hear you and Bernard ...' She decided to give up on the tact. '... cavorting around in the throes of lust just across the landing.'

The drift of the on-going silence subtly changed from bloody-minded awkwardness to struck-dumb stunned. 'I don't suppose you realise how bad it made me feel when your father and I did occupy your spare bedroom...' she added, forced by Freda's lack of response to go the whole way, '... listening to all that rowdy love-mak...'

'We *don't* cavort,' Freda snapped so fiercely Maeve plumped down on the bed. 'Well, just the once when we got drunk,' she conceded, obviously recalling the noisy night when her poor sleep-deprived mother had had to resort to banging on their bedroom door. 'And why would it make you feel bad anyway?' she demanded hotly. 'I mean why *bad*?'

'Because you would be having it and I wouldn't,' she blurted. And with a start she realised that those last words that had somehow rushed out were true. She would be jealous of her own daughter. Jealous of her and Bernard making love while she lay uncherished and alone. Hector might have been domineering and insensitive but he had had the normal masculine equipment which he'd quite often used to good effect. 'I might be a senior citizen widow but I still have my needs,' she muttered to justify herself.

'Well stick some cotton wool in your ears,' Freda tittered. 'I don't like to think of you living all alone in Tooting.'

Why *would* a married daughter want her old mother living with her Maeve wondered for the umpteenth time, grateful for her persistent offer, yet at the same time perplexed and amazed by it.

'Rooting-Tooting-Tooting's got a lot to offer,' Maeve assured her. 'There's ... there's ... the Bec Bridge Club, full of friendly people. One of them, old Wally Woodcock, wants me to be his regular partner - at bridge that is - though I think he fancies me too.' A stupidly girlish giggle inexplicably rose tinkling from her throat and hurriedly she transformed it to a sharp coughing fit.

'I mean it worked when you and father stayed here for weeks on end last year,' said Freda, totally ignoring the joys of Tooting Bec Bridge Club, old Wally Woodcock and her mother's apparent respiratory problem.

Maeve flopped back on the bed, forgetting her teetering haystack of big looping curls, displacing a spiral truss. 'Yes it did work,' she agreed, threading the fallen sheaf back behind one ear, 'but your father was dying then so that made it better.'

'Mother!' Freda exclaimed, and Maeve pictured her pale freckled face turning bright pink, clashing with her orange hair.

'Well it did make it better in one way - you and Bernard could put up with the lack of privacy and extra work because you knew it wouldn't last for good, knowing it would cease, well, when your father ceased.'

Maeve kicked off her slippers, lifted her legs and wriggled her body straight, knowing her compassionate daughter would be bound to respond and that her novel was on hold for the duration.

'We *enjoyed* having you both with us,' Freda stated, rather over-aggressively.

'That was because he was on his best behaviour. You wouldn't have enjoyed it normally. Before he realised he was at death's door he was impossible. You know that.'

Maeve gazed up at the ceiling, seeing a myriad of cracks, wishing Hector had thought to fill them in before getting ill.

'Poor father. He *was* difficult, but not always.'

'Nearly always. He improved towards the end because he wanted to leave a good impression. I could read him like a book.'

Now a long drawn-out silence, like the hollow sound inside a seashell, assailed Maeve's ear while Freda clearly tried to decide whether to defend her dead father or let it go.

'I worry about you being by yourself,' she eventually said, obviously going for the easy option.

'That's really very kind of you,' Maeve said sincerely, 'but I'll just come down and stay with you now and then ... for little mini-holidays. That would be nice.'

'And ... and if you don't want to live in the cottage with us ... how about ... how about ...,' Freda stammered, still foolishly searching for a compromise that would clear her conscience, '... how about we refurbish the mobile home and you move in there.'

'But that's Hermione's,' Maeve gasped, shooting up straight, dislodging a shower of pins and the rest of the stack. The idea of living in that smelly misnomer balanced on piers of bricks in the old walled yard really shocked her. Yet at the same time she was overwhelmed that Freda was prepared to turf out her beloved pig for her because she adored that big fat sow as much as any mother loved a daughter, probably even more so. 'It's very kind of you, but that's Hermione's home,' Maeve reaffirmed.

'She'll just have to learn to live down in Porkers' Paradise with the rest of them,' Freda said in a small voice, and Maeve could tell she was already regretting her reckless offer.

'No thanks Freda,' she stated firmly, letting her off her self-inflicted hook, 'it's very kind of you, but I'll stay right here where I am.'

'But what about your arthritic hip?' Freda uttered in a last ditch effort.

'That will stay here with me.'

'Until you have to have a false one,' Freda said darkly, not responding to her mother's witty quip.

And, as they said their goodbyes, the image of a surgeon smiling down at his pet Alsatian as it gnawed into the sawn-off ball joint of her femur burgeoned into Maeve's mind. I'll keep the original as long as possible, she decided, staring glumly at her reflection. People might always be telling her she was the spitting image of Joan Collins the glamorous filmstar, but did Joan Collins have a dry worn out hip and dry worn out hair? She thought not. But that's what ordinary people got for growing old. *And* dry, though not yet worn out, private bits. But, thank goodness for KY Jelly. Though, unless she gave in to old Wally's advances, there'd be no use for that again.

Dejected, mostly by the latter thought, she gathered her hair back into a scrunchie then plodded downstairs, wondering whether to dump the half-used tube of KY in the Oxfam charity bag, or keep it in hope. In the kitchen she put the kettle on, took two mugs from the cupboard then remembered and replaced one. She took out a single teabag and a packet of digestives, then put the digestives away too. It wasn't worth opening a new pack just for one. Besides, it was only a reflex action because she wasn't hungry.

She took the cup of tea up to the study, sipped it whilst scrutinising the uncomplicated-looking rows of keys on the typewriter. She'd been a typist when she was young but this typewriter was different. Nowhere could she see the normal gap in which to feed the paper, or a roller to wind it round on, or even a carriage return bar. She wished now that she'd shown an interest when Hector had used it.

A snake of guilt slithered uncomfortably through her. But would he have wanted to spend his precious time handing on the knowledge he'd learned on his two week course? Would he have wanted her interrupting his research on the Internet where he worked against the dying battery of his life clock attempting to prove he was the Queen Mother's first child? No, she decided, he definitely would not.

Too damned right, said his voice, quite clearly, inside her head.

Grateful that for once he agreed with her, even though she'd had to wait till he was dead, she re-examined the typewriter, glad that at least the keys were in the same familiar QWERTY line-up as they always had been. She put the empty cup down on the window ledge, surveyed the equipment once more. If only she knew how to switch the thing on. Several times she'd nearly pushed the big red button at the front of the computer, but she didn't dare go through with it, knowing that red always spelt danger. She'd read that dire things could happen when things went wrong: viruses, bugs, crashes. Hector had suffered them all at various times - even before he had a computer! She waited to hear if he'd laugh at her inner jest but he'd rarely been on her wavelength with humour, so why should his spirit change now.

Without hope she flicked through the *Windows for Dummies* library book again. But nowhere could she find the simple instructions she sought: *Press such and such a switch. Insert paper. Start typing.*

There couldn't be much to it, she reflected. Even complete idiots like her milkman had apparently sussed it, as she knew to her cost because he was always delivering late saying it was because he'd spent half the night surfing ...

The sudden ring of the doorbell cut into her thoughts.

Downstairs, she opened the door, seeing Jatinder Singh from next door hovering on the step.

'Suppose you want your ball back,' she said, affably.

'Yes, if it would be convenient for you Mrs Salmon,' he replied, adopting his sing-song Peter Sellers' lilt as opposed to the coarse London accent she'd heard him use with his mates in the street.

She liked him, liked his whole family. Liked the way he always politely asked before going round to their back garden.

'Do you know how to work a computer?' she asked, seizing her chance.

His dark eyes flashed the kind of contemptuous look that said: *Do you mind?* But he merely said, 'Yes, naturally. What is it you would like to be knowing?'

'I just want to be able to switch it on, then type on it,' she replied lamely.

'It's easy innit,' he said, reverting. 'I'm off school 'cos it's an Inset day so I got time to show you now.'

She didn't want to reveal too much ignorance in one go, so let the Inset day remain a mystery. 'It's up in the spare bedroom-cum-study,' she said, leading the way.

'Okay,' he said, dragging a chair up to the desk to sit beside her, 'first of all let's switch it on, then while it's booting up I'll try to locate your mouse.'

Locate her mouse!

His slim brown finger pushed at the apparently non-dangerous red switch and then he turned and looked at her and she saw, for the first time, that this boy next door, whom she'd watched grow up since he was a babe in arms, had sprouted a faint dark moustache.

'Now for your mouse,' he said, grinning seductively.

She glanced round at the door seeing with a tremor of anxiety that he'd pulled it shut. No doubt this boy who was verging on manhood was bursting with testosterone and uncontrollable urges, she thought, as lines of meaningless white words and numbers zoomed around on the black screen behind his head.

'Look,' she squeaked, pointing. 'Look what's on the TV.'

'That's normal innit, it's what the computer does when it's switched on. Now let's get down to it, let's locate your mouse.' He licked his full lips and his lustrous black eyes held hers for long seconds while the computer whirred.

A scene that had no right being inside a woman of her mature year's head burgeoned in full technicolour. She was lying back on red satin sheets, her long bleached hair fanned out across the pillow, her diaphanous nightdress raised. The dark prince of next-door was standing by her. 'Look, I can see your mouse,' he cried, diving at her.

A sudden musical pling plong mercifully brought her back to reality and she saw that the screen had turned turquoise.

'Look I can see your mouse,' Jatinder cried, diving past her and delving under an untidy pile of papers.

'Call that a mouse,' she quipped, hoping he wouldn't notice her hot cheeks. 'It's barely the shape of one, doesn't have ears and its tail's the wrong end.'

'Cor, you're wicked Mrs Salmon,' Jatinder declared, rummaging around Hector's jumble of papers, searching for something else. 'Ah, and here's the mouse mat,' he proclaimed, pulling out a squarish pad emblazoned with the words I LOVE MY WIFE in bold red letters.

And that snake of remorse slithered its way back inside Maeve, winding itself around her heart, squeezing the life out of it. Hector had loved her enough to have this declaration printed on his mouse's mat. She should have been more demonstrative. Should have cuddled him and kissed him more. Been more affectionate, let him know she cared. Then small letters in the bottom right hand corner caught her eye: *But I love my Mouse more. Mickey Mouse Disney Corporation.*

'It's an advertising joke innit,' said Jatinder, obviously noticing the dagger sticking out of her heart, plunged there by Hector, mercifully stabbing the life-constricting serpent at the same time.

Jatinder pushed the typewriter in front of her, placed the mouse on its hurtful mat, then pointed at the screen saying, 'First you gotta learn the lingo. This might look like a telly but it's called a monitor, and those symbols there on the desktop, they're called icons.'

'Where?' she asked, perplexed because she could see nothing approaching a picture of the Madonna or The Pope on the desktop and, besides, he wasn't looking down at the desk, he was looking up at the screen.

'That's called the desktop, the opening screen,' he explained with a sigh.

'Why?' she asked, frazzled already, her brain doggedly clinging to the notion that a monitor was a child who helped a teacher, and an icon was the image of a holy person.

'Because it's like a real desktop innit.' He looked around at the chaos on the real desktop. 'And, like real desktops,' the Peter Sellers' lilt reappeared, 'you have got to be learning to keep them tidy.'

'I'll tidy up tomorrow,' she said meekly, taking the hint, knowing she should have gone through Hector's paperwork weeks ago.

'On the screen desktop you have instant access to files you use regularly,' he said, in his pure Indian politeness. 'See, like this real one on your real desktop.' He picked up her folder containing the first scrawled pages of her novel.

'Yes, I do see,' she said, nodding and slightly frowning, hopeful that she was fixing a look of wise understanding on her face.

'Have you got a headache?' he asked, gawping.

'No, I always look like this when I concentrate,' she said, feeling daft.

'How d'you know? D'ya always look at yourself in the mirror then?' he chortled, back to the London accent of his birth.

Bloody clever dick, she fumed inside. He might be helping her but she was going right off him. 'I just *know*,' she snapped. 'I feel my face muscles tighten and can imagine it looks as if I'm in pain, but I'm not, I'm just concentrating.'

Apparently encouraged by the reassurance that she was concentrating, he continued his lesson in sing-song fashion again: 'Take a document you're currently working on, like, maybe, this.' He picked up a shopping list she'd started writing earlier. 'It can be tidied away in a file named *Shopping Lists* within a folder called, maybe, *Household Notes*.'

'But I haven't got a file for shopping lists,' she wailed, re-flummoxed. All this bloody yackety yack. All she wanted to do was be told how to wind paper into the bloody stupid machine and then how to work it.

'That's just an example innit,' he blared.

'Listen, Jatinder, all I want to know is how to use this sodding typewriter,' she exploded.

He exuded a long deep sigh with the disciplined control of someone obliged to break wind in a church. 'It's called a keyboard Mrs Salmon,' he said.

'Typewriter, keyboard Mrs Salmon, just show me how to damn

well use it,' she yelled, immediately ashamed of setting this obliging youth such a bad example.

'Old people, they're the pits,' he muttered to himself, obviously thinking that her old ears wouldn't pick up his words. His lips tightened and he ran his long fine fingers through his jet black hair. 'What is it then that you are wanting to type?'

'My novel,' she mumbled.

His dark eyes swivelled round to her. 'Neat,' he observed.

'Not neat, I've written fifty pages but my writing's so untidy no-one else will be able to read it, that's why I need to type it out.'

'I'll be setting up a folder and a short cut on the desk top, then all you'll have to do is double click on it. Please, what is the novel to be called?'

'*Twenty Ninety-Five.* I started it five years ago, in nineteen ninety-five, but then put it away.'

'A story set in the future,' he exclaimed, cottoning on quickly, 'Real wicked. I'm right into science fiction.'

Encouraged, she sat back and watched, trying to fathom out what he was doing, but her scrutiny seemed to unsettle him.

He stopped manoeuvring the mouse. 'Listen Mrs S. While I set it up why don't you go down and make yourself a nice cup of tea.'

'Right. I will,' she agreed, deciding to disregard his patronising tone, glad of an excuse to get away from all the concentrating.

Downstairs, as the kettle began to boil, old Wally Woodcock rang.

'Hello Maeve my dear, just checking you're on for bridge this evening,' he said.

'Yes, I'm looking forward to it,' she said. 'And, by the way, do you know how to work a computer, because the young lad from next door is setting Hector's up for me right now but, once he's left, I'm bound to forget something basic, like how to get it going again.'

'Yes, I know enough to get you going.'

And suddenly she wondered if, in bed, with the light out, he truly could!

Three

Inching along in heavy traffic on her way to the Bec Bridge Club, Maeve spotted an exotic magnolia, its delicate curved petals nipped brown by frost. And further along, a slender tree, a smattering of white blossom and pigeon droppings bedecking its fine twiggery. Speeding up past Tooting Bec Common, she noticed the dirty black grass at the verge turned to verdant green a little way in, and that trees and bushes grew tall and strong on their intake of exhaust fumes. How could she even contemplate living with Freda and Bernard in the village of Wood Hill? Here she had everything. Flowers, blossom, trees, walks over lush grass. The beauty of nature, plus shops galore. And people of all races in their colourful ethnic clothes. Tooting had everything.

The ecstatic mood of living in such a wonderful place made her bid wildly.

'Seven no trumps,' she called glibly on the first hand.

Slowly, Wally laid down his cards on the green baize table, his incredulous eyes flashing her the message: *are you stark staring mad!* As she played each card he nervously tugged both wings of his walrus moustache as if intent upon uprooting them. But, even after she'd gone four off doubled, the feeling of well-being stayed with her.

'You're in a buoyant mood, considering,' observed Wally when the results were read out at the end of the evening.

'Just because we came bottom doesn't matter,' she retorted. 'It's fun just playing the game.'

'Fun playing the game with a devil-may-care like you,' he responded fondly, 'and such a pleasure to look at you across the table - you have such mischievous twinkly blue eyes, and the wild disorder of your untamed curls is so very attractive.'

Maeve pushed an escaping spiral back into the splayed leg of a dangling hairpin so she could view him more clearly, shaken to see the look of adoration shining from his dark spaniel eyes.

'Would you like to come out to tea with me tomorrow, I know a nice little place?' he said, rounding the table and lifting her jacket from the back of her chair.

Oh God, he was taking her high spirits as a sign she enjoyed being with him, she realised, as he courteously held out the short red coat for her to insert her arms.

'Sorry I can't,' she declared, rising from the table and lunging her right arm backwards into the armhole.

'That's a pity. Do you have another engagement?' he asked, jiggling the garment in an effort to capture her jabbing left arm.

'Yes, the boy next door is coming in to give me another lesson on the computer.' Maeve leaned forward, contorting her body to try to locate the elusive armhole.

'Maybe some other time?' he persisted, deftly capturing her groping fist and easing the sleeve up her arm.

As she wriggled into the jacket, then fumbled to do up the buttons, he tucked his hand between the nape of her neck and the jacket, smoothing the collar down. She flicked her head, pulling away, as the back of his fingers lingered too long on her bare flesh.

'Maybe some other time?' he prompted, as she turned to face him.

In the depths of their dark sockets, his velvet brown eyes were gleaming with hope as they stared at her.

'Yes, maybe,' she prevaricated, starting to edge away from him towards the door.

He took her arm. 'Instead of going out to tea, maybe you'd prefer a trip to the South Bank - take a look at the new London Eye?'

She stopped walking. To go and see the giant Ferris wheel erected by the Thames for the millennium was something she'd really like to do - with or without him.

'Yes, I would prefer that,' she truthfully answered, deciding she'd go by herself when the weather was warmer.

Jatinder came round after school, as promised, and forced her to go through the procedure of turning the computer off, despite her assurance that it wasn't necessary because she'd keep it switched on all the time.

'Oh yeah,' he said cynically, 'and what if you go off for a week? Know what I mean?'

'Yeah, I do know what you mean, I do speak English,' she snapped, 'but if I went off for a week, I'd keep the computer switched on.'

'Okay. So what about if you go off for a month?'

I'll go off bang and clout you one, as big as you are, she thought, though she'd never hit anyone in her life before this week. *What is it about computers that brings out the aggression in people?* she wondered, thinking of the good-natured Rastafarian she'd hand-bagged.

'I'll never go off as long as a month,' she asserted.

'Not even if you find a rich toyboy who will be wishing to take you off on a cruise,' he sniggered, as if that was the most impossible thing in the world.

But, before she'd thought up a retort, he began issuing orders which she clumsily followed until a message appeared on the screen stating it was safe to switch off.

'Go on then,' he said grumpily.

Past caring, she jabbed the red button and instantly the computer hiccuped, stopped breathing, and the screen went dead. But she felt no jubilation. She knew she'd never be able to remember the complicated procedure once she was by herself.

Then, having gone through all that, he made her switch it on again, standing over her like a menacing school teacher while she attempted to type the usual exercise of *the quick brown fox jumped over the lazy dog*. Only her version of it turned out to be *thhhhe quuickkkk brrrrowwwwwn fooooox jjumpedddd overrrr thee hazy boggg*.

Punctuated by ever increasing testy sighs of impatience, causing sharp puffs of draught on her neck, he kept repeating that she must learn to tap the keys lightly. What the hell did he think she was trying to do for God's sake! Not content with that, every time she nearly fell off the chair with the shock of slicing her hand through thin air and connecting with nothing, he kept blazing that she had to remember that there wasn't a lever to push back 'cos there wasn't a carriage to return.

'It's like going down a stair that isn't there,' she wailed, almost toppling off her seat again, but it didn't cut any ice with him because he just rolled his eyes, grabbed hold of a sheet of paper, shoved it in the printer, then ordered her to click onto the print icon.

Carefully moving the mouse, she eventually managed to do so

and was astounded at the speed the printer worked, though why they'd discarded the old method of typing straight onto paper was frankly beyond her. Jatinder loudly proclaimed that she would soon discover the benefits, but she doubted it. Then, in a gentler, though facetious, tone he said what a giggle it was that whenever she moved the mouse around she made appropriate squeaky noises. 'Just like a mouse,' he unnecessarily explained, adding, 'it's kinda cool innit.'

Before she'd decided whether to laugh at this observation or get cross, he abruptly pronounced that she was ready to carry on by herself and he had to go. Overcome with instant terror, she clutched hold of his arm and begged him to stay longer.

'Don't worry,' he said, shaking her off, 'me dad's old and he can do it.'

His dad's old! His dad's thirty-seven. What did that make her?

'You stay there Mrs S,' he stated, 'I'll see myself out.' And, with that, he leapt up and disappeared from the room.

She heard him bound down the stairs, heard the front door slam, and then there was silence except for the hum of the fully activated machine!

Unbidden moans and whimperings seeped out from her throat as she extracted the first page from the *Twenty Ninety-Five* folder and gingerly started to copy it. The time was two thirty. By three o'clock she was ready to give the whole thing up and chuck the frigging computer out of the window. By three thirty her repertoire of swear words had increased to depths of vileness she hadn't even known existed inside her head. By four o'clock she'd stopped slicing her right hand through thin air but had started crying. By four thirty she'd got the hang of the 'delete' key and was starting to appreciate the automatic word wrap, but, at four thirty-five disaster struck when she accidentally clicked onto the X in the top right corner. Or, to be accurate, disaster *nearly* struck because everything should have been deleted except that the sporty computer gave her a second chance and let her cancel it. She felt encouraged that at least the bloody thing was trying to help her. By five o'clock she'd finished copying five whole pages. She stopped battling with the keyboard and scrolled back, but just as she started reading what she had typed, the phone began ringing. *Go away, go away,* she thought, her eyes not leaving the screen. But whoever it was was steadfastly hanging on.

At last she dived out to her bedroom.

'Maeve Salmon. Who is it?' she snapped into the phone

'It's me mother,' said Freda cheerily, 'just thought I'd let you know our news.'

'Oh, hello,' she said, forcing her voice to sound pleasant.

'Are you okay? You sound odd.'

I'm just bringing myself back from the future.'

'Are you *sure* you won't come and live with us,' Freda said, this time her voice saturated with the concern of a daughter who thought that her mother had flipped. 'Or at least sell up in Tooting and buy somewhere here in the village. Nesbit and Enid Batty have just put *The Bungalow* in Bramble Lane up for sale. That would suit you nicely.'

Maeve sat down on the bed. She'd never considered selling up to live near them. *The Bungalow* would be ideal too. All on one level and just down the road from Freda and Bernard and their FAB Animal Park. A mysterious feeling fluttered inside her chest, like a frightened moth fatally attracted to a scorching light bulb.

'Are you there? Did you hear me?' Freda asked in a worried tone.

'Yes. I was thinking. Maybe I'll take a look at *The Bungalow* next time I'm down.' The fluttering inside her ribcage took on the intensity of powerful eagles' wings.

'That's *great* - but it's bound to go quickly, so come down soon. In the meantime, why not get your house valued.'

Maeve's inside was now crammed with the beating wings of a flock of panicking pigeons. What was she thinking about! She was a townie, not a country person. And she was all fired up to write the novel. Why should she want to move!

'If *The Bungalow* goes, it goes,' she said flippantly.

'But you will get your house valued won't you,' Freda urged.

'Okay, I'll arrange that, but you don't have to worry about me. I like living here on my own.'

'But I *do* worry about you. All of your old friends seem to have died, or gone into retirement homes. And didn't ...'

'Dolly Potter hasn't moved away and she's one of my oldest friends,' Maeve cut in.

'... And didn't your old chums Vera and Jean move miles away to be near their families?' Freda continued, undeterred.

'Yes they did,' Maeve admitted.

'So, that's what *you* should do. Move near us, help out with the running of our Animal Park - that's if you'd like to. You seemed to enjoy it last year. That way you meet people and we'd be nearby to help you when you needed it.'

'I'll see,' Maeve muttered, weakening.

'I don't know why you don't jump at it,' said Freda huffily. 'What on earth do you do to fill in your long empty days now dad has gone?'

'I write ...' Maeve stopped. For reasons she couldn't fathom, she wanted her novel to be a secret. Maybe so she could surprise everybody when it was finished and hopefully published. 'I write ... I write letters to newspapers. I do cryptic crosswords. I play bridge. I'm okay Freda.'

'If you're sure,' Freda said doubtfully, then, changing her tone: 'Now I'll tell you the reason I rang. You know Princess, our pinkest piglet, well she's not really a piglet any more but I still think of them all as babes. Well, we had her mated and, guess what, we heard today ...' Freda's voice had risen to a high-pitched squeak, '... our little girl has conceived. She's in-pig, as we pig breeders put it.' Freda's happy rapture seemed to heat up the phone.

'Oh great news,' Maeve enthused, really pleased. She liked Princess - she was a cheerful colour and seemed a good-natured pig as pigs go. She also knew that to her sadly childless daughter, those pigs were her family.

'And we're having a combined party next month,' Freda continued. 'On the thirteenth of May to celebrate Princess's successful conception and Bernard's fifty-fourth birthday. All the neighbours are coming. You'll come too won't you?'

'Can I let you know?' Maeve stalled.

'I thought you'd jump at it,' Freda said in a hurt voice.

'I would normally only ...' Maeve floundered.

'Oh, I've just realised,' Freda gasped. 'It'll be the first party you've been to on your own.'

'Something like that,' she mumbled.

'Well, it's almost a month away, you might feel more confident about mixing with people by then. And in the unlikely event that *The Bungalow*'s still for sale, you can take a look at it that weekend.'

'Yes, I'd like that,' said Maeve, quite curious to see what the Batty's had made of it. She'd been inside once, soon after the old woman who owned it had died and it had been very shabby.

After they said their goodbyes, during which Freda urged her again to get the house valued, she dashed back to the computer. Now all she had to do was save what she'd typed then pluck up the courage to switch it off.

Nervously, she manoeuvred the mouse arrow onto the little icon of a blank screen, seeing the word *Save* pop up. Relieved, she clicked it then clicked onto the X and in an instant all her work vanished. Panic overcame her. It had been so quick. Too quick. She must have lost the lot. Whimpering pathetically like a puppy who had lost its mum, she double clicked the *Shortcut to Twenty Ninety-Five* icon displayed on the screen. And, miraculously, her novel reappeared. She hadn't lost it. The novel had been saved. She had been saved. She could do it. She could type and save a document. She, Maeve Salmon, could work a computer. Carefully, she went through the procedure to shut it down and as she pushed the red switch turning it off the tune from *The Sound of Music* burst into her head.

'You go to my head like the sound of music, la lala la ...' She was Maria joyfully running to the edge of that mountain, arms outstretched. She rose up and twirled. 'I am sixteen going on seventy,' she carolled, twirling again, dislodging an avalanche of loose curls from the cluster pinned high on her head. God, being a computer literate novelist was *brilliant*.

She opened up her Yellow Pages at the Estate Agents' section, ran her finger down the list. Stopped. Grinned at the peculiar aptness of the name. Picked up the phone and dialled.

'I'd like you to come round to tell me how much my Edwardian end of terrace is worth,' she said to the man who answered, wanting to cut her tongue out even as she spoke those awful words.

She wouldn't sell. She knew she wouldn't. But it would be interesting to find out what it would fetch.

Four

Maeve opened the front door to see a pimply youth in a dark navy suit, an open neck red shirt, and hair sticking up so stiff and spiky you could scrape mud off boots with it.

'Mrs Salmon, right?' he said, tilting his head, smiling cheekily.

'Right,' she confirmed.

He handed over his card showing the quirky name that had made her ring his estate agency instead of one of the better known ones, though now that she'd seen him she wasn't so sure about it. How could a kid like him know the value of her house?

'Steven State Junior, from the S. State Estate h'Agency. Pleased ta meet-cha.'

'I bet you are,' she responded, seeing the gleam of two per cent commission lighting up his eyes as they darted past her shoulder to spy out the hall.

'Would-ja like ta start showing me h'around,' he said, ignoring the barb, inching forward like an over-eager child in a Father Christmas queue.

She stepped to one side, flattening herself against the wall as he bounded in.

'Mmm, nice little *hh*all,' he said, over-pronouncing the aitch in a vain, though she supposed commendable, effort at speech improvement.

In four long strides he reached the end of the hallway where he yanked the kitchen door shut.

'It may not be Buckingham Palace but as halls go in end-of-terrace houses this is not *that* small,' she retaliated, noticing for the first time that maybe it was rather poky.

'Oh, right. No h'offence intended,' Master S. State said, bounding back, leaning against the front door and aiming a small rectangular contraption at the door he had just closed. 'Three point five metres,' he said. 'That's abaht twelve feet,' he interpreted, obviously noticing her blank look.

'I know, I know,' she blustered, not wanting the patronising kid to get the upper hand. And she wasn't going to ask him how he'd measured that without getting on his hands and knees with a tape measure either.

'It's h'infra red,' he obliged, patting the box. 'Bounced back and gave me a reading, know what I mean? Look see.'

She stared at the small screen, impressed.

'Lead on Mrs Salmon,' he said, grinning impishly.

And she found she was warming to him.

'This is the kitchen,' she needlessly said.

'Plenty of scope for improvement,' he beamed, as if that was a plus point. 'Fitted wall and floor cupboards in need of replacement,' he muttered into a tiny tape recorder. 'Formica work top. Compact dining area plus view of small garden from the sink.' He glanced over at her. 'They like that,' he said reassuringly. 'Now, on to the next room.'

But, when she led him into the sitting room her feet started dragging as if gaining weight with each step. This was where she and Hector had sat. Day after day. Month after month. Year after year. She stared at the bright shiny lad, daring him to say anything derogatory about it.

'I'm well pleased ta see you've kept all the original features,' he declared. 'It's, like, so many times people think they're improving their *hh*omes by boarding up fireplaces and what-not, but it ain't the case.'

He paced around, measuring with his device and muttering into his machine.

'Just a couple of coats of paint over that weird little mural and ya could picture yer were back in Edwardian days,' he observed.

'It may be weird and little but it's symbolic,' she stated, staring at the picture she'd painted in defiance of Hector who would have been even more outraged if he'd known that the spring of green water spouting out from the ground represented her, and the orange-brown rock about to crush it depicted him: her despotic husband always ready to put her down.

'Wossit, like, meant to be?' the kid asked, twisting his head, as if studying it sideways would enlighten him. And it seemed to work because, 'I god-it,' he suddenly whooped, 'the green swishes is a kinda weeping willow and the orange is a kinda wonky sun.' He straightened and shot her a proud look as if expecting acclaim for his intelligent interpretation of modern art. She smiled and nodded, not intending to un-enlighten him. 'But it don't go wiv Edwardian, right?' he succinctly added.

'Right,' she agreed, leading him out and up the stairs to the spare bedroom cum study.

'That lot ain't bad,' he commented, jerking his head at the computer paraphernalia on the desk. 'That yours?'

'It is now. It was my husband's. He had a top-lap too but he dropped it when he became too weak to carry it, just two weeks before he died.'

She pictured pale spindly Hector tottering across the room, his precious cargo cradled in his arms, heard his desperate cry ...

'Not a *top*-lap, a *lap*-top,' the youth grinned.

I wasn't too weak to carry it you silly bitch, I slipped on the grapes you'd bloody stupidly left on the floor, Hector's voice raged in her head.

'Wotcha do wiv it?' S. State Junior asked.

'With what?'

'The broken laptop.'

'Gave it to Oxfam,' she whispered, hoping Hector wasn't spookily picking up on that one.

'Ja wanna sell this lot? I'd take it all off your *h*ands.'

'No thank you. *I* shall be using it,' she said with pride. She stared at her new-found friends - monitor, keyboard, computer, all in a beigy mushroom colour which, she'd just spotted, co-ordinated beautifully with her beigy-pink curtains and carpet. As the kid measured and muttered, she wondered why on earth it had taken her so long to become computer literate, for hadn't she been the only female in their group of friends who'd been in the Science stream at school. The only one more interested in *Tomorrow's World* than *Coronation Street*, the only one who had pored over articles about DNA, Lasers and new inventions over the decades since ...

'If ya change ya mind abaht selling yer PC Mrs Salmon, give us a bell,' S. State Junior cut into her thoughts

'I won't change my mind,' she said decisively, deciding to go to evening classes to learn about surfing the Internet.

She led him out to the landing and into her bedroom, that such a short time ago had been Hector's bedroom too. As he aimed his infra-red measuring devise at the opposite wall she looked at the double bed and was suddenly overwhelmed by sadness. To cuddle a hot squidgy hot-water bottle every night was comforting, but not a patch on a hot squidgy man.

'I'll leave you to it,' she mumbled, choked, hurrying out of the room and stumbling downstairs.

'You gotta very sought-after property,' he said later as he joined her in the kitchen.

'How much?' she asked. 'Let's get to the nitty gritty. What's it worth?'

'I'm like thinking wiv the right person you could get one hundred and sixty thousand pahnds.' He beamed, arching his back and rubbing his hands up and down his minuscule buttocks, like an uncle who'd just given a present to a small child.

But she wasn't grumbling. They'd only paid eight thousand for it.

He tapped the side of his nose. 'Maybe even five thousand more wiv the right person. So. Wotcha fink then?' he pushed. 'Do ya wannus to put it on the markit?'

'I'll know in a month's time, the weekend of the thirteenth of May to be exact,' she said, ushering him to the front door. Her door. Nobody else's. Hers.

She tossed and turned unable to sleep. Sat up, peered at the clock, seeing it was 2.22 which pleased her by its lucky digit repetition, but distressed her by its hour. Oh God she was so tired. She slumped back, shut her eyes, and next time she looked it was 3.33 and this time she was even more pleased at the lucky portent, yet even more distressed by its hour. Was it to be 4.44 next time she looked, then 5.55? Was she to get no sleep at all?

She forced her eyes shut again and, after a while, felt herself floating. She looked down, just in time to see a young couple coming in through the door. They stopped directly underneath her and kissed passionately, then the girl pulled away and began scrabbling at the buttons of her blouse, whilst he dug out some coins and keys from his pocket before kicking off his jeans.

From her high vantage point she could clearly see that the keys spread out on the shelf were *her* house-keys on *her* special keyring. Horrified, terrified, she dived down, darting around their heads like an angry wasp, but, ignoring her very presence, they hopped naked into bed and proceeded to make outrageous love. But they couldn't stay there in her home, in her bed. Couldn't keep her keys on her keyring given by Hector after she'd temporarily left him that time. She hovered, reading again his immortal words etched into the metal disc: *Remember Maeve, bloaters are for breakfast but this Salmon is for life.*

She swooped down reaching out to pick up the keys, but her fingers went straight through them. She wheeled round, bombed down again, but the same thing happened. Over and over her fingers brushed through the solid metal. She tried to scream but no sound came out. Yet, strangely, the new inhabitants woke up as if they had heard her.

'We're only trying this place out,' the young woman warned, glaring up at her.

'Yes, only trying it out,' confirmed the man, 'but we don't like peeping Toms so we won't be buying it.'

'But I have to sell up if I decide I do want to move to Wood Hill.'

'Tough,' they replied in unison, immediately vanishing.

She half woke, shivering, wishing she could feel Hector's arm draped over her, feel him spooned against her. As she drifted off, she saw his tall thickset figure gliding down on beautiful angel's wings. 'It's not fair,' she grumbled. 'If I'd have gone first you'd have been the one to suffer. Trust you to take the easy way out.'

He landed with a thump on the pavement outside their house, smoothed down sparse strands of ginger hair, then magically produced an estate agent's sign from under his white gown. Tears of deep emotion fell from his eyes as he pushed the pole into the ground between the gate post and the privet hedge.

'*I, Hector Salmon, once lived in this house,*' he declared in an angelic voice.

Abruptly, he spread his wings, bashing one into the post, then he flapped them vigorously sending feathers flying as he clomped down the pavement, gathering speed, finally taking off right down by the corner shop, eventually disappearing into a thick bank of clouds.

She stared out at the newly erected sign but it was facing the wrong way. Surprised that she could do it, she levitated from her bed and, still lying flat on her back, skimmed out, feet first, through the open top window, righting herself in time to land lightly on the pavement.

She looked up at the sign and there in big bold red letters were the words: SOLD. MAEVE SALMON HAS MOVED TO *THE BUNGALOW* IN WOOD HILL. And, in small gold letters underneath it was signed: *The Dead Salmon Estate Agency*.

Typical, she thought. Still telling her what do even though he was dead. But perhaps from his far-seeing vantage point he could look into the future and see what was best for her. She glanced around, wondering how on earth to get back into bed, but suddenly found she was in it, snuggled up under the duvet.

When next she opened her eyes it was 8.08. Sleepily, she reached over and lifted the phone.

'Freda,' she yawned, 'will you make arrangements for me to view *The Bungalow* as soon as poss. Your father's sent me a sign.'

But, even as she spoke, she knew it was wrong. Why was she letting him dictate to her. She always fought against it when he was living, so why was she heeding him now! Deep inside though, she knew it was her spirit talking, not his, and that she was meanly pinning the difficult decision to move onto his spectral shoulders.

'Sorry, Hector,' she faintly whispered, realising that, as far as she could remember, it was the first time she'd ever uttered those two words to him.

'Sorry too for not saying sorry before,' she apologised, after she'd said goodbye to Freda, realising that she must have been wrong at least once during their marriage, though unable to think of a time.

Just bloody well get down to Hampshire and take a look at it, his voice clearly said.

What, the whole of Hampshire, she thought-sniggered, having a spooky joke with him.

But, as usual when she cracked a gag, he didn't respond.

One hour later Maeve snatched up the ringing phone.

'Hello mother,' Freda said, 'I've made the appointment for you to look round *The Bungalow* tomorrow afternoon ...'

Five

Maeve had rested for half an hour after the long drive down to Wood Hill. Now, Freda was all set to walk to *The Bungalow* with her, but, just as they were about to leave, Bernard dashed in saying that Lardarse had gobbed at a visitor who was furious.

'Lardarse never spits,' Freda cried.

'Well he has this time and *I* can't very well rub llama sputum off the woman's chest.'

'Sorry mother,' she said, 'you'll have to go there alone.'

And Maeve was delighted because, much as she appreciated her daughter taking time out for her, she preferred to look around by herself and make up her own mind.

'I'll show thee round, I say I'll show thee round,' boomed Nesbit Batty, motioning her in through the front door. 'My Enid's out in t'garden tending to 'er rhubarb.'

'How long will she be with her rhubarb?' she asked, disappointed that he'd be the one to give her the guided tour. She knew this couple from when she and Hector had stayed at Freda's and she preferred Enid by far.

'She communes wi' that rhubarb for hours. I say she communes wi' that rhubarb for hours. Has an affinity with all of 'er plants - Brussels sprouts, parsnips, the lot - as thee well knows seeing as thee's sold 'em in thy Freda's barn shop.'

'Yes I have,' she confirmed, glancing around, keen to get on with it. She'd been in *The Bungalow* once before when old Gertrude Smith owned it, but the hall was bigger than she remembered and had been freshly painted in warm terra cotta with an attractive dappled effect that she really liked.

'Buy this place and thee could supply Freda with 'ome grown veggies, keeping all the profits in the family,' he beamed, pinpoints of light blazing off his false choppers, face polished with the cocksure glow of a vendor convinced of a sale.

'But ... but, I could never manage such a big garden,' she gasped, suddenly unsure. She could hardly keep her own small lawn and narrow flower beds under control, so how could she be contemplating the upkeep of a veritable field.

'Don't dismiss it, I say don't dismiss it. The job of growing plants has been made easy by Enid's dedicated digging in of sackfuls of thy Freda's manure.'

As she thought over, then rejected, the idea of making a joke, he ushered her off to the right and through into the large sitting room. She'd been in this room with Freda once, soon after Gertrude Smith had died, but it had been shabby then, not like this. The Battys had really improved it. The mustard yellow walls gave off a cheerful glow where natural sunlight shafted in from the French windows. And the long blue and cream brocade curtains looked rich, yet homely.

With growing excitement she spotted the attractive arched alcove that she'd forgotten was even there, now housing an elegant sideboard instead of Gertrude's old piano. She turned to the opposite wall, seeing useful built-in shelves crammed with magazines and books to the right of the chimney breast. Comfy-looking armchairs were positioned each side of the fireplace to which her eyes slowly became riveted. And suddenly her high spirits sank. That fire surround was so tall and heavy-looking. She turned away, overcome by all the old fears.

'Is something up?' he ventured, the cloud of a receding sale speeding across his sunny face.

'That fire surround. It looks so heavy.'

'Aye, 'tis good solid mahogany is that. Good solid mahogany weighing a ton I wouldn't wonder.'

'That's what worries me. The mantelshelf is so solid-looking, so heavy, so high. It must be top-heavy.'

His eyes flickered uncertainly like light bulbs on the blink.

'But it's connected to the wall, so what does thee mean top-heavy?'

'Don't you see. Day after day, year after year. Slowly but surely that fire surround could be dragging its moorings out of the wall, and, when it is completely free, its top-heaviness will send it crashing down on top of anybody unfortunate enough to be sitting in front of it.'

'Nay, nay. It's never fallen off the wall, not once. Never likely to neither.'

She averted her eyes from his incredulous gaze and saw, through the French windows, Enid, at the far corner of the garden, dabbing her eyes as if weeping.

He caught the drift of her gaze and smiled ruefully. 'She doesn't want to move, 'tis me that's anxious to get back wi' me old mates up north.'

So that was it. Enid was deliberately hanging around out there so she didn't have to show her round. Maeve wondered if she'd be like that back in Tooting.

'Rest assured, that fire surround cannot plummet,' Nesbit stated firmly, manoeuvring her forcibly by the elbow out of the room and across the hall into the spacious kitchen-dining room.

She stood by the sink looking out through the window across the front lawn. The head of a horse and the top half of a girl bobbed along behind the front hedge. *That's a glorious sight I never see in my busy London road,* she thought, the seed of interest that had been germinating inside her suddenly burgeoning into a rampant plant of desire that smothered her erstwhile doubts regarding the fireplace.

She turned, seeing six chairs around a long pine table at the far end of the room. *Perhaps Wally Woodcock or Dolly Potter would come down and visit me, and I could cook dinner and invite Freda and Bernard round to join in,* Maeve thought, picturing the jolly scene, forgetting for a moment that she wasn't good at cooking and had never liked preparing food for others, no matter who they were.

'And here's a useful utility room,' Nesbit announced bounding across the kitchen and throwing open a door.

She peered into the narrow room, picturing her washing machine and ironing board neatly stashed away out of sight there. And excitement grew within her. This was the place for her, of that she was almost sure.

'Enid decorated the 'ole lot,' he said as he led her back out to the square hall, 'learnt to do all the ragging and sponging at a special effects shop. It's called distressed.'

'Where is it?' she asked, thinking she might go there.

'Why, on t'walls,' he answered, throwing her another of his doubtful looks.

'Where's Ontwalls?

'There!' he bellowed, stabbing his finger in different directions around the hall.

Nonplussed, she twisted round, staring into the spaces he had jabbed. 'Are you saying the shop Enid went to is in Ontwalls but there are different branches?' she asked slowly.

'Which shop?' he screeched.

'Distressed. The shop where Enid learnt the special effects.'

'Nay, nay, the special effects're called distressed. I 'aven't a clue what the shop's called.'

He wiped his brow as he led her along a wide passage with strip pine flooring, past a bathroom and two bedrooms, to a door at the end.

'This new bedroom's what I'll regret leaving,' he said, almost dancing in. 'Designed this extension and built it meself.'

She followed him in, stopping dead, pulse racing. It was superb. In front of the double bed, a vast picture window gave a breathtaking view of the back garden which, screened by woods at the back and tall hedges and shrubs either side, was quite private. Mirrored doors on the left wall reflected the view of the patio seen through the window to the right.

'And be'ind the built-in wardrobe is the en suite toilet and shower,' he said, diving past the end of the bed to the side wall and sliding open one of the mirrored doors.

'Best quality sanitary ware, I say best quality sanitary ware,' he boomed, letting her through into the long room, fully tiled in turquoise and blue, the colours perfectly matching the velour track suit she was wearing, a coincidence she stupidly interpreted as another sign. 'And them medicine cabinets dovetail in with t'wardrobes on t'bedroom side - all me own design mark you.'

'It's *excellent*,' she enthused, loving the whole effect, pleased he'd chosen a bathroom suite in sparkling white. Fancy colours were all right in most places, but not in the toilet zone. Especially the toilet paper - all those different colours people went in for, like Freda's favourite pink, making it impossible to monitor bodily eliminations with any degree of accuracy.

'Did thee notice the hair trap over the plug 'ole in the beedett?' he asked as they turned to go.

'No,' Maeve said uneasily, wondering how much hair it was possible to shed in one quick sluice.

'Cracking idea of Enid's. We'd never found a suitable place to clip our toenails so, take heed of this Maeve, if thee positions thy foot on the edge of the beedett you'll find thee can snip away safe in the knowledge that the clippings'll not scatter all over t'floor but will ricochet off the curved sides, lodging in the hair trap, to be lifted out and dealt with later. Thee can have ours, I say thee can have ours,' he said with an air of supreme benevolence, adding, 'it'll be thy first 'ouse-warming present.'

'Thank you,' she quavered, her stomach churning.

Back in the bedroom, again she stood still, all thoughts of bidets and hair traps gone. It was such a wonderful room. Much bigger than hers back home and the mottled blue walls so much more appealing than her grimy magnolia. Yes. Yes. She would live there, even with the top-heavy fireplace and the over-large garden. And, with Freda just up the lane, her life would be perfect. A strange heat rose in her throat like the afterglow of a good curry.

He directed her out of the bedroom into the next room.

'This is where Enid keeps 'er pottery and does 'er sculpting,' he announced, throwing out an expansive hand.

In the centre of the rectangular room stood an old wooden table, its dusty surface laden with brilliant renditions of animals Enid made to sell in Freda's FAB barn shop. Models in the making, shrouded by damp cloths, rose up like ghosts on shelves bracketed to one wall.

'Now to t'third bedroom,' he said, ushering her out and into the next door along. 'Thee could use it as a sewing room or suchlike.'

A sewing room! The last time she'd wielded a needle was when Freda had given her a tapestry set and, to show no ill-feeling for such an inappropriate gift, she'd laboriously dug the blunt needle in and out of the loose weave and, at the end of three months, the picture of a thatched cottage that had been printed on it was covered in her stitches which somehow turned out like Maggie Thatcher on a bad hair day. Better than the naff cottage, but she'd still donated it to Oxfam - a charity that had done quite well out of her she realised.

She followed Nesbit out and into the bathroom next door, overjoyed to see this too had a ceramic bathroom suite of pure white. As if floating on air she looked around, taking in the bath with its gold taps and hand grips. She looked down, admiring the smooth fitted carpet in white and black squares. She looked up - but a sudden stab of fear sent her crashing back down. For there in the ceiling was a trapdoor.

'Aye, that's the way into the roof cavity,' he said enthusiastically, obviously noting where her eyes were fixed, but not the horror-struck look in them. 'And 'tis fully boarded so there's plenty of storage space up there. And 'tis easy to get at. When thee pulls on that cord the hinged door drops down bringing the step ladder zooping down with it.'

'But ... but,' she stuttered, her pulse revving up a gear at the over-graphic description. 'But supposing they hit you on the head,' she quavered, remembering the WW2 bomb that had finished off her piano teacher and thus her hoped-for music career. 'If you were cleaning your teeth say, and the trapdoor sprang open by itself, those steps could kill you.'

'Nay, nay. They never would,' he protested, eyes swivelling wildly to the open door as if hoping Enid - or anyone - would miraculously materialise. 'For one thing they'd never descend without a tug on the cord, and for another the worst they'd do would be to dislodge a filling - they're made of aluminium.'

'I think you'll find they're amalgam,' she retorted hotly.

'Nay, not your fillings,' he said, extracting a grubby hankie from his trouser pocket and mopping his brow. 'The steps is what I meant.'

She knew he thought she was mad, and perhaps she was. But ever since that demolishment of her music teacher, followed a week later by a bomb blast that had ripped her bedroom door off its hinges sending it slamming down on top of her as she slept, she'd had a phobia about things falling heavily and unexpectedly on top of her.

'Hello Maeve,' said Enid appearing as if in answer to his mute prayer.

'I've shown 'er round, I say I've shown 'er round,' he said, 'and apart from 'er peculiar notions that fireplace is about to fall off wall and the ladder leap out of t'loft, I get the feeling she is favourably impressed.'

'You're the first person who's viewed it,' said Enid, dolefully. 'Do you really think it's what you're after?'

Yes, Maeve thought to herself. *Yes I do think it's what I'm after. In fact, yes, I know it's what I'm after. I can see myself living here. Freda could get me a gardener to grow vegetables for her to sell in the shop. I could get the trap door battened up and could make sure I always sat well back from the fire place.* A quiver of excitement ran through her as she imagined moving her books onto their shelves, her pictures and mirrors onto their walls, her furniture into their rooms.

'Yes, Enid. I do think it's what I'm after,' she declared.

'Good,' Enid said in a tiny voice.

And then she remembered the most important thing she had forgotten to ask.

'How much are you asking for it?'

Nesbit and Enid looked at each other, then Enid said, 'Mole, the Estate Agent is dealing with that side of things. You'll have to ring him.'

She hurried back along Bramble Lane. Soon this was to be the road she lived in. Soon she'd be able to pop in and see Freda without the long drive from London. Joyfully, she leapt in the air, clicking her heels, yelping with pain as she landed off-balance and tottered full pelt into the hedge. Still buoyant, though now hobbling, she turned into Nuthatch Lane, reading the peculiarly worded arrowed sign that Hector had organised not long before he died. In bold blue letters on a bright yellow background it stated: *FAB - Freda And Bernard's Private Park - Open to the Public.*

The graffiti that had altered the *Private Park* to *Private Parts open to the Public* had been cleaned off but was still faintly visible, still capable of raising a smutty smile she thought, smuttily smiling.

Sounds of cheering came from the behind the car park field and she knew that the piglets directed by Bernard must be putting on their show. Though they weren't piglets now she mused. They were fully grown porkers.

As she neared Wisteria Cottage, Freda burst out of the gate and pounded up the lane to her.

'What do you think? Tell me,' she puffed. 'I couldn't settle to anything once I'd dealt with the spit.'

Maeve hooked her arm into her daughter's as they entered their front garden and crunched down the gravel path. 'It's wonderful and is in perfect order, but ...'

They stopped walking.

'Yes? You're going to take it. You are, aren't you,' urged Freda. 'Come on don't keep me in suspense.'

'Yes I want to buy it. Come on inside, I have to ring that Mole Estate Agent.'

Freda was laughing out loud as they barged against each other as they went through the door. 'Oh it'll be *fantastic*,' she hooted, 'but are you really going to put in an offer straight away? Shouldn't you get it surveyed first?'

'Shouldn't I get a price for it first you mean, I haven't a clue what they're asking.'

'Oh dear, I should have found out before you came down,' Freda groaned, pulling out a directory, thumbing through it, then jabbing out a number on the hall phone.

'Mole Estate Agency, Orlford, a female voice said as soon as she handed it over.

'I'm ringing to enquire how much you're asking for *The Bungalow* in Bramble Lane, Wood Hill,' Maeve said, grinning broadly at Freda.

There was a muffled conversation then, 'Sorry, it's only just come onto the market, I had to ask Mr Mole himself.'

'How *much*?' she prompted.

'Three hundred thousand.'

'Are you *sure!*

'Quite sure, it's a very sought-after village and single storey dwellings are in short supply. Old people like them.'

'Old people *and* young ones,' Maeve blared, offended by the inference that she was old, even though she was.

'Sor-*ry*,' the woman said, with that annoying inflexion that meant she was anything but. 'Pity it's too much for you, but we do have a cheaper place going in Great Piddlehurst. It's on the sixth floor and there's no lift, but it could suit a young person such as yourself.'

Maeve thought she heard the woman sniggering as, snapping it wouldn't do, she banged down the phone.

'What's up?' asked Freda, pulling out a coil of her rust-orange hair and chewing on it.

'They're asking three hundred thousand pounds and mine's only worth one hundred and sixty thousand. That's what's up.'

Freda's green eyes, so like Hector's, fixed upon her with a look like a cat that had had it's longed-for sardine snatched away from under its nose. 'But I *wanted* you living there,' she exclaimed in the same petulant tone as when she was eight years old and had been refused sweeties.

'You know you don't always get what you want,' Maeve snapped, as she always had. And she half expected Freda to stamp her foot, burst into tears and rush off to lock herself in the bathroom as she always had.

Maeve stayed with Freda and Bernard for two more days and it rained incessantly. Each morning she squelched down the garden with a bucket of corn to feed the chickens and one of their new acquisitions, Emanuel, a peculiar emu with one normal length leg, at least normal for an emu, and one short one - though both extremely lengthy for most other kinds of bird. Luckily, its affliction meant it couldn't run very fast. A comfort for men visitors whom she noticed instinctively placed protective hands over their fly area if the bird approached, the memory of Rod Hull's emu and Michael Parkinson's flailing legs and beak-clutched crotch obviously still vivid in the male psyche and probably passed down to their sons in their genes.

Each day, like the porkers, she got deeper into the mire, though hers was of despondency as well as mud. One hundred and forty thousand pounds extra would buy her a life in a luxury home close to the pigs and her daughter, but all she had was a measly two thousand pounds in a TESSA, put by for a rainy day. But not as rainy as these ones.

Next day, ignoring their cajolements to stay longer, she set off on her long journey back to her old house, and eventual demise, in Tooting.

Six

Maeve's forefinger plonked down heavily on each digit pad as she dialled the number.

'S. State Junior speaking,' said the kid. '*Hhh*ow can I *hh*elp you?'

'This is Mrs Salmon. Just to let you know I will not be moving,' she stated gruffly.

'But why not!' he bellowed in an explosion of commission spiked disappointment.

'Because I cannot afford ...' She gulped noisily. '... I cannot afford ... the property I want in Wood Hill.'

'More properties will be coming onto the market,' he said, in the dulcet tone of a politician sweet-talking a voter. 'I mean, it's like, they're b'ahnd to.'

'There may or may not be more properties coming onto the Wood Hill market, but it is *The Bungalow* I had set my heart on, not others,' she said stiffly. 'And the one hundred and sixty thousand pounds you valued my house at is one hundred and forty thousand pounds short,' she elucidated, trying not to break out into a sob.

'I'm, like, revising my opinion, ' he said. 'If the right person came along, right, you might get five thousand more, right. Or maybe even ten thousand, right,' he added, desperation in his mendacious voice.

'Five thousand, *right!* Ten thousand, *right!* she cried. 'Where do you think I'd get the bloody rest from, *right!*

'So you *hh*aven't got Granny Bonds or nothing like that tucked *hh*away' he adroitly observed, denting her eardrum with the power of his full-blown aitches, and her pride with his Granny Bond reference.

'Sharp aren't you,' she snarled.

'It's been a pleasure to nearly do business wiv you,' he sighed.

'Yer details are on our computer so if yer parents die and leave you some money, just give us a bell, right?'

As she said goodbye she could hear him sniggering. No doubt at the absurd idea that she was young enough to have living parents. Which, of course, she was, though she hadn't. But at his age that would probably be hard to take on board.

Slowly, she replaced the receiver brooding on why, at the end of her last two telephone conversations, young people had openly sniggered at her, wondering if at their age she'd have done the same when dealing with old people. Then remembering that she had!

She went into the kitchen and while she waited for the kettle to boil she consoled herself that at least now she could feel settled. It was almost a relief not to have the hassle of moving. Now she could fully concentrate on *Twenty Ninety-Five*. She would forget *The Bungalow*, forget men, forget sex, dump the half-used tube of KY in the Oxfam bag and throw herself into her work.

Excitement welled as she placed her mug of coffee on the desk upstairs and confidently pushed the benign red button, sending the computer whirring. As it went through the process called booting up, she thought about how her life had taken on this new meaning a few weeks after Hector had died:-

She'd been flopped out in the sitting room staring blindly at the newspaper, hearing the loud tick of the clock inside and the faint hum of traffic outside. *Oh Hector, when you sat opposite me commenting on my every move, I yearned for some space to myself. But now I have it, I find, I don't like it*, she had dejectedly thought, wondering how was she going to fill in the lonely days without him. Playing bridge with Wally Woodcock wasn't going to be enough. But what else could she do? Bowling? The W.I.? Maybe Line Dancing? But she wanted something more than just aimlessly filling in time. She gazed at Hector's photo up on the mantleshelf and his eyes peered back, gleaming, like hooded green marbles. She turned away from the hardness of their gaze. But when next she looked, his eyes had taken on an out-of-character dreamy stare. And, suddenly, the words of a song burst into her mind:

Think about things you'd like to do - you've got to have a dream, if you don't have a dream, how you gonna make a dream come true.

That was it, she realised. That was what was missing. A dream, an ambition. Something to aim for. But what? Then a memory hit her. She *had* had a dream once, and she thought she knew where she could find it.

She'd galloped up to the bedroom, hauled out the deep bottom drawer of the tallboy, and delved into it, plucking out the tent-sized rose-sprigged flannelette nightie Freda had given her one Christmas during her frumpish years, then a couple of ancient cardigans put by to wear in the garden, and a polka dot bikini kept from the sixties just in case, though just in case of what she didn't rightly know now. Looking at the minuscule black-dotted bright yellow scraps of material, she wondered how she'd ever dared wear them in the first place. Wisps, if not whole tracts, of pubic hair must have been on show, and she might just as well have gone topless for all the narrow strip of cloth would have covered her ample breasts. She burrowed down under a full skirted three-tier waist slip and an old sheet that needed mending and there, right at the bottom, she felt what she sought.

Carefully, she'd tugged out the file, pushed herself up off her knees and carried it into the spare bedroom. She'd perched on Hector's swivel chair, placed the file down on his long built-in desk, slid the elastic corner loops off and taken out a sheaf of yellowed paper, the top sheet headed: *TWENTY NINETY-FIVE*.

That was the first time she'd clapped eyes on her unfinished novel since she'd abandoned it five years ago. Her secret writing, her forsaken ambition: the futuristic love story set one hundred years on, in the year twenty ninety-five. She flicked through the dog-eared sheets, seeing page after page of almost illegible scrawl. Half-way down the last page, the writing stopped and her Titanic heart, buoyed up on the swelling sea of hope, suddenly hit an icy snag and sank as she realised she couldn't remember how she'd intended the story to carry on.

Agitated, she swivelled the typist's chair from side to side, then scooted it round and round, pounding the carpet in mounting frustration as she racked her brain. And, as if by centrifugal force, a faint recollection was flung out to the surface: hadn't she written an outline of the plot and stashed it away with the rest?

Head spinning, she had rummaged through the bottom drawer again, at last digging out a slim file lodged at the very back. Through the dull plastic she read: SYNOPSIS to TWENTY NINETY-FIVE a novel by Maeve Salmon 5th of January 1995. Even more giddy with excitement than she'd been with high velocity twirling, she tottered back, withdrawing the loose sheets, seeing there were ten of them, and all written in her neatest hand. It was then that she knew how she would be filling the long hours of her new life. She would write a blockbuster novel. Make it the next Harry Potter but with science instead of magic, space travel instead of broomsticks, explicit sex instead of schoolboy japes. She'd be a second Mary Wesley with a first book published late in life. Her heroine, Venus, would become more famous than calorie obsessed Bridget Jones.

Now, she clicked onto the *Shortcut to 2095* symbol and began reading what she had copied out from her scribbled notes last time:-

'*Venus jumps up, goes to the window, looks out over the tidy lawn. She hears her Great-great-grandfather move, feels his presence behind her, half turns.*

'*That grass used to need cutting twice a week in the summer,' he says. 'Look at it now. Broad stripes grown into it, never changing, always just so. Like the flower-beds that never need weeding and the woodwork that never needs painting.*'

'*Well, that's good isn't it?' Venus says.*

'*It's the reason there are no jobs for the Three-bees, the reason they are solely dependent on their Being Born Benefit. The reason people like you and your contract partner have given up the right to have a child for the dubious advantage of spells of allegedly dull work in order to earn World Currency.*'

'*I haven't given up a thing,' Venus says vehemently. 'I've never wanted a screaming kid.' A picture of the plump pink baby that used to inhabit her dreams flits into her mind and vanishes so quickly she scarcely registers it was there.*'

Electrified, Maeve snatched up the next page to be typed out and began pounding the keys. And, with just a few breaks to eat and drink, she continued all day.

That night, exhausted, she snuggled up in bed smiling to herself as she imagined the words of praise and astonishment she was sure she'd receive from The Novel Group tomorrow - the first Tuesday in May.

Seven

Hands quivering, Maeve folded four pages of *Twenty Ninety-five* into her shoulder bag, then wiped her perspiring forehead. She was nervous she knew, but her damp skin was as much to do with the unusually hot humid May evening. She cast aside the black velour track suit she'd intended wearing and donned her scarlet and white sun dress. Then, anxious to make a good first impression, she slipped her feet into matching red kitten- heeled sandals, not intended for walking.

Eagerly, she set off for Dickens Road but, even by the time she'd reached the corner of the street, the shock waves from each uncushioned step had bashed all the jauntiness out of her. And by the time she'd reached the next road along she was even more hot and sweaty than she'd been before and wishing she'd worn her comfy trainers with their built-in gel shock absorbers.

At last she limped down the front path of 4 Dickens Road and, with pounding heart, sticky armpits and aching hip, knocked on the scruffy front door which immediately flew open revealing a man with a bulging stomach topped by a surprisingly skinny chest, as if his body had been made up with mismatched parts.

'Hugos Thayre?' she ventured.

'Friend or foe!' he shrieked, exposing the neglected 'before' teeth of an orthodontist's advert.

Unsure whether he expected an answer, she mumbled, 'Friend,' and he guffawed loudly, clutching the underside of his wobbling belly as if to prevent it from dropping off.

'You must be Maeve Salmon. Shirley told me to expect you,' he said once he'd simmered down. 'Please do come in. Oh, hello there Shirley,' he called, letting go his tum to wave, 'your new lady's here.'

Maeve turned to see a short rotund woman with small grapefruit breasts and a round face neatly framed by two pale crescent moons of hair. It was as if God had used a pair of compasses to design her, Maeve thought, wishing she'd turn round so she could check on her bum.

'Hello Maeve,' Shirley said in that soft voice of hers. 'So pleased to meet you in the flesh.'

And the round blue eyes ran over her skimpy sun dress in a way that made Maeve wonder if it were true that her flat mate, Parsnip, was only staying with her to help out with the rent.

'Come in Maeve,' beamed Hugos, moving his arm in a dainty balletic arc, motioning her through into a gloomy hall.

'In there,' he said, shoving his arm in front of her and pushing open a drab grey door. The chatter inside instantly ceased and inquisitive eyes stared. 'Go in, sit wherever you want,' he instructed. 'And you Shirley.'

But Maeve found she couldn't move anything except her hand which gripped the strap of her shoulder bag tighter.

Shirley, close behind her, muttered, 'Go on in then.'

So, she pulled forward, towing herself into the centre by the strap, then standing there in a dither until Shirley urged her, none too politely, to get on with it and sit down. Hastily, she threw herself into the nearest vacant chair.

'Sorry Maeve,' called out Hugos, 'that's mine.'

And, now with the wild abandonment of a child playing musical chairs, she launched herself into the next empty one which turned out to be much lower than she'd envisaged, making her screech out like a parrot as she landed heavily down on it. Trying to rearrange her body into a more dignified position, she prayed that her blazing cheeks might make her self-combust and completely disappear.

'This is Maeve Salmon, everybody, she's trying out our Novel Group workshop,' Hugos announced loudly.

Maeve looked up from her lowly position, nodding and smiling inanely at the circle of smiling faces whilst still desperately trying to reorganise her body and limbs to show more decorum and less underwear.

'Here Maeve, take my seat,' said a man with the close isobar lines of a weather chart storm etched into his face. He held out his hand. 'James Joist,' he said, hauling her up, his gale force lines at odds with his sunny smile.

She sat down on his soft, normal height chair, feeling an over-whelming gratefulness, as if he'd donated his one healthy kidney to her, not just his seat.

'Are we all settled down then?' said a woman in a white caftan dress.

Maeve stared, marvelling at the fat fleshiness of her red nose and the heavy weightiness of her earrings, which looked as if they were being worn in an attempt to stretch her plump earlobes into thinness. If she shook her head the dangling metal balls might swing out on their chains and bash her nose Maeve thought, wondering if that's how it got so fat and red in the first place.

'Maeve Salmon. Welcome,' the woman said, edging her face round carefully in her direction. 'My name is Dora Dome and I take these sessions. I'll quickly introduce you to the rest, though I daresay you won't remember many at first.'

As she reeled off six or seven names Maeve reflected that Dora Dome should change her name to Millennium Dome by the look of her.

At last the preliminaries were over and Dora Dome turned to Hugos saying they'd kick off with him. A hush settled on the gathering like a vulture settling on a tree. Hugos explained that he'd give a brief summary of what had previously happened for Maeve's benefit. As he launched forth, Maeve half closed her eyes, concentrating, trying to take in the gist of his story which appeared to be that a married man, named Anthony, was besotted with the postman, called Patrick, and his wife didn't know. With a voice trembling with the passion of a ham actor, Hugos began to read:-

Anthony opened the door a crack and stared into Patrick's eyes. 'We must stop meeting like this, my wife is getting suspicious,' he hissed.

'But I had to knock,' said the postman, 'you've got to sign for this recorded delivery.'

Maeve giggled, but nobody else did, so she covered the sound with a cough. At the end of his four pages there was complete silence except for Shirley who, in hushed tones, said, 'Oh *yes.*'

Maeve looked around the room seeing that the man who sported a tuft of bristles on top of his rather pointed head was resting his lower face heavily in his cupped hand, looking for all the world like a coconut waiting to be shied at.

'I liked the subtleness at the end where the postman slowly and seductively pushes the rolled-up magazine into the letter box. It said a lot,' the coconut man observed, lifting his head revealing an appropriate matting of sparse coarse hair on his chin.

'Thank you,' said Hugos, 'I'm glad you saw that. I was wondering.'

'Pity it couldn't have been the back door though,' Coconut Head added, smirking.

'But then it wouldn't be subtle would it,' observed Shirley, grinning at Maeve and rolling her eyes.

'Just a small nit pick,' said James, the man who'd given up his seat for her and was consequently sitting with his knees up by his chest.

'What is it?' asked Hugos guardedly.

'In the middle you said, neither the neighbour nor his wife *are* suspicious, but it should be *is*. *Is* suspicious. Neither the neighbour nor his wife *is* suspicious. Co-relative conjunctions - the verb has to agree with the nouns. In this case the nouns are singular.'

'Thank you James,' said Hugos between gritted teeth.

'Good point James, but enough of that,' snapped Dora Dome. 'Now we'll move on to our newcomer Maeve Salmon,' she continued, taking up a fat red biro, which perfectly matched her snout, creating a perfectly co-ordinated fat red duo. 'What is its title?' she asked, biro poised.

'*Twenty-ninety-five*,' Maeve croaked, removing the four pages from her bag and, dry mouthed, stuttering a short résumé of what had gone before.

'You were meant to start at the beginning,' grumbled Dora Dome, almost shaking her head then appearing to think better of it. Maeve stared at the dangerous dangling balls and rather wished she'd gone through with it. 'Never mind,' Dora sighed, 'carry on.'

Maeve stared down at the trembling sheet in her hands, then began reading in a voice that quivered even more so:-

In twenty thirty-five when finally gene manipulation could cure all ills, it was decided a rule had to be made controlling deaths in order to keep the population down,' says Venus's Great-great-grandfather. 'I was in my seventies then and I understood, and agreed, that the cut-off age was to be one hundred and fifteen. It made sense then and it makes sense now.' He stretches out his long legs, looks relaxed. 'So you see the Tender Put Down is nothing to fear, not like the terrifying hospital deaths of the early twenty-first century. And, I'm dying to meet up with my Ginny.'

He grins at his joke, dying the operative word.

'But your brain, your memories,' Venus blurts.

Maeve heard herself reading, detached as if in a dream, or more like a nightmare. With frequent stops to swallow the excessive amounts of saliva swilling around in her mouth, she somehow got through until at last she was gabbling out the final paragraph of the fourth page:-

How can he, so intelligent, think he'll meet up with his dead wife, Venus thinks. What is there to meet? A soul of atomic sub-particles? Neutrinos perhaps: no mass, the essence of Ginny flitting around the Universe at the speed of light?

Maeve stopped, shuffled the four sheets of paper in her hands, not daring to look up. Was that silence a stunned one she wondered. Were they completely overcome by the intelligence of her work.

Hugos cleared his throat.

'Yes,' said Dora Dome, 'do you wish to comment?'

Maeve lifted her eyes from the swirls cut into the short pile of the stained beige carpet.

He leaned back, crossed his arms and rested them heavily upon his jutting belly. 'It was a bit far fetched wasn't it?' he said.

Maeve stared at him, astounded. Far fetched! Fucking far fetched. And he was writing about a man buggering Postman Pat!

'Not so much far fetched,' chipped in Shirley, 'but very downbeat. People don't like downbeat. Can't you raise the age of the Tender Put Down so that Venus's Great-great-grandfather can live longer?'

'One hundred and fifteen is the age the TPD comes into force,' Maeve exploded. 'And, for the story, he has to die.'

'Now, now, Maeve,' soothed Dora, 'it's always hard at first to accept criticism. Let's ask our English teacher, James, what he thought.'

And when she said the words *English teacher*, one side of her upper lip actually did curl.

'I think it was innovative,' said James slowly, crinkling an apologetic smile at her, 'but I think it lacks passion.'

'The passion comes later,' Maeve defended sulkily.

'Ah, but you have to hold the reader's attention from the beginning,' he advised. 'Change it just a little to insert more raw emotion. Cut out some of the dry scientific phrases.' He stretched out his arms to enfold his knees. 'And, by the way, when you said that Venus's Great-great-grandfather's colleagues would think he'd gone as mad as a hatter, that is a cliché.'

She was appalled. How could such a kind erudite man be so blind to great literature!

'But keep at it, it could be exceptionally good,' he added.

Could be, she inwardly fumed as Shirley Shakespeare began her reading. *COULD* be exceptionally good. Anyway, how could she change even one word of it after all that effort of typing.

At last the meeting was over and she limped home where, exhausted, she went straight to bed. It was a stupid idea thinking she could write a novel. She wished she was moving down to Freda's away from it all. At any rate she would ring Freda tomorrow and tell her she'd definitely be going to the party on the thirteenth. There, she would join in the fun to celebrate the pregnancy of her daughter's pig and her son-in-law's birthday and forget all about writing, forget all about keyboards, forget all about being an author.

'Oh Mary Wesley,' she cried, 'how did you manage to do it so late in life?'

She kept at it, Hector's voice gently said.

'Who bloody well asked you,' she blasted, 'why don't you sod off.'

And, that night, she didn't even try to oust the soul-crushing guilt snake that shared the bed with her, because she knew it deserved to be there.

Eight

Since that tragic evening when the literary acclaim she deserved had been denied her, Maeve's low spirits had slowly risen. The story of Venus and her partner Jupe in the year twenty ninety-five had become even more meaningful than her real life. Early each morning she rushed to the computer and, with just a few short breaks throughout the day, would often work right through till late at night.

Her only times away from the writing she loved were the evenings she played bridge with Wally Woodcock down at the Club.

This evening, as she drove past the Common towards Tooting Bec, the sudden blast of a horn made her jump, jerking the wheel round.

'Stupid cunt,' a man screamed, his face looming at her, coarse mouth contorting in his ugly mug as he repeated those degrading words.

Shaking, she yanked her window up against the vile dirty passenger in the vile dirty van she had nearly hit. No-one ever spoke like that in Freda's dear little Hampshire village, she thought, tears welling. Down in Wood Hill the only sounds were the twittering of birds and the bleating of sheep. A hot tear slid down her cheek as she thought of what might have been.

'You look upset my dear,' said Wally, staring at her across the bridge table, as usual tugging at his droopy moustache ends as if intent upon tearing them out.

'That's because I am,' she quavered, scrawling her name on her card.

'I know you are still grieving for your Hector, believe me I know what it's like, but it gradually gets easier to bear you know and coming here to the bridge cl...'

'No it's not because of *that*,' she cut in, for some unfair reason riled by his concern. *He'll be calling me diddums next and trying to wipe my nose*, she thought angrily.

'Why then, my dear Maeve?' he asked, leaning across the table and making to take hold of her hand.

'Because some ignorant bloke called me a *cunt*,' she shouted, snatching her hand away.

A silence bombed down on the hall and Wally shot back, face colouring as every head turned. Nobody spoke. Then Wally, weakly smiling, declared, 'How could he call you a *RR*unt.' Emphatically, he rolled the R. 'Just because you're small and slim. That's what makes you attractive,' he continued, warming to his own improvisation, playing to the attentive crowd. 'No way could you be considered a *RRR*unt.' This time his R was rolled so fiercely that, if she hadn't been able to see the vibrations in his tash, she'd have truly considered it to be the grating stutter of a pneumatic drill. But he'd caught the attention of his audience and she almost expected the lot of them to start clapping and demand an encore. Instead there was silence and, realising the excitement of the impromptu speech was over, they slowly transferred their attention back to their cards.   He smiled jubilantly at her, made a minuscule adjustment to the knot of his speckled brown tie then flicked forefinger against thumb under one of his moustache wings.

'Thank you Wally,' she muttered.

'Let's go for a drink after this,' he said striking while her gratitude was hot.

'Yes let's,' she agreed with reluctance, hoping he wouldn't fiddle with his moustache too much during the drinking process.

But by the end of the game her gratitude at his *RR*unt intervention had been coshed out of existence by his clubs' bid. Everyone knew it was asking for aces. Everyone that was except him.

'I've changed my mind about the drink,' she said curtly as they stood to go. 'The game has given me a headache.'

'As you wish,' he sighed.

She looked at his kind face perched on its stringy neck and wished that she fancied him.

'Maybe we can make a date for that trip to the South Bank we talked about,' he said as they left the hall.

'Yes, maybe,' she said absently.

He took out a diary from his tweed jacket, leafed through it, then said: 'How about this Saturday, the thirteenth?'

God, was he never going to give up. 'Sorry, I can't. I'm going down to Hampshire for my son-in-law's birthday party.' At least that was a genuine reason.

Undeterred, he riffled through his diary again. 'Well then, how about sometime next month, say Wednesday the seventh of June?'

'That sounds okay,' she muttered, unable to quickly think up an excuse.

Maeve carried her overnight case out to the landing. As she passed the open study door, she stared in at the non-whirring computer and the blank screen.

'Bye bye, see you after the party,' she foolishly said, raising her free hand and waving.

She arrived at Wisteria Cottage soon after mid-day and, after a snack lunch with Freda and Bernard, went up to rest, exhausted by the long drive down.

Later, refreshed, she threaded her way through a clucking squawking melee as Freda scattered corn to the squabbling ducks and hens.

'Wally Woodcock asked me to go out with him today,' Maeve remarked.

'What a pity it coincided with our party, but you can go another time can't you?'

'I can, but I'll only go once. He's all right as a bridge partner, but he's too old for me.'

'How old is he then?' Freda ceased her measured casting of corn to stare at her.

'Seventy-two, I think.'

'But that's the same age as you.'

Oh God. She'd made a boo-boo. Let the cat out of the bag. But maybe now was the time to tell her the secret she'd kept from her for so long? She took a deep breath, then slowly released it. Perhaps she wouldn't. But Freda would find out when she was dead and saw her birth certificate. Better she was alive to explain.

'No it isn't the same age as me Freda. I'm sixty-eight.'

'Don't be silly Mother,' Freda laughed, grabbing up a fistful of corn and throwing it out to the frantically squawking horde. 'You had your seventieth birthday party two years ago, remember? I was there.' She turned to her mother, casting a sly look. 'Have you been telling Wally Woodcock porkies about your age? Is that what this is about?'

'No. You. I've been telling *you* porkies about my age for all of your life. Once I'd started ... well, it was hard to go back. There was never the right time - until now.'

Maeve could see by the concerned look on her daughter's pudgy, yet beautiful, face, she was thinking her old ma had gone senile.

'I don't understand. You're saying you *weren't* seventy when you had your seventieth birthday party!' Agitated, Freda rotated her free hand fiercely round and round the corn in the bucket that hung on her arm.

'Yes, I wasn't seventy. I was sixty-six. My old friends Vera and Jean knew, and of course your father - that's why he wasn't bothered about not being invited. But by then I'd lived the lie so long I thought I might as well treat myself to a wild bash with a sexy male stripper while I had the energy for it, because by the time I really reached seventy I might not be able to cope.'

Freda's eyes widened into lustrous green traffic lights and her hand, now full of corn, shot up to her mouth.

'Don't eat that Freda,' Maeve snapped, suddenly back to the time when her daughter was two and eating handfuls of sand from her sandpit.

'But *why*?' Freda wailed.

'I've told you before. It'll upset your stomach.'

'Not that. *Why* have you lied. Did you want people to tell you how young you looked for your age? Is that it? Was it your warped way of fishing for compliments?'

'Don't you think I do look young for sixty-eight then?' Maeve flared, realising immediately she'd fallen into the conceit trap that was always her downfall.

'You don't even look *fifty*-eight, you know that,' said Freda vehemently, casting corn with such force at the poor fowl that they careered back, flapping and screeching, feathers flying, as if being raked by a maniac with a machine gun. Abruptly, Freda stopped her bombardment and whirled round on Maeve. 'Why! Why! Why!' she cried, dragging the back of her hand dramatically across her forehead. 'Why?' she added again, for good measure.

'To set you a good example.'

'A liar as a mother is supposed to be a good example!' Freda stamped her wellington boot down, just missing a tiny exotic duck that had ventured forward.

'Because I got pregnant when I was fifteen,' Maeve blurted. 'I was ashamed ... didn't want you ever to know. Nineteen was bad enough - the age that I told you.'

'You were just a schoolgirl?' Freda whispered.

'It was terrible in those days. I left school six weeks before you were born. I wasn't very big and my gymslip hid the bump. I even went in for my exams and matriculated. I'd just turned sixteen by the time you were born. Your dad came home on compassionate leave and we got married. It was expected.'

Freda linked her arm into Maeve's and squeezed it. 'I can't say it isn't a shock, because it is. A big one. But it's all a fuss about nothing isn't it,' she said.

Maeve looked into the eyes of her only child. They were brimming with sympathy. How easy it had been to tell her. Why hadn't she done so years ago? 'I didn't want to set you a bad example,' she muttered.

Freda patted the back of her mother's hand. 'I'm glad you've finally plucked up the courage. Glad you were just a naive young girl then, and not a senile old woman now - which is what I'd begun to think!' She kissed Maeve's cheek. 'But even though this is a significant moment in both our lives, I'm afraid I have to leave you now to help shut all the animals away, then quickly get back to the house to prepare for the party.' With a final consoling pat to her mother's hand, Freda hurried off.

Maeve followed in her daughter's glorious wake, feeling lighter, as if a weighty mantle had just been lifted from her shoulders. And the funny part was that she'd never really registered it had been there. Elated, she grinned at everything that moved, mingling with visitors, goats, sheep and the emu with the mismatched legs who was now her cupboard-love friend. Anyone watching his jerky dash to her side might have thought he was mocking her limp!

Gradually the stiffness in her hip eased away and she was tempted to go down to the stable block to see the new foal. Instead, she was drawn like a smoker to a tobacconist's shop to go to *The Bungalow*, the dwelling she still foolishly dreamed of one day being her home.

She sidled into the barn, past Cynthia Slocumb who, busy serving in her tea room, merely glanced up and waved, past a group of visitors paying the attendant their entrance money, and out into the car-park field beyond the open back doors. When she reached the top of the slope, she turned left into Nuthatch Lane, hurrying down to the T-junction at the end then right into Bramble Lane.

Spurred on by the hopeless dream that if it were still for sale she could somehow afford it, she broke into a trot. But, the sign that emerged in the distant garden had just one predominant word on it. And that word was SOLD. Resisting the temptation to get a closer look and feast her eyes on what might have been, she turned and mooched dolefully back.

Freda was in the kitchen sorting out glasses when she trailed in.

'Do you want any help?' Maeve asked, attempting a jolly smile.

'No thanks. Bernie's going to help me soon. There's two hours yet so why not go up and lie down again for a while - because, even though you're only sixty-eight, you're not getting any younger are you. You aren't, are you?' she sniggered.

'I wish!' Maeve laughed, wondering for a moment if she should knock a further year or two off. But no. Sixty-eight it was. No more lies. She wasn't getting any younger either and really could do with another rest. She went up to her bedroom and quickly fell asleep.

At last her furniture was in and *The Bungalow* was hers. Delirious with happiness, she danced, hooting with laughter, then threw herself vigorously into a fireside chair. It was at that moment that a deep thumping sound set up and she glanced anxiously at the fire place. A babble of screeching voices erupted, masking her scream as she saw that her dread had become a reality and that the strength of the booming vibrations was inexorably shaking the mahogany surround from its inadequate moorings. In direct line, she scrabbled to get to her feet as it started toppling. Louder and louder pulsed the beat, higher and higher screeched the voices, closer and closer came the top-heavy killer. Gathering all her strength, she flung herself sideways and as she slid onto the carpet her eyes opened and she saw she was in Freda's spare bedroom and realised that the babble of voices and thumping beat came from downstairs. Shakily, she hauled herself up and began to get ready for the party.

Nine

Maeve checked herself in the long mirror, seeing with satisfaction that Fidal Bassoon's miraculous transformation of her dry haystack into a glossy upsweep of tresses pinned up in large looping curls had survived her fitful sleep. She held up the hand mirror to view the back, thankful to see that a softening gauze of wispy spirals attractively curtained her neck. She changed the angle, surveying the whole length, seeing with relief that the black and turquoise silk dress was slinky enough to show off her slim figure, but not tight enough to reveal that the cheeks of her bum had slid downwards like half-melted scoops of icecream. She slicked on another coat of coral lipstick, blotted it, took a deep breath and stepped out of the room. Downstairs, she bumped into Freda in the hallway.

'You look great. I must introduce you to Buzz Pike, he's by himself and looking out of things,' Freda shouted above the din, grabbing her mother's arm and yanking her into the sitting room. She manoeuvred her through the flailing arms of dancers to a man clearly ill at ease, standing alone in the corner.

'This is Buzz Pike, he's Irish,' she yelled. 'This is my mother, Maeve,' she yelled even louder to him, before muttering an apology about the volume and hurrying away to turn it down.

Buzz cast her a shy smile as Lulu's raucous 'Shout' belted out. 'Sure I can't hear a thing,' he bawled, screwing up his face and pointing at one of his ears. Mercifully Lulu's lusty rendition was suddenly toned down as Freda reached the control. 'Pleased to meet you, so I am, whoever you are,' Buzz said, his delicately protruding top lip peeling back in a hesitant smile, revealing top central incisors angled slightly back at their meeting edge. He made as if to shake hands then raised his palm, awkwardly circling it, saying, 'Hi.'

'Hi,' she said, anxious to be equally modern, immediately

worrying that her vague hand motion had turned out more like the floppity wave of the queen.

'Hi,' he repeated, circling his flat hand again, then saying, 'Sorry, I didn't catch your name.'

'I'm Maeve,' she said, for some reason deliberately missing out her connection with Freda. They stood and stared at each other and as she gazed into his vivid blue eyes a hot flush slowly spread over her. Confused, she turned away.

'Are you okay Maeve?'

'Yes, I'm fine, just … just need some water, must go … must go to the kitchen and get some.'

'Sure, that'd do it, you're looking very hot so you are. Stay there man and I'll get it.'

Man! she looked down at the scooped neck of her best dress to check if her breasts had vanished, but they were still in situ, jutting forward in 36D fullness, a modest line of dark cleavage visible, at least from her aerial viewpoint.

'Don't move from that spot,' he instructed, handing her his can of beer.

She watched him push his way through the dancers, surprised to see from the back that his sandy hair was long and gathered into a tight pony tail.

'Sorry I had to go,' said Freda, suddenly by her side, 'it was too loud to be able to talk, then I got waylaid by Cynthia. But I've brought you a glass of chilled wine and I've opened the French windows too - it's quite safe, all the animals are locked away for tonight. What did you think of Buzz? He seems nice doesn't he.'

'Mmm,' she said trying to sound non-committal as, still holding his beer, she placed the wine down on top of the TV. 'There's something familiar about him. Where does he live?'

Freda looked uncomfortable. 'He's just moved to Wood Hill from London, though he's obviously Irish. Oh look there's Bernard the birthday boy,' she cried, rushing off.

'Some people have all the luck,' a man close behind her was saying loudly. 'Ignorant as sin, no schooling you know, yet he wins a fortune.'

'Here's your water,' said Buzz pushing his way back beside her.

Murmuring her thanks, she took the tumbler from him and, as their hands brushed in that brief exchange, tingles like mild electric shocks sped through her.

'You're still looking flushed. Are you sure you're okay?' he said, taking his can from her, causing yet more titillating sensations that disconcertingly homed in on her inner thighs.

'Yes. Yes. Just need this water ...' she took a long swig then switched the tumbler of water for the glass of wine and took a large gulp from that too. 'And some fresh air,' she added, fanning herself with her free hand.

'Let's go outside then,' he said, hovering for a moment as if about to touch her elbow, then awkwardly turning and leading the way.

On wobbly legs she followed, wondering why this shy man with the slightly crooked nose, in the ordinary navy cotton shirt and ordinary denim trousers was having such an effect on her. And why she felt that she knew him.

Outside, he breathed in deeply through nostrils not quite aligned. He banged on his chest. 'I love it here,' he said 'the Hampshire air ... the sounds ... just listen won't you ... did you hear that?'

'That was just a pig squealing,' she giggled.

'Aye, it was so it was, but I never heard pigs squealing in Kilburn where I've just moved from. Not animal pigs at any rate,' he added, his eyes immediately darting around as if fearing the village bobby was standing within earshot. He took a gulp of his beer, wiped his mouth with his hand. 'Wood Hill's a magic place, so it is. Do you live in the village?'

'No, I'm just staying with Freda for the weekend. I live in London - in Tooting.'

'London's exciting but Wood Hill's a special wee village,' he said dreamily.

'Yes, very special,' she agreed. 'I *wanted* to live here but the property I'd set my heart on was too dear, and now it's been sold.'

In the gathering dimness of night his kind eyes glowed beneath dead straight, fair eyebrows. It was as if they'd been carefully drawn with a ruler to make up for the slapdash line of his nose. Nervously, she glugged her wine down to the last drop.

'I'll get you another,' he offered.

But she didn't want him to move, wishing to savour the increasing thrill of standing so close to him. 'Thanks but I can wait till you've finished your beer see that mobile home over there in the old yard that's where Freda offered to let me stay permanently it's where her pig Hermione lives,' she gabbled, overcome by nervousness and the need to keep him put.

'But that's *appalling*, offering you a smelly pig sty to live in!'

'No. No, it isn't. It's the greatest sacrifice she could have made. That great porker of hers is the substitute for the child she couldn't conceive. She dotes on her. To offer her home to me was a huge compliment.'

Buzz began to chuckle, a deep gentle rumble that quickly grew to a belly laugh.

'It's true,' she giggled. 'Hermione's her precious baby - and that's not some ordinary smelly pigsty, it's a smelly *luxury* one with several rooms - though the pig is only allowed in one of them!'

'To tell you the truth, I hardly know this Freda,' he laughed, 'but she must be a very special friend of yours ...'

Now is the time to tell him that Freda is such a special friend she is my daughter, Maeve thought, though she said nothing.

'... a *very* special friend,' he repeated, 'to offer her piggy's home to you. Not many would do that.' He bent over, hands on knees, convulsed, drawing her in till they were both howling like loons.

'Oh hel*lo*,' cut in a sophisticated blonde, 'what's the joke?' The woman whom Maeve knew to be Poppy Bambridge flashed her an apologetic smile. 'Sorry to interrupt your fun Maeve, but I've been absolutely *dying* to meet this man.'

Buzz's merriment abruptly ceased. 'Hi,' he said, tracing out a circle with his flat palm, then stepping back a pace

'You're the lucky man who won a million on *Who Wants to be a Millionaire* aren't you,' she pronounced, smiling.

Maeve felt her mouth gape.

'Tell me, was being on television much of an ordeal?' Poppy carried on.

'Indeed it was, but didn't I have nothing to lose and everything to gain.' He looked down, shuffling his feet as if searching for a hole to fall in.

'I *thought* I recognised you,' Maeve exclaimed. 'The straight eyebrows, the vivid blue eyes.' She didn't carry on to mention his strong nose which changed direction by a degree or two just below its bridge.

He reddened, pulled his pony tail forward and fiddled with the ends, and the memory became clearer. It was soon after Hector had died and watching the first man to win that much on British TV had helped take her mind off her new loneliness, though not off the exorbitant cost of the funeral. *I could have done with winning some of that,* she remembered thinking, though still not regretting the extra cost of the brass handles.

'Wasn't your hair loose and shorter then?' she asked as the recollection became clearer. She narrowed her eyes, blurring him but sharpening her memory. 'And, of *course!* The words exploded out like a burst balloon, making him reel back further. 'Sorry, but, of *course,*' she repeated. 'You had a full beard then didn't you.'

'I did, but after I'd won all that money I had no wish to be pointed out in the streets, so I shaved it off and grew my hair longer, tying it back.' He took a quick swig of his beer.

'I was surprised when you had to phone a friend on that quarter of a million question,' Poppy stated.

'Yes, so was I,' agreed Maeve. 'I thought *everyone* knew that the L in LASER stood for light.'

Like a zebra rolling its eyes at a trusted cameraman who'd carried on filming whilst a lion ripped its back apart, his hurt gaze transferred from Poppy to her.

'I knew the answer so I did, but I didn't dare say it without confirmation.' He pulled his ponytail forward, gave it a tug, flicked it back, took another swig from the tin.

'Very sensible,' Maeve gushed, in an effort to make up for her thoughtless words.

'*Everyone* says it's easy,' he said bitterly, draining the tin, obviously unmollified.

'Yes, everyone does,' Poppy agreed, shrewdly not establishing if she was included in the everyone, although she'd as good as said she was.

'As Chris Tarrant always says, it's only easy if you know the answer,' he added, defending as if he'd said all this before and was on automatic pilot.

'I think it's wonderful that you won,' said Poppy, laying her hand on his arm. 'And that final question, something about a bird, had all of us stumped - but not you.'

'Yes it did,' Maeve hastened to agree. 'It had me stumped too.'

'Thank you,' he muttered, crushing the can in one hand.

'Suppose you've bought yourself a mansion and a new car,' Maeve said.

'Bought myself a three litre Jag - it's always been my dream.'

'And wonderful that you chose to spend your money on *The Bungalow,*' added Poppy, 'a compliment to all of us living here in Wood Hill.'

'*The Bungalow!*' Maeve exploded. 'So it was you.'

'What's wrong with me buying it?' he cried. 'It was for sale. I had the money. What's wrong with that man?' He took the already squashed tin in both hands, crushing it further.

'Oh dear,' muttered Poppy, sloping off.

'*I* wanted it,' she grumbled. 'That was the property I told you about, the one I couldn't afford.' She held her empty wine glass upside down and flicked it at the grass.

'I'm sorry to hear that so I am, but it's really not my fault.'

'Course it's not,' she said, flicking again.

Suddenly Bernard appeared at the open French windows. 'Freda told me to get you in,' he called. 'She's lighting the candles on my birthday cake and everyone's to be there. Plenty of time though, she's put all fifty-four on.'

'What about Princess?' Maeve asked as they followed him in. 'This party's for her too. Is she standing by the cake displaying her pregnant tum?'

Buzz, at her elbow, chuckled softly and something about his close presence and the sound of his laugh made her skin prickle.

'When Princess has her litter you'll be a great-grandfather you know,' she joked to Bernard as they crossed the emptying sitting room.

'And you'll be a great-great-grandmother,' he retorted, and immediately she realised her mistake. She whipped round to see Buzz's reaction and was relieved to see that he'd been waylaid by Cynthia, Freda's best friend who ran the barn teashop.

He'll find out soon enough, she told herself, as she pushed her way through the throng into the kitchen-diner. A daughter of fifty-two and a son-in-law of fifty-four wouldn't stay unidentified for long. She glanced at all the people gathered around the table where Freda was setting up a blaze of candles, mentally daring any one of them to say anything. However her powers of thought transference were obviously non-existent for immediately, Esmerelda, that witch-woman from Rugged Farm next door, piped up.

'Hello, en't you feeling old having a son-in-law that age.'

'Shhh,' Maeve hissed fiercely, plunging the bright gypsy face into a swarthy glower. 'Shhh, he's about to blow out his candles,' she added to make sense of it. She glanced back, relieved to see Buzz still talking to Cynthia.

'But Freda en't finished lighting 'em yet,' observed Esmerelda, still clearly miffed.

'She's very quick,' Maeve explained, noting with dismay that Freda had held the match with the flame burning upwards so it had just gone out. She should have insisted her daughter had joined the Girl Guides when she was young, she realised belatedly.

A glass of champagne was shoved into her hand as the last few candles were lit. Silence settled. Bernard stepped forward and with his now fifty-four year old lungs, blew the conflagration out in three prolonged and noisy inhales and exhales of breath.

Happy Birthday revved up and she swore she felt Buzz's presence behind her before hearing his sonorous voice.

When the singing and cheering had stopped, Bernard held up his hands for silence. He drew Freda to him. 'As you all know, this isn't just for my birthday, it's also for the first of our grandchildren to conceive.' He lifted his bubbly. 'So, here's to our Princess,' he said, sounding choked.

'To Princess,' intoned the assembled throng, raising their glasses.

'I thought Princess was a pig,' whispered Buzz.

'She is, she's one of Hermione's grown-up litter,' Maeve confirmed.

And his low contagious chuckle rumbled forth again.

'Shhh,' she sniggered, trying to control herself, 'Freda and Bernard are deadly serious about their porkers, as you can see.'

Freda, eyes glistening like emeralds, lips struggling bravely, looking as if they were doing some weird new form of mouth break-dancing, started to cut the cake.

Maeve glanced around at her daughter and son-in-law's friends and neighbours crammed into the room, seeing the twinkling eyes of people, all on the verge of hysterics. She hoped they weren't also on the verge of divulging the great-great-grandmotherly connection of the forthcoming litter to her. Slices of cake were handed out and she and Buzz took theirs and pushed their way through to a clear space by the sink where they placed their glasses down on the draining board.

'This cake looks good,' he said, taking a hefty bite. 'And it *is* good,' he mumbled, 'go on, you try it.'

Obediently, she lifted hers off the plate and daintily nibbled, then struck by its delicious chocolatiness, began greedily scoffing.

'It isn't often I feel at ease like this with someone I've just met,' Buzz said, leaning back against the work unit, gazing softly at her.

'Nor me,' she agreed, fluttering her eyelashes and flashing him a hopefully sexy grin.

'Your teeth,' he said, tapping his angled incisors.

'Of course,' she snapped, really offended.

'Sure and I never ever thought they were dentures ...' He trailed off looking miserable.

'Well, one of them's capped,' she admitted, to be fair to him.

'Perhaps I should have said nothing, I'm never sure about these sort of things ...' He petered out again, looking even more miserable.

'Yahoo,' called Freda, waving at them from the midst of the throng streaming out to the hall.

Maeve grinned and waved back but strangely Freda bared her teeth, pointing at them, as she swept past.

'What's up with my teeth?' she asked uneasily.

'Isn't that what I was trying to tell you,' Buzz bawled into the quietness that had suddenly descended. 'Yours are covered in cake crumbs.'

And the humiliation that enveloped her was worse than when she'd wet herself at her tenth birthday party, worse than when she'd tipped water all over her boss's lunch when pouring from a tall jug, worse than when her knickers had fallen down to her ankles when climbing the stairs of a bus. Here she was grinning like a lovelorn idiot with brown speckled teeth.

She snatched up her glass, filled her mouth, pumped the champagne up and down, distorting her chin, distending her top lip, feeling her nostrils stretch. She peered down, seeing the tip of her nose lifting with each upward surge of the bubbly. Realising too late she must look like a cross-eyed Miss Piggy, she stopped pumping and looked up to see Buzz staring at her. She swallowed hard, instantly choking on bubbles that rushed down her throat then surged up to her nose.

'Cough up,' he said anxiously, taking the glass from her as she staggered around making rasping noises. He made to bang her on the back, but she ducked away, clinging to the edge of the sink, gasping, wishing she could disappear down the plug hole, or even die, which seemed highly probable as, vainly, she fought for breath. Very, very gradually, she regained control until at last, heart pounding, cheeks on fire, inhaling and exhaling in long tremulous breaths, she let go the sink, and turned to him.

'That was a wee bit scary for you,' he observed.

Still panting, she nodded her agreement, although a *wee* bit scary wasn't exactly how she'd have described it. For wee replace shit, because she'd truly been shit scared. Not because she thought she was really going to expire, but because she thought that when she turned round he'd be gone, having taken his chance to escape.

'Your teeth must be pristine after such energetic ablutions, so why don't you give us one of your lovely smiles again.' Comically, he dragged the sides of his mouth sideways with hooked little fingers, making a face at her.

She giggled through closed lips, then sucked at her front teeth and flicked her tongue around in a final check-up.

He nodded encouragingly.

She looped back a fallen tress.

'Come on, Maeve,' he urged, baring his gnashers.

Now feeling shy more than worried, she parted her lips in what she knew was a false smile.

'Beautiful,' he whispered.

And her already pumping heart missed at least three beats.

'I see you're wearing a wedding ring,' he noted as he handed her back her glass, which, amazingly, still had some drink in it.

'Yes, but my husband's dead,' she rushed, in what she suddenly realised sounded horribly gleeful. She waited for Hector's ghostly reproach but he remained silent. 'Early in January - he just made it into the new millennium,' she added, a sudden sadness gripping her. It wasn't that long ago. Not long enough to fall for someone else. Not after fifty-two years of togetherness, quite a few of which had been good.

Buzz gazed at her and she noticed for the first time that his eyes were exactly the same vivid hue as the Dulux Gloss Blue Jive Liquid paint she'd picked for the paintwork in her lavatory.

'I'm sorry to hear that,' he said, reverently bowing his head, moving it into the sphere of the ceiling spotlight which torched his hair into glowing amber. She stared, seeing two fine threads of silver running through it. Maybe he was older than he looked, she thought hopefully, casting aside her guilt. After all there were no rules to say when you were allowed to fancy another man after your old one had gone.

The sound of a romantic waltz drifted through from the other room ending her traitorous thoughts. Her pulse quickened. Soon he would take her in his arms and they'd be dancing. But he just stood there.

'Shall we go and join the others?' she suggested, attempting nonchalance.

'Sorry Maeve, it's been great meeting you, but I really must go now.'

'Go!'

'Sure, I must get back, it's kind of late for me.'

'But you must have time for just one dance,' she pleaded, all attempts at insouciance gone.

'Never been any good at things like dancing. Always too busy earning a crust.' He started to move away.

'But not now, not now you've won a million,' she coaxed. 'I can start teaching you.' She held out her arms, swayed, smiled encouragingly.

'Sorry, I have to go. Hope to see you again one day, sure I really do.'

And, after another of his stiff waves, he turned, strode out to the hall, opened the front door, glanced back, waved again, walked through, closing the door firmly behind him. And it was all she could do not to fly out into the darkness, grab hold of his pony tail and haul him back in. Instead, she tottered into the low-lit room full of smooching dancers, searching for Freda. Pictures of her snuggled into Buzz's arms filled her tormented mind as she spotted Freda entwined with Bernard. She pushed her way to them, grasped hold of her daughter's arm.

'Just going up to bed, she stated. And, in answer to the surprised look, because her daughter knew her mother was always one for a party, she added, 'Because, as you very well know, I'm not getting any younger.'

Freda nodded, smiling, obviously going along with that because it confirmed what she'd already said earlier. But, upstairs, over three hours later, the party audibly over, Maeve was still tossing and turning, her emotions in turmoil. How could she have these longings for a man who was possibly about the same age as her son-in-law? Yet she knew that she did.

By four o'clock she had reasoned that an attractive man like Buzz Pike must have a wife and family. A wife who didn't like parties and who had therefore stayed at home. A wife he had to hurry back to. A wife in *her* Bungalow, sleeping with the man she'd fallen for. Why oh why, when he'd asked if she was married, hadn't she asked if he was too?

At some time, she must have drifted off for when she next

opened her eyes it was nine o'clock. She unclenched her fists, relieved that the news headlines *Female Salmon knocks out female Pike* must have been in a nightmare, because as she'd hit the Pike woman's head with her handbag in *The Bungalow*, it had seemed as real as when she'd hit the Rasta with her handbag in the library. But much more enjoyable.

The passion for Buzz that had consumed her in the night had now strangely transformed to anger that he owned the home she wanted to be hers. 'It's not *fair*,' she complained, snapping a bite into her Marmite toast, risking the tooth cap dislodgement. 'Buzz Pike gets *The Bungalow* for answering questions everyone could have got right.'

'Not everyone,' sighed Bernard, passing his hand over his hung-over brow. 'The one that got him the million - something about a bird - that was hard. At least, I thought so.'

'Well, all except that one,' she conceded. 'But he won the first hundred knowing that Raindrops Keep Falling on your Head and not your shoulders, knees or balls.'

'Surely not balls,' yawned Freda.

'Well maybe not, but, I mean, I can finish *The Times* cryptic crossword and when I send it in I don't even win their measly fountain pen - finishing that off must be worth a million if Raindrops Keep Falling your Head is worth a hundred.'

'That's the way the cookie crumbles,' said Bernard sleepily, stretching his arms in the air.

'And that's a cliché,' she snapped, noting their ensuing startled looks.

'What's with the cliché?' asked Freda, now slightly more alert. 'Everyone talks in them, so what?'

But she didn't respond. Her novel was a secret between her and the Novel Group, and she intended to keep it like that.

As they cleared the table, Freda suggested going out for a walk to help clear their heads. 'I've organised people to take care of the animals this morning so if you like we could take a stroll past *The Bungalow* - you might see Buzz. It would be nice for you to meet up again. You seemed to get on like a house on fire.'

'No. No, I have to get back to Tooting. I'm in a bridge tournament with Wally tonight.'

She'd fibbed once again to her daughter. But, she couldn't bear passing *The Bungalow* and witnessing the man whose presence made her tingle ensconced there with his wife.

'You didn't mention bridge before,' challenged Freda, her eyes searching her mother's face like piercing green lie detectors.

'To tell you the truth,' she lied again, 'I'd forgotten about it. And, by the way, getting on like a house on fire is also a cliché.'

'Oh, pardon me,' Freda said, stalking to the sink.

And still she didn't let on about her novel, or the Novel Group weirdos who'd made her so hypersensitive about such normal sayings. Though next time she read out there wouldn't be one for them to moan about. She'd bloody well make sure of that.

But, as she drove back to London along the M3, her head wasn't full of her novel as it had been when she'd driven down. The only thing occupying her mind was the shy attractive Irishman - Buzz Pike.

Ten

Whatever she was doing Buzz lurked in her mind. As she crouched, hauling clothes from the washing machine, his soft voice caressed her bad hip. As she drew her bedroom curtains back, the light that flooded in had the sand-gold hue of his hair. As she sat on the lavatory, gazing at the nearest wall tile, the images she used to see in its fine crazing - a dragon breathing fire most often, a fairy on a cobweb sometimes, two mating pigs very occasionally - was now always the profile of an erect man set at an angle, head lodged into the top right-hand corner, long ponytail falling, foot squashed into the tile at the bottom left corner, toes broken or missing to fit in (a prophetic image as it transpired), and a suggestive line jutting upwards from the fine mass of hair-line flaws in his pubic area - a shallow line she found herself absently enlarging with a hairpin on one shaming occasion.

Three weeks passed and she pounded the keys getting faster and faster. Then came the first Tuesday in June and the big decision. Should she go to the Novel Group meeting, or should she continue alone?

By the evening, she had decided. Donning her black velour track suit and her comfy trainers, she headed for Dickens Road, the next four pages folded into her bag ready for reading.

'Hello Maeve,' Shirley Shakespeare's voice called out behind her as she neared Hugos Thayre's house.

She turned, astonished again to witness the roundness of her.

'A lot of people don't brave it twice,' Shirley commented as they walked down the path.

She rang the bell at the side of the peeling door, which immediately opened.

'Ah, Maeve Fish,' Hugos exclaimed, 'so you've come back to us.'

'Maeve *Salmon*,' she corrected, entering the fried onion atmosphere of the dingy hall, perturbed at their obvious amazement that she'd returned.

'Not far off,' he said. 'Fish. Salmon. I'm good with names. Go on straight through.'

Quivering, she pushed open the door and entered, noting that Dora Dome and the coconut head man both sat in the same positions as last time. Unsure, she took the comfortable chair that James had given up for her, immediately leaping up as he walked in.

'No, no,' he said, flapping both hands downwards. 'It's yours dear lady, relax.'

Gratefully, she settled in.

By five past eight, everyone from the last meeting had assembled, plus a sexy looking young woman called Abigail who apologised for not attending last time, explaining to Maeve that she was a nurse and was often on night duty.

Dora asked Shirley to kick off and, as she launched into her novel, *Two into One Will Go*, about two women who openly and happily shared a man, Maeve noticed that even her words seem to float out like bubbles. And she began to wonder if Spud, one of the two women in the story, could in reality be Parsnip, Shirley's flat mate, especially when the orange electrostatic duster on a stick was mentioned, for they were always on sale in the Betterware catalogue, though intended for attracting and picking up dust, not the sensual titillation practised by Shirley's character.

'Well that really got me going,' said Hugos, stretching over his bulky belly and scratching his crotch.

'Got you going!' spat Shirley. 'It was meant to get you thinking. Thinking about how wise those two women were to share a man, not to be bound to him one hundred percent. Just fifty percent of all duties and pleasures. Plenty of time off. The best of all worlds.'

'Well it got me going,' he reiterated, having another scratch.

'Anything else to say anyone?' asked Dora hurriedly.

'With a title like 'Two Into One Will Go,' shouldn't it be two men sharing one woman,' suggested Abigail, quite unabashed by the anatomical pictures conjured up by her suggestion. But then if a nurse couldn't mention such things, who could, Maeve reflected.

'Any other *constructive* criticism?' asked Dora, meaningfully.

Maeve was dying to ask if it was based on real life, but didn't like to.

'No? That's settled Shirley then,' said Dora. 'Now, how about

James Joist, our English teacher.'

Once again, as she pronounced the words *English teacher*, her upper lip hitched up into a disdainful curl.

James opened a black arch file and began reading in a full rich voice with diction as precise as his grammar. It was a historical called 'Civil Roar' and was about the problems of a Roundhead and a Cavalier who were devoted friends.

'A bit stiff,' commented Shirley, provoking a snigger from the nurse.

'Just because you're in the Men's Ward,' giggled Shirley, egging her on.

'Also,' cut in Dora, glaring, red nose pulsating, 'I think you went into too much detail about the Civil War. It's the interaction between the two protagonists that's important. Readers don't want a lecture.'

'Thank you,' said James, surprisingly meekly.

And Maeve realised that skulking amongst their peculiar observations and suspect jokes, was good sound advice, if only one could detect it.

'Now Maeve, it's your turn,' she said at last. *Twenty Ninety-Five*, from where you left off last time if you don't mind. No cutting out great chunks.'

Clutching her four pages, she cleared her throat and squeakily started:-

Venus walks to the centre of her small back yard, sits down in her Virtuality Chair, programs in Sydney Harbour, then lolls back abandoning her body to the instant heat of the Virtually Natural Sun. She closes her eyes, listening to the lazy rhythm of the waves as they break upon the sand. This Virtuality Garden is glorious, absolutely glorious. Winter in England, in the heart of London, who'd have thought it! You were wrong Great-great-Granddaddy, she thinks, the privilege of earning World Currency to buy things like this is worth a contract marriage conceding the dubious right to bear a child.

The sudden scream of a sea-gull snaps her eyes open. She stares out to sea then shoots bolt upright. There they are. Early. She leans forward peering out across the water. A flotilla of brilliant sails is rounding the rocks. Joyous, daring, dipping, falling, righting, almost flying. Fluorescent colours tautly bowed, criss-crossing the sparkling blue water. If today were to be the same as other days, in amongst those vivid colours speeding across the bay there would be a plain black sail.

She grabs up the binoculars, sweeping the sights across the windsurfers to the rocky headland. And, here it comes. The jet black sail. And there he is, balancing on the board - the Black-sail-man. Through the powerful lenses she can see him clearly, leaning out, his long sandy hair streaming in the wind. He flips round, flies towards her, and she activates the lenses to zoom onto his face, seeing the quick flash of blue as he blinks in the spray. Electric tingles speed through her inner thighs. SOOD, she wants him. Wants his arms around her, wants his hands on her flesh, wants ...

'What're you looking at?'

She jumps. 'I didn't hear you there, you startled me,' she blurts, turning to Jupe.

'Come on, what were you looking at?' he persists, pushing his fingers through his tight black curls, staring intently.

She knows he is aware of her discomfort, can feel that her cheeks have flushed red. But why? she asks herself. Their marriage is merely a legal contract. It wasn't her fault he'd fallen in love with her and she'd fallen for someone else. Nevertheless she flounders.

She stopped reading, not daring to raise her eyes. At last James' voice broke the silence.

'Maeve, that was so much better. Before there was no passion. This time it was jam-packed with it ... almost as if ...'

She looked up.

'Almost as if you were writing from experience.'

Around the room she saw quizzical eyes staring at her.

'No. I just have a good imagination,' she mumbled. No-one spoke. '*And* I remember back to when I was young,' she added to break the embarrassing silence, though not really recalling any experience in the past that matched the strength of emotion that was swamping her these days.

'Must have a good memory,' sniggered Abigail to Shirley, continuing sotto voce, 'she must be about fifty.'

And Maeve's heart that had been plummeting, bungee jumped back up again. About fifty - and her aged sixty-eight!

'It's good, but did you say SOOD? queried Conan the coconut head.

'Yes, short for Scientists Of Our Destiny - they run the World,' she explained. 'And Venus wouldn't say God,' Conan murmured thoughtfully, adding, 'I like it - made me think about what it'll be like in the future.'

'The future written in the present tense,' said James. 'Excellent.

You really must carry on, it has great potential.'

She skipped home, hopping on and off the kerb like Gene Kelly *Singing in the Rain*, except it wasn't raining and she twirled her shoulder bag instead of an umbrella. That was until the strap broke and the bag flew over a hedge. When she went to retrieve it, a young woman appeared at an open window bawling that it was bad enough kids for ever chucking things into her front garden and vandalising it but if old people were going to start doing it too, it was time to emigrate.

'Sorry, it was an accident,' Maeve said, dropping to her hands and knees, grovelling in every sense of the word, as she retrieved the flying missile from a clump of broken lupins.

'That's what they all say,' the woman blasted, slamming the window shut.

Next day, Wednesday seventh of June, Maeve kept the date she'd rashly made with old Wally.

Eleven

From across the road by M & S, Maeve could see him standing proudly erect like a soldier guarding the entrance to Tooting Broadway Station from enemy attack. As she crossed with the jostling crowd, she saw him dash to the kerbside to greet her, the wings of his moustache raised like jetfoils on the uplift of his beaming smile. If he'd cut off the dangly bits, he'd look like an old photo she'd once seen of Einstein, she realised. Same deep set, bloodhound eyes, same swept-back luxuriant white hair.

'You look very nice,' he said, crushing her in his arms in a manner quite unbefitting for a platonic bridge partner.

She pulled away, pleased to regain her breath, pleased his tash had settled back to its natural droop, and pleased he'd said she looked nice, though she rather wished he'd said something a little more stirring, like glamorous, or radiant. After all she was wearing her new cream ankle-length skirt with the slit up the side which was the trendiest garment in her wardrobe, thanks to the BHS sale.

'I like your blouse, it's nice,' he commented as they waited on the platform. 'It's a nice colour.'

Nice, again she inwardly groaned. *Nice* blouse *nice* colour. It was scarlet silk and it was fantastic. She supposed she could reciprocate by telling him his cravat was nice. But it wasn't, it was horrible, even worse than the normal dull ties he wore. All that floppy beige-green paisley, meant to conceal the worn oldness of his neck but failing dismally. Already she was wishing she'd turned him down and carried on with her writing.

But sitting squashed up close beside him on the train she found she liked the smell of his piquant aftershave and the feel of his tweed jacket against her bare arm. And, by the time they'd got to Clapham North, she felt glad to have a man by her side again and especially one with whom she could relax, undisturbed by fantasy yearnings. At Waterloo they alighted and wandered down to the river, gawping in astonishment as the top pods of the London Eye came into view, astounded by their great height. They made their way to its base and craned their necks to look up at the giant Ferris wheel.

'It's even more impressive when you're really close to it,' she observed.

'Just like you,' he whispered. 'Have I ever told you how I love the way you do your hair, all piled up on top like that but with untidy bits dangling down.' He reached out to touch a tendril.

'Yes, you have told me,' she said, flipping her head away, feeling her cheeks flush.

'My wife, Nellie, used to blush like that at a compliment,' he said, making to take hold of her arm.

But she side-stepped into a group of people waiting at a hot-dog stand.

'These oniony smells are making my mouth water - let's buy one,' she suggested.

His eyes, nostrils and mouth contracted, as if she'd offered him a large spoonful of syrup of figs instead of a mere hot-dog.

'I'd thought we could eat in the Royal Festival Hall.'

'Suppose it would be comfortable,' she conceded.

So they headed off in that direction, side by side, close, but without touching, except that when walking under the bridge at the very moment a train rumbled over, she stumbled in fright at the sudden noise, causing their hands to make fleeting contact. His dark eyes rolled in her direction, shining with wicked delight, like a fourteen-year-old who'd delved into a bra for the first time and was expecting the full works. *On your bike*, she silently chided, the brief touch having done nothing for her.

Upstairs, in the spacious area alongside the bar, they made their selections from the self-service salad section. They ate without speaking at first, watching and listening to a young Oriental cellist with long straight black hair. Her movements were as fluid as the haunting tunes she played. But as soon as she had finished they began to talk about their first impressions of the stark concrete exterior of the building in which they sat.

'Maybe we were here on the South Bank at the same time all those years ago,' he said. 'Maybe we visited the Festival of Britain and maybe I was standing right next to you. Maybe ...'

His eyes gleamed with adoration like a chimpanzee gazing

enraptured at its keeper.

Perturbed, she butted in. 'Maybe we *were* here at the same time in 1951, but it wouldn't have meant anything because I was nineteen years old then, married, and with a three-year-old kid.' She rammed a small beetroot into her mouth and bit hard into it, feeling its vinegary juices squirt out, then trickle down her chin.

Smiling indulgently, he whipped out a large handkerchief and daubed at her humiliation, transferring the purple-red stain to its pristine whiteness. Silently, he folded it back into his top pocket and she was overcome with gratitude for his consideration and silence. Hector would have guffawed loudly, showing her up, or grumbled at her carelessness. She arrested her unkind thoughts, waiting for the spooky wail of reproach, but nothing came. Had she at last given up Hector's ghost she wondered - or was it he who had given up her?

After they'd eaten, they sauntered along beside the Thames, reminiscing about the air raids they'd lived through as children and, just like Hector and Freda and all the rest of them, he refused to believe her absolutely true story about her grandmother praying to God as bombs rained down.

'I swear it,' she said, 'my grandmother pleaded with Him that she wouldn't be killed and, because of that, the glinting hell bomb that was destined for her house suddenly veered off smack into the middle of our roof.'

'How do you *know* it was destined for her house but suddenly veered off?'

'Because, despite everyone saying I was tucked away safely in the Anderson shelter, I clearly remember looking up and seeing it change direction.'

'No-one in their right mind would look up while bombs were falling,' he said scathingly.

'Well *I* did.'

'Don't see how,' he muttered.

A boat on the river hooted a warning as she drew in breath to explain. It wasn't any use anyway, nobody ever believed her, so she let it out again and they ambled along in silence until he said:

'I was called up in 1943. Ruined my education. By the time I was demobbed I thought I was too old to carry on, though I wasn't really. And then I met sweet Nellie and in six months we were wed...'

She wondered if sweet Nellie had, like her, been too obliging in the knicker area, though he'd never talked of a child.

'... and she encouraged me to go to evening classes where, after three years hard slog, I got my HND in engineering and thus a better job. But her joyous spirit slowly withered as she failed to conceive and in the end, well, we just lived together, more or less like brother and sister.'

She thought of her brother, five years older than her and always trying his best to touch her up or see her naked. Living together like brother and sister didn't have to mean what he had implied!

As she gazed at the floating rubbish sweeping out with the tide, she thought of her sadly childless daughter, how her withered spirit had been revived by the addition of her pig, and she wondered if his Nellie would have become joyous again if she'd taken on a porker, or even a budgerigar, something alive to look after, instead of moping around getting sad.

Tentatively, Wally took hold of her hand and she didn't pull it away, finding she enjoyed being with someone who shared memories similar to her own, especially while strolling along the riverside on such a sunny day.

'Let's go to the Tate Modern in the old Bankside Power Station, it's just opened,' he said.

'Yes, let's,' she agreed, keen to see London's newest gallery of modern art.

But, by the time they'd reached the pub just before it, her hip was hurting.

'You're limping Maeve,' he observed, 'here hang onto my arm. Do you have a stone in your shoe, or something?'

'No, it's arthritis,' she reluctantly admitted. 'It's just that I've walked too far.'

'Oh dear dear. We'll do the Tate another time,' he said, guiding her to an empty table on the pub terrace. 'We'll sit and rest a while. What would you like to drink?'

And as he went inside to order, she gazed at the beautiful but uncrossable new Millennium Footbridge, and was unable to remember when she'd last felt this content. Wally, despite his outmoded dress and old-fashioned ways, was a pleasure to be with, though he didn't make her inner thighs tingle, not like Buzz Pike. That, she realised, was probably the reason why she felt so relaxed.

But, as he drank his beer and she sipped her cider, his chimpanzee gaze of adoration intensified to that of a besotted gorilla, and she became nervous.

'Look,' she said to distract him, 'see how St. Paul's dome gleams in the light.'

He turned his head to look and suddenly she wondered what his thick white hair would look like grown long and gathered into a pony tail. Stupid, she concluded. But, if he wore modern casual clothes and shaved off his vintage moustache it would be an improvement.

He turned back. 'It's truly beautiful. And what a miracle that all the buildings around it were flattened in the war, yet Wren's mighty masterpiece remained standing.'

'Well, that's God for you.'

'What's God for you?'

'That's God for you. Allowing the wholesale demolition of ordinary people's houses but making sure his own stood intact.'

'You *are* joking?'

'No I'm not,' she flared. 'It wasn't a one-off either. He did the same in Cologne. Wanted to keep a foot in both camps,' she mused out loud, warming to the hypothesis.

'You're incorrigible,' he said gently.

She felt herself flush, and turned away.

'You once asked if I could help you with your computer if you ever needed it, but I never asked what you were using it for.'

'If I told you, you'd think I was stupid.'

'No, of course I wouldn't, not you. Incorrigible, yes. Zany, yes. Stupid, never.'

'Well then, I'm ...' she stopped. This was her secret. Hers and the Novel Group's. But what did it matter? He was a trusted friend. '... I'm trying to write a novel,' she blurted.

'That's really exciting,' he exclaimed, leaning forward, eyes dancing. 'What's it called?'

'*Twenty Ninety-Five*. It's a kind of love story based in that year.'

'That sounds interesting. What kind of life have you envisaged for people living so far into the future?'

And swept up in his avid interest she told him all about the terrible Disasters Of The Early Century, known as the DOTEC, that wiped out two thirds of the world population; about gene manipulation that could cure all ills; about the World Government's decision not to allow such treatment after the age of one hundred and fifteen.

'I'd have forty-three more years left then,' he said. 'And, now

I've met you, that would be so very welcome, think of the lovely times that could lay ahead of us.'

Lovely times like two old codgers reminiscing year in year out cooped up in a Retirement Home, she thought, ignoring the warmth of his words, stolidly continuing, explaining about Venus and her black American contract partner Jupe, and about Venus's yearnings for the unknown man with long sandy hair who skimmed the Sydney waves in her London virtuality garden, the only one to windsurf with a plain black sail.

'Is it just pictures she sees?'

'No, no. It's more than that. It's the actual sights and sounds of Balmoral Beach - a large bay on Sydney Harbour. It's real people. Real life, picked up by the virtual reality cameras. It's as if she's really there.'

'So how is it that she can see it during the daytime in England when it'd be night-time Down Under?'

'Because it's released to receiving countries during their next daylight hours.'

She grinned, thrilled by his probing questions and her ability to answer them.

'Which one will she land up with, the sandy-haired so-called Black-sail-man, or her contract partner Jupe?'

She stared at this wiry white-haired English gentleman and, weirdly, saw big black American Jupe.

'I haven't decided for absolute sure,' she said slowly, 'but it's ninety-nine per cent certain to be the Black-sail-man.'

'Pity,' said Wally innocently, 'Jupe sounds a decent sort.'

'He is, but he doesn't make her tingle, not like the Australian.'

Wally's dark eyes sharpened. 'But surely when Venus gets to know this Black-sail fellow she could be in for a disappointment. After all, the attraction's purely physical, based on his looks. She doesn't know what he's really like, doesn't know the heart of him.'

He was speaking as if these characters were real, she realised. As if he knew that she was the one craving for a stranger with long sandy hair, a man she didn't yet know the heart of.

'But she'll *get* to know him and he'll be even nicer than Jupe, I'll make sure of that,' she said vehemently, thrilling to the Godlike power of being a writer.

'It'll be like a children's fairy story then,' he gently scoffed, picking up his dimpled beer glass then putting it down again. 'Except that fairy stories always have real baddies and you seem to have one very nice man Jupe, and the Black-sail-man who's going to turn out even nicer!' He took a quick slurp then ran finger and thumb down his moustache tails patently checking for froth.

What does he mean, it'd be like a children's fairy story? she inwardly fumed, glaring at Jupe's pale alter ego and vowing that next time she got novelling she'd make him really nasty. 'I'd like to walk back now,' she said, scraping her chair back.

'If you're sure you're up to it,' he said in a kind voice.

And she realised that, whilst she could make Venus's contract partner meaner, she had no such control over her real-life bridge partner who was innately kind.

He came round to her side and supported her elbow, helping her rise. And, as they ambled back to Waterloo Station and he continued to bombard her with questions about the futuristic world she'd invented, contentment resettled like a well-loved old duvet. And, as she gabbled away about the majority of Earth citizens, known as the Three-bees because they were solely reliant on their Being Born Benefit, and about Venus and Jupe's Agreed-no-children contract marriage giving them the privilege of earning World Currency, or WorCs, she recognised how wonderful it was to be with someone who was truly interested.

They reached the station, caught a train immediately and, for the whole journey she gabbed on about the world she'd envisaged for *Twenty Ninety-Five*: of the millions of solar generators way out in space, and the cars that could be programmed to get to their destination without their drivers' control, and of roads constructed of strong polystyrene blocks, easily lifted for access to the pipes underneath. And, in next to no time they were back at Tooting Broadway Station.

'Thanks for a lovely time Maeve,' he said, hooking his arm into hers as they left the train. 'It was one of the happiest days of my life.'

'And mine,' she said, really meaning it.

They left the station amidst a scurry of commuters, standing to one side to say their goodbyes.

'Be best for you to take a cab with your poor old hip,' he advised.

And she felt so overwhelmingly grateful for his tender concern that, impulsively, she reached up and kissed him. But instead of her lips contacting soft flesh, they met up with manky hair and she pulled away quickly.

'Sorry Maeve, there's an art to this,' he smiled, drawing back his hirsute curtains with both hands then pursing his lips forward.

Gradually, she yielded to the pleasure of the kiss, but, as his hands relocated to her waist, his drapes flopped back down and she pulled away, rubbing her tickled chin.

'Sorry Maeve, got no control over it.'

'So why on earth do you keep it?' she blared. 'Why in heaven's name don't you chop the whole thing off.'

His hands flew up to the two ferrets flanking his mouth as if fearing attack. 'I've had this tash for nigh on forty years, it's part of me,' he protested.

'Well it's high time it went,' she muttered under her breath.

A cab drew up and as she ducked into it he said, 'I look forward to seeing you at the bridge club tomorrow.'

'Yes, see you at eight,' she confirmed.

It was only when the driver pulled up outside her shadowy house that the desolation hit her. *If only someone were waiting inside to greet me*, she thought, as she paid the fare. *Someone to tell where I'd been and what I'd been doing. Someone who was interested and who cared.*

She turned the key, pushed the door open, mooched down to the kitchen and filled up the kettle. As she waited for it to boil she thought about Wally. Kind, courteous, loving. A man to bring a warm glow to your inner self - but not to your inner thighs!

Feeling too hot, she stepped outside into the cooling air, where glinting silver trails embellished the concrete path. *The evidence of the slugs and snails progress may be beautiful*, she thought irritably, *but their effect on my plants is not.* She stomped back inside for a plastic bag then stomped back out again. As she slid an unsuspecting snail off the underside of a leaf, she thought of Buzz. *What is it about this shy, retiring man that affects me so*, she wondered, peering into the shade of the dark clump. *Is it knowing he is unobtainable? Knowing he is no doubt happily married and living the perfect life in the wonderful Bungalow with his faultless wife and impeccable kids?* Ruthlessly, she tore a slug off a leaf and plopped it into the plastic death chamber with the rest of the condemned creatures.

Indoors, she tied the bag's neck, yanked opened the freezer, pulled out a packet of oven-ready chips and shoved the bag of snails and slugs in its place. As she turned the oven on, she pondered on whether it would be worse to be frozen to death then dumped in the dustbin, which was to be the fate of the pests entrapped in the bag, or to be cremated then scattered under their Peace rose bush, which had been Hector's choice: ironic in view of his aggressive nature, but it's what he had wanted because, (a) 'When I am gone you'll not look after that rose plant properly so it could do with a good feed of bone meal to stand it in good stead,' and, (b) 'It won't cause you too much trouble because it's just outside our front door.' That was when he was in one of his rare martyrish moods. His preferred option, which she had ignored, had been for her to scatter a pinch of his ashes over their bridge table each time she played, then bang on the table every now and then, making his dust rise. His reason, given in a triumphant, though feeble, voice, had been: 'As I obviously get up people's noses at the bridge table now I'm alive, it gives me pleasure to know I'll be carrying on doing so when I'm dead and gone.'

Typical of him, wanting revenge, she reflected moodily.

It was only a joke - why do you think you're the only one with the right to black humour? Hector grumbled.

Why is his touchy spectre for ever bombarding me with narky reproaches and unwanted advice, she thought crossly as she poured boiling water on what looked like his ashes but which were in fact the contents of a sachet of Chicken Cuppa Soup.

You know its your guilty conscience, not me speaking, his smug voice pronounced.

Oh, shut up, she moaned, knowing he was right and that she was talking to herself.

And, thankfully, her brain obeyed, allowing her to drink the soup unbothered by strange thoughts. But, as she waited the fifteen minutes for the chips to cook, her mind started whirring again and she remembered how Hector had declined to play more bridge after their last game with Freda and Bernard during which he had passed out. Freda, thinking her father had had a heart attack, had ripped his shirt open and bizarrely attacked his chest with a sink plunger. No doubt a resuscitation process she'd read about in *Plumbers' Weekly* or the *Pig Rearing Magazine*, Maeve mused, cracking two eggs into a frying pan. When Hector had come to and seen the contraption jutting out, vacuum sealed to his left breast, he'd nearly had a real heart attack, she recalled as she flipped hot oil over both yolks. Panicking, Freda had dragged the plunger off and when Hector had looked down again and discovered that red weals encircled not only his left nipple but his right one too - the rubber plunger having been rammed in a frenzy onto the wrong side the first time - he'd become so enraged, they'd all wished he would have a heart attack - only a mild one of course, just to simmer him down.

She waited for his oft-heard moan that it had been her bad bidding that had made him lose consciousness in the first place, but he, or maybe it was she, remained silent.

Dolefully, she ate the eggs and chips whilst gazing vacantly at the box. Why was she in such a gloomy retrospective mood, having had such a perfect day out with Wally, she wondered as she took out her dirty plate. But she knew why and, after turning the TV off and plodding upstairs, instead of getting straight into her nightdress, she suddenly found she was jabbing out Freda's number and waiting nervously perched on the bed, trying to work out how to pose the vital question to which she had to have an answer, one way or the other. Probably the other, she thought, even more gloomily.

'You've just caught me,' Freda eventually answered. 'I was about to get into bed. Are you okay?'

'Yes, yes,' she faltered. 'In fact I've had a lovely day on the South Bank with Wally.'

'Oh yes?' she giggled, 'and you couldn't wait to tell me - he's proposed to you.'

'Don't be stupid,' she cried, suddenly realising that the suggestion wasn't so far fetched. 'How is Princess?'

'You've rung at this hour to ask about our pregnant pig!' she exclaimed, sceptically.

'Not only,' she muttered. 'How's Bernard's new act for the pig show coming on?'

'Are you really all right?'

'Yes,' she blared. 'Nothing wrong with showing an interest is there!'

'No. No. The new act's brilliant actually, he's already incorporated it into the show and it brings the house down.'

'What is it?' she asked, now relentlessly drawn into the details of a bloody pig show, which Freda with great verve and vigour filled in.

'So that's it,' Freda finished, 'and I've got a busy day tomorrow so must get to my bed.'

'That Irish man, Buzz,' she plunged in. 'You know, the one

who bought *The Bungalow.*'

'Much to your annoyance!'

'Yes, but I suppose with three bedrooms it's much better that a man with a family should have it.'

She held her breath.

'Oh no. He lives there by himself,' her glorious daughter said. 'Quite a recluse by all accounts. Just works in the garden, keeps himself to himself. He's definitely there alone. And I'm really going now - night night.'

'Hang on!' she cried. 'How about if I come down - you know, to see the new act for myself?'

'When?' A stifled yawn oozed through the ear piece.

'Tomorrow.'

'Tomorrow! Yes, just a minute Bernie, I *am* coming. And mother's coming down tomorrow to see your new act.'

'Jolly good,' she heard him say, 'you'll have plenty of time to natter then.'

'Bye bye you love birds,' she trilled, replacing the phone, glimpsing her reflection in the mirror and wondering if her lips had ever stretched to that grinning width before.

Twelve

Next morning Maeve rang Wally and told him she was going away.

'But why,' he cried plaintively. 'Why go away? We had such a lovely day out. I hoped we could do it again. Hoped we could take a bus right to the Tate Modern to save your hip. Besides, you can't go. You're playing bridge with me tonight, remember?'

'Sorry, you'll have to find another partner. My daughter needs my help at their Animal Park. I'll give you a ring when I get back.' She tried to blank her mind to what a cow she was being. But her mind wouldn't blank and guilt filled her like sour milk.

'Where is it that you're going?' he asked in a small grief-stricken voice.

'Wood Hill in Hampshire.'

Deliberately, she kept it vague.

'Don't go,' he said, his voice broken and outraged at the same time.

But, steeling her heart, she pronounced that she had to, then quickly rang off. Upstairs, she passed the open door of the study and glanced in, seeing her *Twenty Ninety-Five* outline lying teasingly on the desk. She didn't want to leave it anymore than she wanted to let Wally down, but some things were greater than ambition or friends. Or so she thought.

As she removed her slippers from the small suitcase, placing them under the bed, excitement grew in her. One forty, and the unpacking was complete. In ten minutes she'd go outside, ostensibly to see Bernard's new pig act, but the second it was over she'd be off to seek out Buzz.

Hastily, she stripped off her comfy travelling clothes and donned her shocking pink top and narrow black trousers. She re-did her hair, whipping it up into an elasticised band, twisting long strands into billowing curls and anchoring them on top with fine hairpins.

She hurried downstairs, through the kitchen and out the back door, bounding into the glorious, hot, manure-tinged air. *Unforgettable - that's what you are ...* her inner voice sang as her trainers pounded the rough grass of the back garden. *Unforgettable - though near or far.* Faster and faster her feet flew over the down-sloping lawn. Now he wasn't that far, just the length of a pig show away. Her heart swelled as she sped through odours and sounds coming forth from the pig unit, taking the spring water rivulets in her leaping stride, sending ducks and chickens squawking and scattering in her bombing path.

But, as she wheeled round through the gap in the hedge into the adjacent field she flagged to a halt, heart thumping, lungs rasping, hip throbbing. She flopped forward, hands on knees, hair pins falling, sweat beading her forehead. Her shadow, hunch-backed and heaving, seemed to mock her effrontery at forgetting how old she was.

At last, still breathing heavily, she straightened, hands clutched around her ribs. Through her muzz of hair she spotted Emanuel, head cocked on one side as he stared across. Even to a wonky emu she must look a sight, she realised, glad to see there were no visitors around. She bent down, searching through blades of grass for fallen pins, retrieving enough to anchor dangling coils back up on top.

The snorts and snuffles coming faintly from behind the hedge suddenly revved up to excited squeals and she knew that Bernard must be on the point of releasing them from the yard to make their processional march across to the show arena. The show that Freda and Bernard were under the impression she'd come specially to see, she thought guiltily, setting off again, glancing down to her left and seeing her daughter emerging from the end stall of the stable block, bucket in hand. Freda waved, then urgently flapped her free hand, shouting, 'You'd better hurry or you'll be too late for the start.'

Obediently, she quickened her step, passing the open doorway of the barn to the right, glancing in to see Cynthia clearing a table in her tea room area. She glanced up, cast her a buck-toothed grin. 'You'd better get a move on,' she warned, 'there's no-one about, the show's due to start very soon.'

Okay, okay, she thought, putting on a final spurt, if I drop dead through heart failure, it'll be all thanks to you and Freda. The awful picture of Freda ramming her rubber plunger onto her left breast came into her mind. She winced, then imagined the obituary Freda would write if she snuffed it: *Maeve Salmon, my mother: tragically I couldn't get my plunger to her bosom in time to save her. All she wanted was to see our FAB pig show, but sadly she just missed it.* If only! she mused, hearing the chatter of the waiting audience as she drew near. If only she could miss witnessing the antics of the pigs, as attractive as they were, and could get straight down to witnessing Buzz Pike, who was even more appealing!

All the bench seats around the oval show ground were taken, and the spaces between were filled with people sprawled out on the grass. She wended her way through legs and bodies, searching for the chair Bernard had said he'd put out for her, spotting it by the opening kept clear for his entry. She hurried over, removed the *Reserved for Salmon* sign, and sank down on it.

'Thought that Salmon was gonna be part of the show,' whined a young kid somewhere to her left.

'It's not gonna be a fish show ya dumbo,' jeered an older, though still childish voice, 'it's *pigs*, got it!'

But the faint strains of a Sousa march arrested their spat and soon Bernard was marching into the ring, tape recorder dangling from his shoulder, squealing pigs marching in four pairs, behind him. Abruptly the babble ceased and the applause commenced, gradually taking up the beat of the music as the cumbersome army of fully-grown porkers progressed in.

She knew that, because of her delicate condition, Princess had been banned from performing until after the birth, a prohibition which, according to Freda, upset the pig because she enjoyed showing off her exceptional bright pinkness. *Ridiculous that Freda should imagine she understands the pig's feelings* she mused, suddenly catching a glimpse of her shocking pink top. *She could equally well imagine she'd worn this to show herself off to Buzz* she thought, realising with horror that she had and rather wishing she'd gone for the plain navy T-shirt.

Bernard strode over to a bag whilst the pigs spread out, facing each other in pairs a little way apart. At least with the preggers pig missing it left a more manageable eight she reflected as Bernard delved in, lobbing out frisbees which were adroitly caught in the clamping jaws of the four pigs facing him. Skilfully they began throwing and catching back and forth with their partners, each time stepping backwards to widen the gap. She wondered if there were any rules precluding pigs from playing cricket for England. They not only had they the advantage of actually *being* English, they also knew how to catch!

Gasps and spontaneous applause burst out as the gaps widened. She stared, amazed at the strength of the sideways neck flip for it seemed that with this daily performance Repetitive Strain Injury must inevitably kick in, but no signs yet, they were patently enjoying it. Suddenly Bernard stepped in, catching each frisbee, putting an end to the game.

As the tumultuous applause died down, the bell-like sound of a celeste began chiming out the Dance of the Sugar Plum Fairy. And laughter welled up as the pigs vast bodies started twirling, hammy legs flashing on pig-trotter points. And, from the joyousness of their spins and leaps they also clearly loved dancing. On the final pirouette they all sank down, forelegs and snouts flat to the ground, hind quarters lifted. And, apart from the lack of tutus and the bum holes on blatant display, they could have been real ballerinas.

Grunting and snorting, they scrabbled themselves up to their feet and galloped over to Bernard, milling around him, squealing and squabbling in anticipation of their reward. As he dug into a plastic bag, the squealing sharpened to screams, each cavorting pig abruptly silenced as an apple was shoved into its mouth, until finally seven lucky porkers crunched with noisy relish and one lone porker screeched in anguished hysteria. Quickly, Bernard plugged its gob with a fruit and then pushed one more into each of the gyrating spittle-edged mouths.

As he was doing all this, a weighty seesaw was being hauled into the centre by two burly men, both of whom remained standing by its side. Bernard showed the porkers that the apple bag was empty, then ushered the fattest pig away from the group, guiding him into the centre and onto the peculiar-looking seesaw's large flattened end.

'This is the newest, and final, act in our show,' Bernard announced. 'And this is Pudding. He's our heaviest pig, weighing in at 30 stone - which is about 190 kilograms.'

Whispers of amazement swept round the arena like a gust of wind.

'You will see,' Bernard continued, 'that the high end of the seesaw has hoop handholds allowing three people to sit one behind the other up there. But, we do need to have three whose combined weight is greater than the pig's, don't we?'

Voices were raised in excited agreement.

'Children, you tell me why we want the combined weight to be more than the pig's weight?' demanded Bernard.

'To send Pudding flying,' screamed the kids.

'Quite,' said Bernard, 'so to help us out, Charlie who weighs 17 stone, or 108 kilos, is going to start us off.'

One of the two burly men grinned round at the crowd, clasping his large hands together above his head, then he cocked his leg over and sat astride at the lowest position.

'Now let's have two children who weigh at least 7 stone, that's 45 kilos, for Ted here to lift up and tip the balance.'

As children dashed into line, Esmerelda Oven, the witch-woman neighbour from whom Freda and Bernard rented the field, walked into the ring, a magnificent blue and yellow parrot on her shoulder.

'This is Cocky, en't it my beauty,' she announced, lifting him off and gingerly placing him on to a pad Ted had just secured to Pudding's large head.

A silence settled as they all surveyed the weird scene. A big pig with a parrot on its head stood on what looked like a giant's fish slice waiting to be flipped. Bernard walked along the queue of volunteers and picked out a stocky boy aged about twelve and a hefty young girl, sending them over to Ted.

As Maeve watched the fun, her thoughts turned to Buzz. Come *on*, she thought impatiently, get the pig and parrot flying then I can sneak off! But Ted was taking his time and making great play of the difficulty of lifting the girl. At last he'd heaved her up behind Charlie. Anticipatory sounds came from the audience and the girl astride the seesaw giggled nervously. But, as Ted apparently found the strength to lift the boy up, dangling him over the highest space, a silence settled. When that child's weight was dropped down, the pig must surely go flying. Tantalisingly, Ted held the boy aloft for long seconds before finally letting him down. But, just as the balance shifted, Pudding stepped off, the parrot soared up, the seesaw dropped down and Maeve jumped up with the rest of the crowd, clapping and laughing. And another huge roar went up as Cocky made a clumsy attempt at looping the loop, before flapping back down screeching and squawking on Esmerelda's outstretched arm.

Bernard, Charlie, Ted, the children, all eight pigs, Esmerelda and Cocky took their bows to uproarious applause before the children, giggling, hands clapped to their mouths, returned to their seats and their beaming families. As Bernard and the pigs marched out, the wild clapping was replaced by a babble of voices as the audience stood ready to leave.

Now was her chance. Now she could slope off with the crowd without being noticed. She looked around furtively and headed back towards the barn, weaving through noisy groups, knowing that Freda and Bernard would be fully occupied with the animals. But suddenly Freda leapt out at her, making her screech in alarm.

'God Freda, don't do that. You nearly gave me a heart attack,' she gasped, not revealing that that was the second time she'd nearly done it in one afternoon.

'Sorry,' Freda laughed, obviously not detecting how close to extinction her mother had nearly been. 'I was on my way back from mucking out Felix the foal, but just had to come up to see what you thought of it.' The emerald eyes in her chubby freckled face gleamed expectantly at her.

'Ah yes, the new act. It was *brilliant*.'

'Good, it was worth your while coming down for then,' she said. 'Now let's make the most of you being here by having a cuppa and a chat together inside.' She linked arms and started to pull Maeve towards the gap in the hedge that led to their back garden.

Deftly, Maeve untangled herself. 'I must get some exercise first. I ... I was just going off for a little stroll.'

'Good idea,' Freda agreed, 'after the long drive you must still be stiff. I'll come with you.'

'No. No. You've got things to do. Why not get all your jobs out of the way, then we can chinwag.'

Freda's green eyes, so like Hector's, stared at her and she felt herself redden.

'Okay,' she finally pronounced. 'You're right. I do have things to do - see you back in the cottage later.'

Eagerly, Maeve set off for *The Bungalow* and her beautiful Buzz.

Thirteen

In the countless times she'd run this scene through her head Buzz had always been there in the shade of the magnificent oak tree in his front garden, kind of waiting for her. But now, (she realised, quite unsurprisingly) there wasn't a sign of him.

She stood dithering behind a tall bushy protrusion in the beech hedge, peering across the long front garden, her eyes gradually taking on a rhythm all of their own, sliding from the wide kitchen window on the left, past the front door and on to the tall narrow sitting room window to the right, then back again, as if following a never-ending tennis rally. But there was nothing. Not a shadow of movement in either room.

Maybe he was in the beautiful bedroom at the rear, gazing through his picture window, or working in the back garden, or maybe even out? She ceased her measured eye movements and tottered giddily towards the gate. She would just walk in and knock at his door, she decided. But what would she say if he answered? *Something about you turns me on so I've come to gaze at you!*

Unable to think of a better tactic, she retreated again behind the bushy protrusion, eyes back to their rhythmic searching: kitchen window, front door, sitting room window, front door, kitchen window, front door, sitting room window, front door, back and forth, back and forth, scouring *The Bungalow* until all the foamy pink hope had worn away like a rusty old Brillo pad.

Dejected, she walked to the gate, meaning to open it, but her courage failed and she gave up and turned to go, taking a last look behind her and spotting a man in the distance walking towards her. And her heart seemed to swell up with the renewed lather of hope. He was too far off for her to be sure, but it looked a bit like him. Still, she didn't want him to see her hanging around just waiting for him, so she feigned interest in a colourful bird and, miraculously, at that very moment, the front door of *The Bungalow* opened and Buzz stepped out.

'Hi there. I thought I saw someone.'

'Hi there,' she called back, exaggerating her withdrawal of attention from the bird.

'It's great to see someone else interested in our feathered friends so it is,' he said, circling the empty milk bottle clasped in his hand.

'Yes ... yes, they're ... they're fascinating, I'm very interested in them,' she said, watching her saviour fly off

'Would you like to come round the back to see more?' he offered, placing the bottle down on the step then walking gingerly down the path towards her on bare feet. 'I was digging early on and they come down for the worms and grubs.'

Would I! Would I! Would I!

'I think I just about have time,' she said, guilefully glancing down at her watch, 'but don't you want to put some shoes on first?'

'I hardly ever wear them - just when I'm digging I put boots on. I've got tough feet.'

She followed him round the side and, as they reached the back wall of *The Bungalow*, he held up his hand.

'We must creep quietly from here,' he whispered, turning sparkling eyes to her before tiptoeing forward.

Stealthily, she followed.

'Look,' he said softly, motioning her beside him. 'See, right over there, on the apple tree - you know what that is don't you.'

She stared at the old gnarled tree where he pointed, eventually spotting a greenish yellow blob. 'Is it an escaped canary?' she hazarded.

'You're a hoot so you are,' he snorted. 'I guess you know as well as I do it's a male greenfinch.' Then: 'Oh be Jaisus, Maeve, you bring me luck. Look over there on that tree in the far corner - a Lesser Spotted Woodpecker, that's a rare sight so it is.'

He remembered her name! He did, so he did, so he did!

'See! See it,' he whispered excitedly, pointing. 'See, it's a male.'

She slitted her eyes, at last seeing a tiny black and white bird and wondering how, from this distance, he could see its masculine appendages.

'Look at its gorgeous red crown,' he marvelled as it flew off.

'Ooo yes,' she enthused, silently wondering at the weirdly inappropriate name because that Lesser Spotted Woodpecker couldn't *be* lesser spotted if it tried, seeing as it was spotless and covered in stripes.

'I'm trying to make the garden more attractive to birds,' Buzz said. 'You can see, I've just mown this lawn and intend to keep it as it is now - really neat and short.'

She stared past his perfectly formed feet to the grass which was indeed really neat and short, astounded that birds even noticed such aesthetic details.

'It does look nice.'

'Sure, the robins and thrushes love it.'

A picture of robins and thrushes promenading around the short clipped grass billowed into her head. 'I can imagine,' she murmured.

'Sure, a closely cut lawn exposes the slightest movement of worms - but, hey man, you know that.'

'Mmm,' she agreed, shutting down her new internal film showing the birds relaxing in miniature deck chairs, eyes closed, wings outstretched, smiles on their beaks.

'And insects can be reached easily too.'

'Mmm,' she agreed again.

His devastating blue eyes held a quizzical look as they gazed at her and she racked her brain for something more intelligent to say.

'Yes, sparrows would like that too,' she finally said, completely failing.

'Aye, the Passer domesticus, they're becoming more rare lately.'

'Ah yes, the Passer domesticus,' she echoed, 'they're becoming much more rare lately.'

She nodded, adopting a hopefully well-informed look.

They walked towards the large vegetable plot where some birds were pecking at a newly dug tract, changing tack half way there and heading for a patch of untidy, weed-ridden, long grass to the right of it.

'I see this is your next job,' she commented, daringly adding, 'to cut the grass low to attract your domestics.'

He cast her a queer look, then light seemed to dawn and a quiver of laughter ran through him. 'You're really funny,' he hooted. 'I'll be calling those sparrows my domestics in future, 'tis a good name for them.'

And she joined in, laughing merrily, hoping her blush didn't show.

'Actually, I'm leaving this crop of spring weeds to seed so that the finches and collared doves will come down and eat them - they'll be a grand sight so they will.'

'So they will,' she agreed, deciding that to parrot him would be the most whimsically appropriate strategy.

'But once they've seeded, I'll give it a rough cut - I've ordered a rotary mower specially for the job.'

'It must be nice winning all that money so you can buy what you want,' she offered, at least on safe ground there.

'Sure, having money is better than being hard up, if only for economic reasons,' he replied, apparently seriously.

Now a quiver of laughter ran through her, setting up unladylike snorts. His Irish logic replayed in her head and she exploded with laughter.

And suddenly he was erupting too.

'Sure Maeve I don't know what's so funny but I haven't laughed this much for years,' he gasped. 'You're really good for me. Have you time for a cup of tea?'

Have I! Have I!

Composing herself, she again guilefully looked down at her watch, saying, 'Yes, I just about have time.'

He led her to the wrought iron table and chairs set out on the patio, the wall of the sitting room behind, and the wall of the new extension jutting forward to the left.

'Take a seat Maeve, I won't be long,' he said, bounding to the French windows and disappearing inside.

She sat down, glanced through the open bedroom window, seeing an unmade bed and the mirrored doors of the wardrobe and shower room entrance on the far wall behind. She sighed, thinking that her unmade bed could have been standing there if she'd had more money. A robin flew down close by and began pecking at cracks in the paving. At least she could identify that one she thought gratefully.

Buzz appeared, tray in hand. He placed a plate of biscuits in the centre, handed her a steaming mug, then sat down opposite fiddling with a fingernail. And, peculiarly, they both became tongue-tied, politely throwing in occasional remarks about the garden, the lovely warm day, the work to be done on the vegetable plot and, again, the fact that he intended to buy a new mower. All the time he concentrating on his nail, carefully picking at it, until eventually a substantial strip tore off, whereupon he spread out his fingers and glared at the jagged edge as if his picky finger and thumb had had nothing to do with it.

'Won't you just look at that,' he said in apparent amazement, dropping the rough strip of nail onto the table. 'Would you be having a nail file on you?'

'No, I'm not even carrying my handbag, but I have one at home.'

'What, a handbag?'

'No, a nailfile. But also a handbag.'

Then silence descended again whilst he set about shredding the nail even further. But a question had been lurking on the tip of her tongue and, even though she knew the answer, it would no longer hold back.

'Are you married?' she blurted, taking a gulp of her tea in feigned nonchalance.

'Yes, I am.'

'Yes!' she spluttered, snatching a tissue from her trouser pocket and choking into it.

'Yes, to Sophia - she's Italian,' he said, as if that explained everything, 'from Rome. I met her when she came over to work in Aberdeen to improve her English.'

'Well that was a joke!'

He cast her an uncertain look. 'Sure it was, but she didn't know that then,' he said, defending the no-doubt proud dark beauty to whom he was wed.

'What job did she do in Aberdeen?' she asked, just to ameliorate her rudeness, because in reality she couldn't give a bugger what that Sophia woman did now or then.

'She worked in the canteen making wonderful pizzas - I think I fell in love with them before I fell in love with her.'

'Oh,' she whispered, not wanting to hear that vile love word.

'We got married but I was mostly offshore on the rigs.'

'What did you do?' she asked, dully.

'I was just a lowly steward. You know, made the beds and cooked for the men who did the real work. But it was well paid for what it was, and I got to see all the glorious sea birds.'

'Why did you leave then?' she asked, sucked into a conversation she had no real wish to continue.

'Sophia didn't like the Aberdeen weather.'

'Who would?' she muttered sulkily, lifting her mug, taking a sip, then banging it down, shooting tea up all over her chest.

He eyed the splatters scattered across her shocking pink T-shirt, then coloured, averting his gaze. 'So we moved down to London,' he carried on doggedly, 'not just for the warmer climate. She also hankered for art galleries, museums, concerts, and the kind of life only on offer in capital cities.' He stopped, his lovely face turning dreamy. 'She wanted softer weather...'

She spat on the tissue she'd used earlier to choke into, then beat at her breasts in an effort to get rid of the brown stains.

'... a softer life for her and the baby she was carrying then ... our dear son Georgio, though I always call him Georgie.'

'Sounds like you did the right thing moving,' she said, giving up on her T-shirt and starting to dab at droplets of tea on the glass top.

'She forgot you also need money to take advantage of most of those things. But, away from the North Sea I couldn't get a well-paid job.'

'But surely in London you could,' she cried, screwing the sodden tissue into a ball and somehow resisting the urge to chuck it full force at him.

He placed his mug down, pulled his pony tail forward, tugging and smoothing it.

'No, not me man,' he said, flicking back his silky security blanket. 'I couldn't get a well-paid job because I wasn't qualified to do anything, so I did menial work at a supermarket close to our council house in Kilburn.'

She tucked the tea-soaked tissue ball into a wrought-iron loop under the top, wishing he'd shut up yacking about his bloody wife.

'And, even though I worked my way up to assistant manager, and even though we did manage to buy the house, to be fair to her, our life was bleak.'

'To be fair to her?' she exclaimed, snatching a ginger nut from the plate and shoving it whole in her mouth.

His eyes turned away, gazing unseeing into space.

'Yes, she ran off two years ago to live with a fellow Italian in his villa in the sun. A life amidst her own people, speaking her own language. Who could blame her? And our Georgie was grown up with a life of his own, and her new bloke, Giuseppe, well, he sounded a good sort.'

'That's very generous of you,' she whispered, half closing her eyes in an effort to hide the elation she knew to be strobing from them.

'And I don't even see Georgie now. He went off backpacking round the world six months ago and I've not heard from him since.'

She thought of Hermione's piglet named Georgie, now a fully grown boar. 'Georgie is a pig ...,' she started.

'Yes I know he is. He should contact me. We were close. But he is my son and I love him and maybe he phones or e-mails Sophia, sure I don't know.' He paused, turning troubled eyes on her. 'It's been hard to get used to a life without them, even harder than revealing my ignorance on TV.'

Impulsively, she reached across and patted his hand. 'It was very brave of you,' she said, guiltily remembering how she'd scoffed when he'd had to call a friend to establish a patella was a kneecap and not a female newsagent, a Spanish dish or a foreign brothel.

'It's good talking to you Maeve,' he said shyly, 'I don't make friends easily, but you seem, well, a kindred spirit.

And her kindred spirit rose.

'But, what am I doing,' he cried, 'you said you didn't have long, and here I am keeping you.'

'No, no,' she protested, regretting her mendacious glances at her watch.

'I know you're too polite to rush off, but your friend Freda is no doubt expecting you back.'

She opened her mouth to put him wise, then shut it again.

'Did you say you helped her out with her Animal Park?' he asked, rising.

'Yes, it's known as FAB CAZ, short for Freda And Bernard's Children's Animal Zoo.' Reluctantly, she stood to go. 'My husband thought up the CAZ bit, it was meant to be CAP, short for Children's Animal Park, but he organised the signs - just before he died.'

'So, it's good to have FAB CAZ to take your mind off your loss,' said Buzz sympathetically as they walked round the side. 'Tell me, what sort of things do you do there?'

'Oh, sometimes I sit in the barn collecting entrance money and selling stuff from the shop, sometimes I feed the chickens, sometimes I hose down the pigs, all sorts really.'

'She's dead lucky to have such a good pal,' he observed.

And, still she said nothing.

At the gate, they stopped. 'I don't know anyone else interested in birds,' he murmured, 'and, as you might guess, they're my passion.'

'Mine too,' she mumbled, glad no-one else could hear her.

He opened the gate and reluctantly she stepped out of his heavenly aura into the lane.

'Maybe you'll come and watch them with me again some day,' he said, shutting the gate firmly behind her.

'I will. I will. When?'

'I know you're busy at FAB ...'

'How about ten o'clock tomorrow,' she cut in.

His eyes widened. 'Okay, I look forward to it,' he said in a soft voice that made her legs go wobbly.

God, she hoped she hadn't seemed too eager, she worried, as she tottered back to Wisteria Cottage, anxious to get her hands on the Bird Book she'd noticed on Freda's book shelf.

Fourteen

Her head was reeling. Even though she'd pored over Bernard's *Bird Spotting Book* for most of last night, she was finding it harder and harder to hide her ignorance as they watched big ones, little ones, colourful ones and dull ones fluttering and twittering in Buzz Pike's garden. Maybe her confusion was because Bernards' bird book had been so old it was priced at two pounds, ten and six, but, in all honesty, she didn't think so because birds couldn't change their plumage any more than leopards could change their spots.

'Look, there's a male greenfinch,' she dared say once about a greenish yellow bird which looked the same as the one she'd mistaken for an escapee canary.

He'd given her a sharp glance, then said, 'No, that's a male siskin, smaller, though similar in colour.'

She decided then to risk no more guesses, just listen and learn. And, thankfully, just when she thought her head would actually explode with the knowledge she was trying to pack into it, he said, 'I'll go and put the kettle on - would you like tea or coffee?'

'Coffee,' she said gratefully, 'shall I come in and help?'

'No, you sit on the terrace and enjoy the garden. You'll probably find that robin will hop up to be near you, he's a friendly wee bird.'

'Ah, yes, the turdinstraw,' she said, sinking down onto the chair, glad to remember the Latin name of at least one bird family.

He cast another of his sharp looks then doubled up, saying, 'You're a scream, so you are.'

And she joined in the merry laughter though she hadn't a clue what it was all about.

'Turdinae, turdinstraw,' he chuckled as he went off.

She leant back, tilting her head, closing her eyes, not wanting to clap eyes on one more bloody bird, turdy or otherwise. Slowly she relaxed in the warmth of the sun, gradually she drifted off.

'Are you really a twitcher? his voice suddenly burst into her ear, making her jump and squeal. 'Sorry I startled you,' he apologised, placing a steaming mug in front of her. 'It's my bare feet, they make no sound.' He placed a saucer on top of the mug. 'Helps keep it hot,' he explained. 'Are you really a twitcher?' he asked again, taking the seat opposite and staring hard at her.

'Well, sometimes when I'm tired I jerk a bit,' she admitted.

'What on earth are you talking about?'

'Twitching.' (There was silence.) 'You know, an out of control movement, takes you unawares.' (More silence.) 'You know, like when I jumped just now when you startled me.' (Continuing silence.) 'You know, twitching, like this.' She jerked her head three or four times creating sharp daggers of pain in her neck and dislodging a thick hank of hair.

Slowly, he rubbed his nose, following its crooked ridge with his digit finger. She smiled through the blonde veil, then, unsure what to say, gathered the fallen tress up and secured it with a repositioned clip. Still he rubbed his nose and stared. Nervously, she giggled.

And that seemed to do the trick because he guffawed loudly, then spluttered, 'You had me going there, so you did.' And he began twitching his head and shoulders like a lunatic, saying: 'See, I am a twitcher like you!'

And, as was becoming the norm, in full ignorance of the joke, she joined in the hilarity, twitching her arms and shoulders but not her neck which was still jabbing darts of pain from before.

'I've been thinking,' he said, when they had simmered down. 'With a name like Maeve, you must originate from Ireland like me.'

'No, I'm a Londoner, born and bred.'

'Then why Maeve? It's an Irish name, so it is.'

'Apparently when I was born I was a mauve colour,' she reluctantly explained, 'so my mum and dad used to call me Mauve but, as it wasn't a proper name, they christened me Maeve. At home though, I was always Mauve.'

'I really like that,' he laughed.

And, as usual, his chuckling was infectious and soon they were squealing and snorting like two frolicsome pigs. It was then that she realised the attraction of this man. It wasn't just his shy gentle nature and attractive looks, it was because he laughed so easily, unlike Hector. But then, Hector hadn't won a million pounds and been able to buy the house of his dreams, she remonstrated with herself, suddenly guilty to have harboured such unfair thoughts.

'Mauve suits you, you're a purple kind of woman,' Buzz observed.

And while she was trying to figure out if this was a good kind of woman to be or not, he added, 'It will be my pet name for you.'

His pet name for her! That meant she was someone special. That meant he intended seeing her again - didn't it? She snatched the heat retaining saucer from her mug and took a large gulp in an effort to hide her intense feelings, but the tears that immediately sprang to her eyes weren't from the deep emotion of his words but from the blistering agony of scalding coffee.

'I expect you wonder why I'm known as Buzz,' he commented, his eyes following the flight of a passing bird.

His gaze turned to her when she didn't reply. 'I was christened Aldrin,' he continued, uncertainly, 'that being ... that being my mother's maiden name. Are you all right Mauve?'

'Yes, I'm okay,' she whispered, thrilling at his use of that pet name for her, despite the pain in her mouth.

'So, when Buzz Aldrin went to the moon,' he continued, 'I was nicknamed Buzz after him. Are you sure you're all right Mauve, you've gone all red in the face.'

'Just burnt my ...' Suddenly she realised she'd be able to work out his age now if she knew what his age was then. '... my throat, but it's okay now. How old were you when Buzz Aldrin went to the moon?' she asked, with feigned nonchalance.

'Let me see. I started working on the rigs when I was twenty. It was a year or two after that, maybe more.'

She glanced down at her watch, suddenly keen to get back to Freda's to look up the date of the first moon landing in their encyclopaedia.

'I can see you don't want to listen to my blather,' he said in a prickly kind of way, 'so I won't be keeping you.' Quickly, he drained his mug and jumped up, staring down at her.

'What you were saying was very interesting, but I suppose I should get back - help Freda a bit.' She cast him a hopefully placatory smile.

And it seemed to work because all signs of dudgeon had disappeared by the time they reached the front garden.

'It's funny, I'm a Pike and you're a Salmon - our meeting must be meant,' he observed as they stood together.

And, wanting to establish if he meant *meant* because of their fishy names or if he meant *meant* because she meant something special to him, on a stupid impulse, she decided to test him.

'Tomorrow I have to drive back to Tooting,' she fibbed, every fibre of her body vibrating, alert, waiting to pick up on any sign of disappointment, no matter how small.

'Have a safe journey then,' he said, showing no sign of anything whatsoever as he gaily threw open the gate.

'I don't, I don't have to ...' she stuttered.

'No, I'm sure you don't. With a thriving business like FAB CAZ, Freda can afford hired help. You get back to your own home and relax. Do you good. Maybe see you around next time you're down.'

Then, with a cheery smile and a flat-handed wave he turned and, without even so much as a backward glance, strode back down the path, leaving her wanting to cut out her smarting tongue on two counts.

Still angry at her own stupidity, she marched into the cottage to find Hermione lounging across the sofa, gently snoring, and everyone else out. As she passed to get to the book shelf, the pig opened one eye, grunted convivially, then dropped back to sleep. Maeve wondered if the sow lay there for hours on end through old age or boredom, or if she was showing off, miffed at the way her offspring had taken centre stage, quite literally, leaving her, their mother, as a non-participatory onlooker. A fact of nature, she realised, wondering how old she was in pig years.

She lugged the heavy encyclopaedia down off the shelf, then sat down and flicked her way through to: *Aldrin, Edwin Eugene, known as Buzz, the second man to set foot on the moon in 1969.*

That was it, the information she needed. If he'd been, say, twenty-two in 1969, that meant he'd been born in 1947. And that made him fifty three. Oh God, fifteen years her junior. A kind of derisive snort came from the sofa.

'Who asked you!' she blared.

But, Buzz hadn't been sure, had he. Maybe he'd gained his nickname later, when he was older. Considerably older. Maybe he was nearer to sixty now.

Or maybe barely fifty, Hector's infuriating voice cut in.

'Who bloody well asked *you!* 'she blared again, though this time not to the supine porker. Nevertheless, the piggy eyes sprang open and, emitting loud squeals of fear, the sow scrambled off the sofa and blundered hurriedly out of the room. The sound of the pig flap banging shut as she exited the cottage through the special opening in the wide kitchen door sounded, to Maeve, like the clang of a prison gate slamming shut on a condemned man. Or condemned woman in this case. A woman condemned to yearn for a man she could never have because (a) he was too young, (b) he was married, albeit separated, and (c) the only birds he seemed interested in were the tweety feathery kind.

She trailed out to the kitchen and started to prepare the evening meal. As she viciously shoved stuffing up the chicken's arse she wondered if Buzz would ever eat poultry or if he'd balk at the idea because it had once sported feathers and a beak. There was so much she didn't know about him and never would now.

'I'm going back,' she told a startled Freda that evening. 'Just remembered a bridge tournament I'm in at the weekend.'

She dialled Wally's number. 'I'll be back for Sunday night's duplicate match,' she informed him.

'Oh, sorry Maeve, I'm fixed up.'

And the dog in her manger was infuriated. 'Who with?' she snapped.

'Dora Dome, she's a new member. She says she knows you from the Writers' Circle.' Then, to her chagrin, he added, 'She's a very nice person and apparently brilliant at bridge.'

Fifteen

Back home Maeve pounded the keys, fired by new passions. Now Venus's yearning for the sandy-haired man who skimmed across Sydney Harbour each day in her virtuality garden became a sickness, an all consuming ache. And, while she hungered to feel his lips upon hers, her contract partner, Jupe, was being subtly seduced by red-nosed Geranium, a brilliant scholar on the same course as him at the Buckingham Palace University.

Days passed. The characters in *Twenty Ninety-Five* became all engrossing, more meaningful than real people in Maeve's life. Venus continued to lust for the far away stranger and Jupe began to fall for Geranium's wily charms. But, that wasn't meant to happen! She re-read her outline seeing with consternation that Jupe wasn't meant to become attracted to *anyone*, let alone a clever-dick female with a colourful conk. And, by this stage in the story, Venus should have got together with the man of her dreams, not just sat back pining for him.

And, as if a sudden strike of lightning had stabbed straight through her thick skull to light up her brain, she saw quite clearly that Venus and she had become one. Shocked at the revelation, she impulsively clicked on the X to delete the whole humiliating lot. But, when the dear computer queried her rash decision, she snatched at its second chance and clicked 'cancel'.

Feeling quite dizzy at the near obliteration of months of hard work, she slumped back, gazing blindly at the screen. And, slowly, the words came into focus and she read the last lines she had typed: *Geranium looks coyly up at Jupe as they enter the lecture hall in Buckingham Palace University and he smiles tenderly back down at her.* Suddenly struck by another bolt of lightning, she realised that that was Dora Dome looking coyly up at Wally as they entered the bridge club and that now Jupe and Wally were indisputably one and, like Venus, she was about to carelessly lose him.

But she couldn't! She enjoyed playing bridge with him and, although he was old-fashioned, he was a kind gentleman who had gazed at her with adoration - unlike Buzz who, like the Black-sail-man, remained distant and unattainable.

She ran to her bedroom, jabbed out Wally's number on the bedside phone and listened to her heart thumping out of time with the ringing tone.

'Hello, who is it?' he answered, and she nearly dashed the phone down with the shock.

'Oh, hello, it's me,' she replied awkwardly.

'Hel*lo* Maeve, fancy hearing from you,' he answered in the kind of affable yet remote voice of someone who'd once been close, but wasn't any more.

'Yes, turning up like an old penny,' she quipped, hoping Dora Dome wasn't listening in on his extension and spotting the cliché.

'We won last night,' he gloated. 'Dora was superb.'

'Well done. I'm very ... pleased ... for you,' she said, the words pushed out like stiff icing sugar from a forcing bag.

'Thank you Maeve.'

'I can partner you on Wednesday,' she rushed.

'Oh.'

There was a pause.

'Unless you've made other arrangements,' she said tartly, all sugary stiffness melted away in a rush of red hot spit.

'Well, Dora did say ...'

'But what about me your regular partner,' she wailed.

'You didn't say how long you'd be away so I couldn't just put my bridge on hold till you returned, could I?'

'No, you couldn't,' she muttered, knowing that was reasonable.

'So, goodbye then, thanks for the offer.'

'You're welcome. Goodbye.'

Dolefully, she trailed back to the computer. 'So you are to be my life,' she bawled at the pipes zooming round and round the screen apparently saving it. 'You are to be my reason for living. *Twenty Ninety-Five* is to fill up the hours I have left on this earth.' And, even as she ranted, excitement welled. Jupe would see through that Jezebel Geranium, she'd bloody well make sure of that. And Venus would meet up with the Black-sail-man and he'd fall for her impish charms, and the two men would battle over her and she wouldn't know which one to choose. She plonked down on the swivel chair, span round once, then set off typing.

And, apart from the time spent sleeping, buying food and eating it, she stayed there solidly for what seemed liked years but was probably more like a fortnight.

Twenty thousand words on and Venus was still in the doldrums. Still fantasising that she and the Black-sail-man would get together, though, at the same time, becoming more upset by the remoteness of Jupe who, like a nectar-seeking bee, was being sucked ever deeper into Geranium's hot red petals. Just like her, Venus had lost the two men in her life and, as she pounded the keys, she found her heart ached even more than her fingers.

Another week passed and the story took an unexpected twist. Out of her control now, Venus had belatedly recognised that Jupe was a good man, and that a good man was hard to find. As she pondered on whether that phrase was a dreaded cliché, the phone rang and she dragged herself to the bedroom ready to let forth an earful to anyone trying to sell her double glazing or a conservatory.

'Hello, who is it?' she said warily.

'Hello Maeve, this is Wally,' said Wally in a good man sort of voice.

Jupey, I've missed you. Have you ditched the red nosed bint! she wanted to scream. Instead, she said:

'Hello Wally, why have you rung?'

'Just ... just to see how you are.'

'Very well thank you.'

'Good.'

'How are you?'

'Very well thank you.'

Oh God, this was awful. They were like two foreigners practising English together.

'How is the bridge?' she asked, unable to think what else to say but not really giving a toss.

'A disaster,' he moaned. 'That Dora Dome - well you must know about her problem,' he said, his good man sort of voice turning accusing.

'What problem?'

'Her drink problem. She showed me up at the club - even more than you did when you shrieked out that C word.'

She bridled. Why did he have to bring *that* up.

'She kept overbidding, even worse than you do, then ranting and raving when we didn't make it, slurring her words, calling me *old walrush tash*, telling me in front of everybody that I was *shtupid.* Even telling me I was old-fashioned. I mean, *me!*

She wasn't quite so drunk then, Maeve reflected.

'She's a different person when she's sober - good fun, polite, intelligent.'

Yeah, yeah, she thought, yawning.

'When I came out with it and told her she was an alcoholic she denied it saying she never ever drank on Tuesdays to prove to herself and to everyone else that she could give it up whenever she wished. But, well, I tell you, I'm never playing bridge with that woman again, even on TT Tuesdays. I should have known by that nose.'

'So, I suppose you want me back,' she said, nasty inflections edging her voice into sneering mode.

'We were a good team,' he wheedled.

Then she remembered her Venus. How her cold unsympathetic treatment of Jupe had been the reason he was falling for another's charms. And, even though Dora Dome was safely out of the way, there were plenty of other lone women keen for a partner down at the club - at the bridge table *and* in bed.

'Okay, you're right. When's the next game?' she said briskly.

'Oh Maeve,' he sighed, '*thank* you - tomorrow evening at eight.'

'See you there then. Goodbye.'

She sat opposite him at the table, trying to concentrate on her cards, but her eyes kept drifting up to gaze at him. That wasn't her old Wally. This was a brand new one, pale pink lips on full display, devoid of moustache. He caught her eye and she hastily looked back down again.

'Do you like it?' he whispered, running forefinger and thumb down the furrows in the pale nude skin each side of his mouth.

'I suppose you cut it off for *her*?' she retorted, sniffily.

'Get on with the game,' grumbled her left-hand opponent, but, by the embarrassed look on Wally's face she knew she'd hit the nail on his head. He *had* lopped off those two thick hairy wings for that drunkard Dora. Morosely, she snatched up her cards, set them out in order and, despite her full complement of Aces and Kings, said 'Pass.'

'God, that was awful,' grumbled Wally at the end as their opponents conducted a joyful inquest. And those four words became his mantra at the end of every hand.

During the game in which she was the dummy she studied him as he played their combined cards. Not only were there the newly-exposed fleshy grooves flanking his mouth, but equally fleshy horizontal grooves had just appeared in his forehead, no doubt reflecting the intense activity going on in his brain. She looked around the room seeing other faces fixed into stern frowns. Maybe they all laughed and sang when not concentrating on the cards, she cogitated, though it was hard to imagine. He glanced up and she saw that his upper lids did not retreat as most people's, with the skin neatly packed away between two narrowly spaced curved lines. His didn't seem to fold at all but were more like two mauve-tinged half moon shells, obliterating the tops of each brown iris, even with his eyes apparently fully open. The lower lids, by contrast, dropped loosely away exposing moist rose tinted linings. He looked up again, caught her hard stare - and winked! A brief flashing movement that pleased her, but not her left hand opponent who witnessed the brief flutter and muttered dark threats about calling the director to complain about signals being passed.

'Bet you wish you'd played with Dora,' she sniped, when at last the long tournament was over, knowing her play had been awful.

'No ... no I don't,' he answered unconvincingly. 'She and I did do better than tonight I admit - but I missed you.'

'Missed me. Missed me for approximately ten minutes before you set up with her.'

'Fair dos, Maeve. The way you just went off, after our lovely day out, I, I ...' He floundered, helping her on with her jacket. '... I thought, you couldn't give a fig for me. And I knew I was ...' He lowered his voice. '... I knew I was, well, falling in love with you.'

'You had a bloody funny way of showing it!'

'It's not my way, to chase after women who don't want me,' he mumbled, his fingers tapping all around his mouth as if searching for the comfort of a lone hair. 'And Dora, when sober, did seem attracted to me as a person - not just for my skill at bridge.'

She gazed at him, wondering if they'd ever managed a grand slam - at the table or in bed, realising that she'd experienced neither for a long while, and was missing both. And, somehow, that wink had got her going.

'Would you like to come back to my place for a drink,' she offered rashly.

'I'd *love* to,' he declared.

And sitting in her red Skoda, watching in her rear view mirror as his dark blue Volvo tailed her home, she felt her pulse quicken. He might not be the big strong black American Negro called Jupe of her novel, he might not be the Black-sail-man or his alter ego, sandy-haired shy Buzz, but he was a man who fancied her, and he was coming to her house!

She poured a little water into each tumbler of Malt, handed him his, then plonked herself down beside him, taking a sip and then giggling like a gauche schoolgirl as he raised his arm across the back of her shoulders and drew her to him.

'I've missed you,' he whispered, squeezing her far shoulder so hard that she feared the chunky foam shoulder pad of her best cardi would be permanently deformed.

'Likewise. I've missed you too,' she said, tugging it free from his mangling grasp.

'It's so good that you're my partner again,' he sighed, voice emotionally breaking. 'How about we go on another trip up town together?'

She blanked her mind to a blossoming picture of Buzz. 'Yes, let's,' she agreed.

'Oh dear MAEVE!' he cried, strengthening his vice grip.

And her whole being thrilled. It had been years since a man had called out her name in the throes of passion. She leant back into his draped arm, closing her eyes.

'Maeve! *MAEVE!*' he screamed louder.

And, overcome by the heat of the whiskey and of his ardour, she turned to kiss him. But, instead of witnessing a potential lover's face contorted with desire, she saw an old man's mug crazed with pain.

'What's up?' she cried, terrified that instead of being in the throes of lust he was in the throes of a heart attack.

'It's my shoulder,' he moaned, lifting his arm up, then dropping it heavily down.

'Yeow!' she screamed, as its full weight struck her.

'I can't get it off,' he cried.

'Shh! The neighbours might hear,' she sniggered.

'Move *off* me,' he bellowed.

And she shot forward, away from him, now truly worried that young impressionable Jatinder might be able to hear them through the party wall.

'Thank Christ,' he moaned, as his arm flopped down.

Why does getting old make things so bloody difficult? she inwardly raged. *Would it really have been so difficult for God to have thought up a joyful way of dying, something to really look forward to, instead of this slow frustrating deterioration first?*

'Sorry,' he groaned, slowly circling his shoulder, 'just a touch of the old rheumatics.'

'Tell me about it!'

He tapped her gently on her hip, making sympathetic noises. 'How is it?' he asked.

And somehow the gentle tapping became smooth caresses. And somehow the smooth caresses led to a safe low-armed cuddle round her waist. And somehow the safe low-armed cuddle incited a kiss. And somehow Wally's soft warm lips on hers became Buzz Pike's. She pulled away, gasping.

'Oh Maeve, Maeve,' he panted, 'we're a good bridge partnership aren't we?'

She nodded.

'So how about we make it more permanent?' He slithered off the seat, stiffly balancing on one knee. 'Maeve my dear, I love you, will you do me the great honour of becoming my wife?'

No, no, she screamed. *Jupe isn't the one, he's just her contract partner, not the love of her life.* And, in that flash, she knew she had the ending of her novel. Or, at least, she thought she had.

'It is, it is ... it is indeed an honour your asking me,' she faltered.

His intently staring eyes darkened to two black pools, sucking her into their depths.

'Indeed a *great* honour ...' she floundered, '... but, no, no thank you very much. If we were married it would spoil our game.'

'Bugger the game, it's you I want,' he bawled.

And she realised she didn't really know this man at all because, firstly, she thought bridge meant everything to him and, secondly, she didn't think he ever swore.

He bowed his forehead down onto her knees and, tentatively at first, she stroked his hair, and suddenly she was a kid again, sitting in the vet's waiting room, stroking the thick white fur of her cat who was meowing pitifully because of the marble jammed inside his ear. And she was overcome with the same feeling of anguish and guilt at being the one who'd inflicted the pain.

'Let's get to know each other better first,' she stalled.

'Oh thank you, you're right, yes thank you,' he said, looking up, grimacing.

'What's up?'

'My knee. Can you help me - I'm stuck.' He held out his hand.

She stood and helped haul him up to his feet, but taking his weight sparked a sharp jab of pain in her hip.

'Bloody arthritis,' she railed.

'*And* bloody prostate.'

'Why bloody prostate?' she asked, bewildered by this change of direction from dicky joints to dicky male bits.

'Makes you get up to pee in the night. Not funny you know.'

'No, not funny at all,' she agreed, ushering him out to the door, imagining what wedded bliss *that* would be.

'Well you did say we should get to know each other better,' he said as he stood on the doorstep, 'so it's something you ought to know about me.'

Not quite what I had in mind, she thought, deliberately not telling him that she too had to get out several times in the night and she didn't even have a prostate.

The trill-trill of the Lesser Spotted Woodpecker in Buzz's garden grew ever more insistent. She ran her fingers through his silky pony tail, easing off the elastic band, setting his gleaming sandy locks loose and, deftly, he flicked all the combs and pins from her hair, releasing her cascading tresses. Oh Buzz, she whispered, their swirling manes entwining as he span her into his arms, Oh Buzz, why won't that frigging bird stop! But the aggravating trill-trilling relentlessly carried on.

She lifted her eyelids then dropped them back down but, in that foolhardy movement, everything vanished. Buzz where are you and where is your beautiful garden? she cried into the white fog that had obliterated everything except the insistent call of that bird. She heaved herself over, stretched out, grabbed its hard smooth body and yanked it up intent upon throttling it but, instantly, its strident trill trill ceased.

She opened her eyes, seeing with amazement it had transformed to a phone. 'Hello,' she yawned into it.

'Mother, sorry if I woke you. Were you having a siesta?'

'Kind of. Couldn't sleep last night so lay down for ten minutes after lunch ...' she looked round at the clock. '... and here it is five past four.'

'Sorry to disturb you, you obviously needed it, but I had to let you know. Buzz Pike has had an awful accident.'

She shot up.

'He was using his new rotary mower and somehow got his bare foot caught under it.'

She fell back onto the pillow, grisly pictures filling her horror struck head. Chunks of dripping flesh festooned trees and shrubs whilst vultures flew overhead and Buzz lay silently on red-stained grass, a whole foot missing.

She let out a moan.

'It's horrible isn't it,' Freda whispered, 'every toe on his right foot was torn off.'

'Thank God,' she gasped.

'Thank *God!* erupted Freda. 'Thank God that all his toes have been torn off. That's sick.'

'I mean, thank God it wasn't any worse,' she explained, not going into the gory ankle stump detail.

'Bad enough,' she muttered, unimpressed.

'What happened to them?'

'What happened to what?'

'His chopped off toes.'

'Apparently the paramedic gathered them all up in a plastic bag but the surgeon only sewed the big one back on.'

'Why just the big one?' she asked, trying not to dwell on the mental image of a plastic bag filled with his redundant toes looking exactly like the plastic bag of badly butchered chicken thighs stowed in her fridge.

'Because the big toe was the most important one for his balance and it would have taken too long to do microsurgery on all the rest.'

She remembered the ages it had taken her to sew the thumb back onto one of Freda's mittens, each stitch meticulously placed so that everything lined up. And that was only in easy moss stitch.

'Apparently they've tidied up each stump by sewing a flap of skin over each jagged bone.'

Once again the splintered red stained bones and flapping skin of the chicken thighs sprang revoltingly into her mind and she decided to dump them.

'He's in Great Piddlehurst Hospital for probably a whole week more,' continued Freda, 'and the reason I've really rung is that he's asked to see you.'

'Me!'

'He said you're the only one in the village he feels he knows, and that is so funny because you're not even in the village, are you?'

'I will be. I'll come straight down,' she impulsively stated, immediately remembering the Novel Group meeting she was meant to be attending in a little while.

'You'll be too late to see him tonight,' Freda advised, 'but come down anyway and stay with ...'

'No, no,' she interrupted, 'it'll take me time to pack so I'll set off early tomorrow morning.' And, even as she spoke she wondered why she was still holding back from telling Freda about her writing and the group, realising it was probably to save face if she failed.

As she changed into her midnight blue trousers and baggy black top, she thrilled at the thought that soon she'd be receiving glorious accolades for her next four page episode, and that tomorrow she would be visiting poor sweet helpless Buzz. She tried not to dwell on poor dear hopeful Wally with his soulful eyes and enlarged prostate.

Sixteen

'You know where it is, Dora's already in there,' said Hugos Thayre as he let her in. She pushed the door, twisting her head round to look into the dimly lit room. Dora's glowing nose swivelled round at her like an usherette's torch.

'Oh, hello Maeve, you're the first,' she gushed. 'So pleased you could come again - I wasn't sure if you would.'

'Oh, and why not?' she asked sweetly, taking a seat.

'Oh, you know ...,' Dora said, lifting her bum and pressing back into the chair, her full weight precariously balanced on red stiletto heels and amazingly stick-like ankles, as she pulled her dress straight underneath her. '... you know, the fact that you know that bridge playing Wally too.' She slid back down, sending the voluminous amounts of yellow and blue striped material back into disorder.

'The fact that we have a mutual friend called Wally, wouldn't stop *me* coming,' she retorted, quite surprised that dipso Dora had the gall to mention him.

'Not mutual as far as I'm concerned, he fiddles with his moustache too much and so old fashioned, I mean his clothes are a joke. I didn't know there were that many shades of brown.'

'For your information, he doesn't have a moustache any more.'

'Ha! He must have shaved it off for me. I mean, it was ridiculous, like snogging the backside of a horse.'

'And, I suppose, you'd know all about that,' Maeve countered, pleased with the witty spite, though miffed to learn that on such a short acquaintance they'd snogged. And him on one knee proposing to her so soon afterwards.

Shirley Shakespeare, smiling roundly, entered the room, quickly followed by Conan the Coconut Head, James Joist the teacher, Abigail the nurse and, lastly, Hugos Thayre the host, who twisted the dimmer switch round to full blazing wattage, making her wish she'd taken her sun glasses with her. Seats were noisily taken, papers pulled out and glasses put on.

'We're all here now so we must get cracking,' stated Dora briskly. 'And we'll start with you Hugos. Is it still the same title?'

'Yes, *Postman's Knock*,' he confirmed, hunching his thin shoulders forward so that he looked like a narrow-backed, over-stuffed, winged chair.

And as he began reading his story about the man who was in love with his postman, Maeve tried to follow the plot, but her mind kept drifting to whether she should make Venus travel to the other side of the world to meet up with the Black-sail-man, in the same way as she was driving down to Hampshire to meet up with Buzz. And, if so, whether she'd be disappointed when she really got to know him, or whether they'd truly fall in love.

She glanced up, seeing Dora's glinting gaze upon her, so she placed one finger to her chin and frowned slightly in a show of intent listening. But Hugos only read for a few seconds more, before his four pages were up.

'Anything to comment Maeve?' asked Dora, smiling wickedly.

'No. No. It was ... interesting. It was ...' She stopped, her feeble words giving up on themselves.

'Try to be more specific,' Dora chided, 'say what you found interesting.'

'I thought he really brought the postman to life,' gushed Shirley, saving her.

'Well for crying out loud he *should* be able to bring him to life seeing as how he *is* one,' exclaimed Conan. 'He delivers my junk mail every morning.'

'That's enough of that disparagement,' Dora said crossly. 'You've been coming to these meeting long enough to know that just because you happen to *be* something doesn't mean you can automatically write about being that something - at least not so brilliantly that the character leaps off the page.'

'Especially if you happen to be something sometimes and not other times,' Maeve blurted, thinking of Dora being a drunkard most of the time, but not on Tuesdays.

'What do you *mean*?' Dora asked.

'Well ...' All eyes were latched onto her now and she wished she'd kept her big trap shut. 'Well ... if you happen so be something sometimes and not other times, like, say, a ... a prostitute. A prostitute would sometimes be a mother, sometimes a daughter, and only sometimes a prostitute.' There was silence, which she felt obliged to fill, digging herself in even further. 'Or ... an alcoholic,' she ventured, averting her eyes from Dora. 'An alcoholic is mostly in a drunken state, but not always ... some days she ... or he ... can keep off the booze, some...'

'And which one are you, prostitute or alcoholic?' cut in Dora, killing herself.

And from the hoots of laughter all round the room, she knew Dora had got one over on her. She gave what she hoped was a sporty smile then busied herself tidying stray wisps of hair.

'Enough of this,' Dora finally said, though still smirking. 'If you've all had your say about *Postman's Knock*, we'll proceed to Abigail - have you named your novel yet?'

Abigail, looking fetching in a skimpy black and orange number that revealed the fleshy top mounds of impressive white breasts at the neckline and sturdy white thighs at the hemline, said, 'Yes, it's called *Ward of the Beast*, at least that's its working title.'

Maeve wondered if the ward in question related to a poor little orphan or to Abigail's hospital.

Pushing her long fringe to one side to give her eyes full vision, Abigail shot off, gabbling out the words as if intent on breaking a record for speed reading. At the end of four pages she stopped, visibly panting, breasts rising and falling dramatically.

'Well, has anyone any comments on Abigail's work,' asked Dora, once the quivering flesh had subsided.

'I don't think that the beast in question would be drinking herbal tea,' stated Conan, creating faint rasping sounds as he stroked his chin.

'Does it *matter*,' exploded James Joist. 'Does it really matter what the beast drank when the word *who* has been used instead of *whom*. That the beast drank herbal tea is of no importance beside that blunder.'

'Here we go again,' muttered Dora, and, strangely, Maeve found she was on Dora's side.

James' eyes disappeared into the depth of his frown, glimmers of reflected light pulsating through sparse bits of eyebrow. 'It is the grammar that matters,' he thundered. 'And the fact of the matter is that the pronoun, who, is used as the *subject* of a verb and the pronoun, whom, is used as the *object* of the verb. Got it!'

And she half expected him to fling a piece of chalk across the room.

'Thank you for the grammar lesson,' Dora said, tight lipped, 'but time's getting on so we'll go onto Maeve now.'

And, by the way the room started spinning, Maeve thought she was about to faint. But, no such luck, so, with trembling hands, she extracted her four sheets and started explaining.

'This is the part where Jupe, who you may remember is ...'

'Should that be whom?' whispered Shirley.

'Just get on with it,' grumbled Dora.

'You may remember that this is the part,' she amended, 'where Jupe, who is Venus's Agreed-no-children contract husband, is arriving at the Buckingham Palace University ...'

'Buckingham Palace University!' cried Shirley. 'I don't know what the Queen would have to say about that.'

'It's in the year twenty ninety-five so she wouldn't say anything,' Maeve said forcefully, 'because she'll be dead - as we all will.'

'Oh dear,' said Shirley, plump fingers flying up to her lips in alarm, as if it was the first time she'd ever realised her mortality. And, Maeve had to admit that stating it so baldly had made her feel quite queasy too.

'This isn't starting where you left off before is it,' accused Dora. 'You didn't mention Buckingham Palace last time.'

'It is, more or less,' she replied, trying to cast aside thoughts of her own extinction. After all, she might be well on the way to her allotted three score years and ten, but most of the time she felt about twenty-two.

'What do you mean more or less. Either it *is* where you left off last time or it isn't,' quibbled Dora.

'I'm reading from where Venus starts to lose Jupe to Geranium, a girl with a red ...' She stared at Dora's alcoholic hooter and made a mental note to omit all mention of the redness of Geranium's nose.

'Well let's get on with it,' Dora said grumpily.

So she took in a deep breath and launched forth:-

So deep in his day-dream of having a son or a daughter is Jupe that he hasn't noticed that the bus has rounded the old Queen Victoria monument in the middle of the road, but suddenly it stops. And there it is. Buckingham Palace University. Solid and strong. He alights with the noisy, jostling crowd of students, instantly caught up in the familiar excitement of a new day. As he crosses the quadrangle and enters the Grand Hall, he thinks of the rich queen and her family who once lived there, whilst, at the same time, hundreds of her destitute citizens slept in cardboard boxes out in the streets. A Three-bee's life nowadays must surely be better than ...

'Hi Jupe!'

He glances round. Pushing her way through the crowd is Geranium the girl with the red no ...

Maeve stopped abruptly, glanced over at Dora who frowned irritably and pointedly looked down at her watch.

Pushing her way through the crowd, she began again, *is Geranium the girl with the red no ... notebook.*

A chorus of angels let rip in her head for the heaven sent improvisation. She took another deep breath and carried on.

Jupe waits for her to catch up.

'It's the Old Throne Room Lecture Hall this morning,' Geranium states, looking coyly up at him, flashing a seductive grin.

She takes up a position beside him, matching his long loping strides with hurried short ones, until they arrive at their destination and enter the hall which is already jam packed. They climb the broad treads to vacant seats near the back and edge along a row of students where they squash in together. Jupe looks around with interest.

'The thrones must have been down there,' says Geranium, pointing, nudging up closer to him, her no ... no ... .'

Maeve just remembered in time.

Her no ... notebook glowing red.

Instead of two thrones fit for a king and a queen, a tall stool stands alone, a panel of glowing lights and buttons by its side. As the students whisper together, Geranium gets out a strange pack of cards. 'A few of us have set up a club,' she tells him, 'you know, a real one, not in cyber space, one like those they used to have before the DOTEC, when people used to really meet together to play games. Would you like to come along one evening, give it a try?'

'Where do you meet?' Jupe asks, tempted by her warmth, so different from the coolness of his contract wife.

'At my place ...'

But, before she has time to elaborate, the lecturer marches in and silence settles.

She stopped reading, kept looking down, waited for someone to say something. Anything! But nobody did. If she couldn't have seen their feet she'd have imagined they'd all left. Slowly she raised her eyes wondering why they all look so stunned. Wrist arched high, Conan tweaked at the tufts of hair on the top of his head, looking as if about to say something.

'Yes?' she blared.

'Why did you say Geranium had a red notebook? Is the colour significant? If not, why put it in, it's a pointless detail,' he said critically, his busy hand shooting up in a sharp upward flourish as if doffing an invisible hat.

Suddenly and unexpectedly she wanted to burst into tears.

'Forget the actual colour of the notebook,' Hugos rapped. 'This *is* meant to be the year twenty ninety-five so why a *notebook* for *God's sake*. Why not a camcorder or computer that records sight smell and sound, something futuristic, for *God's sake*,' he repeated, sending her even closer to the blubbing brink.

Through the mist of unshed tears she stared miserably at Dora's nose, flashing like a fucking Belisha beacon as it tracked each speaker. That hooter had robbed her of the acclaim she would have indubitably received if she'd stuck to her typed script. What would it have mattered if she'd offended her. Besides, she should be speeding down to Wood Hill now, ready to visit the hospital early tomorrow. Ready to comfort Buzz instead of sitting here being mortified by this lot.

She wiped her hand across her eyes, looked around, seeing James Joist's penetrating hazel gaze upon her. He smiled encouragingly.

'Cut out the notebook,' he said kindly, 'it's a red herring ...'

'Red notebook don't you mean,' squealed Shirley going off into bleats of laughter, sending the rest of the sheep baaing.

James smiled warmly at her and waited for the flock to settle down. 'But I think the idea of your novel is brilliant, a futuristic story with love interest. Science is the buzz word today ...'

Buzz, oh why did he say buzz, she thought, seeing a picture of his shy face and toeless foot.

'... and so I think you will find that if you look through *The Writers' Handbook* or *The Writers and Artists' Year Book* to find a publisher interested in that genre, you could well find yourself in print.'

'You really think so!' exclaimed Dora, sounding narked.

'I do,' he said, beaming at Maeve. 'Just cut out the red no ... no ... notebook!' He turned and stared pointedly at Dora, then beamed back at Maeve.

He had guessed she realised, wanting to grab him off his chair and dance around the room with him.

'Before we finish, what the heck is a DOTEC?' asked Abigail.

'An acronym for Disasters Of The Early Century,' she replied, glad to have the chance to explain.

'*Which* early century?' asked Conan.

'This one of course,' she snapped, amazed he couldn't see it. 'Isn't it obvious. In the year twenty ninety-five they'd be looking back at the disasters that happened in the early part of the century - the century that started six months ago.'

'What were the Disasters?' asked Shirley, her soft voice edged with fear.

'There were lots, too many to go into now, but they wiped out two thirds of the world's population.'

'Oh dear,' said Shirley, 'it is fiction isn't it.'

'Of *course* it is,' she exploded. 'How could it be anything else. My story's in the year two thousand and ninety-five, and we live in the year two thousand.'

'No need to get irate Maeve, it's what we're here for,' admonished Dora.

'Shouldn't it be DOTEM then?' said James gently. 'Disasters Of The Early Millennium.'

She stared. 'Maybe so,' she agreed meekly, not having thought of that.

'So why does the World Government give special privileges to those couples who contract not to have children?' asked James, quite reasonably.

'Because world resources can cope better with the depleted population. In my story there are no starving people and the planet's wealth is distributed to everyone as their Being Born Benefit.'

'I still don't know what the Queen would think,' muttered Shirley as they stood to go. 'Students racing around the corridors. I mean she lives in that palace.'

'Goodbye computer,' she inanely said. 'Goodbye *Twenty Ninety-Five*. I can't wait to get back to you, but some things are greater even than you.'

As she carried her grip downstairs, the phone started ringing.

Seventeen

'Glad I've caught you,' Freda said breathlessly. 'I've just heard that Buzz is back home in *The Bungalow* so there's no need for you to visit him in hospital.'

'Not visit him,' she wailed, disappointment searing through her like a blow torch flame.

'He's discharged himself against the doctor's orders, said he couldn't stand it in there.'

'Of course he couldn't stand it, he's is not a hospital sort of person,' she cried.

A quizzical silence oozed out from the earpiece and she became fearful that her daughter had cottoned on to her feelings.

'Of course he can't stand it, not with his toes missing,' she said, mustering a pathetic quip to put her off track.

'It's nothing to joke about mother,' Freda snapped.

'I wasn't joking. He couldn't stand *it*, or stand *up*, in hospital,' she blustered. Then, saving herself from more foolish utterings, a sudden thought hit her. 'Maybe you got it wrong and it was someone else from the village who'd discharged himself from hospital.'

'No, no it *wasn't*,' she said.

'Listen Freda, will you. Gossip can be like Chinese whispers, the last person to hear what's being passed on gets a garbled mix-up of the facts.'

'No, no, it wasn't like that.'

'Well, how do you know he discharged himself?' she flared. 'You always were argumentative.'

'Because he rang me up specially so I could let you know, so you wouldn't have a wasted journey,' she answered hotly. 'I'd told him you'd be visiting. And I am *not* argumentative.'

'That was very considerate of him,' she murmured, trying to control the quiver taking over her chin. 'But I've packed my bag, so I'll come down to Wood Hill anyway.'

'Of *course* you will. He still wants you to visit him, silly. He said he didn't want you wasting your time driving straight to Great Piddlehurst.' As her emotions soared like a skylark, Freda added, 'He said something about you having a mutual interest in birds. That's news to me I told him.'

Oh daughter, how could you let me down so!

'I'm *becoming* interested - remember I was reading Bernard's Bird Book,' she retorted, wishing she'd spent at least a few hours of the last weeks studying more bird books instead of squandering them all on her novel.

'I'm glad you're getting interested, it'll help you fill in your lonely hours without father,' Freda said in a syrupy kind of voice that made Maeve want to throw up. Though, in fairness she supposed, not knowing about the novel, Freda must assume she filled in her days doing crosswords, dusting, and gazing at the wallpaper. Still, even though she knew her daughter meant well, the patronising tone made her want to slap her legs.

'By the way,' Freda brightly continued, 'he said he didn't know you were my mother.'

'You *told* him,' she exclaimed. 'You *told* him. *Why* did you tell him?'

Oh how could my only child let me down so badly, twice!

'Because you are,' she said, sounding nonplussed. 'You are my mother so why try and keep it from him.'

Because even though I am your mother I fancy him like crazy, her inner voice raged.

But, overriding the inner voice rantings, her normal voice calmly said: 'Oh, no reason, just a bit of fun to see how long it would take him to catch on, but you've succeeded in finishing that harmless game off.'

'Sor-*ry*,' she said, clearly anything but. 'See you later - you'll come here first?'

'No, I think I'll go straight there - as he's asked for me.'

She pulled up behind a blue car with a DOCTOR ON CALL notice displayed in its window. She eased herself out, and tottered stiffly down *The Bungalow* path, heart pounding like a meat pulveriser. As she reached the door it flew open and a large man loomed out at her.

'Doctor Radio,' he said briskly, sticking his hand out and

pumping hers, 'you must be Maeve Salmon?'

'Yes, is Buzz all right?'

'As right as a man who's amputated his toes and stupidly discharged himself from hospital can be,' he said without smiling, flapping one hand, urging her in. 'I'm glad you came before I had to go because we need to talk. Come in quickly and see him.'

She followed him down the passageway to the open bedroom door at the end. As they entered, Buzz lifted his head from a flat meagre pillow, his sandy stubble glinting as it passed through a ray of light. Wanly, he smiled before flopping back down.

'Hi Maeve,' he whispered, weakly lifting his arm and circling his flat palm, 'sure I'm grateful you've come.' And, immediately, his arm drooped down, together with his eyelids.

'Oh Buzz, Buzz,' she whispered, overwhelmed by the sight of his sparse sandy lashes brushing his pale sombre face. 'How are you feeling?'

'I'm fit enough in myself, but my big toe is agony,' he murmured, eyes still shut tight.

'The one that's just been sewn back on do you mean?' she asked, to be sure.

He opened one eye. 'Yes, that's the one,' he confirmed, a delighted grin lighting up his face like a sudden flash of sunlight in a sombre sky.

'I've been explaining to him,' said Doctor Radio, 'he can't stay here alone, not so soon after the operation. He was under the anaesthetic for eight hours and that's left him weak. Not only that, the four toe stumps weren't clean wounds, they were jagged and messy, and skin flaps were ...'

'Jaisus,' cut in Buzz, 'they're my toe stumps you're talking about and it makes me feel sick.'

'You'll be feeling even more sick if infection sets in, which it could,' blasted Doctor Radio. 'Even gas gangrene. So don't stop me explaining about your wounds to your friend here.' He wiggled his finger violently in one of his ears as if dispelling his anger. 'You should be in hospital, you know that, so don't talk to me about feeling sick,' he added for good measure.

'Well he's here now,' Maeve observed timidly, 'so ...'

'Taking the law into your own hands and hiring a private ambulance like that,' he continued, glaring at Buzz. 'And you a National Health patient.'

'Don't you think you *should* go back,' she ventured, suddenly scared for him.

'They've given me a tetanus jab,' Buzz said wearily. 'And they say they've sewn skin flaps over the stumps - so that should protect them from infection.'

'*And* make them look nicer,' she added, to cheer him up.

'Yes that too,' he said, faintly smiling, 'but I'm not going back,' he reiterated. 'On your head be it,' snapped Doctor Radio.

And she refrained from the obvious, seeing that neither of them looked in the mood for witty quips.

'He says he can pay for a nurse and physio to come in regularly,' said the doctor moodily, at last addressing her. '*And* domestic help, but he refuses to have a stranger living in. He wants someone he knows and likes.'

She hugged herself, shivering in anticipation of what she hoped was to come.

'Someone who is prepared to stay here with him night and day,' he confirmed.

And a crooner with palm court orchestra started singing inside her head: *Night and day, you are the one, only you beneath the moon and under the sun, whether near to me or far ...*

Her eyes latched onto Buzz's now wide open orbs and, as the music faded, quivers ran all over her and her legs began shaking. He wanted her to live here with him - day and night, night and day. Abruptly, she plumped down on the edge of his bed.

'No, NO,' he screamed, Get OFF!'

She shot back up, appalled.

'Not near my foot! Don't you ever sit anywhere near my foot. Don't you ever even touch the duvet.'

'Sorry,' she mumbled, stealing a glance at the doctor. Was he making a mental note of her unsuitability? Was he about to insist that Buzz went back into hospital rather than risk living there with her?

'So, might you be able to stay here, just for a while, to keep an eye on him, make sure he's safe?' the doctor asked, ignoring the drama of her potentially foot-crushing bum. 'He explained that he hasn't known you very long but said you get on well together - said he didn't like to ask you himself.'

She gazed at Buzz who was self-consciously staring up at the ceiling, his loose sandy hair fanned out on the thin pillow. The first thing she'd do would be borrow some plump feather ones from Freda she resolved, longing to pamper him. He turned his head and his eyes stared into hers with the imploring expression of an unwanted pet pleading for its life.

'I'll stay for a few days,' she agreed, trying not to whoop and grin too broadly. Then she remembered her fear. 'Provided that trapdoor in the bathroom ceiling is battened up.'

Two pairs of eyes stared in amazement at her.

'Sure, if that's what you want ... you organise it will you.'

'And I warn you I'm no good with blood or bedpans,' she added.

'Mr Pike says there'll be a nurse here during the day, so she'll take care of those things,' the doctor assured her, while Buzz returned his gaze to the ceiling, his beautiful face flushed pink.

'I'll stay for a while then,' she confirmed, even though the matter of night time predicaments had been left unresolved.

'That's settled then,' said Doctor Radio brusquely.

'Just for a few days mind, I haven't packed enough for very long,' she said, suddenly nervous again. She hardly knew this man and here she was agreeing to live with him! She almost expected Hector's ghost to put in his two penneth, but amazingly he remained silent.

'As my good companion,' Buzz whispered, smiling weakly, closing his eyes again.

As your good companion for starters, she thought wickedly, almost breaking into a skip as she accompanied the doctor out to the front door.

As he opened it, she glimpsed a figure coming in through the front gate.

'Ah, Sister Anna,' Doctor Radio called, 'I'm glad you've got here so quickly.'

A dark voluptuous young woman in nurse's uniform bounced towards them.

'How is Mr Pike?' she asked.

'Come in. Very weak, should still be in hospital, but you know how cantankerous some patients can be, especially those not accustomed to money. This is Maeve Salmon by the way, she's agreed to stay with him for a few days. Good luck,' he added, promptly hurrying off.

She stared aghast at this Florence Nightingale who seemed to have stepped straight out of a *Carry On* film.

'Pleased to meet you Maeve,' she said with an open friendly smile, 'Mr Pike is lucky to have you.'

And immediately she started to like her. And, when she caught sight of the engagement ring on her left finger, she decided she liked her even more.

While Sister Anna was attending Buzz, Maeve found a cordless phone in the kitchen and rang Freda.

'I'm staying here at *The Bungalow*,' she told her.

'Okay, see you here for dinner - about seven o'clock.'

'No, I mean I'm staying here, at Buzz's, for a few days.'

'What sleeping there!'

'Yes, sleeping here. But not in his bedroom.'

'Of *course* not,' Freda cackled, as if it was the looniest thing she'd ever heard. A pause followed which Maeve instinctively knew foretold of a change of mood. 'So, you'll move in with him, but not with me,' she finally said in a huffy, hurt tone.

'Yes, because with him I can move out whenever I want to - without upsetting anyone.' Surely Freda could see that.

'You could have done that with me too.'

Maeve pictured her daughter's pouty lips and was just about to make a standard retort when, through the kitchen window, she spotted a tall female striding down the front path. 'Must go, there's somebody coming,' she said, glad to get away from that wrangle.

She opened the door.

'G'day, does Buzz Pike live here?' a bright-eyed young woman with broad nostrils and short gingery-black hair enquired.

'Yes he does.'

'I'm Abolene Fisk his new physiotherapist, better known as Fizzy the Physio. Is Sister Anna here?'

'Yes, come in,' Maeve said, motioning the athletic-looking woman in.

'Are you Mrs Pike?'

'No, no, just his friend,' she giggled.

Fizzy raised a thick dark eyebrow, clicking her tongue in a suggestive fashion, edging Maeve's giggles to the high-pitched warbling of a car alarm.

Silly bitch, act your age, she probably thought you were his mother, Hector scoffed.

She wouldn't have clicked her tongue if she'd thought that, Maeve silently argued, though she knew he had a point about acting her age: she was acting idiotically girlie.

'Come on in,' she said, winding quickly down. 'My name is

Maeve Salmon - I'll take you down to his room.'

'Strewth, a Pike and a Salmon together. I wonder which one will win.'

'What do you mean?'

'Don't pike eat other fish?'

I hope so, she thought, as she knocked on Buzz's bedroom door.

Three days since she moved into *The Bungalow*. Three days of witnessing how his appalling taste in furniture has mucked up the beauty of Enid Nesbit's distressed walls and tasteful colour schemes. Three days of nothing to do except sit in his bedroom with him, staring through the picture window on the lookout for bloody birds. Hour upon hour of it, only relieved by his requests for endless amounts of tea, or sometimes coffee 'to make a nice change'. Big deal! She'd tried to get him doing crossword puzzles, but he couldn't work out the cryptic clues and wasn't interested anyway. All the housework and cooking was being done by apple-cheeked Mrs Norris from the village, and all the gardening by Esmerelda Oven, that weird neighbour of Freda's. God knows what she was digging into his vegetable plot. Probably dead badgers or some other innocent sacrificial creature killed by her coven. On the morning that Carl the carpenter came in to batten up the trapdoor you could hardly move for people busy at work.

Fizzy the Physio and Sister Anna had been in each day, Fizzy to exercise him and Anna to dress his stumps and keep an eye on the colour of the stitched back big toe. And, Maeve was finding that although his presence still excited her, she was bored stiff.

'What's the matter Mauve?' he asked.

Yes, he still called her by her pet name, though that *had* ceased to thrill her.

'Nothing,' she said, thumping the tray down on the bedside table, then pulling up a chair and flopping down on it, ready for the wondrous excitement of spotting yet more beaky winged things.

'There is. You've lost your verve, lost your sparkling wit.'

'So are you going to sack me then,' she blared, violently beating a spoonful of sugar into his tea.

'Steady on there Mauve, you'll smash that mug. Won't you give it to me.'

He stuck out his hand and she shoved it at him, slopping some onto the sheet.

'Doesn't matter,' she snapped, 'your laundry woman will see to that.'

He sighed and dabbed at the stain with a tissue. 'What exactly do you mean, will I sack you. How can you ever sack a friend?'

He gazed intently at her and she turned away, staring blindly out of the window.

'Come on, tell me what's up. Don't you like living here?'

How could she tell him she was bored out of her skull and missing her novel. She continued to stare, spotting what might be a jay. She took in a breath to tell him, then let it out again, unable to bear the thought of gabbing incessantly about another flaming bird, as if she could care.

'I thought you said you wanted to live in Wood Hill' he said softly. 'I thought this would be an opportunity for you to enjoy *The Bungalow*, the place I was fortunate enough to be able to buy instead of you. I thought it would be fun for both of us - but it isn't, is it?'

She turned to look at him, seeing the desolation in his beautiful eyes, the unhappy downturn of his tender mouth. She was meant to be helping him recover, not giving him this grief.

'I *love* living here with you, but you've got all that money to throw around and you're so generous with it ... I know you don't want me to have to do any of the hard work, but I do need more to occupy me.'

He patted his golden stubble, silently scrutinising her, and the piercing depth of that look made the inside of her chest go hot. Why hadn't she kept her trap shut, she thought miserably. Would he now tell her he didn't need her any more and that she should go?

But instead he held up both hands in a gesture of surrender and said, 'Sure you need more to do, an energetic girl such as yourself.'

An energetic *girl*. He'd called her a girl!

'I wasn't thinking Mauve. Well I was. I was thinking I didn't want you, my only friend, to have to do tedious domestic chores, not when I could afford to pay. But, if you want to take on the shopping and cooking, or the cleaning, or the washing and ironing, or the whole bally lot, I'll gladly stop forking out on Mrs Norris.'

'Good God NO,' she shrieked. 'Good God NO,' she shrieked again.

'Well man, what *do* you want?' he asked, running bitten-down

124

finger nails through his long flowing hair. 'Tell me, how do you fill your long days in Tooting?'

Now he was bloody well sounding like Freda. Her long days. Her poor dull long days. As if, like him, she was friendless. As if like him she thought spying on birds while they went about their business was wild living.

'My long days, as you call them, do not seem long to me because I am writing a novel and the hours fly by.' Snappily she crossed her arms over her inwardly boiling chest.

He looked astounded. 'Writing a novel. That's a big commitment man. Why have you never said?'

'I don't know,' she mumbled. 'I haven't even told Freda.'

'Not told your own daughter,' he exclaimed as if she'd been withholding something momentous from her, like she was actually a test tube baby with four identical clones.

'I wanted to finish it, then surprise everyone by getting it published. It's been my secret.'

'Sure you're a very secretive person, Mauve.'

'I am not.'

'You are secretive Mauve. Not only didn't you tell me you were writing a novel, you also didn't tell me Freda was your daughter. I had to find out from her.'

'Thought you knew,' she muttered, feeling the fire inside her boiling chest rising up to her cheeks.

'No I didn't know, and I find it hard to believe. Did you adopt her?'

His eyes bored into hers and her cheeks burnt even hotter as she shook her head.

'Well you must have been just a kid when you gave birth.'

She stared at her feet. 'Yes, I was a kid, a schoolgirl of sixteen,' she confirmed, not daring to look up.

There was silence and she knew he continued staring, though she hadn't raised her eyes.

'It must have been hell for you at such a tender age,' he said softly.

She thought of what heaven it had been until she and her baby, Trixie, had had to move out of the comfort of her parents' home to live with the fiery soldier husband she hardly knew who had just been demobbed. The fighting had stopped in Europe but war quickly broke out in their rented flat and, as well as socking her just the once, he'd insisted they call Trixie Freda.

'Yes, it was hell,' she confirmed. Then, in a sudden flood of fairness to Hector she added, 'Well, just at first that is.'

'Freda must be a lot younger than her husband,' he said, his gimlet eyes piercing into her.

'Yes, yes. She's much younger,' she mendaciously concurred.

'How old is she then?'

Oh God! She'd been forced to lie to her daughter for years, now this! How deep in an ocean of falsehoods was she prepared to sink. 'Forty,' she whispered, knocking twelve years off and reaching rock bottom.

'Ah, so you're fifty-six,' he said smartly, 'just two years older than me.'

And the rest, guffawed Hector. *If he's fifty-four, you're fourteen years older and, with your track record, old enough to be his mother.*

And, if he hadn't been dead already, she'd have truly killed him.

'But forget age, it's of no importance,' said Buzz. 'Let's talk about how I'm going to keep you here while I convalesce.'

'You still want me to stay?'

'Of course. Aren't you the only person I really know in Wood Hill. And you're good company too - at least you were at the start. But mostly I want you to stay because I know how much it means to you to be living here in *The Bungalow.*'

So that was it then. He was doing her one great big favour.

'It doesn't mean much when it's not mine,' she said moodily. 'It was owning it I wanted. It was living permanently close to my daughter. To be free to help out with her Animal Park, not being tied here with ...' she petered out, appalled at what she'd been about to say.

'You're not tied here all the time,' he cried. 'It's eight days since the op. I'm not in so much pain. There's no infection so far. I can move my sewn-on toe a wee bit, and I feel stronger ...'

'It didn't come out right,' she cut in. 'I didn't mean tied, I, I meant ...'

'You could go shopping, go and help Freda - do whatever you darn well want,' he continued angrily. 'But, even though I've slept right through every night, I have to have someone here - just in case I get out of bed and fall down. At least, that's what they all tell me.'

'Of *course*, I'll stay. And I don't want to go shopping *or* help Freda.'

He flopped back on the mound of soft pillows borrowed from

Freda and closed his eyes. 'Thanks Mauve. But I'll not have an intelligent woman like you bored silly, if you don't want to do those things, you must write your novel here.'

'But I write on a computer. And I don't think I could do it any other way now.'

'Okay, let's buy one for you.'

'No. No. It's all stored away inside my own one at home.'

'Well you could leave early tomorrow and drive to Tooting to fetch it - and be back before evening. That's if you're up to it.'

She thought of the weighty-looking computer, the printer, keyboard and monitor, all upstairs, needing to be carried down and carefully positioned in the car. She thought of the long two-way journey. She thought of her hip. 'No, I don't think I am up to it,' she admitted.

'Sure and I'm a pig-ignorant fool,' he exclaimed. 'Of course it'd be too much, with you so dainty and petite, how could you lift all that equipment, what was I thinking of.'

'But perhaps Bernard could take time off from FAB CAZ to drive me there and maybe Jatinder could help with the dismantling and lifting,' she said, thinking out loud.

'Who's this Jatinder then?'

'The teenage son of my next door neighbour. He knows about computers and is big and strong.'

'Why not give him a ring right now then - see if he's able?'

Excitement rose in her overwrought chest.

'I'll go get his number,' she said, diving out to her room, hauling her grip out of the cupboard and extracting her flip-up pad from it. Quickly, she found the Singh's number, dived back to Buzz and tapped it out on his bedside phone.

'Hello, who is it there please?' Jatinder's mother answered.

'This is Maeve from next door, only I'm not next door, I'm down in Hampshire. Is Jatinder there?'

'Praise be that it is you,' she cried. 'I am meaning - your house - it has been burgled.'

Eighteen

'They haven't taken everything Maeve, just the electronic equipment,' Bernard shouted above her din. But his words did the opposite of pacifying her and she howled even louder into her tear-sodden duvet.

'I wish they'd taken my jewellery instead, *and* this bed with all its pillows and the sheet and duvet ...'

'Then what would you be crying into?' he said, in a pathetic attempt to jolly her out of it.

'I wouldn't be cr-cr-crying,' she sobbed, sitting herself up, 'n-n-not if they'd l-l-l-left my computer.'

'Hector's computer,' he pedantically pointed out.

'He's dead,' she bawled, 'it's mine now.'

'But it's not the end of the world, you can buy another one the same,' he said gently.

'I *can't* get another one the same because mine had *Twenty Ninety-Five* inside it.'

'What's twenty ninety-five got to do with anything?'

'*Twenty Ninety-Five* is ... is ... is the nov-nov-novel I'm wri-wri-writing,' she blubbed, out of control again.

'You're writing a *novel*,' he exclaimed, as if the only thing he thought she was capable of writing was her will.

'Ye-e-e-es. And it's all been stolen.' She was astounded at the height her voice had managed to pitch.

'Didn't you have a hard copy?'

'What ... what ... do ... do you mean?' she squeaked.

'I mean, didn't you print it up onto paper?'

'Only four four pay-pay-pages at a time to read out to the Nov-Nov-Novel Group.' She slumped forward on the edge of the bed, knuckles brushing the carpet.

'The Novel Group!' he gasped, sounding even more thunderstruck, as if a Lesbian Group or a Jazz Rock Group would have been more likely.

'Yes, the Nov-Nov-Novel Group, and once I'd read my four pages to them and made any alterations they suggested ...' her voice was now rising to a most spectacularly high crescendo '... I binned the lot. Even my first scrawled notes.'

'But surely you made a back-up copy?'

'Can't you get it into your thick head,' she screeched, flinging herself upright. 'No. I did *not* make a back-up copy. Jatinder said that I should, but I wasn't sure how to.'

'Oh dear,' muttered Bernard, his bright eyes now wilted like dead cornflowers. 'How far had you got?'

'Over fif-fif-fifty thousand words,' she wailed, slumping back down again.

'Oh dear,' he said again, somehow infuriating her.

She shot up again, tears spraying out. 'Oh fucking dear is right,' she sobbed, grinding her knuckles into her eyes before collapsing, head on knees, howling into her pink trousers.

There was silence, save for her sobs. At last she opened her eyes, seeing the pale pink cotton spotted with blotches of damp cerise. She looked up at Bernard. He was standing quite still, digit finger draped over his nose, thumb stuck into his mouth, like a frightened toddler.

'All I have left is my outline which I'd stopped following, so oh fucking dear is right,' she said again, strangely pleased to be able to shock him. Maybe a blaspheming mother-in-law would make him realise the enormity of the tragedy that had struck her.

'The police might find it,' he ventured, backing away from her as if she was an unknown dog he feared might attack him.

'Like your pig might frigging fly!'

Obviously defeated in his attempts to mollify her, he shrugged, saying, 'I'll go down and make us some tea. Then I have to get back to help Freda - we're short-staffed today. Do you want to stay on here to sort things out?'

'No. I have to get back too, to be with Buzz for the night.'

He gave her a funny kind of look, then said, 'I'll go down and put the kettle on, you stay up here for a few minutes to recover.'

'I'll *never* recover.'

'Look on the bright side Maeve. The police have talked to you, talked to the Singhs, and they're working on it. You never know ...' He trailed off, then shuffled out, obviously even failing to fool himself.

A picture of Hermione trotting full pelt towards high cliffs then sailing off into space before bombing snout-first onto the rocks flashed into her mind. Pigs might fly. They never fucking well did.

She heard him clomping downstairs. Dear kind Bernard. Freda's husband whom she loved as a son. But not even he could find the right words to console her because they didn't exist. Tears welled again, spilling over, flooding her cheeks, running under her chin and down her neck. She fell back on the bed feeling the trickles change direction, encircling her neck in their hot noose.

Over the sounds of her snuffling distress, she heard a bell ring, then the muffled sound of voices. Hope rose. Maybe it was a policeman calling to pass on good news. She sat up, wiped her eyes, strained her ears, hearing the sound of light footsteps bounding up the stairs, then suddenly the door flew open and Jatinder crashed in.

'Mrs S, it's the pits innit,' he said, high emotion shaking his already wobbly voice.

'Yes Jatinder, it really is the pits innit,' she wept, pushing herself up and allowing herself to be enveloped in his slim young arms.

'You've grown,' she stupidly noted as he crushed her to him.

He loosened his grip, held her out from him, his dark eyes holding hers for long seconds. He inhaled deeply then blurted, 'You must be gutted.'

'Yes Jatinder, I am gutted,' she agreed, even managing the glottal stop.

He handed her a tissue and she blew her nose.

'Did you, like, make a back-up copy of your novel, like I told you?'

She shook her head, flailing her hair into a new assortment of tangles.

'Then I have a confession to make.'

'I'm not your priest,' she groaned, spying a large sprung hair clip on the side table.

'I did it,' he said.

'You did what?' she asked, snatching it up and guiding a fallen tress into its snapping jaws.

His dark troubled eyes turned away from her.

'Sounds serious. Who did you murder?' she said, her attempt at a merry laugh coming out as a strange little yelp.

'Not a murder! I did *it*.'

'What, you stole my computer?'

'Goodness gracious me, no.'

'Well what then?' she asked impatiently. Couldn't he see she was in a state and could do without all this cross questioning and Peter Sellers' impression.

'I did it. I made a back-up copy of your writing.'

Slowly his words drifted down through her ear canals and seeped into her brain: *I did it. I made a back-up copy of your writing.*

'But ... but ... why? When? ... That's ... wonderful. Where ... where ... oh ...' her words stumbled out like drunken youths ejected from a pub in ones and twos. Overwhelmed by the joy of his words, she burst into tears again.

He took out a small rigid square from his pocket and handed it over. 'Here's the floppy disc - mind you don't wet it wiv all that crying, yeah. It's all on there, all your writing, as far as you'd got two days before you went away that is.'

She took it from him and gazed at the black square he'd called a disc. MF2-HD IBM FORMATTED 1.44 MB was printed in black on silver on it. A stick-on label had M.S. TNF written in black felt pen.

'What's that, Manuscript The Next-door Fool?' she tittered, on the verge of hysteria.

'You what? Naw, it's Maeve Salmon *Twenty Ninety-Five*, innit.'

'But why did you copy it?'

'Basically, I was, like, curious to know what you were writing about.' He looked down at his feet as he shuffled them. 'So last time you asked me to help - remember, you'd unplugged it to use your Hoover and forgot to connect it back again?'

She nodded, recalling leaving him to sort it out while she went downstairs for something.

'Well, I made a back-up copy then didn't I - partly because, like, I guessed you hadn't, despite what I'd said. And, partly, well, like I said, I was right curious to know what ... what someone your age was, like, writing about.'

Ignoring the 'age' word, she cackled manically. 'Come to me you darling boy,' she babbled, joyfully hugging him to her.

'What ... what're you doing?' stuttered Bernard as he came back in.

'Jatinder has saved me,' she cried, releasing her grip on him.

Bernard flashed her yet another dubious look, and she could tell he was wondering if he should report back to Freda.

'He made a back-up of my novel on this,' she explained, jubilantly wiggling the square disc at him and bursting into emotional tears again.

'Now all you gotta do is buy a new PC innit,' stated Jatinder.

She dabbed at her eyes with her soggy tissue. 'Can you write down the kind it was, so I can buy the same - so I'll know I'll be able to use it?'

'Sure, where's a pen and paper.'

'In the office.'

He followed her into the room where dusty patches in the shape of the computer equipment stood out on the desk top. She handed him a pad and a biro and he scribbled away.

'Dunno how much this lot'll cost, but that's the sort of PC and accessories you had before,' he said, ripping the top page off.

She took it from him. 'What did you think of it then?' she dared ask.

'It was okay, but if I were you I'd get more RAM and at least twelve giga...'

'No, not what did you think of the PC. What did you think of my novel.'

'Oh, *Twenty Ninety-Five*. It's ...'

She held her breath.

'... it's, like, well cool innit.'

She stared, aware that her eyes were shining and her lips were grinning at the fantastic knowledge that she'd achieved the highest accolade possible from one of today's modern youths. 'Yes, it's, like, well cool innit,' she agreed, causing her dear son-in-law, who'd just wandered in again, to cast her another peculiar look and agitatedly ruffle up his neat hair.

'Only one thing I didn't like ...,' added Jatinder, knocking the grin off her face and the shine off her eyeballs with one deadening swipe of superfluous words, '... I didn't like the main dish in it, that Venus, she's a selfish cow isn't she, lusting after the Black-sail-man when she's got Jupe, a perfectly nice, honest, respectable contract partner at home.'

Oh God, is that how it seemed? she thought in an agony of doubt as she handed him her spare set of keys and Buzz's phone number and address in case of more trouble. *Am I that selfish cow lusting after Buzz when I have a perfectly nice, honest, respectable, bridge partner living close to my home?* she asked herself as Jatinder left.

'I'll just give Wally a quick ring before we set off,' she informed

Bernard after she'd hastily packed all her best underwear, more makeup and more clothes. 'Just let him know what's happened and that I won't be playing bridge for a while.'

'Okay,' said Bernard, 'I'll carry your case out to the car and wait for you there. But don't be long, we're really short of help today.'

She tapped out Wally's number on the hall phone.

'Come *on*, come *on*, be in,' she muttered, overpowered by the urgent need to talk to him.

'Wally Woodcock here, who is it?' his kind voice obediently replied.

'This is Maeve ...'

'Oh Maeve, my darling girl, where are you?'

'I'm at home.'

'Oh good, I've really missed you.'

'But I'm going back straight away,' she jumped in, suddenly scared by his warmth.

'You can't!' he exploded.

'But I am.'

'Is it because I was too forward last time, you know, asking you to marry me?'

'Yes ... no,' she dithered, 'I was very flattered that you did me that honour. No, I'm needed by ... I'm needed in Wood Hill.'

'*Surely* your daughter should have learnt to stand on her own two feet by her age.'

And, dishonestly, she didn't enlighten him. He'd never find out she wasn't staying with her, and Freda would never find out how she'd let him hold on to a falsely bad opinion of her.

'And, by the way,' she added, remembering why she'd ostensibly rung. 'I've been burgled and they took the computer.'

'Oh my dear, that's *awful*, what about your precious novel?'

So she explained about Jatinder and the back-up disc and he seemed almost as relieved as she was. The sharp beeps of Bernard's car hooter cut through the air so, hardening her heart to Wally's pleadings to 'at least come and visit me before you go', she said she couldn't because Bernard was getting mad at the delay.

'They're lucky to have you,' he grumbled.

Another sharp beep sounded.

'I really have to go.'

'Before you ring off, quickly, give me their phone number and address.'

So, feeling guilty, she did, not enlightening him that she

wouldn't be staying there. And, after she'd replaced the phone, she felt even more guilty when she realised that, apart from Jatinder, he was the only one who truly cared about her writing.

Cow, she told herself, as she settled into Bernard's car. Nasty cow, so horribly unfair to your perfectly nice, honest, respectable bridge partner.

But, nearly two hours later, as they pulled up outside *The Bungalow*, all thoughts of dear white-haired Wally had been superseded by darling sandy-haired Buzz.

Nineteen

Fizzy the physio was just opening the door as Bernard dumped Maeve's case down on the step, apologising that he had to rush off to help Freda.

'G'day, are you right Maeve?' Fizzy asked brightly, transferring it into the hall.

'Very right thanks,' she answered, 'how's Buzz doing?'

'He's more like a lazy koala than a bouncy kangaroo, but he's getting there. He'll be glad to have you back - all men like a woman for company at night.' She raised a suggestive eyebrow, causing Maeve's cheeks to burn.

As Fizzy bounded off, Maeve realised that, these days, she was not only blushing all the time like an immature teenager, she was feeling like one. She dashed to the bathroom then skipped down to Buzz.

He looked up from his bed and smiled sleepily. 'I heard you come in. It's good to see you back. Did you remember to bring some milk in?'

'Good to be back and, no, I forgot the milk,' she said, the thought flashing through her mind that for a cow such as herself that was some joke. 'But what I have got is a back-up of my novel,' she said, hoiking the disc out of her bag and brandishing it at him.

He gave her a blank look.

'Thieves had stolen my computer,' she explained, suddenly realising he knew nothing of the trauma she'd been through. 'And I hadn't made a copy of *Twenty Ninety-Five*. Can you imagine how awful that was - weeks of work gone in one felonious swoop.'

'Aye, I can imagine, it'd be like if I missed seeing a wheatear as it passed through.'

'It's nothing *like* that,' she bawled, realising how little he understood and thinking the best place for a sodding wheatear to pass through would be a cat

She plumped down. At least Wally had known how she felt and had shown some concern. At least he knew how much it meant to her.

'Okay, okay, keep you hair on, or should I say up,' Buzz annoyingly smirked.

'But the angel who lives next door had made a copy, so I was saved,' she explained, hoiking a fallen tendril up and threading it into a hairpin.

'Did they take anything else?' he asked, completely ignoring the miracle of Jatinder's divine intervention.

'Just the TV and video recorder,'

He sat up. 'Jaisus, you must be shattered!'

'No I'm *not*,' she flared, wondering how he could be so thick. 'This is all that matters.' She wiggled the back-up disc at him again, but he scarcely glanced at it.

'What about any valuables, like jewellery?'

'No, that was all left - I've brought most of it back here with me.'

'You must be relieved.'

'No I'm *not*,' she shouted. God, he might send shivers running all over her but he was bloody exasperating. '*This* is all that matters,' she said again, wiggling the disc so energetically that she suddenly wondered if the novel might get flung clean out of it.

'But you must be feeling awful,' he persisted. 'Haven't I heard people say they feel contaminated knowing that somebody has been through their belongings.'

'No I *don't*. This is all that bloody matters,' she yelled, ramming it under his nose.

'All right, all right, I get it,' he said, frowning boss-eyed at it. 'And there's no need to swear man.'

Oh God, this wasn't how it was meant to be. How did she expect him to realise how important it was to her. He wasn't like Wally, involved from the start.

'How did the burglar get in?'

'He forced the kitchen window up. Mr Singh's going to fix it for me.'

'That's good. Sister Anna was in earlier,' he said, smoothing his white cotton sheet in slow sensuous movements.

'What did she have to say?' she asked, staring jealously at that sheet, wishing it were her.

'She said she's a bit concerned about my little toe.'

'Which one?' she asked, mesmerised by the seductive sweepings of his hand.

'Why the one that is a stump of course, why would it be the other.' He stopped his disconcerting stroking and stared hard at her.

'Oh *that* one.'

'Yes, it isn't healing properly. That's why it still hurts.'

'I didn't know it did still hurt,' she said, shocked again at what a cow she'd become. As if writing fiction could be more important than the reality of toe stump pain, as if writing a poxy novel was more important than having four toes missing and one reattached one.

'But Fizzy doesn't let me give up - makes me hop around the room battling with my elbow crutches. She and Anna are a couple of good kind girls.'

'Yes they are,' she said in full agreement.

He lifted the jug of water beside his bed, started pouring it into his glass.

'Would you prefer a cup of tea?' she asked, wanting to make amends, and also feeling parched herself after the long drive.

'Sure that'd be nice. But, first, tell me, how do you expect to use that disc there without a computer?'

'I can't. I'll have to get a new one, and a monitor, and a printer. But I'll have to wait for the insurance money.'

'No you won't. While the kettle's boiling, look up a supplier in the Yellow Pages and order whatever you want. You know I can afford it and I must keep you happy now that you're moving in.'

Moving in. She was moving in!

'It'll be fun to have you here permanently as my companion,' he added, stretching out his hand, but as usual pulling it away before actually touching her. 'I've grown accustomed to your face ...'

And suddenly, she wasn't so sure. She jumped up. He might be inadvertently spouting *My Fair Lady* lyrics at her, but what about her empty house.

He stared at her anxiously. 'You could let out your house in Tooting to give you some income,' he said, as if reading her thoughts. 'And, if you don't mind my asking Mauve, what does your income consist of?'

She dropped back down. Oh God. How could she say that on

top of Hector's measly pension from the Bank and her new widow's pension, her only other income was a State pension of her own. How could she let him know she was an OAP!

His eyes seemed to slice through her like an MRI scanner counting her annual growth rings.

'I have a widow's pension,' she muttered, hoping that widow's pensions were given to young widows as well as old ones. She made a mental note to ring up the DSS to check on it.

He continued his laser staring.

'And a few investments,' she added, feeling her face grow hot as she exaggerated the importance of the two thousand pounds she had in a TESSA.

'Sorry Mauve, I was rudely staring but, honest to God, I was thinking how like Joan Collins you looked, except you're blue eyed and fair-haired.'

She smirked, growing hotter.

'Same broad smile, high cheek bones, elfin face.'

'Mmm,' she squeaked, touching her chin with one finger, looking down at her feet and suddenly realising she'd transformed in an instant from glamorous Joan Collins to gormless Frank Spencer!

'Except she's a lot older than you of course,' he added, as if worried he might have offended her.

'Mmm,' she squeaked even higher.

'Both finely built like sparrows.'

She looked up, caught his stare.

'Be Jaisus you look flushed, I'm embarrassing you. And I shouldn't have asked about your money, that's your affair. But honest to God man, letting your house out wouldn't just give you extra income, it'd give you protection from more intruders as well.'

This is what she had dreamt would happen, but now that it had it all seemed so fast - and so final.

'You could do it on a six month let,' he added, again as if reading her mind. 'And by then I should be up and walking, and you'd be free to go - if you'd a wish to.'

She shivered at the barely hidden meaning in those words. If she'd a wish to. And, if she hadn't a wish to, she could presumably stay.

'Good idea,' she said, breezily.

'And by the way,' he remarked, grinning broadly, 'I soon sussed out that you haven't a clue about birds.'

'You swine!' she shrieked. And they both collapsed in hysterics. But, when the snorting and squealing had simmered down, their eyes locked, and the way he looked at her made her pulse quicken. 'I could watch them with you ...,' she started, hoping the loud thudding of her heart wasn't seeping through her ribs and into his ears, '... and you could teach me.'

And, as her brain was picking up on what else he might teach her besides facts about birds, he asked her to pass him his bottle in which to pee.

Twenty

Rashly, she'd put the letting of her house in the hands of Steven State Junior, from the S. State Estate Agency, the easiest option as he already had the details on his file. Also, he had assured her he would only let it to someone *h'absolutely* perfect, and that she had no need to do a thing except sign the forms which he would send when the right tenant had been found.

'We will remove your personal h'effects into the spare bedroom-stroke-study then lock that room away,' he had stated, making her thankful she'd removed the KY Jelly from the bathroom cabinet and brought it down with her.

Meanwhile, at *The Bungalow*, Carl the carpenter, had finished building a desk and putting up new shelves in the third bedroom. Charlie, the odd job man who plays a part in the new pig act, had painted the walls a ripe cantaloupe melon colour and Mrs Norris had thoroughly cleaned everything. Following directions given by Jatinder over the phone, Maeve had managed to install the contents of the back-up disc onto the new PC which sat shimmering with promise like an eager virgin waiting to be switched on. (Which sounded a lot like her - except for the virgin bit.)

She was now dying to get on with the novel but, mindful of her duties as Buzz's companion, she sat at his bedside first thing, trying to get him interested in one of the straightforward crosswords with uncryptic clues, but it quite obviously bored him and the only clue that aroused any excitement was, surprise surprise, one to do with a bird. Soon after that he started droning on about a thrush he'd spotted on the lawn and, to amuse herself as much as him, she said that *he* hadn't spotted it, it was spotted already. And, though he did pause a second for one single 'ha', it just encouraged him to spout on even more about it. How much palaver can you generate from a ten inch speckled brown bird, she wondered tetchily.

'What about the poor snails they bash to death on hard stones,' she said, deliberately controversial. 'Think of the headaches they have to endure before being ripped apart by those speckly sadists.'

And this time he chortled, saying he liked having her with him because they had such jolly good laughing sessions together.

And, morosely, she wished he'd said he liked having her with him because they had such jolly good love-making sessions together.

Then came more bird talk until Fizzy arrived.

'How's he doing?' Maeve asked as she showed her in.

'Okay - aren't you Buzz. Got some movement in his big toe which proves some nerves have joined together, just got to get his confidence up now.'

Not just his confidence, Maeve thought balefully as she left them to it.

But as soon as she stepped into the study, breathing in the heady mixture of new wood, fresh paint and Windolene, all thoughts of Buzz disappeared. She sank down on the new chair, switched on the PC, and started pounding the keys.

Venus has ignored her old friend Satty for years but now, lonely and keen to show off her high-tech luxuries unavailable to ordinary three-bee citizens, she invites her round. They sit together in Venus's small virtuality garden in the heart of London experiencing the sights and sounds of Sydney Harbour and, when the Black-sail-man appears in the colourful flotilla of windsurfers, Venus confides in Satty telling her that despite being married to her contract partner Jupe she has fallen for this sandy-haired stranger who lives on the other side of the Earth.

To Venus's surprise, Satty informs her that she is a member of a World Government committee whose purpose is to keep communications open with Australia, the only country not to have joined the Planet Earth Union.

'Maybe I can get you over on a near-space rocket plane to see him in the flesh,' Satty says, apparently bearing no grudge for having been cold-shouldered by Venus for so long.

Two days later, Satty vid-phones inviting Venus and Jupe to dinner at her place the next evening.

'Have you been able to organise my trip to Sydney?' Venus asks her.

'Just wait and see,' she enigmatically replies.

That means she has, Venus guesses, deciding to get her hair cut into a slicker style at one of the expensive salons in The Old Harrods Shopping Mall. But what would Jupe think? He always raved about what he called her unruly mop. But, SOOD, what does it matter what he thinks. It's not him I'm out to impress!

'Hello Maeve, can you spare a minute?' asked Sister Anna, poking her head round the door. 'It's about Buzz.'

She hadn't heard her arrive she'd been so engrossed. Quickly, she saved what she'd written, worried by the tone of Anna's voice.

'I'm not concerned about his wounds, they're clean and slowly healing. It's his lack of motivation that bothers me,' Anna said. 'He needs something other than those blinking birds to think about. Fizzy agrees with me.'

'Like what? He's not interested in crosswords or playing cards or ...'

'He said he wanted to learn to use the computer.'

'What!'

'Apparently, when he was at work he'd relied on others knowing how to use them and he always meant to go to evening classes but never did.'

'Well, I'll try and teach him - the little I know at least.'

'That's what I thought, so I've organised a wheelchair to be delivered tomorrow - one narrow enough to negotiate internal doorways. Either Fizzy or I will get him in it and manoeuvre him in here.'

'Okay Buzz, are you sitting comfortable?'

'Sure, as comfortable as I can be with half of one foot missing.'

'Don't exaggerate, it's not half of a whole foot, that would mean you'd only have the heel and a short bit. And, look on the bright side, you've got four toes that will never plague you with corns.'

'Big deal,' he muttered.

Maeve didn't go on to explain that she'd said the last part with feeling, because the corn on her small toe was giving her gyp (which probably meant it would rain).

He leant forward from his new wheelchair. 'Okay, so how do you work that typewriter then.'

'I ... I think that first of all you must.' She stopped. How could she teach him when she'd only just learnt herself.

'And how d'you get a picture on that TV screen?' he added.

Think of how Jatinder taught you, she told herself, think of how he put it. She closed her eyes and concentrated on trying to recall his actual words and gradually that first lesson filtered into her mind, so clearly that she might have been back in her home in Tooting.

'First you gotta learn the lingo,' she said. 'That's called a keyboard. And, this might look like a TV, but it's called a monitor, and them symbols there on the desktop are called icons.'

He stared hard at her then looked down at the desk. 'Where?' he asked. 'Where are the icons on the desktop?'

'*That's* called the desktop, the opening screen, because it's like a real desktop innit,' she said. 'And, like real desktops,' the Peter Sellers' lilt of Jatinder impinged itself, 'you have to learn to keep them tidy.'

'Why are you talking like that? And this desktop couldn't be tidier, there's nothing on it but that thin file and the computer stuff.' He slumped back. 'I was never any good at learning,' he sighed.

'Just try and concentrate. It's not computer *stuff.*' Jatinder's polite Peter Seller's lilt forced itself through again. 'You have to learn the names. This is the monitor and the opening screen is what's called the desktop.'

'Why are you speaking with that Welsh accent again?'

'I'm *not!* Do you want to carry on, like, or not?'

'Yes,' he said meekly.

'Well, on the desktop you have instant access to files you use regularly,' she explained, keeping her voice level. 'See, like this real one on the real desktop.' She picked up her *Twenty Ninety-Five* outline file, with an uncanny sense of déja vu.

'Yes, I do see,' he murmured, nodding and slightly frowning, and she knew he was trying to fix a look of wise understanding on his face, because she remembered trying that one on herself.

'Have you got a headache?'

'No, I always look like this when I concentrate,' he said, as she knew he would.

And, as she knew she would, she replied:

'How d'you know? D'ya always look at yourself in the mirror then?'

'I think I'd like you to wheel me back to my room,' he said stiffly. 'I was never any good at learning and it's too late to start now.'

She stared at him, seeing the hurt on his face, the dejection in his slumped shoulders. When she'd reached this stage of gloomy dejection Jatinder had packed her off to make a cup of tea, but, with his lack of toes, she couldn't do that.

'Oh Buzz, I'm sorry,' she cried, impulsively throwing her arms around him. 'What a cow I've been.'

'I'll go along with that,' he muttered damply into her neck.

They stayed locked together, neither of them moving, and passion swirled around her innards in great eddies of yearning. Go on, do something, her mind thundered over the pounding surf of her heart. Rip off my blouse, anything. But be quick about it - my back is killing me.

The feeling of soft moist lips on her cheek sent a roller breaking over her, sucking her further into the power of its undertow. But a sharp rap on the door made her shoot back, squealing.

Mrs Norris's rosy face appeared, followed quickly by the rest of her. ''Tis toad in the hole today,' she stated.

If only! Maeve thought.

'So what does you fancy tomorrow then?' Mrs Norris asked coming in and standing close beside them, hands rhythmically smoothing her apron over her rounded tum.

Were the beady staring eyes picking up the wet imprint of Buzz's lips on her, Maeve wondered, reluctantly dabbing a tissue at her kiss-scarred cheek.

Mrs Norris sighed again. 'Well, what *does* you fancy then?' she asked impatiently.

'I fancy ... I fancy ... (Go on, why not spit it out, tell her the truth. Tell her what you fancy is Buzz, naked and making passionate love to you.)

'I don't know what I fancy,' said Buzz, apparently unfazed by her untimely entry. 'How about you Maeve?'

'I don't know either,' she lied.

'How about salmon and chips,' offered Buzz, snorting. 'Sure don't you both get it. Maeve *Salmon* and computer *chips*.'

'Honestly,' sighed Mrs Norris, giving up and marching out of the room as they dissolved into hysterics.

But the hysteria that had overtaken her was nothing to do with his corny joke. It was an outpouring of joyous emotion because his lips had just touched her.

'I'll give you another lesson tomorrow,' she offered eagerly.

'No way!' he replied.

*   *   *

I'm not attractive. That's why he doesn't want to carry on with me.
Maeve looped fallen tendrils behind each ear, staring intently into the mirror. Her skin was still good, she could see that. And her cheekbones still showed up high and strong, not hidden by podgy fat. Maybe it was her hair. Buzz liked everything to be tidy. Perhaps it was too undisciplined for him. Perhaps she should have it cut into a neater style. Although what would Wally think, he always raved about it. But, what did it matter what he thought. It wasn't him she was out to impress!

She dashed to the phone.

'Freda, will you make an appointment with your hairdresser for me - as soon as you can. The roots need retouching and ... and ....' She could hardly bring herself to say the words but she forced them out, 'and ... and I might get it cut into a neater style.'

There, she'd done it. But she didn't have to go through with it. She'd see if Freda's Great Piddlehurst Raymond seemed as good a hairdresser as her Tooting Fidal Bassoon before making the final decision.

Twenty one

'Good heavens. You're never Freda Field's mother!' exclaimed Raymond, waving his comb in the air.

'I was very young when I had her,' Maeve said, affecting modesty, already liking him.

He motioned her to a chair, deftly flinging a black gown over her front. 'Mrs Field said you wanted your roots touched up and that you were thinking of going in for a new style,' he said, angling and flapping the wide sleeves for her arms insertion.

She sat in the black leather seat and stared at her reflection, seeing that with the clever camouflage of black gown on black chair, her head stood out on its own as if it had been decapitated. She noted with alarm that her hair, glinting in the spotlight, looked at its very best, which always happened whenever she got within lacquer-spraying distance of a hairdresser. The same as a toothache always vanished within a mile of the sound of a drill.

'Cup of coffee while you look at ideas?' Raymond asked, handing her a thick magazine, its front cover displaying a young model with orange hair jutting out in spikes so pointed and solid looking that if her head had been fixed to her neck by a universal joint you could probably aerate a lawn with it.

'Yes please, I'd love a coffee,' she murmured, already deciding she'd drop the idea of a re-style if that was the kind of thing they went in for.

'Marlene, get Mrs Salmon a coffee and bring her that other mag, there's a dearie.'

A girl appeared, her short white hair sporting shocking pink stripes in the long thick fringe. *I once had some pink candy stripe curtains like that,* Maeve remembered, wondering what had become of them. As Marlene handed over the new magazine, Maeve could see the back of her head in the mirror. A triangle had been sculpted into the pure white hair, shorn almost back to her

146

scalp and coloured jet black.

'Would you prefer white or black?' the young girl asked.

'No, I'll stick to my normal ash blonde,' Maeve said firmly.

'Not your hair, your coffee!' Marlene spluttered, clapping her hand to her mouth and giggling loudly.

'I'll have white,' Maeve mumbled, briskly thumbing through the magazine and staring blindly down at a page.

'I don't think that one would suit you,' Marlene sniggered, draping a towel round her neck.

'Might do,' she argued, focusing on the West Indian dreadlocks, for an instant truly wondering whether to give it a try, just to save face.

Marlene disappeared then came back holding a cup and saucer which started rattling ominously as Maeve took them from her. Nervously, she placed the flooded saucer down then raised the dripping cup to her lips but, halfway up, she found her forefinger was stuck in the handle and, with a yelp of claustrophobic fear, she shook the imprisoning china loop, screeching as great sploshes of boiling coffee pierced through her gown.

'Hang on!' cried Raymond - as if she had any choice. He bounded to her, grabbed up her hand, forcibly yanking her lodged finger out of its painful imprisonment. Then he whipped the towel from round her neck and shoved it at Marlene, bellowing instructions for her to insert it under her skirt. As Maeve suffered the indignity of it looking as if Curtain-head was dealing with her incontinence, Raymond glared at the cup, saying, 'Their handles are too tight, they're all the same,' - as if they grew like that through inherited pottery genes and he didn't have the power to smash them all up and buy new ones.

'Would you like another cup?' asked Marlene, who'd finished with her intimate nappy installation and was mopping the floor.

'No I would not!' Maeve asserted, vigorously shaking her head and dislodging a flurry of pins and several curls in the process.

'I see that your intricate coiffure is rather insecure,' observed Raymond.

She drew back her hair to see him and nodded.

'But it suits you beautifully, especially with those gorgeous softening tendrils.' Gently, he lifted one that garnished her neck then let it fall.

'Thank you,' she whispered.

He took out more pins, drawing out a thick hank of hair and

running it through his hands again and again as if gently hauling a flag up a pole.

'I think it's best to leave it,' Maeve said. 'Just touch up the roots.'

But he was obviously in no mood to relinquish the rich rewards of a revamp. 'Is it naturally curly?' he asked, twirling his hands together as if scrubbing up for an operation.

'Not since I grew it long about twenty years ago. Now I have to loop it round into curls and secure each one with pins and clips - it's a lot of bother but I like it.'

'Ah,' he murmured, back to hoisting up the non-existent flag again. 'It's the weight of all that length that pulls it straight.' Deftly he unpinned the rest, and flapped it all out loose. 'Gorgeous,' he gushed, 'but, as you say, difficult to maintain.'

But what is the alternative? she worried. She didn't want spikes or stripes or anything outlandish. She wondered what Buzz would want, realising for the first time that, as far as she could remember, the only time he'd ever mentioned her hair was to tell her to keep it on. Then she thought of Wally who said he loved its spontaneous wildness.

'How about if we cut it short on top encouraging its natural curl, giving it height and thus the impression of length without the bother of all that hardware to hold it in place?'

She gasped and shook her head. 'No, no. That would be far too drastic.'

He placed a hand on her shoulder. 'Only the crown, the rest would be merely trimmed a little to strengthen the ends. It would be neater and much easier to deal with,' he said coaxingly.

Wally would hate it of course, but what about Buzz. Surely he would like it.

'Okay,' she said recklessly, 'go ahead.'

'Oh hi-ya,' said Buzz, hardly even glancing at her as she barged into his bedroom. 'Anna brought in her scrabble today but it's a tedious game so we packed it in. But, guess what I saw.'

She stood still quivering, waiting for his eyes to alight on her.

'I don't know what you saw, could it be a bird with an exquisite *crest*,' she suggested, leaning back against the door post and sliding one foot up it.

'Jeez, no, it was a *black* woodpecker.' His radiant face and dancing eyes turned to gaze at her. 'Can you imagine man, a *black* one. It was on that tree there and I could see its red crown and crest and its bright yellow eyes and ...'

'Great,' she snarled, stamping her foot down and storming out into the study where she threw her handbag down and punched the on-switch of the computer. While it whirred itself into action, she stomped out into the immaculately clean kitchen and jabbed the kettle on. How *could* he not have noticed, it looked so different - so fabulous.

'If you're making a cuppa, I'd like one,' his voice faintly called.

'Would you like a cup for your precious poxy woodpecker too,' she snarled, though not loud enough for him to hear.

She caught sight of her reflection in the window and wondered again what Wally would think of the new prim look.

'Sure and you've had your hair done,' observed Buzz when she shoved his tea at him.

'Sure and what do you think of it,' she mimicked nastily.

His lambent eyes, as blue as swimming pool water, gazed soulfully at her, then sharpened as he took stock.

'Well bloody well say something,' she snapped, not able to bear the suspense.

He cleared his throat.

'Yes. What?'

'I don't like it when you swear Mauve, it's not ladylike.'

'Not ladylike! Not sodding ladylike! Bloody hell. And do you think it's gentlemanly-like to ignore a lady's new hairdo. No wonder I'm not ladylike,' she shrieked, knowing she sounded pathetic but unable to contain herself. He was so *disappointing*.

His eyes compressed to two thin fluorescent blue slits. Moments passed. 'It's good that you've had the top cut short - now all those pins and combs and stuff won't be dropping out all over the place.'

'All those pins and combs and stuff dropping out all over the place!' she exploded. 'Well pardon my hair for existing. Pardon me for pinning it up to make it look nice. Pardon me for not having had a crew cut the minute I set foot in your pristine bloody bungalow.'

And suddenly she found she was howling. Great sobs of delayed grief, replaying the horror of seeing Raymond wielding his scissors, snapping through tress after tress, watching it float to the floor, swept away immediately by Curtain-head, as if they'd never existed. Umpteen years of growth lopped off while others chatted. She raked her fingers up through the massacre and, as they shot out unimpeded into space, her howling grew louder. She wanted her intricate haystack back. Already she missed it.

'Mauve, stop all that noise won't you. Come closer, let me look properly at you.'

Sobbing, she lolloped to him.

'It's nice and soft looking.'

'I don't *want* to be nice and soft looking.'

'Jeez, not you Mauve, not you personally, not you all over, just your hair. Your hair is nice and soft looking.'

'And what's the use of that,' she wept, 'no-one's likely to touch it.'

'I'd touch it, if only I could reach,' he said timidly.

'Go on then,' she blubbed, dropping to her knees by the side of his bed. 'Go on. I dare you. Feel if it *is* soft.' And unbridled sobbing revved up again.

'Hush Mauve, please.'

And she felt his hand pat lightly on her cropped curls as she buried her face in his duvet to muffle her grief.

'Hush,' he instructed again.

And this time his fingers ran through them. And then again. And again.

She held her breath, but it burst out in the gulps and hiccups of a distraught child.

'There, there,' he said, his probing fingertips now tentatively massaging her scalp.

And the thrill of his intimate touch slowly calmed her.

'Nice,' he murmured. 'Your new hairstyle feels nice. I really like it.'

She looked up at him, wiped her eyes with the back of her hand, took out a tissue from under his pillow and blew her nose. 'Do you?' she said. 'Do you really like it? You're not just saying that?'

'Yes, I do like it.'

She smiled through her tears, seeing in a softening blur the man she was now certain she loved, his eyes shining like the Mediterranean on a sunny day, his hair gleaming like a sandy beach just after the tide had gone out.

He cleared his throat and smiled back at her. 'Yes, I really do like it,' he reiterated. 'It reminds me of the pom-pom crest on a large exotic duck I once had.'

'A pom-pom crest!' she cried, hands flying up to her puffy crown. 'On a large exotic duck!' she howled, levering herself up to her feet.

'It was a beautiful duck,' he said, in apparent bewilderment.

And as she marched from the room, she refrained from yelling back the word that rhymed with duck, for it wasn't exotic *or* beautiful.

She barged into the study, threw herself down and began beating the keys:-

Satty opens the door, grabs Venus by the shoulders and holds her at arms length, gushing how wonderful it is to see her again, and how wonderful she looks. A big bearded man appears at her side whom she introduces as her husband, Zarro.

'And this is my husband Jupe,' Venus responds, pulling him into view, noting the surprise on Zarro's face as he takes in his colour.

'I like your new hairdo,' Satty states as she guides them along a passageway to a room at the end. She opens the door, stands back, eyes sparkling. She says, 'Venus, you go in first.'

Venus smiles her thanks, steps inside then gasps, seeing a tall handsome sandy-haired man - the image of the windsurfer she sees each day on Sydney Harbour.

He steps forward, shakes her hand formally, and she hopes he doesn't feel its tremble. 'Hi, I'm Tron,' he says with a grin, 'Satty told me a red-head was coming. You must be Venus.'

She nods, the shock of seeing him there making her incapable of speech!

'Satty tells me you've been watching me wind-surfing each day - I've seen the virtuality cameras tracking us from Balmoral Beach,' he says in his antipodean twang.

'Yes. Yes, I have,' she says, words at last forming. So it really is him! And he is even more devastating in the flesh than he is in Virtuality.

Twenty two

Maeve had had the devastating news that morning that her stolen computer wasn't listed as a special item on the insurance form and was therefore not covered. Buzz had brushed it aside as being of no significance of course, but she felt indebted to him and, in an effort to be more useful around the place, had peeled the potatoes for the evening meal and was just starting on the onions when the phone rang.

'Hello,' she sniffed, wiping a tear away with her onion perfumed hand, setting up more eye smarting

'Oh good, it's you mother,' said Freda. 'Guess who rang today - your friend Wally Woodcock.'

'Wally! Oh God!!!' she cried, blinking fast and hard.

'He seemed to think you were staying here with me.'

'I did say I'd help you out ...'

'I know. He said. And he sounded most disapproving, made me feel like a wicked slave driver. And actually you've only helped out once since you've been in Wood Hill, and that was just to sponge down Jesus who wasn't very dirty anyway.'

'Georgie,' she sniped. 'Remember you changed his name in case it offended people.'

'Georgie, Jesus, whatever. You know I always revert to his original when visitors aren't around,' she snapped, as always angry because she'd been picked up on the name of her first born: the piglet who, according to her, had been born dead, then had risen up from it.

'I know you think I'm pedantic,' Maeve said, 'but it would be the same as me reverting to calling you Trixie when people weren't around.'

'Yes, I know,' she sighed grumpily, 'you've told me a hundred times, it was father who made you change my name to Freda. But forget that. What's with this Wally? Why did you tell him you

152

were staying with me to help out?'

'I dunno,' she mumbled, realising she sounded more like her own daughter as a kid than her adult mother.

'Anyway, I told him where you were staying and he says he's driving down to see you.'

'What!' she bellowed, in a discharge of horror and onion tear drips.

'Must go, Goolie's ramming at the door.'

'That's what'll be happening here soon,' she sniffed to the purr of the disconnected phone.

All day she was tense. They all noticed it. Sister Anna even offered to get her some tranquillisers. When Mrs Norris came in and saw she'd done the vegetables, she offered to cook Maeve's favourite meal tomorrow, then got all tetchy when she couldn't think of a favourite one, or even one that was merely just nice. Esmerelda Oven came in from the garden and handed over a bunch of frondy carrots saying: 'They en't orchids but they taste better.'

'How do you know,' Maeve had churlishly responded, 'have you ever tasted an orchid?'

To which Esmerelda had dashed the carrots down, muttering indiscernible words like a witch casting a wicked spell. Which, knowing her involvement with the Great Piddlehurst and District Sacred Coven, she probably was actually doing.

'Are you right?' Fizzy had asked, eyeing Maeve as she barged, bottom first, into Buzz's bedroom, a tray of tea and biscuits in her hands.

'Right what!' she snapped, banging it down.

To which Fizzy and Buzz exchanged meaningful glances. But, when the man who wants to marry *you* is expected any minute to come knocking on the door of the man you want to marry, it would be unnatural not to get a little het up, she reasoned, offering him a biscuit from the tilted plate and shooting the lot onto the bed.

'I guess her novel's not working out,' said Buzz in a loud whisper, picking up bits of digestive and eating them.

'Or, she's not got enough to flaming do,' sniped Fizzy pointedly, not even bothering to whisper, picking up an unbroken custard cream and the two halves of a Nice biscuit. 'Here, help me get Buzz up. Grab the crutches from the corner there and bring them over,' she ordered, directing Buzz's arms into his brown checked dressing gown as he leant forward.

And, glad to have her mind taken off Wally's impending visit, she did as she was bid, standing at the ready and trying not to dwell on the fragment of ginger nut she glimpsed as he manoeuvred his legs over.

'There's a bit of damage to his cartilage and ligaments,' Fizzy said, 'but he's been lucky that it's ...'

'LUCKY!' Buzz exploded, jerking his dressing gown tightly around himself. 'Do you call having your foot mutilated lucky man?'

Fizzy started again, 'I was going to say you were lucky to ...'

But the sound of the door bell suddenly screamed out its horrendous warning stopping her voice, and Maeve's heart, dead in their tracks.

'Well, aren't you going to get it Mauve?' said Buzz irritably when no-one moved.

She tightened her grip on the crutches.

'Go *on*, I'm busy,' Fizzy snapped, dragging them from her.

Slowly she moved one leg. Slowly she moved the other. Slowly she walked out of the room, along the passage, to the front door. Slowly she took in a deep breath. Very slowly she opened the door a crack.

'Hello Maeve,' said Bernard, 'I've called to pick up some potatoes to sell in the barn, but thought I'd knock to see how Buzz was before going round the back.'

'Bernard!' she burst out in a sudden whoosh of released breath, flinging the door open and flapping him in. 'It's so *good* to see you.' And she only just held back from showering kisses on him.

'Are you okay?' he said, backing off.

'Fantastic,' she confirmed.

Wally Woodcock roved through her brain all night long. Hour after hour she had to endure his loud lamentations about her lopped locks and his whining whingings about her wanton ways. Each time she awoke, the languid rumbling snores of Buzz drifting through his open door drove her mad with envy. She thought of closing it and hers so she couldn't hear him, but that was the supposed point of her being there - to help if she heard him call out in the night, so, in fairness, she couldn't. Gradually she drifted back to sleep and into the Wally nightmare.

But she couldn't stand it and forced herself awake, though her eyes remained closed. She lay there for a while until the parched dryness of her throat impelled her to the kitchen where, eyes still half-closed, she filled the kettle. As she did so, she was amazed to hear a key turning in the front door lock and Fizzy's greeting 'Cooee'. *Why is she here at such an ungodly hour?* Maeve muzzily wondered.

'Curtains not drawn? Are you right?' Fizzy asked, peering in the dim kitchen.

'Tired,' she yawned, 'do you want a drink?'

'No thanks, has Buzz had one yet?'

'No. but if you think he'll want one at this hour I'll make one,' she offered, taking down his blue tit mug and spooning some decaff into it.

'I'm getting him up and in his wheelchair once I've checked on his toes,' Fizzy said as Maeve poured the hot water.

'His *lack* of toes,' she sleepily sniggered, flopping down at the table with her drink.

But Fizzy was humourless this morning, snapping shouldn't she be dressed and hadn't she seen the time.

She had no idea of the time except to know she'd got up extra early to avoid more of Wally's nightmare visitations. What was it about her she wondered, first it was her dead husband's spirit filling her head and, as soon as he'd had the decency to vamoosh, up comes wailing Wally to haunt her.

She had just raised her arms in a long lazy stretch when the ring of the doorbell arrested her. Probably the postman, she dozily thought, flopping her arms down, pushing herself up, shuffling out and, with her hand cupped over her mouth to cover a gaping yawn, opened the door.

'Hello Maeve,' said Wally.

'Oh my God you're here,' she gasped.

'Oh my God your hair,' he gasped back, in an unintentional parody of her words.

They stood staring at each other in silence whilst she tugged her black satin dressing gown up round her throat to conceal her bare chest.

'Well aren't you going to invite me in then, it's been a long drive?' he groaned.

'Sorry, yes, sorry, please come in.'

But instead of passing her by, he lunged at her, sweeping her into his arms and, before she'd had time to duck away, he was passionately kissing her.

'And who might we have here?' Buzz's voice said.

She ripped herself away, swung round seeing the bug eyes of Buzz in his wheelchair and Fizzy behind him.

'This is Wally Woodcock,' she muttered, wiping her mouth clean.

'Sure and where have you sprung from?' asked Buzz, slumping back.

'Where's your loo?' Wally replied.

'Never heard of it mate,' said Fizzy.

'Where's your loo?' repeated Wally louder, jigging around.

'Is it spelt like Waterloo?' asked Fizzy, seriously.

'No, like water closet,' Maeve said briskly, ushering him past them.

'You wait,' Wally ordered, shooting inside the bathroom and slamming the door shut.

She hovered outside, hearing the intermittent surges of his prostate-impressed bladder coming through the door. *Oh God, what am I to do?* she wondered, knowing that the first thing must be to get herself washed and dressed, and to comb her hair, because from the glimpse she'd caught of herself in the bathroom mirror before he'd shut the door, she could see what a slut she looked. And, after that she'd have to work out how to tactfully get rid of him.

The door opened and a relieved looking Wally appeared.

'Oh Maeve, I've missed you so much. But what have you done to yourself? How can you look like this at gone eleven in the morning?'

'Gone eleven!'

'I've never seen you look so unkempt,' he moaned, trying to grab hold of her.

But, nimbly, she dodged away.

'I got up late because ...' How could she tell him about the recurring nightmares about him. 'I got up late because I overslept,' she foolishly said, not holding his gaze.

Meanly taking advantage of her momentary lack of vigilance, he snatched hold of her hand, wailing: 'Why? Why? Why?'

Why was it people were always asking her questions in triplicate, she wondered, not knowing to which of the many dilemmas he was referring.

'Why are you staying here?' he enlightened her.

How could she tell him? And how could she tell him she was hoping to spend the rest of her life here, when he'd just driven all the way down from Tooting Bec?

'And why did you get up late?' Wally persisted, clearly unimpressed with her first answer.

They stood staring at each other and in his intense gaze she fancied she saw the unspoken question: Was it because you spent the night in bed with that man?

'I had a restless night,' she muttered, tempted to tell him why, but deciding against it. He was too good a friend and, before Buzz, they had meant something to each other. 'Let's go and sit down,' she suggested, leading the way back through the now empty hall into the bright sunny sitting room. 'Take a seat,' she said motioning him to the ghastly orange and brown striped armchair set several feet back from the fireplace. Through the open French windows she spotted Fizzy and Buzz, in his wheelchair, talking to Esmerelda down by the vegetable plot.

But, instead of taking the seat she'd suggested, Wally sat on the dung brown three-seater sofa, within falling angle of the high mantle shelf.

'I'll make you a drink, then quickly get dressed,' she told him.

'No. Just come here and sit next to me,' he commanded, patting the space by his side.

She glanced out at Buzz.

'*Please* Maeve,' he begged, 'there are things we have to discuss.'

She pulled her dressing gown even tighter around her neck in an effort to entrap odours she was fearful her unclean body must be emitting, then sat down at the far end, just about out of range of him and the mantle shelf.

'So tell me, why did you get up so late?' he prodded, sliding along, edging up close to her.

'I had a restless night,' she said, turning her head away so the tainted breath of her unbrushed teeth wouldn't reach him.

'Why?' he asked, inching his arm up over her shoulder (a rash move, in view of the last time).

'Because I was having night... night...' she turned, saw his gentle kind face. 'Because I was having night-dreams about you.'

'Isn't this most interesting,' Buzz's voice proclaimed. 'And what did you dream about him Mauve?'

She leapt up, span round to see him leaning forward from his wheelchair at the open doorway.

'Fizzy, I'm sure you're busy,' he said, 'so won't you just get me over to the pair of them, then you're free to go.'

With a feeling of icy dread, she watched Fizzy manoeuvre him up the small step then trundle him over the pink-sprigged tan carpet, angling the chair so that he faced them. Fizzy levered the brake on, rolled her eyes at Maeve, then with a quick 'G-bye' and a parting smirk, rushed off.

'And what did you dream about him Mauve?' Buzz asked again, his sharp blue eyes never leaving her.

'It *wasn't* a dream it was a nightmare,' she stated, deciding to come clean (at least in one sense) and wondering how she'd come to be in this real living nightmare, with the two men in her life witnessing her at nearly lunchtime looking and smelling like shit.

'She said it was a dream first,' Wally pronounced triumphantly.

'It's of no account to me what it was. And if you've driven all the way down from London to see her you must stop and have lunch with us. She's obviously very special to you.'

Did she imagine the challenging look in Buzz's eyes. Was he wanting Wally to deny their friendship was special. Or could he truly not give a damn?

'Thank you, I do need some sustenance,' said Wally. 'But before that, I'd like the three of us to talk together.'

'I must go and get washed first,' Maeve muttered, beating her malodorous retreat.

Ten minutes later, her ablutions finished, she was in her bedroom trying to decide what to wear. Twenty minutes later, with nearly every item of clothing she'd brought down with her strewn across the bed, she was in gibbering despair. 'Nothing looks right since my hair massacre,' she groaned to her ugly reflection in the long mirror.

I always thought you looked good in that red all-in-one thing said Hector, quite clearly.

He'd returned! His ghost had returned to haunt her. And, at that moment, she couldn't have been more pleased.

'Good idea,' she whispered.

Of COURSE it's a good idea. I always knew what suited you best you silly bitch. It's just a pity you didn't realise it sooner, saved you looking such an idiot so often.

But, not having the time, nor being in the mood for an argument, she let it rest, belatedly realising that letting things rest would have been the best policy to adopt when he was alive, saving what probably amounted to years of rowing before *he* was laid to rest. Sad really, she thought, as she sat on the bed and shoved both feet into the legs of the red cat suit, hauling it up only to find that the zip was at the back instead of the front. Whimpering in panic now at how long she was being, she wriggled out of it, twisted it round, inserted both feet again, pulled up the zip, then grabbed up her nearly-new red kitten heeled sandals, slamming both feet into them.

At last she was ready to face them.

Twenty three

Mrs Norris was just placing a slice of toast topped with bubbling hot cheese down on a large dish when Maeve ventured in.

The granite eyes, set in the homely red face, glared at her. 'I only called in to pick up my money and I find the two of 'em fiddlin' around grating cheese and slicin' bread,' she said tetchily. 'Your friend there said 'e could do it but I said to him, cooking is woman's work. There's two more slices under the grill - suppose you're capable of serving them up.' She looked Maeve up and down. 'Even though you is all togged up like a dog's dinner.' Then, with a roll of her eyes and an upward jerk of her chin, she left.

Buzz glanced over his shoulder, giving a weak smile before turning back to Wally who faced him across the table, though his gaze was on her. Averting her eyes from them both, she clacked over to the fish slice left at the ready, then concentrated on shovelling two more slices up from the grill pan and piling them on top of the other two without flipping them over. *Woman's work*, she thought irritably, not at all minding doing it, but not for that reason. She placed the dish on the table, handed out plates, then perched nervously on the end chair, Buzz on one side, Wally the other.

'Wally tells me you're very close friends,' said Buzz, sliding a slice onto his plate, then licking his fingers.

'We play bridge together if you call that close,' she said sullenly.

'Isn't that what he told me,' said Buzz, biting a seemingly carefree semicircle into his toast, flapping his hand in front of his mouth as the hot cheese hit home.

'Maeve, you know it's more than just playing bridge,' scolded Wally, lifting a floppy piece of cheese-laden toast to his mouth, then putting it down again. 'And you don't have to worry, Buzz has explained you're his housekeeper. I'm sure you don't have to be shy about our closeness in front of him.'

His housekeeper! Her eyes, out on metronome stalks, flicked a fast beat between them.

'It's to your credit,' Wally continued. 'You haven't just sat around moaning about your meagre pension, not like some OAPs. No, you're feisty. You've got on with it.'

Inside her head she fancied she heard Hector's raucous laughter.

'You mean my meagre *widow's* pension,' she corrected, brain racing. 'My meagre *widow's* pension,' she repeated.

Wally was smiling at her in a soppy lovesick sort of a way. 'I've missed you,' he said, in his gruff old voice. 'But now I know you're only here to organise Buzz's household until he's back on his feet I feel better about it. And, by the way, could you get us some cutlery.'

What the *hell* had Buzz been telling him she thought, diving across the room, snatching up knives and forks from the drawer and quickly distributing them. She plonked herself back down, grabbed up a slice in two hands, fiercely snapping her teeth into it, shooting hot runny cheese down her chin.

'Here, let me,' offered Wally, getting out a large white hand-kerchief with a faint purple stain on it and dabbing the humiliation off her.

'*I* could have done it,' she muttered, flicking her head away.

'Beetroot,' Wally explained to Buzz, disloyally pointing out the purple stain now smudged with cheese, 'from the last time we ate together at the Royal Festival Hall.'

He cast a fond glance at her as she sat stiff backed and mortified while he folded the shaming evidence away. Only twice in her whole lifetime had she sent food squirting out of her mouth and each humiliating episode was now preserved indelibly on his bloody hankie, to be exhibited at any time. On this morning's evidence, not only would Buzz think she was a covert slut, he'd also think she was a messy eater needing constant mopping up.

She stared anxiously at Buzz but he looked away saying, 'I can get myself around with this wheelchair, so I'll leave the pair of you to it.' His eyes, blue as a coral sea, latched onto hers. Did she imagine a ship called Happiness sinking in their azure depths? 'Because you obviously mean a lot to each other,' he added, pushing down fiercely on each wheel as if intent on winning a disabled marathon.

No! No! she wanted to shout after him as he bashed into the

door jamb then readjusted his line of exit and zoomed out. No! No! It's you that I want, not him. It's you who I want to sail off into the sunset with, our Happiness isn't wrecked.

'Now I understand the situation I feel much better about it,' Wally said, still stupidly grinning at her.

'About what?' she blared, jumping up.

'About your hair,' he said, rising also.

'My hair!'

'Yes, I suppose as senior housekeeper in charge of several members of staff you don't want to look too wildly glamorous.'

Yes she did, that's exactly what she did want to look. Wildly, *wildly* glamorous for her beautiful Buzz. She ran her fingers up through the cropped curls, regretting their clean quick exit, yearning for the muddle of loops that used to perch there.

'It's easier to keep control over workers when you look tidy and more mature,' Wally went on digging his long knife in.

'More mature!'

'Yes ... older,' he needlessly clarified, 'that hairdo succeeds in making you look older which is no bad thing when you're in charge of staff,' he added, twisting the knife so hard that she gasped.

'At least my clothes are bright and modern, not dull and old-fashioned like yours,' she blasted, infuriated that the stupid old buffoon should dare to talk to her about her looks when he stood there dressed like an off-duty undertaker.

He stared at her in an almost full-iris display of astonishment. He stared down at himself. 'But these are my best clothes,' he said plaintively.

'Bought in the last century by the look of them,' she scoffed, edging away from him, dying to go after Buzz.

'Of *course* it was the last century - just like your red boiler suit. The last century was only seven months ago,' he hooted.

'Boiler suit! This is a cat suit I'll have you know. A catsuit that makes a statement. A cat suit that is scarlet. A catsuit that is bold. Not tame and safe and conservative and nondescript like your out of date stuff.'

A look of pain sped over his face as if she'd viciously tightened a thumb screw. 'Whatever. Cat suit, dog suit. You always look fetching,' he said generously. 'And, if you don't like my clothes I'll buy new ones. But, for now, let's go out for a drive because we can't talk here very well.'

She looked around the room, devoid of anyone but them. 'So *why* can't we?' she asked, throwing out her hand. '*Why* can't we talk here?'

'Buzz told me there were nurses and physiotherapists and cooks and various other people coming in and out all the time,' he explained in a lowered voice, taking hold of her arm. 'So come on Maeve, let's go for a spin, park somewhere, then go for a walk. I'd really like that.'

'No need, we can walk in the garden,' she objected, pulling away from him.

'Please,' he wheedled, 'I want to be close to you - and undisturbed.'

She stepped back in horror, grunting as she bashed into the wall.

His labrador eyes stared, silently begging. If he'd have had a tail it would have slowly wagged. 'I don't know this part of the world - you could point out the sights,' he cajoled.

'All right,' she sighed. After all, it wouldn't take long and after that he'd go home and leave Buzz and her in peace. 'But we'll go in my car,' she stipulated.

'A Skoda!' he exploded, as if she'd suggested taking him out in a hearse.

'So! What's wrong with a Skoda?'

'What's right,' he muttered.

'It takes me safely from A to B, that's what's right. And it was bought by Hector.'

'Oh, sorry, didn't realise it had sentimental value,' he said, hand flying to his cheek, its back displaying a network of stringy veins, the colour of blue/black Quink.

'Not sentimental value. He only bought it because it was cheap. But to me it's a vehicle that makes a statement, that statement being: I am me and I don't care what others might think. So, Wally Woodcock, if you're so insecure you think sitting in such a car is beneath you, well, tough luck, that's your problem.'

'I see,' he whispered. 'I didn't mean to offend. Yes I see now. That car is just right for you. The colour of a radish and zany.'

'The colour of a *radish*!' she shrieked, quite liking the zany.

'Well, maybe not a radish, more a tomato.'

'A *TOMATO!* First a ruddy radish, then a bloody tomato. It's fiery. Fiery blood red, not a sodding salad item.'

'Oh dear, oh dear,' he murmured, 'yes, I should have said that:

fiery blood red - the same as that fetching outfit you have on. Yes. Fiery. Blood red. More exotic than a radish, or a tomato. Yes, much more you.'

She saw he was upset and, after all, he was a good old friend who'd come a long way to see her, and she was giving him unnecessary hell.

'Okay, we'll go in your car,' she pacified him.

'I don't mind going in your Skoda,' he said anxiously.

'Too late, it'll save my petrol. We'll go in yours.'

She let him usher her outside and down the front garden path to his old Volvo parked in the lane behind Buzz's green Jag. She noted the covetous look he cast at it as they passed.

'That's what I'd like,' he said. 'Whose is it?'

'Buzz's, but he'd only driven it a couple of times before his accident.'

'Bad luck for him - he must have some money.'

'Yes, he must have,' she agreed, without explaining.

He opened the passenger door for her and as she took her seat and he bent closely over to pull out the seat belt, a whiff of Pink Camay Soap and underarm excitement wafted into her nostrils.

'I'm quite capable of clicking that in,' she said briskly, grabbing the metal end from him, holding her breath. She'd never minded fresh masculine perspiration - quite liked it in fact. But Pink Camay Soap! And he had the nerve to turn his nose up at her Skoda!

With obvious effort, he straightened, slammed her door shut, then hurried round, easing himself in to the driver's seat.

'Okay Maeve? Then we're off,' he said, switching on the engine and pumping the accelerator.

She'd long realised that, to Wally, his car was symbolic of what he was: safe, sure, unflashy, with only him knowing what power lurked hidden beneath the bonnet. A power he immediately demonstrated, backing at high speed, jamming the brakes on, then shooting forward, miraculously missing the gleaming wing of Buzz's Jag by the width of a bra strap.

'Turn left into Primrose Hill,' she yelled, her head forced back by the G force.

And, obediently, he yanked on the wheel just making it into the narrow lane that ran up the side of *The Bungalow*, careering along on the wrong side.

'Move over,' she shrieked.

And with another hard yank at the wheel, they were suddenly zooming along the very edge of the ditch that ran down the left side.

'For God's sake slow down,' she cried, guessing that this macho motoring, so unlike his normal staid progress, was laid on to impress.

'Thought you liked to live in the fast lane.'

'Not this fast in this lane!'

'Have you missed me?' he shouted above the roar of the labouring engine as Primrose Hill began to act out its name.

'Have I what?' she bawled, not wishing to answer that.

He changed down to second. 'Have you missed me?' he bellowed into the relative quietness.

'Wow!' she exclaimed.

'Does that mean yes,' he asked, casting her a puzzled look.

'No it does not! It means, WOW I've just seen a sparrow hawk skimming along the top of that hedgerow.'

She pointed, exalted by the bird's timely intervention and astonished to realise that she knew what it was, knew it belonged to the Falconiformes Order and knew that she was genuinely excited about it.

'I'm not interested in a sodding sparrow or a hawk,' he bellowed, not just revealing his true nature normally hidden under his gentlemanly veneer, but also his complete ignorance and indifference to birds. And him a Woodcock too, she mused, smiling to herself.

'I don't know what you find so funny,' he grumbled, also revealing that his eyes were still on her, not on the road.

'Just concentrate on your driving will you.'

A long drawn-out silence followed during which remorse began to fill her like bad cream in an old eclair. Poor Wally was obviously suffering enough without her being nasty to him. Suddenly they veered across the road into a small car park set into the woods, bouncing madly over ruts before abruptly halting, sending her shooting forward into the seat belt then catapulting violently back again. Automatically, she reached up to adjust hair pins, combs and fallen curls, but not even that massive jolt had had any impact. *Well, at least there is some advantage*, she thought, rubbing her whip-lashed neck.

'Alone at last,' sighed Wally, turning to her.

'So we are,' she responded flippantly.

And suddenly, in one completely unexpected lightning move, he had twisted round and was plonking his mouth on top of hers, his hand clasping the back of her head so she couldn't move. She struggled but his grip tightened. She struggled some more but though his grip remained hard, his kiss somehow softened. She gave up squirming. After all, it wasn't unpleasant, his tongue had remained in its rightful place and no doubt this one long last kiss before they parted was meaning a lot to him. Slowly, his grip loosened and his fingers began seductively stroking her hair. And to her surprise she found his tender lips and sensuous touch quite comforting. It had been a long time since she'd been connected in any way to a man, and it wasn't as if it was going to lead to anything. But, as the kiss lingered, he began moaning, low at first, growing gradually louder. And, peculiarly, he wasn't Wally any more, he was the big black Negro, Jupe, and she was his contract partner, Venus, young and lovely. She stretched out one arm and clasped hold of his shoulder. He moaned again, with even more passion, and, swept along by his ardour she forced him back against his seat, twisting her torso, pressing her bosom against his tweed-jacketed chest. He shrieked in a sudden paroxysm of ecstasy, then his whole body slumped. God, he couldn't have come, not now in his best beige trousers!

Awkwardly, she twisted herself away from him.

'Thank God your weight's off me,' he howled.

'My *weight's* off you! God, it was only my top half and the whole lot of me's barely eight stone.'

'My problem has come,' he wailed without moving, his eyes tightly shut.

'It wasn't *that* premature,' she soothed.

'What wasn't!'

'Your, you know ...'

'*I* haven't come,' he bawled. 'It's my problem that's come. My back has gone.'

'Gone where?'

And she swore he deliberately hit her.

Twenty four

Maeve tossed and turned all night long, replaying the scenes of yesterday's drama. Wally in agony, unable to drive. Her starting off on the long walk, mercifully all down hill but killing all the same, especially with kitten-heeled sandals. And not one other passing car driver with whom she could hitch a lift. By the time she'd reached *The Bungalow*, the biff on her nose was hurting, her hip was raging and she was half dead.

She staggered indoors, called out to Buzz who didn't answer, and then rang Freda. Mercifully she'd just dealt with her pigs and had popped inside to pick up her Channel-doused hankie to lure Goolie and Goofy her weird goats to her. But, as soon as she learnt what had happened, she abandoned the goat enticement and drove straight round.

As they hurtled into the car park she could see him, still in the driver's seat, staring upwards, his back in a peculiar arched position.

'How are you?' she asked through his open window.

An innocent, well meant enquiry, which provoked a totally uncalled for long drawn out groan incorporating the words *hooow dooo yoooo bluuuudy weellll thiiiink.*

'Not good then,' she observed, ducking back quickly, in case of another spontaneous nose bashing.

'I'll ring for an ambulance,' Freda rapped, whipping out her mobile and jabbing its tiny pads.

As Freda started to give directions, Maeve ventured inside the car, sitting down beside him, comforting him with soft words of encouragement and gentle strokes to his clenched fist, though it was hard to keep up with the latter as it ceaselessly beat on his chest. She wondered if those knuckles had been the ones that had hit her.

'Ooo Maeve ...' he gasped tenderly, and she was rewarded to

hear his brave attempt to make up for his earlier ingratitude.

'Shh Wally, save your strength, you'll be okay,' she whispered, doggedly caressing the fist still rhythmically beating his breast.

'Oooo Maeve ...' he started again.

'No need to speak, stay calm, you'll be okay,' she repeated.

'Ooooo Maeve,' he screeched, lunging forward, shaking her hand off, 'for Christ's sake *stop* it!'

'Just trying to help,' she cried.

He didn't reply, just took up his former arched-back position and slow rhythmic pounding. And so she sat there in silent contemplation, worried that no-one, least of all him, would understand that for those last heady seconds when she'd led him on and even made advances to him, she wasn't Maeve in the year two thousand, she was Venus in twenty ninety-five.

But the sound of a distant siren, followed soon after by the sight of a blue light flashing intermittently through the trees, took her mind off her troubled thoughts. Then suddenly an ambulance burst into view, heading straight for Freda who stood in the centre of the lane, waving and pointing to them. It veered round, bouncing into the narrow car park and screeched to a halt beside the car. It's siren and flashing light abruptly ceased and a uniformed man and woman leapt out.

'Blimey, she doesn't look too good,' exclaimed the man, flinging her door open.

'Not me,' she bellowed. 'Him!'

'Are you sure?' he persisted, clapping his hand on her forehead and staring at her throbbing nose.

'Well, my hip *is* hurting from the long walk,' she confessed.

'Bugger her hip,' shrieked Wally, suddenly clearly articulate. 'It's my bloody back that's gone out.'

Once again revealing the true man beneath the veneer, she reflected, wondering if she could inject a dark side to Jupe when next she got novelling.

The man and woman muttered things to each other then to Freda, then scurried to the ambulance where they lifted out a stretcher which, with one click of a lever expanded upwards like an ironing board which they trundled round to Wally's side. But as they prized him screaming from his seat and forcefully flattened him out onto it, his cries abruptly stopped. Gingerly he sat up. He looked around at them all, smiled sweetly, said: 'It's all right now, it's gone back.'

'Gone back!' she exclaimed, alarmed. This ambulance crew had come out specially. What would they think!

'It's a miracle,' cried Freda, overdramatically, and, in her case, being an atheist, quite hypocritically.

'It's been a waste of our time then,' griped the woman, as Maeve feared she would.

'Not necessarily,' said the man, thoughtfully stroking his chin. 'We could still take him to the hospital to get him checked over.'

And Maeve wondered if Tony Blair's plan to make the NHS more efficient had resulted in putting them all on piece work. They seemed very keen.

'No thanks, I'm okay now,' said Wally, apparently not at all bothered by their waste of time and petrol. With surprising agility, he threw his legs over and stood up.

'What were you doing to make your back go out?' asked the woman, staring at him suspiciously.

Please don't say Jupey! Maeve silently beseeched as Wally's dark eyes swivelled to her.

'Just twisted round to do a bit of bird spotting,' he said, the sides of his lips twitching.

And the way the ambulance woman smirked, Maeve half thought she'd picked up, as she did, *just twisted round to do a bit of bird snogging.*

Back at *The Bungalow*, Buzz sat in his wheelchair listening to them all gabbling out the story.

'You can't travel back tonight man,' he said to Wally. 'But Mauve has taken the only spare bedroom to be her study.'

'MAUVE!' exclaimed Wally. Did you call her Mauve?

'Just a private joke,' said Buzz shyly.

'And, her study ... that sounds very ... very settled. Not at all the temporary arrangement I'd been led to believe.' He glared challengingly at Buzz then turned the spotlight of his glare round to her.

'It seems to mean a lot to her you know, writing that wee story so ...'

'*I* know that. Of course *I* know that. It was *I* she turned to at the beginning. And it isn't a *wee* story, it's a full-blown novel. But, converting your spare bedroom to her study, that's a bit, well, long term isn't it.'

She listened to the two of them, astonished that they seemed to be verbally slugging it out to stake their claim on her. Despite Wally's kiss being surprisingly pleasant she knew it was still Buzz she wanted. And very soon Wally would go back to Tooting Bec and she'd be alone with Buzz. But then Freda had to go and stick her great big oar in.

'Wally, you can't drive home, not after what you've been through and, besides, it's getting late. You can stay with us, we have a spare room.'

Yawning widely, she entered the kitchen finding, to her amazement, that Buzz was already there, sitting in his wheel chair drinking tea.

'I'm more independent now I can use this chariot,' he said in a clipped voice, 'and Fizzy says it won't be long before I feel safe on the elbow crutches, so you're free to go whenever you've a wish to.'

'But ... but, I don't want to go!'

'You do. It's obvious you want to get back to be near Wally.' He turned the chair in a tight half circle so his back was to her, then quickly span it round again. 'Why did you never tell me there was this man in your life? I feel an eejit getting you to come and live here. I thought I was doing you a good turn, letting you stay in the place you couldn't afford. But all the time you've been itching to get back to him in Tooting.'

'No. No. I *love* being here. Wally isn't the man in my life, not like you mean. He's just a good friend, my bridge partner.'

She bent forward so that her face was level with his, clasped the arm rests, leant closer, sending the chair shooting backwards and her stretching forwards.

'Mind my foot!' he bawled, kicking out with his good one, just missing her as she let go, crunching painfully down on all fours.

'Don't you *ever* get near my foot like that again man,' he shouted as she pushed herself up with the ungainliness of a rising cow. 'Go back home, why don't you. Play your stupid bridge. Go out on jolly jaunts with Wally - yes, he's told me all about your romantic walks along the Thames. *He's* only got a dodgy back, *he's* not a cripple.'

'You're only a temporary one,' she argued, rubbing her bruised knees. 'You'll be walking in no time. And Wally hasn't only got a dodgy back, he's also got a problem with his prostate.'

'What do you mean, *also*. If he can't lie down flat, that is *because* of his back.'

'Not pro*strate*, pro*state*. He's got an enlarged one.'

There was a moment of bewildered silence. Then, 'Ah-HA!' he burst out, 'and how would you know *that*.' He said it triumphantly, as if it was a vital piece of evidence he'd cunningly wrought from her.

'He told me. Really, Buzz, he is just my bridge partner.'

'Well that's not what he thinks. And you don't go telling a woman intimate details on the size of your privates if you haven't got designs on her, and that's a fact.'

'Not his privates! His *prostate*,' Maeve bawled, losing patience with him.

'Same thing: privates, prostate, male genitalia,' he said flushing, pushing the wheels of his chair back and forth, darting to and fro.

'It's *not* the same thing. A prostate is an internal male gland about the same size as a walnut - but it often gets bigger with age.'

He stared, his eyes as hard as blue ice. 'That's what you tell me, he said in obvious disbelief. 'But anyway, it doesn't matter if it's the size of a walnut or a coconut, it doesn't matter if it's a male gland or ... a you know what. You've only got to look at the man, look at the way he looks at you to know ...'

'That's not my fault,' she wailed.

'Yes it is Mauve.'

'Don't call me Mauve, the joke's worn thin.'

'That's true. You're not mauve, you're scarlet. A scarlet woman.'

'Well if that's what you think I *will* leave,' she cried recklessly.

He span the chair round, pushed fiercely down on the wheels, smacked once again into the door jamb, readjusted the line and bombed out. 'That *is* what I'd like,' he called back.

And then the realisation hit her.

'I can't move back because my house is let out,' she called to the empty hallway.

She listened to the silence, wondering if he'd heard, wondering if he had if he was deliberately ignoring her. Well, in that case, blow him. Blow him and his tiny bird brain. She'd go back with Wally in his safe Volvo and stay with him for a while.

Suddenly the phone rang and she snatched it up.

'Hello.'

'Hello mother,' said Freda, 'just thought I'd let you know that Wally's gone.'

'Gone where?'

'Gone back home of course. He was looking after the goldfish of the kids next door and it needed feeding.'

'But he didn't say goodbye to me.'

'No, that's why I'm ringing. He asked me to do it for him. Said he'd see you when you'd finished what you had to do with Buzz. He sounded upset.'

Disappointment overwhelmed her. How could he do that to her. How could a man she'd snogged so enthusiastically bugger off without so much as a peck on the cheek. Especially as the man she truly fancied had just sacked her. So where could she go now?

Go and live with our Freda, Hector's voice said.

'You've been moping around for two days,' said Freda. 'What's up? Don't you like being here with us?'

How could she tell her she missed Buzz *and* Wally too. How could she tell her that as she lay on the same bed that she had lain on with Hector for the six months before he died, she found she was missing him too. How could she tell her that at sixty-eight she was just as much of a mixed up kid with regard to men as she'd been as a teenager. In fact, even more so.

'I'm missing my computer and being able to write my novel,' she said, plumping for a reason that was safe and which was also true.

'Well Bernard can go and get it back from *The Bungalow* and we can install you up in the attic where father used to work. I use it as my studio, but we can share it.'

She knew that was a most generous offer. She'd been up there and seen that every bit of space was full of art paraphernalia, and paintings finished and on the go. Freda was doing well with her art work, selling everything she did. How could she take one square inch away from her?

'No. Even though Buzz is now so independent he doesn't need me ...' (she'd repeated this story so often she was even beginning to believe it herself.) '... he'll probably want to use the computer himself occasionally.'

Freda stared hard at her.

'And he bought it so it's his not mine,' she spelt out.

'It was very sudden your leaving,' Freda observed. 'Had you had a row or something?'

She averted her eyes from the penetrating gaze. 'No, Sister Anna and Fizzy kept saying they wanted him to stand more on his own two feet.'

172

'That makes sense even though he can only put his weight on one,' Freda smirked, the green strobing light of her X-ray vision apparently switching off, satisfied with the image it had picked up. 'And by the way, I meant to say,' she added, 'Wally rang while you were out collecting entrance money in the barn. He asked if you'd ring him back - though he sounded strangely formal - called you Mrs Salmon, would you believe.'

And her Salmon heart fairly leapt against the tumbling despair that had been sweeping her downstream. One of the men in her life at last wanted to talk to her.

She waited till Freda and Bernard were both busy outside then punched out his number.

'Hello Wally,' she crooned.

'Oh, hello Maeve, or should I say MOWve, ha ha, ha. How's Buzz?'

'Don't know, I've left there and am staying with Freda.'

'Oh.'

That was all he said. Just *oh*. Then there was silence.

'Aren't you pleased,' she asked, skittishly.

'Did he kick you out? Did you kiss him too? Did you maybe put his other foot out of action in the process? Or do you only specialise in backs?'

'No I don't. No I didn't,' she raged. 'And neither did he biff me on the nose which, incidentally, still bloody well hurts.'

An icy silence froze her ear, making her head ache.

'Are you still there?' she asked.

'Yes.'

'Okay, tell me, why did you ask me to ring you?'

'Because I'm playing bridge with Dora Dome again tonight - it's safe because it's Tuesday, her non-alcoholic drink day - and I want to check whether two diamonds over one no trump means ...'

She banged the phone down. How could he still be carrying on with that red nosed bint - instead of this red nosed bint! That's not what should happen, in real life or in fiction. She stomped upstairs, slumped down on the bed, stared out of the window across the lane to Tinker's Field, above which a kestrel hung motionless in the air. *What am I doing hanging around here?* she thought, seeing it suddenly dive.

She dashed downstairs to the hall phone, dialled Buzz's number, glad that the cottage was empty save for Hermione whose snuffling grunts could be heard coming from the sitting room.

'Mr Pike's residence. 'oo is it?' answered Mrs Norris.

'This is Maeve. Maeve Salmon,' she whispered.

'That'll be the Maeve Salmon 'oo left him in the lurch, I take it.'

'It wasn't in the lurch. I was *told* to go because he was sufficiently mobile to manage by himself.'

'Sufficiently mobile to fall down while using them crutches,' she sniffed.

'Oh,' she cried, 'is he hurt?'

'Luckily 'ee had a soft landing on top o' that Fizzy on the bed.'

Jealousy clutched her innards in a painful grip. She should have been the one he had a soft landing on, not her. She pictured agile Fizzy, her long aboriginal legs entwining him as they lay laughing together.

'Fizzy were hurt though,' continued Mrs Norris. 'The crutch whacked her in an appropriate place.'

'What appropriate place?'

'Why her crutch of course. Bang on it. She were in agony. And Mr Pike, well, according to Sister Anna who walked in on them, he were red as a beetroot, with Fizzy lying underneath him writhing in agony, clutching herself. You know what a shy man he is. More at ease with feathered birds than with wenches.'

'I'm coming straight round.'

'But ... but ...' she heard her say, as she threw the receiver down.

'Where are you going straight round to?' asked Freda, close up behind her.

She squealed, spinning round, staring straight into the sleepy eyes of her daughter.

'Good God, you scared me to death. I thought you were outside!'

'No, I dropped off on the sofa - unlike me.'

'I thought you were the pig, all that grunting and snoring.'

'Charming,' she yawned. 'So where is it you're going off to?'

'To *The Bungalow* if you must know.'

'I *see.*'

'No you don't,' she retorted, knowing that she did really.

Mrs Norris opened the door. 'I tried to tell you,' she complained, 'Sister Anna is taking Mister Buzz to the 'ospital - getting his foot checked over by that Doctor Radio, the one he first saw.'

Maeve pushed past into the familiar hallway with its warm terra cotta dappled walls. She should still be living in this heavenly place, she belonged here, she was part of it.

'I don't think he'd mind if I worked on my novel for a bit, do you,' she said edging forward.

'Well, I don't know 'bout that. You've officially moved out as I unnerstand it. Wouldn't it be trespassing?'

'No it wouldn't,' she said firmly, squeezing past her.

'Well, I aren't so sure,' Mrs Norris muttered following her through the hall and round the corner into the wide corridor.

Maeve glanced round as she pushed open the study door, but, thankfully, Mrs Norris had turned back and disappeared.

She sank down on the swivel chair, switched on the cherished PC, waited in the warm melon glow of the study, stroking the smooth wood of the desk while the computer whirred. Contentment settled as familiar lines of incomprehensible white words and numbers flashed around on the black screen. This was where she should be. Writing her novel was what it was all about. Forget men. Forget kisses. Forget sex. This was more satisfying. (Untrue, she realised later, but she was in a funny exultant kind of mood, like a novice on her first day in a nunnery.)

But, just as she was about to start typing, she heard the faint voices of Buzz and Anna, then Mrs Norris. Footsteps sounded. She swivelled round, her eyes latching on to the open doorway.

The bandaged foot shot into view first, quickly followed by the rest of him and his wheelchair. 'So, you've come back to write your wee story,' he observed as Anna manoeuvred him round.

'If that's all right with you,' she whispered, not holding his gaze.

'I'm certain that's all right with him,' laughed Anna, pushing him in, 'he's been dead miserable since you left.'

Maeve tried to contain her grin, but it burst out, wide and revealing. She raised her eyes to look at him. God, he was gorgeous.

He pulled his pony tail forward, tugging at it with alternate hands as if milking a cow. He smiled anxiously at her. 'Haven't you got so far with your story,' he eventually said, 'of course you must carry on.'

She remembered his last angry words: *Yes, that's what I'd like - YOU TO GO.*

'Thanks,' she said gratefully.

'Think nothing of it,' he replied, sounding strangely formal.

Then she remembered where he'd just been. 'What did they say at the hospital about your foot? Will you soon be walking?'

'No, they said my toe flaps aren't yet healed so I must still keep my weight off it.'

'They said you must persevere with the crutches,' admonished Anna. 'Keep your weight off that foot, yes, but they said you *must* move around.' She turned to Maeve. 'It's not good for him lying in his bed all day or being pushed in this wheelchair.'

Buzz flicked his pony tail back. Leant forward, his brilliant blue eyes boring into Maeve. 'Honest to God, I'm scared to move without someone with me,' he burst out, 'so will you *please* come back here to stay?'

'I will, I will,' she cried, now not even trying to restrain the wide grin that had broken out.

'Thanks Mauve ... I mean Maeve,' he said, flopping back with a contented sigh.

Twenty five

''Bye, thanks for having me,' Maeve trilled.

'It's hard to keep up with you these days,' sniffed Freda, pecking her cheek, 'never in the same bed two nights running.'

Hopefully not, she thought wickedly, throwing her grip in the car, jumping in, giving a parting wave. She wore her pink cotton trousers and long-line black T-shirt. Great for the warm breezy weather. And, hopefully, great for impressing Buzz. Worn with her lace-up white trainers, she had aimed for an athletic look.

Anna was just coming out of the front door as Maeve jogged down the path.

'He's in his bedroom - says he's going to have a go at his crutches again,' she said, 'but only if you'll walk beside him.'

'I'll walk beside him through the lonely night,' Maeve warbled, provoking an amused smile from the comely nurse.

'Fizzy's taking a few days off because of ...' Anna patted herself. 'You know, the crutch - very painful. So you mind how you fall.'

'I will. I will,' she sang, her mind full of heart-stopping images.

Eagerly, she bounded down the wide corridor and barged into his room.

'Welcome back,' he said, waggling his bandaged foot at her.

Oh my sandy-haired man, I knew it would be you. Your wife and child mean nothing, it is obvious.

He sat on the edge of his bed leaning back, his low-scooped black singlet revealing muscular shoulders, his grey shorts exposing pale legs dusted with gold. His good bare foot nestled in the shagpile carpet, the other was held out awkwardly in front of him.

'I missed you,' he said simply.

And, without thinking twice about it, she bent down and kissed him.

'Watch out for my feet,' he mumbled through their attached lips.

Flustered, she pulled away.

'Honest to God it was a lovely kiss, but I was worried about those socking great trainers you're wearing.'

'How about if I remove them,' she said skittishly, tugging at the laces, sniffing as she hauled each one off, dreading to pick up on foot, or pig, odours, but thankfully only detecting the merest whiff of a corn plaster.

She wriggled her toes in the thick pile, suddenly too bashful to follow through.

'I'd love another kiss from you,' he prompted, 'but what about Wally?'

'I've *told* you, we're just bridge partners, and now he has a new one. Someone I know called Dora Dome. He's probably making eyes at her right now.'

'Before revealing his large prostrate,' he sniggered.

'Pros*tate*,' she corrected.

'Pros*tate*, pros*trate*, it's of no matter. Won't you come and sit here beside me.'

Demurely, she perched down on his good foot side, wondering whether to go into the biological details with him again, but deciding against it. Why try educating him at such a crucial time.

'Was it another kiss you were offering?' he reminded her, nodding at her bare feet.

'If you like,' she murmured, not daring to look at him.

'Oh yes, honest to God I *would* like.'

She turned at the intensity of his words, saw a look of profound longing, like an orphan who'd spent the whole of his life yearning for someone to love him.

But, mindful of her recent activity in that area, and not wishing Buzz's back to go out, or anything else for that matter, she said, 'Okay, go on then.' Then she closed her eyes and puckered her lips, waiting for him to decide on the full force of it.

'Oh Mauve,' he sighed, snaking his arms around her and smacking his lips on hers with such powerful passion she was knocked off balance and, with a little shriek (which detached their lips) they both fell flat back, her two feet and his good one still moored to the floor - like an old movie love scene.

He cleared his throat. Just let him say anything about bloody birds she thought warily as she stared at the ceiling. But she needn't have worried.

'When I met you at Bernard's party, I somehow knew you'd be

special to me,' he said in a foggy voice, 'but I didn't dream I'd feel such ... such heat.'

'Nor me,' she squeaked.

'So, it'd be okay to ...'

'Yes. Yes!'

'D'you mind doing it for me then, save me moving?'

'Do it for you!'

'Yes, it'd be easier for you. And I'm so hot.'

'Do what?' she asked to be certain.

'Why, open the window, of course.'

'Oh, ha-ha. Ha-ha-ha. Yes, yes, of *course*,' she babbled, leaping up, diving over and jerking the securing handle.

As she turned back to the bed, he wiggled his bandaged foot in the air.

'If you're in favour of carrying on,' he said softly, 'would you mind if we laid down lengthways so I could rest up my foot.'

'No. No. By all means, please do,' she said, the words coming out as if she'd agreed to him taking his jacket off at a formal function instead of tacitly consenting to canoodle with him on his bed. Magnanimously, she waved her hand at the king-size divan to re-emphasise her agreement. 'Be my guest,' she said even more stupidly.

'Thank you Mauve,' he said, swinging his legs up, shuffling his body round.

'Not at all.' *Oh God, will I ever stop this absurd prim-speak.*

'Now that I'm pros*tate*, why don't you come and join me,' he said, raising his head and grinning proudly at her.

'Pros*trate*,' she muttered, now cursing herself for slipping from frigging formal to poxy pedantic.

'Whatever, just come to me won't you.'

'Certainly.' (Fuck it!)

'Come *on* then,' he urged, patting the space beside him, smiling encouragingly.

Heart pounding, she dived round the other side, wondering how best to traverse the broad expanse of blue-tit-patterned duvet to get to him.

He smiled again, crooked his digit finger several times, beckoning seductively.

Heart now slamming rhythmic sledge hammer blows into her ribs, she clambered up and, in the sideways crawl of a geriatric crab making its way through soft sand, fought her way to him, glad she'd worn trousers instead of a skirt, and glad for once that her crown of hair had been cropped short so that only the long sides draped forward.

'It's hard for me to twist round with this foot,' he said in a gruff voice, as she neared his side. 'So ... so ... might you be willing ... to place yourself here?' Flushing, he spread his legs apart.

'Between the gap, with me like, on top of you?' she squeaked, to be utterly sure.

'That's ... that's what I had in mind,' he confirmed, the allurement of his smile now converted to timid awkwardness. 'So long as you keep clear of my bad foot that is.'

'I'll try,' she said, raising her near-side knee to launch herself over.

'Watch it!' he bawled.

And she knew that for once it wasn't just his bad foot he was worried about.

Knee arrested in mid air by his timely warning, she darted her nearside hand over his torso, whizzed her now quivering knee over and down between his legs, transferring her weight nimbly onto it as she cocked the other knee over to squeeze in beside it.

'Poetry in motion,' he murmured as she crouched on all fours, dangling over him.

She stared down into his twinkling eyes, dreading that gravity had pulled her flesh into Spitting Image distortions.

'Why not take the weight off your knees, rest down on top of me,' he suggested, lightly stroking her cheek.

Her pulse now thudding erratic rhythms inside her temples, she lowered herself down, suddenly wondering what Freda would think if her wildly beating heart conked out and she died in these circumstances. Wickedly, she almost wished that it would just to shock her.

'Oh Mauve, you're as light as a feather,' Buzz said softly, the back of his hand now stroking her throat, calming her cardiac excitement, arresting mad thoughts.

And, as is normal in such circumstances, the throat stroking led to shoulder stroking and upper chest stroking. And as is also normal, inside his shorts, she felt his ardour twitch. And as with all men, his wrist contorted almost to breaking point as he tried to get his hand inside the front of her T-shirt. And, as with all women, she did her best to assist by straightening her arms and arching her back, at the same time fervently wishing she'd put on a different bra.

'Oh Mauve,' he sighed as his hand hit home and began caressing the British Home Stores circa 1991 dingy off-white cotton brassiere edged with torn lace.

Oh Buzz, she silently moaned, *your touch is thrilling beyond belief but I'm too old to hold this position for much longer.*

'Can you get it off for me?' he said suddenly.

'What do you mean?!' she asked between gritted teeth, immediately on the alert again.

'Your bra, can you get if off for me.'

'Oh, sure,' she tittered, gratefully slumping down, twisting her arms up under her over-long top to undo the back. But pain bit into both shoulders with rodent teeth, as she struggled with flat crooked hooks.

'Indeed, it's enjoyable having you lean down so heavily upon me,' his muffled voice said, 'but I can hardly breathe man.'

So she pushed herself up to her knees, sitting back on her heels and twisting her arms back.

'Wouldn't it be easier without this?' he said, tugging at the black cotton and giving a nervous laugh.

'It would, but then you'd see ...' She stopped, not wanting to explain that once she'd got her top off he'd witness what vile underwear she was wearing!

He fixed her with an anxious blue gaze. 'Sorry Mauve. I can see you're coy, and I like that in a woman, sure I really do. But I'll close my eyes if that'd make it any easier.'

'It would,' she said, knowing that those obdurate fasteners would be easier to undo without the T-shirt to contend with.

'Okay,' he said, his lids snapping down, 'let me know when I should open them.'

In an instant, she'd wriggled from her over-long top, twisted her arms back and forcefully yanked the flattened hooks apart. Deftly, she whipped off the bra, flinging it full force over the bed and onto the floor. *Better to blatantly expose my fulsome boobs than that shaming garment*, she thought, trying to remember which knickers she'd put on. She eased herself down on him.

'Okay, you can open them,' she crooned.

'Oh Mauve I haven't had a woman to love me for so very long,' he said, pressing her to him.

'Oh Buzz, I haven't had a man to love me for ...' Then she remembered Wally, and let the words fade into heavy breathing.

'It'd be easier if you could kneel up a little,' he whispered and, as she obliged, he began kissing her chin and neck, making his way downward. But the ecstasy of the passion was outweighed by the agony in her hip and knees. *Oh God help me!* she inwardly screamed. And, as if in answer to her silent prayer, the phone started ringing.

'I'll get it,' she cried, pulling away, sorry to lose contact yet grateful for the Almighty miracle.

'No. No. Leave it, it'll stop,' he gasped, clasping the nape of her neck and pulling her back down again.

As his lips found their way to her cleavage, her emotions swirled with the agony and pleasure of opposing forces, and the invincible phone kept on trilling.

'I'll *have* to answer it,' she said at last, vigorously pulling away, just as her heavenly Saviour gave up and hellish silence bombed down.

'Oh Mauve, we're not getting any younger are we?' he sighed, drawing her back to him.

'No, we are not,' she fervently agreed, glad he'd included himself in it.

'Why are you pushing away?'

'Cramp! I've got cramp in my toes,' she cried, now understanding about God moving in mysterious ways, for cramp in her foot was a truly Masterly stroke, though absolute agony. Stiffly, she scrabbled over his leg. Slowly and painfully, she crawled to the far edge of the bed.

'Cramp can painful,' he consoled as she scrambled into sitting position, swinging her feet to the floor.

'*Very* painful,' she concurred, bending forward to massage her left foot's splayed toes.

'I missed you when you left,' he said softly.

She sat up quickly. 'I missed you too,' she whispered, feeling dizzy on two counts.

'Mauve, oh MAEve, I'm coming over to you, bad foot or not,' he cried, pushing himself up and shuffling along on his bottom.

'Ooo, my cramp,' she groaned, leaning down to grab at her toes again. God, this was more agonising than the hip and knee pain this had released her from.

As she massaged her foot, she felt the bed bounce as he progressed towards her, then his fingers inserting into the waistband of her trousers. Abruptly, she sat up.

'You're shivering,' he observed. 'You must be cold, we should shut the window.'

'I'm not cold, it's you. Your tah ... tah ... touch sends electric sh ... sh ... shocks through me.'

He pulled on the elasticated band and now she was terrified he was about to see the waist-high, rose sprigged, off-white cotton knickers she'd bought for 99p she'd just remembered she was wearing.

'Electric shocks is it?' he said, laughing softly, 'Sounds more painful than cramp.'

'No, not painful, just tingly,' she said, shivering anew as, now, she felt his warm breath on her shoulder.

'Just tingly, like this?'

And with relief she felt his fingers withdraw from the knicker zone and start fluttering like a butterfly up and down her spine.

'Yes,' she gasped. 'Yes, just like that.'

He lifted her hair, placing a moist kiss on the back of her neck and the worries about humiliating underwear transferred to her neck and whether she'd washed it that morning.

'How's the cramp?' he said thickly into the right-angle of her neck and shoulder join.

'It's ... it's gone, it ... it must be you ... you affect me,' she stuttered, feeling quite faint.

'You affect me too,' he said gently, 'and I have a proposition to put to you.'

'You're propositioning me!' she giggled.

'Yes. How about we become engaged?'

'Become engaged!'

'Yes, become engaged.'

And even though his proposal was beyond her wildest dream, a part of her wished he'd said he loved her first, then asked her to marry him, like old Wally had.

'I should like that,' she said, twisting round to hug him.

But then the bloody phone started up again.

'Oh God not now!' she exploded.

But He didn't intervene and its unabated call for action carried on.

'Is *I should like that* a yes?' Buzz said. 'Be quick and tell me.'

'Yes,' she blurted.

'Thank you Mauve, that's wonderful. Now hadn't you better pick up that phone.'

Twenty six

Phone in hand, the length of her forearms pushed closely together to conceal her voluptuous nakedness, Maeve tilted her head to the receiver. 'Hello,' she said, grinning down at her fiancé lying stretched out on the bed gazing up at her.

'Canna ye tell me if that isa the home of Buzza Pike,' said a clipped female voice.

'Yes, Buzz Pike lives here.'

'I have justa heard he had alla his toes cut off.'

'Just on the one foot,' Maeve corrected.

'That'sa bad enough. Tell him it'sa Sophia and I'd like tae have a word with him.'

And then it dawned on her. This So-feee-ya was his wife. Her fiancé's wife. The man who could only say *engaged* because he was already married.

'It's Sophia,' Maeve said bleakly, shifting her free arm to continue the cover-up, holding the phone out to him.

He made as if to take it and, in the profound depths of his anxious eyes, she swore she saw pleasure. Then he let his hand drop.

'Tell her ... tell her ... tell her ... sure, it isn't a good time now.'

Reorganising her elbows to touch together, she awkwardly placed the receiver back to her ear.

'I hearda. Maybe I ringa back later.'

'How did you find out about the accident?' Maeve blurted.

'Our bairn, Georgio, rang the supermarket where his papa worked and found out he was no longer there, but they giva him his phone number and told him about the accident. He should wear shoes, I always didda tell him.'

'I told him too,' Maeve said indignantly.

'Anda who are you?'

'I am. I am ... a friend who's helping look after him.'

'Then maybe we'll meet because Georgio and I wanta to come to

184

England to see him. Please gie me his address.'

She put her hand over the phone, mouthing, 'She wants your address.'

And he smiled, so faintly it hardly showed, but she saw it.

'I don't know if that's wise now, in view of ... us,' he whispered. Then louder: 'Ask her for her phone number so I can ring her at a more appropriate time.'

'I hearda. My number is ...'

Maeve curled her body over, wrists still touching, clumsily writing the phone number of her fiancé's wife on the pad kept by the phone. Quickly, she said goodbye. Even more quickly, she dashed round to her bra on the floor the other side of the room. Turning her back on him, she inserted her arms and angled her breasts into its dingy shame.

'Fancy her ringing!' Buzz exclaimed.

She turned her head, saw his eyes were shining.

'Perhaps you'd rather call it off,' she muttered, interlinking the crooked hooks, turning to snatch up her T-shirt strewn out on the bed, desperate for its opaque concealment.

'No, no. Hasn't she made her own life. Did she say how she found out this number?'

'Yes, Georgie got it from where you used to work,' she said, dragging the top down over her head, glad that though his eyes had followed her, his mind had patently been elsewhere. 'They told him about your accident too.'

'I'm so glad my Georgie tried to find me,' he said, his already gleaming eyes now spewing out shards of happiness like a spitting sparkler on Guy Fawkes' Night. '*And* I'm glad that Sophia rang when she found out about my toes.'

'Found out you'd won a million, more like,' Maeve sniffed.

'Did she mention it?' he asked sharply.

'No.'

'Well, she doesn't know then. She's never devious, not like some people.'

She thought of their massive age difference and her heart sank. *What will happen when he finds out about my deviousness?* she thought miserably.

'Do you remember why you came in here?' he said, patting her knee in a chummy fashion.

'No,' she said blankly.

'It wasn't to make love on the bed, nor yet to get engaged, it was

185

to help get my confidence up on my crutches.'

How could he be thinking of those kind of crutches? How could he be thinking of getting his confidence up when, if that phone hadn't rung, it would have been his manhood!

'So, won't you get them from the corner for me,' he remorselessly carried on. 'Then stand by for action - though don't stand by as close as Fizzy did - I swear that she tripped me.'

He coloured, looking more embarrassed at the memory of his plummet onto his lithesome physiotherapist than he had for the whole of their bare intimacies of the last hour. And she couldn't make out if that was a good or a bad thing.

'I feel so at home with you,' he said, seeming to intimate it was a good thing.

She handed one crutch to him and, gingerly he stood up, placing one hand on her shoulder as he balanced wavering on one foot. She thrilled to the warmth of his hand permeating the cloth of her T-shirt. With extreme care, he inserted one arm in the open metal loop then, with a grateful sigh as if he'd accomplished some amazingly complex task, he carelessly swung it round, smacking it into her shin.

With an effort, she gritted her teeth, withholding a scream.

'Sorry, I get nervous,' he said airily, plonking the rubber end down full force on her bare foot, shooting the grit from her teeth in a howl of pain.

How much agony can a woman endure in less than an hour? Maeve thought, limping alongside him as he took three tentative hops. He dragged his eyes from their full concentration on the floor, casting an anxious look at her.

'You don't look up to supporting me if I fall, so I'm packing it in while I'm winning,' he declared, hopping back to the bed and plumping down on it. 'Take these away,' he ordered, shoving the crutches at her. 'And while you're propping them up in the corner, will you be handing me that bird book before you go off and put the kettle on.'

She trailed out to the kitchen, the joy of his proposal completely obliterated by his wife's phone call and his unusual bossiness - taking her for granted already, like a long-standing wife.

Or a mother, Hector sniggered, sending her plunging further into a black pit of gloom.

Next morning, they silently ate breakfast together, Buzz in his wheelchair.

'Now that your wife is back on the scene, don't feel you have to ...' she at last started.

'Will you listen to you. I don't feel I have to, I *want* to,' he said, shovelling in a huge mouthful of cornflakes. 'I have to get legally divorced first of course,' he said between crunches, 'but that's just a formality.'

She had tossed and turned all night, worrying about everything, but mainly how she was going to tell him how old she was. She opened her mouth to speak, but he began first.

'The first thing I want to do is buy you an engagement ring,' he pronounced.

She stopped mid-bite of her toast.

'Let everyone know we're an item,' he added.

She dropped the slice down. 'What, even tell Freda?!'

'Sure, and Anna and Fizzy, tell the whole world.'

Awkwardly, she fiddled with the wedding and engagement ring already in place. She'd been married for fifty-two years, and Hector had only been dead for just over half a one. How could she remove them, they were a part of her? She listened hopefully for Hector's spectral advice, but for once he didn't offer any. Trust him to keep quiet, just when she needed him, she thought balefully.

'I can't take these off, my fingers have got fatter,' she truthfully explained, though she knew they could be cut off by a jeweller.

'Well, I'll buy you one to wear on your other hand. Something you can flash about.'

'But, but ...' she knew now was the time to confess, give him a way out of this farcical engagement. 'But, but, you ...'

'But, nothing,' he laughed. 'You can drive me into Great Piddlehurst and we'll get you a diamond fit for a queen.'

'You'll have to use your crutches then.'

'Why not the wheelchair?'

'How do you think I'd manage to get it in and out of the car then push you into a jeweller's shop, be reasonable.'

'You're a hard woman so you are, but okay, it'll be an incentive for me to learn how to use them. Now be a good fiancée won't you, and cook me two soft boiled eggs and toast, well done, cut into strips.'

And she wondered if Hector had been right and Buzz was after a substitute mother, not a wife, which, agewise at least, made her the perfect choice, she realised sinking back into the gloomy pit from which she'd been climbing out.

Twenty seven

'You're what!' Freda shrieked.

'You heard.'

'Engaged!' she shrieked even shriller, her pitchfork, draped with dung-soiled straw, now quivering in her hands.

Hermione let forth a rapid burst of derisive snorts then scampered out and down the ramp to the peaceful clucking and baaing outside the mobile home.

Trust her bloody sow to side with her, Maeve thought morosely.

'To *Buzz*,' Freda exploded. 'I had my suspicions about you. Oh yes, I'll admit that. Bernard told me a few things that shocked me about you and that young Indian boy. But I never really thought you'd seriously go for a man who is probably only my age!'

'Older actually.'

'Not much older I bet,' Freda said, chucking her pitchfork down. 'Go on then, how much older?' she challenged, glaring.

'Two years,' Maeve said, now almost enjoying shocking her. Prim little miss!

'Two years!' she shrieked, back into high decibel, high pitched screeching again, and Maeve wished to God she'd stop, it was doing her head in. 'A toy boy the same age as my husband who will be my stepfather,' she cried, slapping her mucky hand dramatically up to her forehead.

'He has to get divorced first,' Maeve said, now positively relishing her ability to outrage her.

'He's still married! That's even more appalling,' she screeched, suddenly snatching up the pitchfork and aiming the points at her.

Confident Freda wouldn't really run her through, she decided to divulge everything.

'And he has a son called Georgie - so you'll have a step brother and a swine with the same name,' she said, dodging sideways just in case.

Freda rammed the curved tines into the dung-strewn straw at her feet with such abandonment and force Maeve feared she was to have another toeless person in her care, but she adroitly missed her welly boot by a straw's width. 'I don't know what Bernard will say about this,' Freda said fiercely, lifting it again and scraping the soiled tines clean on the side of the barrow.

Maeve sloped off, thinking it unwise to divulge that her daughter's dung-splodged forehead could also do with a scraping.

As Maeve walked down the passageway, she could hear Buzz's voice from the bedroom.

'Is that you Sophia?'

She stopped dead.

'Sure, it's convenient now, it was good of you to ring.'

Guiltily, she tiptoed forward towards the half-open door.

'Aye, they're healing, but I don't know if I'll ever be able to walk properly again.'

Like an iron filing to a magnet, she drew closer.

'The Sister says I might walk with a rolling gait.' There was a short silence then he burst into peals of laughter.

And depression gripped her. Being able to make him laugh was *her* attraction, not his poxy wife's.

'No, not that kind of a gate sweet ...' Abruptly he stopped. 'Not a rolling gate. I mean, can you picture a gate rolling along.' Again, he laughed. 'A rolling gait is a way of walking - like a sailor on board a ship.'

She tried to creep away from the misery of his merriment, but her feet remained stuck.

'And how's our Georgie?' he said, in such a low voice she could only just hear him.

She tip-toed closer.

'Oh, be Jaisus, is he all right,' he burst out. 'Wasn't I wondering why he'd never rung me. I have to see him, you know what I'm saying.'

She turned to hurry away.

'Oh that's wonderful,' he whooped, 'so he'll be coming with you.'

He hadn't mentioned her at all, she thought miserably, as she crept away. Nor Sophia's bloke Gis-pepi, or whatever his name was, the 'jolly good sort' his wife had shacked up with. She filled the kettle, switched it on, her mind in a turmoil. If his wife and their son were coming over from Italy, they'd have to stay. So, would she have to move out to Freda's and would it be his wife or son who took over her bedroom? Then the thought hit her with such force that her hand shook and the coffee granules in the teaspoon scattered all over the floor. Maybe that Sophia woman would take up her rightful place with him in the marital bed. Maybe once she witnessed the kingsize divan in the luxury room with the distressed walls and the picture windows looking out onto the vast garden with its flocks of frigging birds, she'd want to stay permanently. She pictured the Italian beauty snuggled up close to him and a tear fell into his blue tit beaker. More tears dropped as she poured the boiling water and her mind went racing off on its disaster course. That woman had wanted the good things in life and had had to put up with a council house in Kilburn. It was that woman who had left him. What about when she saw his new set-up, learnt of his money. Tears fell, plopping into the decaff as she realised she had no part in their close family trio. She placed the mug on a tray with a plate of biscuits, wiped her eyes, and staggered out to him.

'What's the news?' she asked with assumed cheeriness.

'Sophia and Georgie, they're coming over to see me. He really does care,' he babbled, eyes sparkling like brilliant sapphires.

'Didn't bother to contact you for months though,' she sniped.

'Indeed he couldn't - on his round the world trip he was badly gored by a rampaging cow.'

'Where?' she asked, shuddering at the thought of long pointed horns stabbing into God knows what.

'Bombay.'

'No, I mean where on his body did the cow get him?'

'Apparently in each buttock - he was sensibly running away.'

'Better than some places,' she sniggered, provoking a sharp look of reproach.

'It's not funny, Mauve,' he chastised, 'he lost a lot of blood. When he'd healed enough to travel he went back to Sophia and Giuseppe in Italy.

Giuseppe! He was still in the equation. At least that was a bit of good news.

'While you drink your coffee, I'll work at my novel,' she said, suddenly wanting to be alone.

As she entered the study, she heard him say: 'Why's she put salt in it?'

She switched on the computer and as it went through the process of booting up she remembered the last part she'd written. Venus was at her friend Satty's and had just met up with Tron, the sandy-haired man she watched in her virtuality garden each day.

Maeve slumped back in her seat. Tron didn't have a wife and child though, did he, not like *her* sandy-haired man. Still, she was the author, she thought, perking up. She could be God. They were her characters, she could do whatever she liked with them. As the white words and numbers tumbled around the screen, she recalled what Wally has said on their day out in London: 'It'll be like a children's fairy story,' he had gently scoffed. 'Except that fairy stories always have real baddies and you seem to have one very nice man Jupe, and the Black-sail-man who's going to turn out even nicer!'

Well, she'd show him! She'd give Tron a dark side. Galvanised, she brought the end of the novel onto the screen and set off, fingers flying.

Venus grins round at Satty, grateful to her for engineering this meeting. Grateful too that her old friend bears no grudge for having been ignored by her for so long.

'And this is Jupe, Venus's husband,' says Satty, pulling Jupe forward.

'My CONTRACT partner,' Venus says, casting Tron a flirty meaningful look.

Tron runs his fingers through his long sandy hair, eyes hardening as he stares at Jupe. 'Hi,' he says, not smiling. 'What's a Negro like you doing in London?'

'The World Marriage Contract Agency matched me with Venus,' Jupe explains, 'and I wanted to study at Buckingham Palace University to be a SOOD so ...'

'You! At Buckingham Palace Uni. You! A Scientist Of Our Destiny,' Tron exclaims, voice sneered with incredulity.

'Yes, Buckingham Palace University is the most prestigious on the planet and I'd won a place there.'

'Sounds like you've done well out of it mate. Couldn't do that if you were a darkie in Australia. And you've even clicked for a most beautiful woman.'

Venus's heart races as his brilliant sapphire blue eyes turn to her. She flutters her eyelashes, feels herself blush as his gaze drifts down to her breasts.

A heavily-pregnant woman comes up behind him. She taps his arm and he turns, his expression softening when he sees who it is. Satty hands the woman a drink of iced water.

'Bria,' Satty says to the bulbous woman, 'I'd like you to meet Venus, my old school friend - and this is her husband Jupe.'

Bria's eyes dart between Venus and Jupe, then she beams at Venus, murmuring greetings before casting the merest flicker of a cold smile at Jupe.

Tron slides one arm around Bria then tenderly cups her bulging belly in his other hand.

'Bria is my wife,' he tells Venus. 'And this is our burgeoning child.'

Venus drags her eyes away from the hideous bulge, catching Satty's glinting stare and Jupe's dark velvet quizzical look. She wishes she could run away from them all.

Twenty eight

Maeve thrilled at his need for her, but wished to hell he'd get a move on. This journey from his bedroom along the passageway to the sitting room was taking for ever and she needed to get out and go to a special shop.

Leaning heavily on his elbow crutches, bad foot raised up behind him like some giant wading bird, Buzz tentatively swung his good foot forward.

'I'm feeling a little more sure about these things now,' he said upon its safe landing no more than ten inches in front of him. Wobbling on one leg, he lifted the crutches once more, placed their rubber feet down just ahead of his foot, hopping forward again. 'But don't leave my side will you,' he added, nervously glancing at her.

At last they arrived at the sitting room doorway, too narrow for their side-by-side advancement, so she stepped in ahead. From the sharp intake of breath that that evoked anyone would think she'd been a Siamese twin who'd just been brutally ripped from him. Wildly, he flung the feet of the crutches forward, taking a giant hop, landing right by her side. If he could manage that kind of leap when driven to it, why hadn't he done it before she brooded, snatching a look at her watch.

She helped him into the orange and brown striped armchair where, smiling contentedly, he zapped on the TV.

'I'll just watch a bit of the Test Match before going outside,' he said. He must have seen the look of dismay on her face, for he added: 'Don't worry your head about it, Sister Anna's due here soon so you don't have to stick around. I'll wait here safely till she's here to help me.'

'Okay. Just a couple of things I want to buy in Orlford, won't be long,' she announced, plonking a kiss on him.

He grinned up at her. 'Bye bye, my little fiancée,' he whispered tenderly, and her spirits lifted. She'd almost begun to think their engagement had been a fantasy dream and his patent happiness was because his wife and son were about to re-enter his life.

She managed to park right outside *Lovely Lynda's Lingerie*, the most exclusive underwear shop for miles around. Eagerly, she dived in.

'I'm Lynda. How can I help you?' said the young woman behind the counter, her cap of maraschino cherry hair, bobbing a glossy welcome.

'I'm looking for something ... glamorous.'

Lynda scrutinised her through a barrier of stiff raven lashes, pursing her dark maroon lips into an almost black blob. 'We have a fan*tab*ulous chiffon negligée in crimson - it'd look fan*tas*ticle with your ash blonde hair.'

'No, no. It's not a negligée I want. It's a bra and knickers I'm after.'

'No prob*lee*mo, you'll find individual items over there on the left' - she extended one arm languidly in that direction - 'and matching sets to the right' - she extended the other arm in the other direction, like an air stewardess pointing out the escape routes.

Twenty minutes later, having rooted through a treasure trove of sexy underwear, Maeve staggered back to the counter clutching two sets: a scanty bra and matching panties in black silk edged with fine red lace, and an unusual silver satin duo which gleamed with a pewter sheen.

'Thirty-six *D* cup?' Lynda queried, raising the black silk bra and a pencil drawn eyebrow.

'That's right,' she confirmed, surprised that the hairless black arc was that mobile.

'Lucky you,' Lynda commented flacking out white tissue paper, positioning the black bra in the centre of it. 'I'm a thirty-six A. Try shaking those about when you're dancing. You can't.'

Maeve looked at her chest, barely concealed under a flesh-coloured fine knit kind of tank top and saw what she meant. She'd have to go like the clappers to get any movement from those two.

'Has anyone ever told you you're the spittin' image of Joan Collins, apart from she's dark, of course,' Lynda said conversationally as she niftily folded the black knickers on top of the bra. She looked up, eyes sharpening, 'though she's obviously had collagen or Botox injections of course,' she added, patting at her own smooth upper lip, staring intently at Maeve's.

Bitch, Maeve inwardly fumed, why did she have to draw attention to those few vertical lines etched into the flesh above her top lip like a meagre pelmet.

'I hear she has a penchant for younger men - bril*liant*o for her age,' she chattered on, oblivious.

There was a pause while Maeve guessed Lynda waited for her to reveal if she had a penchant for younger men and if she *was* Joan Collin's age, which she more or less was, but she didn't let on on either count, so Lynda resumed her careful packing, lifting the silver satin briefs, her head flipping from side to side as she studied them. Maeve stared at the dangling garment, suddenly anxious that her droopy buttocks would show below those high-cut loose fitting legs. Clearly not satisfied with something, the painstaking Lovely Lynda laid them down and rooted out the label with long, black painted, square cut finger nails. She bent down to read the small print, then leant forward across the counter, blatantly staring down at Maeve's nether regions.

'Your hips *are* ninety-seven centimetres are they?' she queried, transferring her weight back, making no attempt to hide her clear scepticism. 'That's about thirty-eight inches in old money,' she added to make sure.

And, though still smouldering from Lynda's tactless reference to her faint pleating of flesh, and now irked by her doubt about her bum size, Maeve nevertheless marvelled at this young woman's efficiency. No-one was going to get out of her shop with the wrong size.

'My hips are thirty-seven and a half inches actually,' she said proudly, not revealing her new worry about its possible low-slung redistribution.

As the meticulous wrapping continued, she wondered how Joan Collins coped with a bum pulled down by years of gravity when she stripped off for her man. Actresses all seemed to have face lifts, but she'd never heard of buttocks lifts, though maybe they existed, she mused, wondering how much a nip and tuck job on saggy cheeks might cost.

'Got a new man friend?' Lynda asked, apparently casually, as she taped the tissue paper down.

'Mmm.'

'Thought so,' she said, placing the fragile package inside an expensive-looking blue and gold carrier bag with rope handles. 'Women who've started a new relationship always want sexy new underwear. But, once the Rubicon's been crossed, they rarely shop here again. That'll be ninety-six pounds, fifty-four pence please.'

And, though she'd already worked out what the total would be, that huge amount for four tiny scraps still made her gasp. Two weeks of her OAP pension blown on a whiff of lingerie, she realised, as she tugged her credit card out of its tight-fitting slot in her purse. No way could she ever afford to have Botox injections, or her buttocks lifted, not even just one of them.

As Lovely Lynda glided out from behind the counter, leading her to the door, she studied her rear end. But she really didn't need to. It was, as she knew it would be, rounded and pert, just as her own used to be. She wondered if Sophia's backside had given in to gravity yet. Malevolently, she hoped it had.

It wouldn't be long before her Rubicon was being crossed she wickedly hoped, taking the gold and blue carrier bag out from the car then hurrying down the front path. As she drew out her key, she heard a car stop, its door slam, then Sister Anna's voice calling: 'Sorry I'm late, I got held up.'

Oh God, she'd been away well over an hour and Anna had only just arrived. Supposing Buzz had decided to go out into the garden on his own. Supposing he'd slipped! She opened the door then stood aside letting the Sister in first. After all, she was trained for such events.

'He was in the sitting room when I left,' Maeve sang out after her, hastily tucking the bag out of view behind the umbrella stand.

But when she followed the comely nurse in, she saw his chair was empty and the French windows were open. Visions of him face down on the terrace, crutches strewn around, blasted her mind.

'He'll be making the most of the glorious sunshine,' Anna stated, unconcerned, sauntering across the room to the open doorway.

Buck up, buck up, Maeve inwardly urged, though keeping well back behind her, unlike her febrile imagination which had dashed way ahead.

'Hiya,' she heard Buzz say as Anna stepped out.

'Careful!' Anna grunted, as Maeve barged past her.

'Thank *God*, you didn't fall.' she cried, seeing he was sitting safely at the table looking over at them. She reached his side, hovering, unsure whether to kiss him in front of Anna or not.

'He can get about all right on his own you know,' Anna chided, sauntering up, placing her bag on the table and sitting down next to him.

Deciding against the kiss, Maeve took the chair opposite, feasting her eyes on her man. 'He's always so nervous,' she explained.

'Well just ignore it. He has to gain confidence and he won't if he sees you're so anxious.'

'Sure isn't this a glorious day,' Buzz observed, his dazzling smile vying with the brightness of the clear August sun.

He seemed oblivious that they were talking about him and Maeve wished she knew if his overt happiness was caused by the weather, his new-found family ... or herself, his brand new fiancée.

Anna unzipped her bag. 'I could re-dress your toes out here if you like,' she offered.

'Sure, that'd be great,' he said, scraping his chair back from the table and angling it round at her.

'You look happy,' she remarked, as she lifted his foot onto her lap and began unwinding the bandage.

Hurriedly, Maeve leapt to her feet, ready to make her escape from a forced viewing of what she guessed would be horribly mutilated stumps ranged alongside a big toe cobbled together with vile black stitches.

'That's right enough Anna, I am happy, very happy, a lot of things have been happening here, haven't they Mauve?'

Maeve stood stock still. Was he about to break the news of the impending visit of Sophia and Georgie?

'Such as what?' Anna asked, removing a pair of scissors from her bag, making Maeve's stomach flip.

His dancing eyes latched onto hers. 'I'm surprised at you Mauve, haven't you told her yet?'

'Told me what?' Anna asked.

'Shall I tell her myself then?' His eyes, now latched onto hers, were practically jigging.

'Might as well,' she muttered, waiting for the joys of the looming visit to unfold.

'We're engaged,' he said jubilantly.

And her spirits rose.

'Who?' Anna asked, halting all toe tending activities. 'You and who are engaged?'

'Why, Mauve of course.'

'Maeve!'

'Yes, me and Mauve,' he confirmed, 'and one day soon she's going to drive me into Great Piddlehurst for me to buy her a ring.'

'Why ... why, that's brilliant,' she stuttered.

'Sure, it will be brilliant, I want her to have a diamond,' he chuckled.

And the three of them fell about, though in fact it wasn't much of a joke, it was more the excitement of it all. And, for Maeve, the relief that he hadn't mentioned those other two people.

'There's just a tiny snag and that is we can't get wed till I'm legally divorced,' he annoyingly explained.

And she hurried off saying she'd make them all a cup of tea as he started babbling on about the forthcoming visit of his wife and son. It had been too good to hope for and, besides that, she wanted to hide her bag of new underwear in her bedroom - as well as escape the incredulity etched into Sister Anna's bulging eyes.

Carefully, she drew up outside the jeweller's shop, Buzz on the pavement side.

'Don't you look like a sweet little baby monkey,' he chortled as she started to haul herself out of the driver's seat, battling against the upward slope of the steep camber and the door that kept falling back on her.

'Is that any way to speak to your intended,' she grunted, at last tottering out onto the road then staggering round to the boot to get his crutches out.

'Oh dear,' he exclaimed, as she handed them in to him.

'Come on,' she coaxed. 'Fizzy and Anna have both said you're up to it.'

'Oh dear,' he said again, placing one on the driver's seat and positioning his arm into the open metal hoop of the other one, then brandishing it in the air.

Risking a bash on the head, she grabbed hold of the metal rod as is flew past, then guided its rubber foot down into the gutter.

'Holy Mary,' he burst out, 'you've only gone and put it down in that dog turd.'

Muttering embarrassed apologies, she took it from him,

scraped the soiled end on the kerb, then handed it back again.

Carefully, he reinserted his arm.

'I can manoeuvre my left leg easy enough,' he said, poking his trainer-clad good foot out and placing it down on the pavement. 'This is how Fizzy said I should do it,' he muttered as if reassuring himself, twisting round to take up the other crutch, inserting his arm, then positioning both sticks out on the pavement ahead of his outstretched foot.

'So far so good,' she encouraged, crouching with arms outstretched, on full red alert.

'You look like David Seaman poised for a goal kick,' he sniggered.

And, while she was trying to decide whether to be offended or not, with absolutely no warning, he suddenly pushed down full force.

Fully alert, she shot a hand out to protect his fast rising head from crashing into the top of the door frame.

'Shit!' he aptly bellowed as she lammed him off-balance, transferring his weight onto the turd smeared crutch end that shot from under him sending him crashing down.

'Sorry, oh, sorry, sorry,' she whimpered, grabbing hold of his arm to haul him up.

'Why in God's name did you hit me?' he roared, jerking his arm away with such angry force that she too lost her balance and tumbled on top of him.

'I was saving your head from bashing the car.'

'What, worried about your precious Skoda!' he sneered, sending her over the blubbing brink.

'Well, that was a giggle,' Maeve tittered as they finally reached the shop doorway - she having been helped up by a burly man who had growled words of comfort as he dabbed at her tears with a tissue. Buzz having been hauled up by the man's equally burly wife.

'A giggle!' he thundered, nearly catapulting himself off his crutches with undisguised rage. 'Wasn't being spread-eagled on the pavement with you on top of me the most humiliating event of my entire life.'

As he spoke Maeve pushed at the door which pinged their arrival, then held it open for him to hop in.

'Good morning, sir, madam,' said a thin sallow man standing

behind the glass counter twisting his bony hands together. Lit by an overhead spotlight, he looked like an actor making a jolly good attempt at playing Scrooge.

'Good morning,' Maeve sang.

With obvious effort, Buzz let go his scowl, releasing his straight eyebrows back to separate entities. Smiling with equally obvious effort, he perched himself on a conveniently placed stool. 'Hi,' he at last managed, rotating his flat hand.

'You've got bubble gum stuck to your shirt,' Maeve hissed loudly, immediately wishing she hadn't when she saw his eyebrows regroup into one angry line again.

'And a leaf in your hair if you don't mind my saying,' the man observed, adding, 'Is everything all right sir, you look rather hot.'

Maeve saw that her fiancé's handsome face had flushed crimson. 'It's just that we fell ...' she started to explain.

'For each other,' Buzz burst out, casting her an even more furious look that knitted his eyebrows together so firmly they appeared to have grown like that.

Oh God. This wasn't how it was meant to be when buying an engagement ring. She'd patently embarrassed him by thinking their fall on the pavement was a cracking good yarn to tell.

'Fell for each other - how romantic,' the man gushed, clasping his hands to his narrow chest.

'Yes it is,' said Maeve, hoping Buzz would soon reorganise his features to look more pleasant.

'Yes it is,' Buzz snapped.

'So, how can I help you?' asked the man, looking expectant.

'I wish to buy her an engagement ring,' Buzz confirmed tersely.

The man re-twirled his hands, saying brightly, 'Certainly sir, would it be diamonds you are after?'

'Yes.' 'No.' They said in unison.

Buzz looked at her angrily. 'Mauve, we agreed,' he said, his eyebrows edging ominously close again.

She fluttered a smile at him, then at the assistant. 'He calls me Mauve - it's his pet name for me, so I've decided I'd like an amethyst.'

It was a brainwave that had only just struck her. She'd always loved the beautiful colour of amethysts - and it would save any comparison between a big flashy diamond in a new ring, bought with the money he'd won, and the three small dull ones in her old one, bought with Hector's hard earned cash.

Disappointment dimmed the gleam in the assistant's eyes but his smile remained fixed. 'An unusual choice,' he murmured, drawing out a large tray from under the counter and placing it on top for them to see. 'Here is a selection of new ones.' He bent down, drew out another tray. 'And here are our antiques.'

'Ooo I like that one, see, it winked at me,' she exclaimed.

She looked up and saw Buzz gazing at her with a delighted grin, a clear hairless gap above the bridge of his nose, back to his agreeable self again.

'How about this one,' she suggested, pointing to one of the antiques.

The assistant leaned forward, studied a tiny tag then went to a notebook, turned to a page and silently read. He looked up, his eyes back to shining. 'It is an excellent choice madam. That ring was made by the famous French designer Vever. With its flowing leaf detail on the gold shanks you can see it is a fine example of Art Nouveau. The Siberian amethyst is the best one can get. The ring is eighteen carat gold. It is very good value at fifteen hundred pounds including VAT.'

'Oh, that's much too much,' she gasped.

'We'll take it,' Buzz said, whipping out his credit card.

'So you really did fall for each other,' sniggered Bernard when she went round to tell them her news later.

'Yes, but two onlookers quickly got us to our feet.'

'Your feet and his *foot*, don't you mean,' said Freda contemptuously. 'I don't know how you could get engaged, you've hardly known him two minutes.'

'Three months actually, May the tenth, Bernard's party.'

'I'd never have invited him if I'd known.'

'But it was his birthday!'

'Not Bernard. Buzz!' she exploded.

'But you encouraged it, remember? You said how well we got on together.'

'Let's have another look at it,' she said, grabbing hold of her mother's hand across the table. And, although it was her right hand, and although it wasn't a traditional diamond engagement ring, it obviously still upset her. Maeve knew that in her daughter's eyes the wearing of Buzz's ring was two-timing her father, even though he was no longer with them. And part of her felt the same. She waited for Hector's opinion to enter her consciousness, but he seemed to have left her.

'At my time of life,' she ventured, deciding to try to explain, 'you must grab what you want, you ...'

'You've *always* done that,' Freda cut in, leaping up and stalking to the back door. 'You've *always* grabbed what you want,' she reiterated, pulling the heavy door containing the pig flap open with such force it seemed in danger of ripping off its hinges. 'Always just thought of yourself,' she said bitterly, slamming out.

'She's going to feed the porkers,' said kindly Bernard, 'but, congratulations, I hope when he's divorced and you are married you'll be very happy.'

And, unexpectedly, she wasn't sure. She stared at the three small, lustreless diamonds set in the worn gold ring, tightly ensconced on her finger above the equally embedded wedding ring. *Is it possible to wipe out all those long years in one clean sweep?* she wondered, rather doubting it.

Glumly, she drove back to her shiny new man.

Twenty nine

Two days had passed since her gloomy doubts and she was now wholly convinced. Buzz was her man - and at her age every day counted! So, here goes, she thought, padding into the kitchen where he was sitting staring down at his *Bird Twitchering Magazine* opened up on the table beside his bowl of shredded wheat.

'I have something better than that to show you,' Maeve crooned, standing in front of him.

'Oh yes,' he murmured, not lifting his gaze.

She pulled her black satin dressing gown down off one shoulder. But he kept looking down.

She coughed, rotating her bare shoulder in slow sensuous movements.

Still he looked down.

She coughed harder, this time raking phlegm into her throat to sound sexy. 'Look Buzz,' she said, in a low husky voice, 'I have something to show you.'

'Sounds like you've got a sore throat,' he said, at last looking up at her.

Quick as the flash of a humming bird's wing, she let the dressing gown drop, reorganising her stance into a model pose to show off her new black silk and red lace underwear to best advantage.

He stared at her, bug eyed.

And, at that dramatic moment, the phone started ringing.

She remained immobile. One hand resting on her jutting left hip, the other kind of pointing in languid fashion at her right boob.

His perplexed eyes turned meaningfully to the telephone on the worktop at the other side of the room. But she stayed rooted to the floor, unwilling to turn her saggy bum on him

'Well, aren't you going to get it?' he said irritably, his eyes now darting explanatory looks at his crutches propped up against the wall.

But still she didn't move.

'Come on, buck up!,' he bellowed. 'Whoever it is will hang up soon.'

Hoping that this would indeed be the case, she remained put, but, whoever it bloody well was did *not* hang up soon, so, clamping her buttocks into rigid tightness, she turned and minced across the floor in small restricted steps, snatching the receiver up and spinning round in one fluid movement.

'Hello,' she sighed, leaning back against the worktop, relaxing her cheeks.

'Hello. Is Buzza there?' said that voice with the Italian-Scottish accent that she knew was *her*.

'He is,' she said through jaws clenched even tighter than her buttocks had been.

'Guid, I'd likea tae talk wi' him.'

'Who *is* it?' asked Buzz crossly, shooting his hand out.

She marched over, shoved the receiver into his grasp. 'It's *her*,' she announced. 'Your wife.'

And, as he purred 'Hello' into the phone, the doorbell rang and, half glad, half piqued not to hear his half of the conversation, she grabbed up her dressing gown, shrugged it on, tying the soft belt as she ran out to the hall. Probably Fizzy, recovered enough to work again, she thought, flinging the door open and staring straight into the velvet brown eyes of Wally. But not the old Wally she used to know. On his chin was a finely sculpted beard shaped like a curved W, the outer prongs hugging his jaw line, the middle one rising straight as a match stick up to his lower lip. Not only that, he was dressed peculiarly.

'Maeve,' he sighed, eyes ranging all over her. 'Do you live in a dressing gown?'

'No I don't,' she said, bridling. 'What are you doing here! And why are you all togged up like that?'

'I can't stop thinking about you. Has Buzz's foot healed? Are your duties here finished? Can you come home?'

Shocked by the things he was saying as well as his changed looks, she stood mutely scrutinising him. His open black puffa jacket revealed a purple T-shirt shirt with some sort of logo sprawled across it. His black baggy draw-string action pants were tied at his waist, each long leg hanging low over white and silver trainers.

'Well, say something,' he said plaintively. 'Don't just stand there gawping. At least ask me in.'

But, not waiting for the invite, he pushed past her, cupped her face in his hands, brushed an unspecifically targeted fleeting kiss on it, then carried on in.

'You know where the loo is,' she said, recognising the signs.

'Yes. *Don't* go away,' he ordered as he sped off.

She breathed in deeply, smelling the sweet fragrance of lavender wafting in his wake. But Wally was a man who should smell of toast and marmalade, or even pipe tobacco, not lavender, she thought, her head reeling on numerous counts, but mainly the fact that he was there!

'Next week!' she heard Buzz joyfully shriek from the kitchen, blasting all other thoughts from her mind.

So, they were coming next week. Dejected, she mooched to her bedroom and, with the door ajar so she could hear Wally's exit from the bathroom, snatched up a top and some trousers and hastily wriggled into them. Her fiancé's wife would see his beautiful home, his new self-assurance, and fall for him all over again, of that she felt sure.

'This way Wally,' she called, hearing the bolt pull back.

As she rammed her feet into her sandals, his beaming face peered round the doorway.

'What's with the crazy face hair, and why are you all tarted up like a teenager?' she asked, the words coming out more bluntly critical than she'd meant them to.

'*You* can talk,' he snapped, all signs of a smile peeled off by the sharp edge of her tongue.

She looked down at her scarlet top and blue jeans.

'But I always dress like this. You've always dressed like an old person.'

'And you always used to have lovely long hair swept up high, *now* look at it,' he retaliated, eyes darting to the floppy overgrown mess on the top of her head. His shoulders drooped and he fingered his bald upper lip as if missing his old tash.

She sat down on the bed and patted the space beside her. 'Here, why not come over and join me,' she said in a soft tone designed to make up for her earlier harshness.

He plumped down, slumped forward, elbows on knees, chin in hands, only the central prong of his weird beard visible.

'I did it for you,' he mumbled. 'You said I was too old-fashioned.'

And she wanted to throw her arms around him for pandering to her whim and for looking so unhappy. Instead, she patted his upper arm, then leant her elbows on her knees too, head down, running her fingers through her floppity crown. They sat in silence, united in the regret of their personal hair loss.

'It was good of you to change because of me,' she eventually said, 'but who advised you what to wear.'

'Justin, my neighbour. He went shopping with me - I've bought a whole new wardrobe.'

She stood up, stared down at him, saw that with his thick head of white hair, arty beard and more dramatic clothes, he did look quite stylish. 'It was a bit of a shock, but already I'm starting to like it,' she admitted. 'How old is this Justin?'

'About nineteen. I decided against the earrings. Thought they'd make me look a prat. Didn't realise I would anyway.'

'No. No, you don't look a prat,' she protested. 'That's a really striking T-shirt, the purple makes a bold statement against the pure whiteness of your hair, so much better than the shades of brown you used to wear - what's that written across the front of it?'

He pulled back his puffa jacket revealing the picture of a fishing rod with a fly on the hook and the words *I love salmon fishing.* 'Couldn't get one that said just Salmon,' he said gruffly, not looking up.

'Oh,' she gasped, both touched and appalled. Then she remembered that last time they spoke he was off to play bridge with dastardly Dora. 'What, couldn't you find one with a picture of Dora the Millennium Dome on it,' she scoffed.

'Don't mention that woman.'

'Why?'

'Her tongue is too scathing.'

'Oh,' Maeve said, guiltily knowing her own tongue was also on the scathing side. 'What other clothes have you bought?' she asked in her most mellifluous voice.

He lifted his head and she saw for the first time that in that worn face there was beauty, like finely crazed china.

'I have navy cotton chinos, a brown leather jacket, an English rugby shirt. All sorts. Stupid really.'

'No, no,' she protested again, truly liking the sound of it. 'It's me. I'm set in my ways of how to view you. You look much more ... dashing.'

And the hope that flared in his eyes made her want to swoop down and hug him.

Faintly, she heard a key turning in the front door, then Anna's *cooeeing* to Buzz.

'Have you had breakfast?' Maeve asked.

'No. Couldn't sleep for thinking of you so set off at six.'

'Nor have I,' she said, blanking her mind to the sizzling hot dish she had planned to replace the usual bowl of cereals. 'So, what if I drive you to a little café I know in Orlford. Sister Anna's arrived, so Buzz will be okay.'

'Oh Maeve,' he sighed.

And once again she realised that she did prefer her proper name to that stupid Mauve one.

After they'd eaten a full English breakfast, they staggered down the broad tree-lined High Street to the watercress beds at the lower end of the town.

'I know I acted boorishly before, rushing off without saying goodbye. It was true, I did have a goldfish to go back and feed, but I could have popped in on you first. No, I was running away because I couldn't bear the thought that Buzz had made you a permanent study in his home - and that he had a pet name for you. I realise now he was merely being a kind generous employer. But surely his foot has healed enough for you to be relieved of your duties. Please say you'll come back soon.' He had taken hold of her right hand as they sauntered along the slender path between the fast moving shallow stream and the vast beds of floating greenery.

Will he feel my new ring? she wondered. *Will he ask about it? And, if he does, will I tell him? But how can I? He will be devastated.*

'Is that a new ring?' he asked, suddenly stopping, lifting her hand and peering down at it.

'Yes, it is. Look there's a trout over there. See, in the shallow water by the brown stone.'

'Who gave it to you?'

'See how it flashes.'

'Yes, I can see.'

'No, the fish not the ring. Look at it.'

'Who gave it to you?' he persisted.

'Buzz,' she said sheepishly.

His deep set, soulful eyes bore into hers as he let go her hand.

'It looks expensive. Why did he give it to you?'

'Because ...' she turned away from his intense stare. 'Because we're engaged,' she blurted.

And later as, soaked to the crotch, she drove him back, he explained it was his complete devastation that made him shove her into the stream.

One full day since the soaking and Wally's exit from her life and Maeve was almost feeling back to normal.

'Why didn't you invite Sophia and Georgie to stay here?' she stupidly remarked in an effort to make up for her, what he called, peculiar, mood of yesterday. She even made a special effort to say So-fee-a, instead of her usual sofa with an 'i' in it.

Buzz lay his binoculars down on the table, his face alight. 'Honest to God, it was on the tip of my tongue to ask them but I wasn't sure if you'd mind.'

'I don't mind,' she said, averting her eyes from his and spotting a bird hovering high up in the distance.

'But where would they sleep?' Buzz asked.

He obviously hadn't gone over that scenario once, let alone the million times she had, she thought, seeing the bird dipping and rising in flight towards them.

She turned her eyes back to his, seeing the excitement within, like barely visible currents in the depths of a swimming pool.

'I could go and stay at Freda's,' she even more stupidly offered.

'Would you really. That's great - I've a kingsize bed, so you know what I'm saying ...'

Miserably, she nodded.

'Yes, maybe Georgie could share it with me - though, on second thoughts, perhaps not - don't want his clodhopping feet anywhere near mine. They're size twelve,' he said proudly.

A fluty *too-loo-eet too-loo-eet* sang from above, and her heart sang with it. There was definitely no question that the Italian wife was to sleep in with him. Too-loo-eet. Too-loo-eet!

'Is that a wood lark?' she ventured

He turned the binoculars to the bird now hovering just a short way off. 'It most certainly is,' he marvelled, 'similar to a sky lark but shorter tail. Was that how you knew it?'

'Yes, it was,' she confirmed.

Reading his illustrated *Guide to Birds* in bed most nights had been a labour of love as well as an aid to sleep, but now she'd identified one of the rarer ones, she felt surprisingly elated.

'For someone who knew nothing, you're developing quite an interest,' he observed, 'that's something else I like about you.'

And, as the bird set off on its switchback flight she reflected that he still had never said that he loved her.

Thirty

Maeve opened the door to Fizzy.

'G'day. Forgot my key Where is he?' she said, marching in in long strides that aptly demonstrated the healthy restoration of her damaged crotch.

'Just coming - he's trying to use his crutches on his own,' Maeve said, wondering if Fizzy would wince at the memory of those painful whacking sticks, but she showed no outward sign.

As they waited for Buzz to appear, Fizzy kept tapping her foot, sighing impatiently and glaring down at her watch. Maeve thought she preferred the old more relaxed physio to this one who was, no doubt, restored to over-zealous enthusiasm by her recuperative spell off work.

At last Buzz emerged round the corner, bad foot held up high behind him, furrows of concentration on his face.

Maeve started towards him but Fizzy held up her hand. 'Leave him to it,' she firmly stated, 'we'll wait in the sitting room.'

Maeve looked doubtfully at Buzz then back to Fizzy. 'Are you sure he's safe?' she mouthed, hoping he wouldn't see.

'Of *course* I'm sure he's safe,' Fizzy bellowed, striding off.

Reluctantly, Maeve followed. Even more reluctantly, she perched down beside Fizzy on the sofa. *Probably Buzz stands less chance of plummeting without me there to flatten him with a careless lam of my hand,* she thought ruefully as she waited on tenterhooks for his appearance. Fizzy drummed her fingers on the side of the chair, looked down at her watch, let out a long humphing sigh.

And, at last, Buzz entered. He didn't look across at them, so deep was his attention on the precise placement of his crutch ends on the carpet and his safe take-offs and landings. Cautiously, in short measured hops, he made his way to his chair.

'What kind of wimpy wombat are you,' Fizzy chided as, at last, he eased himself down. 'Even little kids don't make that sort of drama out of it.'

'They don't have so far to fall,' he mumbled.

Then, despite his obvious mortification at her open derision, Fizzy leapt up, stood towering over him, and gave a lecture about doing more exercise.

Even when he changed the subject by telling of their engagement, she stayed fully committed to her theme, just briefly pausing, saying: 'Good on yer mates, can't say I'm surprised I've seen the signs - it's the way you look at each other. Now, Buzz, the nerves in your reattached toe have had to regroup ...'

Now it was Maeve's turn to jump up ready to make a quick exit, not wishing to hear gory intricate details.

'No, you stay Maeve, you ought to hear what I'm saying,' she rapped.

Reluctantly, she sat down again, hoping she wouldn't feel too nauseous.

'Now Buzz, you haven't sustained much nerve damage so you've been flaming lucky - that's confirmed by the way you can wiggle your toe, that's when you've a mind to ...'

Maeve rotated her hand back and forth surveying her ring, trying to blank her mind to Fizz's raging torrent of words.

At last the outflow appeared to be plugged and the only sound to be heard was the faint swish of papers as Fizzy flicked through her notes. 'You had your tetanus jab in the hospi ...' she started up again.

'I *did*,' he interjected, 'and, honest to God, it hurt.'

Fizzy rolled contemptuous dark eyes at Maeve, saying, 'Did you know you were engaged to a baby?' Thoughtfully, she pulled at the fleshy lobe of one nostril. 'I only need to come in maybe once a week from now on. The prognosis is good, but you've got to help yourself by exercising that toe. Maeve, your job is to remind him to wiggle it. You never know,' she'd added, casting a wicked glance, 'once you two are wed, it might prove quite titillating!'

And, just as when Bernard had talked about their marriage as fact, a frisson of fear shivered through her. *But why?* she wondered. *He attracted me from the very first moment we met. To be his wife is what I want. Isn't it?*

The minute Fizzy left, Buzz rammed his arms in the metal hoops, clasped the handholds and, muttering words which included *bloody* and *show her*, careered into the hall then sped up and down the passageway in a series of giant hops. And Maeve, nervous at his new-found recklessness, stood hovering in the kitchen doorway, phone in hand ready to dial 999. But, somehow, even though the pine-strip floor was shiny, he didn't fall.

Maeve and Buzz came in through the French windows and Buzz hopped confidently ahead, clearly in a hurry to get to the loo.

Maeve ambled into the kitchen where Mrs Norris was neatly folding a J-cloth.

'I'm off now but there were a call for you,' she said, wiping her hands down her apron, 'someone called Wally. Sounded in a state, I said you was just outside with Mr Pike and I'd go and get you, but he just put the phone down. Blooming rude if you ask me.'

As soon as Mrs Norris had shut the front door behind her, Maeve punched out his number, but there was no reply. Irrationally disappointed, she wandered down to the study and carried on with her novel.

Hello Venus,' says Satty. 'I thought I'd tell you the news, Bria gave birth to a boy last night and they're calling him George.'

Venus thanks her for ringing then leaves the vid-phone, her mind in turmoil. She pictures the baby cradled in Tron's arms, hears him say: thank you for giving me a son, and welcome to our house dear Georgie.

'Hi,' says Jupe, coming in the front door, 'how has your day been?'

'Sooding marvellous.'

'Sorry I asked,' he snaps, going to the dispenser for a rosehip shake.

'You know the couple we met at Satty's the other day,' she begins.

'Yes, they were very hostile to me.'

'I noticed. She's had a son.'

'Let's hope they bring him up without colour prejudice. And talking of colour, see what I've bought,' he says, pulling out a purple T-shirt with some sort of fish pattern emblazoned on it.

Miserably, she wonders if he's bought it to impress that red-nosed Geranium woman with whom he plays cards.

Abruptly, she stopped typing, hurried to the kitchen and tapped out Wally's number again. Still, there was no reply. Could he be at the bridge club partnering Dora Dome at this very moment? A thin slimy worm of jealousy wriggled through her. But why was she feeling like this! How *could* she be so confused about men at her age? It was just as bad as when she was young, if not worse, the only advantage now being that if ever she did manage to get one of them to cross her Rubicon there'd be no risk of pregnancy. A kind of OAP benefit she thought, smiling to herself.

'What're you looking so pleased about?' Buzz said as he swung in.

'Um ... I was seeing the funny side of ... of Wally accidentally pushing me into the stream.'

'Funny! The only thing funny was that he didn't show the slightest sign of remorse at having soaked you and ruined your sandals. And then he went charging straight back to London. What was that all about? Why did he come down here anyway?'

'Well, we're good friends - I expect he wanted to flaunt his new image.'

'That'd be it, he said, hopping over to the fridge, 'maybe he wanted to dash back to a new lady friend, to show off - like a peacock displaying to a peahen.' He opened the fridge door, sniggering at the idea of it.

Or a great tit displaying to a red nosed reindeer, she morosely thought, suddenly realising that though he *said* he'd changed his looks because of her, he'd chopped off his precious moustache in the first stage of his transformation for that drunkard Dora, scathing tongue or not.

'By the way, I had a phone call from Sophia,' Buzz said nonchalantly, taking out a bottle of milk and pouring some into a beaker. 'They're arriving on Wednesday.'

'Wednesday!' she exclaimed, her heart giving one great thump then seeming to stop altogether.

'What's *wrong* with Wednesday?'

'Nothing.'

Then she remembered that other newcomers were supposed to be arriving on that very day too.

'It's the day that the piglets are due,' she informed him with relish, leaving unsaid, but scudding deliciously around her mind: *so all the swine will be arriving at the same time.*

'They're getting a taxi at Heathrow and coming straight here,' he said, ignoring the coincidence. 'So, can you fix it to sleep at Freda's?' He balanced on one leg, took a swig, then wiped his lips dry.

'One night or two?' she said miserably.

'She didn't say, maybe longer.' His sapphire eyes shone more brightly than her amethyst. 'Jeez, I can't wait to see my Georgie,' he gushed, tipping the glass to his mouth with joyful gusto.

'I'll start packing then,' she muttered, watching drops cascading through his stubble, like balls bouncing down a pintable.

'No need for that is there? Isn't it only the night time you'll be away. You'll be here with all of us the rest of the time.' He patted his chin with the tea-towel saying: 'I think you'll hit it off with Sophia.' Then he stood there grinning and nodding as if trying to convince himself.

I expect I will, she thought, though which bit she'd hit off first she wasn't yet sure about.

'Oh, and by the way Mauve, don't you think you should get your hair cut before she comes, it's getting very untidy.'

She'd already made an appointment with Raymond, but no way was she going to keep it on *her* account, she inwardly seethed, deciding to cancel.

But, next morning, as she finger raked her flopping hair back off her forehead, she decided to get it trimmed into submission just once more before growing it back long once the I-ties had left. Thankfully, they wouldn't be staying long. Or so she hoped.

Thirty one

Tentatively, Maeve pulled the front door open. A middle-aged olive skinned woman and a tall dark young man stood there, both crookedly inclined to counterbalance the weight of their bulky suitcases. Two pairs of black eyes stared at her.

'Sophia! Georgie!' Buzz cried, his flying crutch sharply rapping Maeve's ankle as he sprang out from behind.

'Ow, ow,' she yelled, clasping the painfully battered projecting bone.

'Och, Buzza, it'sa so guid to see you,' Sophia exclaimed, diving eagerly in just as Maeve righted herself.

'Ow, ow,' she yelled again, as the heavy suitcase bashed into her hip sending her lurching across the hall. But she might as well have been invisible for all anyone noticed. Sophia dropped the heavy weapon down, grabbed Buzz's head in her hands and manically pecked each of his cheeks eight or nine times before releasing him. No doubt this exuberant sanitised form of greeting would soon be mandatory under EC law, Maeve thought morosely, though glad that there'd been no lip contact or spit interchange.

'Dad! You look wicked with that long hair tied back like that,' laughed the young man as he lugged his even bulkier case in. 'But how's your poor old foot then,' he said, slamming the suitcase down and just missing his father's good foot by the width of a mosquito leg. Without waiting for an answer, he grabbed hold of Buzz, enfolding him in his arms and patting his back as if consoling a baby.

What about me? I am injured, in every way, Maeve thought miserably, though not failing to be touched by the young man's tender concern for his dad.

As the Pike trio stood in the hall delighting in each other, she studied Sophia. She was slim, medium height, handsome rather than beautiful in a hard-faced kind of way - perfectly made up and horrendously elegant. A faint dark line smudged the space between her nose and top lip, as if soft black pencil had been erased by a dirty rubber. Raven hair, pulled back into a tight chignon, was scraped back so harshly that it pulled back her skin, giving her the equivalent of a face lift. An expensive-looking embroidered silk jacket matched her straight knee-length emerald skirt. Nice legs, high-heeled green sandals.

Maeve was glad she'd kept her appointment at Raymond's, but wished she'd worn something smarter. The statement she thought her fluorescent pink top would make when she'd put it on, seemed to have changed from *I am bright, warm, confident and carefree* to *I am brash, bold and cheap.*

'Will you look at thisa place,' Sophia enthused, grinning at Georgie, throwing out her arm to encompass the large square hall.

'Yeah, looks great,' he agreed, eyes latching onto the walls. 'I like the distressed look.'

What about my distressed look! Maeve thought-wailed, eyeing the rim of his near ear, peppered with a line of holes, two of which were fitted with gold studs, one with a small silver ring and the rest left empty, the cavities in various degrees of closure.

'Are you all right Maeve,' said Buzz, obviously picking up her jagged vibes. 'Won't you come over here, meet the family.'

She stepped forward, trying to rake up a welcoming smile, but she could tell it was coming out crooked.

Sophia's manicured hand took hers in a brief limp hold. 'Sure and is thisa your hoosekeeper?' she asked, the Scottish-Italian lingo now further refined with an Irish touch.

'Be Jaisus, no,' hooted Buzz, shining eyes darting from Maeve to Georgie and back to his wife again. 'This is Maeve Salmon - remember, you spoke on the phone.'

'Och aye. Maeve, nice to meet you. Of course I remember, you're staying here tae looka after him.'

'She looks after me, and ...' Buzz began, his scared-looking eyes now darting back and forth between his wife and wife-to-be, '... and ... and we're engaged,' he rushed, hopping backwards with the force of it.

And Maeve wished he'd at least put his arm round her before transferring his gaze to his wife.

'Engaged!' she exclaimed. 'But we're not yetta divorced - it's nae legal!'

'Georgie, I'll show you where you're sleeping,' Maeve offered, anxious to get away from this unwelcome turn in the conversation.

He gave her a sympathetic smile, heaved up his suitcase, and waited for her to lead the way. Firmly she turned and walked away from them. As she headed off she heard Sophia say: 'But you won alla that money. You coulda have had *any*body.'

Abruptly she halted to hear his reply, yelping as now Georgie's suit case butted her into a forward totter.

Above Georgie's profuse apology, she heard Buzz say: 'But it's only Maeve I want. She makes me laugh. She cares for me. And she's here.'

Mollified, though not entirely, for he still hadn't mentioned the L word, she set off again, Georgie following.

'Most of this is my mother's,' he puffed.

More than a one or two night stay, she thought glumly, as they entered her study.

'This is where you'll sleep. Hope it's okay,' she said, indicating the mattress Mrs Norris had made up on the floor.

Georgie gazed down at it, then he looked round at her with a troubled expression. And, suddenly, in that handsome tanned face, she saw the insecure shyness of Buzz. At least, the insecure shyness displayed when they'd first met but which, she suddenly realised, was fast disappearing as he grew used to the power his new money bought.

'Did dad tell you about my accident?'

'He told me a bull gored you.'

'It was a cow,' he corrected. 'And the scars make it painful for me to sleep on anything with no give in it - like a mattress on a floor. I've tried and it's terrible, I didn't sleep a wink.' He ran his hands lightly over his skinny buttocks to indicate where the pain had been.

Automatically, she stroked her bum where both sets of luggage had whacked her.

'Maybe you could swap places with your mother,' she suggested. 'You could sleep in my room next door where she was going, and she could bed down here.'

He glanced around the room, shuffled his feet. 'She wouldn't put up with sleeping on the floor, especially in an office like this,' he said awkwardly.

'But the walls are a lovely melon colour, surely she could just for a night or two?' she reasoned, wondering who this fussy Mrs Sophia-particular-Pike thought she was.

He shrugged. 'We may stay longer. Giuseppe has had to go away on business for a month and she soon gets bored on her own.'

A month! A fucking month! Or, more accurately, a non-fucking month!

'Is there a B-and-B I could go to?' he asked. 'That would settle it.'

'I tell you what,' she said, a scorching spear of inspiration suddenly searing through her, 'you can sleep at my daughter's instead of me. There's a comfortable bed there, it's just down the lane - and I can sleep in here with my computer.' She didn't go on to say that she'd also be resident in *The Bungalow*, thus keeping a watchful eye on his mother. 'I could get on with my novel without disturbing you too,' she added, just spotting another bonus.

'Your novel!'

'Yes, I'm in the middle of writing it.'

'Would you allow me to read it sometime?' he asked tentatively, fiddling with one of his earrings.

And, contentment seeped into her like bath water heating cold bones. This likeable son of Buzz's was holding no grudge against her for being his father's intended. In fact, more than that, he was taking an interest in her.

'I'd love you to read it,' she said, 'but it's not printed up yet. After we've eaten I'll run you round to my daughter's, so sort out what night things you'll be needing.'

Freda rang soon after she'd dropped Georgie off to tell her that Princess was showing all the signs of going into production. Voice trembling with emotion she said: Oh mother, I feel so blessed.

A pronouncement that oddly moved Maeve.

As she lay on the made-up bed on the floor, she tried to imagine what was going on - in the heat of the delivery room in the mobile home and in the heat of Buzz's bedroom. Would his wife have secretly slunk in there with the aim to seduce him? Would he give way if she did? Maeve listened, but she could hear nothing except for the thumping of her fast-beating heart.

They sat outside in the garden drinking the Chianti Sophia had brought with her. Maeve was glad the sunny spell of weather was lasting. Better to be out in the fresh air than cooped up inside with *her*. Georgie had jogged back from Freda's and joined them and, although he stretched and yawned a lot, his eyes were wide awake and sparkling.

'Last night was *brilliant*,' he enthused. 'I've never been present at one birth before, let alone eight of them ...'

Maeve glanced over to see if this would impress his mother, but she didn't even seem to be listening, her eyes and attention fixed upon Buzz.

'... Freda took me into the mobile home and ...'

'You wanta to be careful of those things, they're dangerous,' Sophia inexplicably warned, in a belated show of interest to her son.

'What's dangerous about them?' Maeve asked, astounded.

'D'ye not ken, mobile phones, they givea off waves that fry your brain,' she answered contemptuously.

'Mobile *home*, not mobile *phone*,' laughed Georgie, flashing an apologetic smile at Maeve.

And she was glad to see that at least the woman had the grace to look embarrassed as she mumbled that she must have misheard.

'It was my job to make sure each piglet was latched on to a teat as soon as it was born,' Georgie rushed on. 'They were so sweet, so small and wriggly. But then, after the fourth one came out, Princess got into a panic and tried to scramble up. You should have seen Freda and Bernard move!'

Maeve remembered that Hermione had panicked whilst giving birth to her only litter, rising to her trotters then smashing down on five of them. She wondered if Princess had been one of those that Bernard had resuscitated by blowing into its snout. Freda had told her afterwards that he'd blown so hard he'd seemed intent upon exploding them and it was a miracle that four of the five squashed ones survived!

'You arrived at just the right time,' said Buzz, an aura of pride shimmering round his entire body as he gazed enraptured at his son.

'Yeah, I did didn't I.' He turned his bright eyes to his mother. 'You should see their place mum: pigs, goats, chickens, ducks, sheep, a foal. The farm is called FAB CAZ and it really is that - FAB!'

Sophia raised her glass, smiling at Buzz. 'Oor bairn takes after you, dotty aboot the wild creatures.'

'And there were chipmunks, rabbits, a donkey, and even a llama,' Georgie gabbled on, in unnecessary corroboration of her words. 'And my bed was very comfy, so thank you Maeve.'

'I'm glad,' she said, warming more and more to this enthusiastic young man, rejoicing that one day, if all went as planned, he'd be her step son.

Sophia tilted her head back, closed her eyes. 'If only it hada been hot and sunny like this in Aberdeen,' she murmured.

'Sure, it was pretty grey and cold,' agreed Buzz.

She opened her dark thickly fringed eyes. 'Or luxurious likea thisa in London ...'

Buzz glanced uncomfortably at Maeve. 'It's not all good,' he said, 'it often rains and you try finding an NHS dentist.'

'Butta you can go private now so it doesn't affecta...'

'How did you know Buzz had won the money?' Maeve cut in meaningfully.

Sophia's eyes flickered.

A wood pigeon cooed.

'I told her,' said Georgie. 'Before I contacted Jim at the supermarket where dad used to work, I rang our old number, but the man I spoke to there didn't know where dad had moved to. Probably in a mansion somewhere, he'd said. And when I asked what he meant, he told me about him being the first man to win a million on a TV show.'

'Is that why you came over?' said Buzz softly, addressing her.

'Och, no,' she said vehemently. 'It was when the man atta the supermarket told him aboot your accident, it seems ye'd rung him from the hospital.'

Buzz frowned. 'Yes, I did,' he said slowly, 'I remember I was lonely and needed to talk, so I rang Jim. There was no-one I knew well in Wood Hill. Until Maeve that is.'

'So how d'you ken it wasn't the smell of your money that lured *her* here,' she said, the sweet smile on her lips at violent odds with the nasty words coming out of them.

'How *dare* you,' Maeve cried, jumping up and just holding back from thumping her one.

Buzz's eyes turned brittle. 'She's not like that. She's never asked for a penny off me. The only thing I've bought, apart from the amethyst ring, is her computer - and she didn't ask for that. She doesn't keep on about expensive holidays, and places in the sun, and new cars, not like ...' He stopped. '... not like some people.'

Maeve unclenched her fists and flopped back down in the chair.

'Well all righta. I'm sorry. But it *was* because of the chopped-off toes that we came,' she insisted. 'Just because we're separated ita don't mean I don't care. And Giuseppi too. It was he who suggested it.'

'Holy Mary, and that was good of him,' spat Buzz. 'Was that before or after he heard of my million?'

'It's notta like that,' she sighed.

Thirty two

Freda rang up next morning.

'Georgie wants to stay a while and help, so I said I'd make sure you hadn't any plans for him first.'

'No. No plans. Just sitting around yacking. He'd be bored silly here. I know I am.'

'Well, you've made your bed, now you must lie on it,' she said, a barely withheld snigger trembling her voice.

No doubt Freda was revelling in reciting the unsympathetic proverb she'd repeated to her ad nauseum when she was young, Maeve thought dolefully, brightening a little when hit by an artful reply.

'I know I've made my bed,' she said, 'and it's not easy to get down to, or up from, when it's on the flipping floor - not with my hip.'

'That's not what I meant and you know it, but if you really find it difficult I'll borrow or hire a bed to put up in the attic for Georgie, then you can have yours - in the room you declined,' she just *had* to add.

'Thanks, but I'll hang on, Sophia should go soon,' she stated, knowing she wouldn't.

As she replaced the phone, Fizzy's smily face appeared at the open kitchen window.

'I've called to see how Buzz is coping with his crutches,' she said, looking and sounding back to her old sunny self.

Maeve rushed out to the front door. 'Come in, come in,' she carolled, over the moon to see a friendly face.

'Is that Fizzy's voice?' called Buzz, from somewhere.

The pounding of crutch-ends beating on floor boards sounded, then Buzz zoomed into view in a series of giant hops.

'Strewth,' Fizzy gasped, 'I should have called you a wimpy wombat sooner!'

Sophia hurried into the hall after him, flacking her newly

varnished silver talons in the air.

'Meet Sophia, my ex-wife,' said Buzz, grinning crookedly at Fizzy.

'Not ex!' Sophia exclaimed. 'Notta yet.'

'Pleased to meet you,' Fizzy muttered, turning to Maeve and making such a comical face it was hard not to laugh. 'Buzz, I reckon you can start to put light weight on that foot now,' she said, 'but I'd like to check it before you do - make sure the skin flaps have healed cleanly.'

'We'll go into the lounge,' said Sophia, annoyingly taking charge.

As the three went off, Maeve decided to walk to Freda's to get some fresh air, see the new piglets and to be somewhere she felt at home.

Clapping and cheers could be heard as she crossed the rough field used as a car park, heading for the barn.

'En't expecting' any entrance fee from you bein' family,' said Esmerelda, on duty at the desk.

'Hi Maeve, good to see you again,' called Cynthia Slocumb from behind her tea room counter as Maeve walked through.

'Hi Cynthia, very *very* good to see you too,' she sang, grateful beyond reason to hear what she knew was a normal greeting.

She sailed through, stepping out onto the field just as Bernard and his small army of Large White porkers exited from the show arena. A hubbub of chatter and shrieks of laughter came from the crowd as they started to leave. A gang of excited children ran ahead of their parents, catching up with the pigs and marching alongside. Bernard spotted her, waved, and called over: 'I'll get this lot back into Porkers' Paradise, then see you in the cottage - Freda should be there soon too.'

Joyfully, she yelled back her agreement, another deluge of thankfulness flooding over her. Here she was someone. Here she could be seen.

She watched the people coming from the show, spotted Georgie among a group of them. He wore black jeans and black shirt, enhancing his gentle dark looks. She saw a pretty blonde with two children in tow casting him flirty glances. Yet another older woman attracted to a younger man, she mused, wondering what it was about these Pike men. Maybe it was their charming bashfulness that brought out the mothering instinct! She fiddled with her new ring in a sudden fit of anxiety. Then she saw the hunger in the blonde woman's eyes and knew for sure that to mother him was not what she had in mind.

Georgie looked around, his face lighting up as he caught sight of her. *This handsome, kind, young man is a son for Buzz to be proud of,* she thought, watching him trot towards her, for the first time understanding how very much Buzz must have missed him.

'Wotcher, Maeve, isn't Bernard's Pig Show fabulous,' he raved, air kissing her cheek.

'It really is,' she agreed.

'I *love* this place,' he said softly, 'I wish I could live here.' He held her gaze for an instant, then looked down at his feet.

To have him living here would be such a pleasure - but, with him, came her, Maeve realised, dismayed by the thought.

'I'm just going up to see the new piglets before going into the cottage,' she told him.

'I'll walk with you,' he said, shortening his long stride to match her pace as they set off.

As they approached the gap in the hedge, her mind dwelt on his mother. Would the pull of Buzz's million be stronger than the pull of Giuseppe and his house in the sun? Or, was she being unfair to her? Was Sophia truly just concerned about his accident? She wished it were possible to read Sophia's mind. And Buzz's too for that matter. Was he still in love with her? After all, it was she who had left him, not the other way around.

'Just look at that idyllic scene,' sighed Georgie, interrupting her brooding thoughts.

They had turned into the long garden and were wending their way between a scattering of noisy ducks and hens. Two bleating kids eyed them from a safe distance. Adults and children were looking over the wall of Porkers Paradise where Bernard was just reinstating the pigs. She sniffed in the aroma of her daughter's precious family, heard their grunts and snorts, wondered where Freda intended to house the new litter when they grew bigger.

They stopped walking to gaze at the pig unit and all the activity

'I love all the animals, but pigs are my favourite because they're so intelligent and proud and have got minds of their own.'

'Proud! Minds of their own!' Maeve gently scoffed.

'Yeah. Didn't you know that. See Pudding, the big one, he refused to let Esmerelda put Cocky onto his head yesterday - went mad, flailing and bucking and snorting. I think he knew that to stand in front of everyone with a parrot perched on his head made him look stupid.'

'So that's why Esmerelda was in the barn and not the show ring,' Maeve observed, deciding not to point out that to have the great boar standing on the flattened end of a giant seesaw, waiting to be flipped, in front of everyone, could also be considered a trifle humiliating to anyone with half a pig-brain, but Pudding hadn't apparently balked at that yet.

'Yeah, everyone mucks in here, that's another thing I like about it, and the jobs are so varied.' They set off again. 'Have you ever been present at a birth?' he asked as they walked up the sloping lawn.

'Only Freda's,' she said, dead-pan.

'Pity,' he said, his mind clearly full of the wonders of pigs and not seeing the joke. 'You should have seen the way they come out fully formed miniature pigs, it's so cool,' he enthused, still clearly overawed by the experience.

'It is something of a miracle,' she agreed, 'especially as it only takes three months, three weeks and three days to grow the whole litter from scratch.'

This was a wondrous fact often told her by Freda. Don't you see the beauty of it, she always raved: three, three, three. It proved to her that pigs were special, and, Maeve had to admit that the repetition of the digits was a lucky omen in her book, even if it only meant they were lucky to get the whole irksome business over and done with in such a short time.

'Growing them from scratch. Sounds like pork scratchings. Like planting a pork scratching and in three months gathering their piglet fruit,' Georgie snorted.

And, just as with Buzz, she was drawn into his infectious laughter.

A kerfuffle of pig snorts and squeals started up behind them.

'It's as if they're laughing with us,' he chuckled.

'Yes, I bet they're saying: Nine months to make just one measly baby who can't even walk. Snort snort! Three months three weeks three days to make a litter of perfect piglets who can stand on their own feet. Call yourselves superior. Ha ha!'

And they both cracked up again, their squeals blending in with the pigs'.

As they staggered on, she looked up to Wisteria Cottage at the top of the slope, seeing it through fresh eyes. This was the picturesque home her daughter had invited her to share with them, the home where she was welcome, the home she had declined, the home that was devoid of a certain Italian woman but where her kind humorous son slept, a home that suddenly seemed so appealing.

Georgie eagerly lengthened his stride as they drew near the old walled yard, housing the mobile home.

'I can't wait for you to see them,' he said, as if they were his own family he was dying to show off.

She puffed up the ramp behind him, through the swing doors and into the maternity ward straight ahead. Even in the warmth of the August day, a heat light shone down on the piglets turning them rosy as they squirmed at Princess's milk bar.

'Aren't they *great*,' gushed Georgie.

'They truly are,' she agreed, feeling a certain pride. After all, if all those years ago she hadn't kidded Bernard it was a pet pig and not a peacock Freda had wanted to cure her lack-of-baby-blues, he wouldn't have bought Hermione and none of this would have occurred.

After they'd feasted their eyes on the babies for a while and clucked sympathy at the poor beleaguered sow, they wandered off to the back door of the cottage.

'I do *love* it,' Georgie said again, as they entered the warm ambience of the kitchen-cum-dining room. And she wondered again if his mother would love it too, though she couldn't imagine her and her expensive sophistication appreciating dung-strewn straw, barmy goats and cumbersome swine.

A week passed and Sophia's perfume hung about *The Bungalow* like the sweet scented badness of rotting apples. Wherever Buzz went in the house or garden, she followed, like a lion stalking a deer, though in this case a cat stalking a one-footed pigeon, she thought balefully, seeing he was an easy prey. The oleaginous voice slithered into her ears day after day, gradually dissolving the little wax of faith she had in her fiancé's wife's sincerity.

Maeve grew to hate the coy smiles and batting eyelashes aimed at Buzz, wishing she could also hate Sophia's home-made pizzas, though, of course, they were delicious. Goaded by her culinary skill (learnt in Italy and perfected in Aberdeen, she bragged) Maeve decided to make her own speciality of cauliflower cheese.

She watched Sophia closely as she forked a minuscule portion into her mouth, seeing the instant crinkling of her elegant snitch and the slight shudder as she swallowed it.

Sophia looked up, catching Maeve's close scrutiny. She smiled sweetly, then in a puke-making falsely caring voice, said, 'Eet woulda have tasted better witha the mascarpone instead of the cheddar.'

Maeve clamped her jaws shut tight, withholding the urge to yell that good old British cheddar was better than all that foreign muck.

Buzz took it in though - he of course being ignorant on the subject of cauliflower cheese, it possessing neither feathers nor wings.

'That's a good tip to know, isn't it Maeve,' he said beaming and nodding, apparently delighted at how well they were getting on. But, though he'd unwittingly let her down on the cheese front, he did back her up with the oven-ready chips, licking his lips and praising the way she had spread them out evenly to cook. 'If they're not carefully distributed on the tin some remain white and hard,' he explained to Sophia, adding, 'And aren't they a perfect combination with the main dish.'

To which she said: 'Aye, cauliflower cheese and oven chips go together justa like *tripe* and onions.'

And her emphasis on *tripe*, did not go unnoticed by Maeve.

Sophia showed no signs of leaving, even though for three days it rained solid, provoking her to many deep sighs, gloomy looks and nasty remarks about English weather.

Go back to bloody Italy then, Maeve inwardly fumed, but the intruder stayed put, sleeping in Maeve's bedroom and infiltrating lines of expensive Italian clothes into her hanging space.

'How about we twa go to see a movie?' she suggested to Buzz in her peculiar assortment of accents.

'Don't forget Maeve,' he protested, darting his eyes at her.

'Aye, she can come too,' Sophia said, shrugging one shoulder at Buzz in a flirtatious way then flashing Maeve a smile that came and went with the speed of an elastic band stretched tightly then abruptly released.

But she'd had enough. 'No thanks,' Maeve said stiffly.

'Nor me, sure I'd like to but it would be awkward with this foot,' said Buzz, rallying to his fiancée's defence.

Or is he? Maeve wondered, realising it really would be difficult for him to hop along a narrow row of cinema seats full of people.

'Whatever was I thinking aboot, of course it woulda,' Sophia sympathised in softly spoken words that failed to disguise her phoniness - to Maeve at least. And she was sick of it. Sick of her flirtatious looks, sick of her invasion of her space, sick of seeing Buzz beguiled by his wife, even though he was engaged to her and Sophia was officially shacked up with another man. She'd had enough.

As soon as Buzz and Sophia went out to the garden together she went to the kitchen and rang Wally.

'Hello,' he said in a weary voice.

'Hello, it's me. How've you been?'

'Oh Maeve, it's so good to hear you. I'm not feeling good. I got caught speeding when I left you last time and I have to pay a fine but it was because of you I was so upset and I truly *truly* do miss you.'

'See you tomorrow then - about two o'clock?'

After he'd joyfully given directions and said goodbye, she dialled the number of her old friend, Dolly, who lived just a mile or two from Wally.

'Hello, Dolly Potter here, whoever you are you'll have to speak up if you want me to hear you,' she eventually answered.

So, Dolly had got even deafer, Maeve realised, clearing her throat, then bellowing, 'It's Maeve. I'm ringing to see if you could you put me up in your spare bedroom, just for tomorrow night.'

'No need to blast my head off,' Dolly grumbled. 'I said speak up, not shriek. I'm not an imbecile!'

'Sorry,' Maeve meekly apologised, dejection enveloping her like a cold dark fog. Now, even her old chum was turning against her.

'But, of *course* you must come,' Dolly continued, her angry bark transformed to a tranquil purr. 'We'll have so much to chat about. Stay longer than one night - why don't you?'

'Okay, I'll pack enough for a week - though I'll probably only stay for a couple of nights,' Maeve added, the strong blast of friendship blowing the gloom away, but also clearing her head to remind her how Dolly never stopped talking, and that two days was probably as much as she could endure. *But, at least getting away from Wood Hill for a few days will give me a break from So-feeya, and time to work things out,* she thought, pleased.

'I'm going to stay with my old friend, Dolly, in London, just for a day or two,' she told a startled Buzz and Sophia when they came back in from the garden. She deliberately omitted to say she was stopping off at Wally's first, not wanting to turn the smirk of delight that had lit up Sophia's face into a full radiant grin.

Thirty three

Slowly, Maeve drove along, looking out for the tall silver birch Wally had said grew in his garden. Finally, she spotted it on the right, towards the end of the street. She stopped, peering through the drizzle, seeing a detached Victorian house, number seventy-three. That was the one, and she was relieved to see there was one parking space right outside. She steered across the road, driving past the gap, before quickly reversing into it, coming to an abrupt halt as her back wheels rammed into the kerb. Groaning with frustration, she realigned the car, then backed in at a shallower angle, surprising herself with the perfect kerb-hugging line she'd achieved on just the second try - *a record for me*, she reflected. The familiar jolt of her bumper hitting the car behind alerted her to discontinue reversing and get into forward gear. Carefully, she inched forward until she judged there was a clear even space front and back. She switched off the engine, then sat back and closed her eyes. At last she was at Wally's. At last she was away from the rotten atmosphere of her fiancé's wife. At last she could relax.

As she stood out in the rain hauling her grip from the back of the car, a dull thumping sound drew her attention to a man banging on the window of the house next door to Wally's. As she caught his eye he began vigorously waving. No doubt Wally's young sartorial adviser being friendly, she mused, waving back before locking the car doors then dashing down the garden path to the shelter of the deep porch.

She peered at the three bells, pressed the one labelled 'Flat 1 Woodcock'. Immediately, there came the faint sound of an inner door opening, then another, louder, then the door facing her was flung open and the beaming clean-shaven face of Wally appeared.

'Maeve, oh Maeve,' he whispered, cocking his head to one side and stretching his arms out.

'What a journey,' she moaned, staggering into them.

He clasped her to him and, exhausted from the perils of spray from motorway lorries, suicidal pedestrians on busy roads and kamikaze drivers who kept hooting at her, she stayed encompassed in his embrace, not even wanting to pull away.

'Come in, come in,' he finally said, guiding her from the first lobby to another with stairs going up to the top flats, then in through his open door ahead. 'Welcome to my home my dear,' he said, shutting the door firmly behind them, then snaking his arm round her waist, guiding her across a small hall, round a corner, and into a high-ceilinged spacious room.

'Are you very wet,' he asked anxiously.

'No, just my hair, as I ran down your path.' she shook her head, flicking a few drips off, noting his look of disapproval at her re-trimmed locks.

'If you want the bathroom, go back and turn right - it's the door facing you.'

Grateful for his consideration, she went in and, instead of doing the normal tidy up, she flailed and flicked at her hair to try for the haphazard look he so admired. But the short crown of curls wilfully settled back to neat perfection, and even the shoulder-length hair simply swirled around a bit before settling primly back. In a last ditch attempt, she lunged her head down, narrowly missing the basin, before launching it back up again. Dizzily, she peered into the mirror to discover that nothing had changed except that now her face had the look of a blood orange.

'Sit down,' he beamed when she tottered back to him. 'Rest while I make us some tea, then we can talk.'

Gratefully, she flopped down in a comfy-looking armchair. Loudly, she screamed as its back shot flat down, the footrest leapt up, and she was thrust supine.

'Get me up,' she shrieked, staring up at his chandelier, close to tears. Not only was her priggish hair upsetting her, a joke chair at the end of her long and hazardous journey was too much to bear.

'Sorry, the recliner mechanism's gone all loose,' explained Wally urging her to push down on the arms while he pressed down on the footrest. As, slowly, the chair and she retrieved their normal sitting shapes, she found that Wally was gazing at her with a thoughtful penetrating look, making her wonder if he thought she'd gone all loose too. But maybe that was just a figment of her tired imagination.

'I'll go and put the kettle on - don't push back again,' he said at last, turning and leaving.

She looked around, her attention immediately caught by a silver-framed, black and white photo on the small glass-topped table beside her. She picked it up, stared at the dark haired young woman with the soft expression, guessing it would be Nellie, his long-dead wife. Suddenly, she realised how much easier it was for her to really dislike the hard-faced Sophia. If she'd been sweet and gentle like Nellie, her emotions would be in even greater turmoil than they were now. But maybe Sophia was sweet and gentle when she and Buzz were alone together? Maybe their marriage would stand a chance if she wasn't there?

Wally kicked the door open, staggered in with a tray, awkwardly placing it down on the table beside her.

'Help yourself,' he offered, removing a mug and a couple of biscuits for himself, then taking the chair opposite. 'Now we can converse,' he said, heaving a long thankful sigh, obviously glad that that arduous chore was over.

'I want to go back to live in my own home,' she blurted, the knowledge having just fully hit her. Then she thought again. That would mean giving up Buzz and living so near to Freda. 'At least for a while,' she amended. 'But I can't, because it's let out for over four more months.'

'Stay here then,' he offered, slowly baring his narrow waisted long incisors and scraping the cream off a split Bourbon with their cutting edge.

That is how I like to eat them too, she marvelled, noting they had more in common than just bridge.

'I can't stay here, you know that.'

'What's happened Maeve? Last time I came to visit you in Wood Hill you were perfectly happy to stay there - with your fiancé.'

The added postscript seemed to have been said more in sorrow than anger, she realised.

And so she launched forth, telling him about Sophia and Georgie and her invisibility, and how she liked Georgie very much, but couldn't stand her. And how she wasn't sure whether Buzz still had feelings for his wife, even though he sometimes seemed to dislike her.

He pulled out a large white handkerchief, flicking crumbs off his lap. 'You know I love you, don't you,' he stated in a matter-of-fact voice, not raising his eyes.

And gratitude filled her. It wasn't just seeing that familiar beetroot stained hankie, reminding her of his kindness (the runny cheese had obviously washed out), it was hearing the L word for which she so pined. She waited for Hector's thoughts on the matter, but he'd given up speaking to her, yet again. She fiddled with her engagement ring as she stared at the man who professed to love her.

'Well, say something,' he begged.

'I ... I ... I'm glad you've shaved your beard off.'

'Because of you,' he said softly, his rheumy eyes brimming with damp adoration.

'You shouldn't have. It doesn't really matter what I think,' she muttered, guiltily running her fingers through her shorn crown.

'It matters to me.'

He jumped up and she saw how the narrow-legged trousers he wore, teamed with a matching navy open-necked shirt, made him look taller and slimmer, quite dishy even.

'Must go to the bathroom,' he suddenly rapped, making a dive for the door.

She looked around the room again, seeing the similarities with her own sitting room, just a couple of miles away. A handsome marble fireplace with ornamental flutes and curves, set firmly into a flat marble base making it impossible to fall. Sash windows, coved ceiling, picture rail, deep skirting board ...

Wally re-entered, the relief on his face no doubt echoing that of his bladder. He walked to the window, looked out at the street.

Eventually, he said, 'Did you notice the red MGB sportscar behind your Skoda.'

'No, I ran in - it was raining.'

'It's my young neighbour Justin's pride and joy. He's spent months doing it up and watches over it like a mother hen.'

The memory of the jolt as she backed into the space assailed her mind. It had been a rather more forceful bump than was her usual.

'He was watching from his window,' she said, the significance of the strangely energetic wave now hitting her. *God, I hope I haven't chipped his paintwork*, she inwardly panicked, knowing that the height of a sportscar bumper must be considerably lower than that on her Skoda.

Wally sat back down, leaned towards her. 'Go on, stay the night,' he urged, 'this is a two-bedroomed flat - in case you were wondering.'

'I can't, I've arranged to stay with my old friend Dolly Potter who lives at Clapham Common. I told her I'd get there before eleven tonight. I told Buzz I was going there too.'

'Better make the most of you then,' he sighed.

The ring of a doorbell suddenly pierced the air.

'Wonder who that is,' said Wally, glancing at his watch, then hurrying out.

There was the sound of doors opening, then a muffled conversation. She looked around again, noting that all the upholstered chairs were covered in a bluish-grey fine textured fabric, so much more tasteful than Buzz's. But then that would apply to the seats in an airport lounge, or a grotty train, she realised, knowing the comparison meant nothing.

'Look who's come to see you,' beamed Wally, ushering a slim young man in.

She recognised the face and swallowed hard. Had he come to remonstrate and demand her insurance details?

'This is my very good friend Maeve Salmon. This my very good neighbour Justin Jones,' said Wally innocently.

Justin Jones cast her an embarrassed grin. 'Hiya Maeve, saw you arrive - thought you'd clouted my car, that's why ...' He stopped, stuck out his hand, grabbed hers and shook it energetically. 'He's told me a lot about you - said you looked glam for your age, and you do.'

Pleased by the *glam*, and annoyed by the *for your age*, she nevertheless felt herself flush.

'See, I told you she blushed, just like my Nellie,' exclaimed Wally, as if showing off a prize rose.

As knowing looks passed between them, she wondered how much these two unlikely companions confided in each other. She hoped he hadn't gone into the distressing details of his back going out in the car or his shoulder on her sofa.

'I did give it a little tap,' she blurted, giving in to her conscience.

'Give what a little tap?' exclaimed Wally, no doubt wondering if he'd missed something meaningful during one of their painful grapplings.

'His car. I gave his car a little tap as I parked.'

'I know, I saw you,' whooped Justin, 'but I've had a butchers and there's no harm done - nineteen seventy-one, they knew how to make cars then: chrome bumpers, black leather interior, the lot, it's wicked.' Then he grinned round at Wally, saying, 'You said she was honest mate, and that just proves it.'

A momentary stab of guilt at how dishonest she was being with Buzz was overtaken by pique at being talked about as if she wasn't there - once again. 'If it's honesty you want,' she said curtly, 'I thought the clothes you advised Wally to buy were ludicrous at his age.'

Justin, dressed in jeans with raggety holes in the knees and a bright turquoise shirt, looked shocked. 'Not ludicrous for a great bloke like him, he's so young at heart.'

And suddenly she was seeing her old codger bridge partner with new eyes: a man looked up to by young trendies, or at least one of them.

And, later, when Justin insisted that they went round to his place for her to meet the family, she saw Wally with even newer eyes, seeing the warmth with which he was greeted by Jennifer and John Jones, Justin's forty-something parents, as well as Jack, Justin's nine-year old brother. In amazement, she watched Wally lark around with the giggling boy, fists high, mock boxing. When a scruffy looking dog bounded in, tail wagging furiously, Justin grabbed hold of its collar, laughing, 'It's a wonder Jacqueline hasn't knocked you over before now, the way she always flings herself at you.'

'Yes, be careful,' Maeve warned.

'Don't worry, we don't want his back going out again' said Jennifer, 'so we don't let the dog out unless Justin or John is here to hold her off.'

Did she imagine the knowing twinkle in her eyes as she mentioned the back. Did he tell the whole family everything?

Justin dragged the excited dog away and Wally ushered her to the sideboard, where a lonesome fish swam around in a large tank.

'Meet Jewel,' he said. 'Do you remember I had to get back to feed a goldfish? Well this is the one.'

'He's a star,' said Jennifer, 'always looks after the fish when we're away.'

Jennifer hooked her arm into Wally's and squeezed it affection-ately.

And the warmth of this contented, ordinary, family, and Wally's acceptance into it touched Maeve. It was something she and Freda had never had and it was beautiful to be part of, if only for a while.

'Why not come round this evening and play cards with us?' Jennifer suggested as they made to go.

'I'd love to,' Maeve said eagerly.

'Can I let you know, after we've eaten,' said Wally, surreptitiously raising an eyebrow at his neighbour, though not so surreptitiously that Maeve didn't see it.

And suddenly she wasn't sure if she'd prefer to play cards with the family, or risk another passionate foray with Wally, risking dodgy joints - and her fragile engagement.

They'd eaten two individual M & S ready-made meals of liver, bacon and mash, beautifully served up by him on white gold-edged plates. To follow came treacle pud, hot from a tin.

'Here, let me top you up again,' he said, refilling her glass for the umpteenth time.

She took a long sip, hearing the calming hum of traffic from outside, seeing the dimmed pink warmth of the small dining room inside. And mellowness seeped into her like the syrup soaking into her pud. She took another slurp, looked across at Wally. His dark wet eyes gazed back adoringly. And a sudden fit of anxiety gripped her. This was all too cosy. Too safe.

'I'd like to do shomething daring,' she pronounced.

'Like what?' he asked, sounding hopeful.

'Like ... like, a parachute jump.'

'What, with *your* old hip.'

'That'sh bloody dishparaging.'

'Not disparaging, practical. Let's face it, you couldn't even jump off this table.'

'Yesh I could,' she said, promptly kicking off her high-heeled sandals and leaping up to her feet.

'No you couldn't,' he argued, like a big kid.

'Could. Could. Could,' she giggled, clambering up onto her chair.

'Hey! Mind that wine glass, it's one of my best ones,' he warned as she lifted one foot onto the plain pink tablecloth.

'Never mind the blooming glassh, what about me,' she cackled, slapping her hands down more than halfway across before lifting the other foot up to join the first, her bottom raised high in the air. His face was now so close to hers she could see the network of veins in his eyeballs, like wiggly streets on two maps.

'Get down!' he roared.

Hysterical with laughter at what brilliant fun it all was, she stayed put, seeing his gaze drop to her breasts which she could feel were dangling close to nipple exposure. 'I feel jusht like a runner on the blocksh, *ready, shteady* ...' she made a jerky movement as if to *go*, just to tease him.

'No, no!' he shrieked, flapping his hands. 'Shoo, shoo. Get back. Get down.'

'Only joking!' she screeched, her ensuing cackle cut short by a sharp stab of pain in the bent nape of her neck.

'Get down before you ruddy well break something,' he commanded, darting his hand past her and moving the cut glass cruet set to one side.

'Yesh, your're right, I'm breaking my neck,' she conceded, awkwardly pushing herself up and, in so doing, propelling her head slap into the dangling lampshade, sending desiccated flies and spiders sailing down in a cloud of dust.

'Now look what you've done, there's a fly in my pud!' he bellowed.

'Waiter, waiter, there'sh a fly in my shoup,' she parodied, killing herself as she turned and stepped to the table's edge, where she stood, arms twirling.

'GET DOWN!' he hollered, dashing round, one hand outstretched.

'Okay, I will,' she pleasantly agreed, launching herself off in a gigantic leap that almost cleared the back of the chair. But not quite.

Thirty four

'So you're not playing cards with us then,' observed Jennifer dryly as she tucked her into the bed.

'Oh, oh, it's agony,' Maeve howled, pain stabbing rhythmically into her back like a mechanical dagger, her right ankle, swollen to bursting point, throbbing a fast counter-beat.

'How's your hip,' asked Wally anxiously.

'It's my back!'

'But how's your hip? She's got arthritis in it,' he explained.

'It's my back. And my ankle,' she wailed. 'They're killing me.'

'But how's your hip?' he persisted.

'Bugger my hip,' she shrieked, screwing up her eyes, sending tears squirting out.

'You should have seen the way she leapt,' he said, almost admiringly. 'Quite amazing. I never thought she'd fly off with such reckless abandon.'

Through her agony, she listened with a modicum of pride, wondering how many women of her age would do that.

'She must have been stark staring mad,' stated Jennifer the ex-nurse, jabbing her scalpel into Maeve's burgeoning ego.

'More likely drunk. If she'd been sober she wouldn't have landed in such a relaxed skew-whiff heap.'

'And that hip of hers would have shattered,' established the know-all nurse.

'Lucky then,' Wally murmured.

Lucky! Sodding lucky! Maeve silently railed. *Call this kind of torment lucky.*

'Very lucky,' Jennifer confirmed.

'She *had* said she'd help clear up the kitchen after the meal, but of course she couldn't,' Wally stated in a disgruntled sort of a way, as if she'd purposely nearly killed herself to get out of it.

And, once again, she was being talked about as if she wasn't there. *Have I turned invisible yet again?* she wondered, raising her head, looking down to check that she, at least, made a bump in the bed.

The beaming face of an astronaut greeted her, his head encased in a large shiny bubble.

'Young Jack sometimes sleeps here when Jennifer and John want a night out,' explained Wally, who must have been watching her. 'He was crazy about *Toy Story* so I bought this duvet cover for him. It's Buzz.'

'Buzz!' she exclaimed, shooting her slumped head back up again.

'Oh dear.' He looked embarrassed. 'Not your Buzz. Buzz Lightyear.'

'For future reference, if you're buying another duvet cover, I'd prefer Mel Gibson,' she grunted.

'See what I like about her. She's so wacky and entertaining,' said Wally, proudly.

I've gone invisible again, she thought, immediately drifting off as Jennifer, in an impressive understatement said: 'The sedative I gave her should work soon.'

She lay curled up in bed, half asleep, senses lulled by the darkness and the drowsy drone of traffic from outside.

'Wakey, wakey,' Wally suddenly whispered in her ear.

She kept her eyes shut, hearing the rattle of a cup on saucer as it was placed down near her head, then his footfalls and the swish of a curtain before a sudden glare of light lit up the darkness beneath her lids, turning her vision orange.

'What about Dolly, she's expecting me,' she cried, blasted into instant full consciousness.

'It's all right,' Wally soothed, bending over her as she squinted up. 'I remembered her name and found her number in the telephone book. She understood.'

'What did she say?'

'What didn't she say!'

'She always yacks.'

Maeve thought back to the time she had stayed with her loquacious friend when she'd left Hector. It was only Dolly's verbal diarrhoea that had driven her back to him.

'I think the gist of it was that you were always crackers so she wasn't surprised you'd jumped off a table and sprained your ankle.'

'More likely *broken* my ankle. *And* my back.'

'She sounded surprised you were still alive. Trying that kind of thing at her age when her bones are brittle, she'd tutted, going on about the dangers of osteoporosis for at least ten more minutes, by which time I'd virtually stopped listening. Then, thinking she'd weirdly changed the subject to the maintenance of phones, I said that I occasionally wiped mine over with Dettol, which launched her off on a tide of advice about cod-liver oil, et cetera, until I finally managed to get a word in to explain that it was my phones and not my bones I'd been talking about. She then charged on about my obvious deafness and advised me to pay for a hearing aid because her free NHS one affected her bowels. Luckily she didn't go into unsavoury details because she raced on to a new topic stating that she didn't know how you could spend any length of time living out in the sticks, because the country always played havoc with her eyes. Finally, I managed to cut into her torrent of words, lying that I had to go because I'd heard you groaning from the spare bedroom - to which she had sniffed that she'd gone to a lot of trouble making up *her* spare bed and you'd had to selfishly jump off the table into mine.'

He laughed, and, in that gleeful merriment, Maeve thought she recognised not only enjoyment at Dolly's peculiar utterances, but delight that she was laid up in his spare bed and not in Dolly's.

And, even though she could have done without the suffering, she felt comfortable to be in his home with him. As she gazed up at him, a sharp pain spiked into the dull ache that had taken over her ankle. She winced, clasped her hands together - and felt the shock of her new ring.

'I must speak to Buzz,' she groaned.

Wally's body slumped as if the puppeteer holding him up had let go of the strings. He opened his mouth, as if to argue. Closed it again. Took a deep breath, let it out in a long sigh. 'I'll bring the phone in here so you can talk privately,' he said, shuffling out.

'Hello Buzz.'

'And wasn't I just talking about you Mauve, how are you?'

'In agony. I can't walk.'

'Join the club,' he sniggered, quickly adding: 'Sorry to hear that so I am, are you at your pal Dolly's?'

'Um, no. I couldn't get there. I'm still at Wally's - I popped in to see him first.'

She stared up, seeing a cobweb in the corner of the high ceiling, waiting for the fallout, but he seemed remarkably unaffected by the news.

'Fizzy came in today and told me I could put weight on my foot and dispense with the crutches, so hadn't I better get them over to you,' he said brightly.

His jolly response was not in line with a man desirous of getting his beloved fiancée back, she realised.

'You called me Mauve, so I suppose Sophia's out of earshot.'

'That she is, and almost out of my life. She'll be leaving soon.'

But, strangely, that news failed to cheer her.

'And what about Georgie, I suppose he's going with her?'

'No, no. He's staying, helping me get the garden in shape, carrying on where I left off, turning it into an even more bird-friendly area.'

'I'm *really* pleased,' she said, perturbed at the realisation that she seemed to feel happier about eventually returning to the company of her step-son-to-be than to her husband-to-be. She extended her right hand, twisted it from side to side, observing the ring. And sadness embraced her in its glinting purple light.

'The medication I'm on is making me feel woolly-headed,' she half fibbed, knowing the confusion she felt was more to do with him than the pills she was taking.

'You're always woolly-headed,' he said gently. 'That's what I liked about you.'

He said liked, *in the past tense, and still hasn't uttered the love word*, she thought, strangely relieved.

'So when do you think you'll be back then?' he asked.

'Apparently it'll be about a week before I can drive. Do you think you can manage till then?'

'Sure, it'll be great, just the two of us.'

Again, strangely, that statement didn't upset her, though she knew that it should have.

'What reason has Sophia given for leaving?' she asked out of curiosity more than anything.

'No reason from her. I just told her she's stayed long enough and had to go, so she agreed that she'd get back to her Giuseppe.'

'Thought he was away.'

'Due back tomorrow by all accounts. Good luck to them - I think they're suited to each other.'

No need to ask in which way they were suited to each other she reflected after they'd said goodbye, it was patently obvious.

She sat in Wally's fireside chair, a small blow-up pillow in the small of her back, foot propped up on an old wooden box, a large spongy pillow cushioning its top. They'd eaten scrambled eggs on toast from trays on their laps and, between them, had nearly finished the crossword.

'I've got to go out for more food,' he said in a hard-done-by sort of voice, as he arose from the un-reclined recliner that she'd refused to sit in - he seeming to have more or less mastered its mechanical looseness, its back only shooting flat down once, two days ago. As he had awkwardly clambered out of it and wrestled the back up straight, he had laughed in a sad sort of way, saying the chair was used to that position because, before he'd become so busy, he'd always had a horizontal snooze after lunch.

'Why not have a little siesta before you go shopping,' she suggested now.

'No time. No time. What will you do while I'm out?' he said tetchily as he shifted the dirty plate and cutlery from her tray onto his with the maximum amount of noise and fuss.

'Suppose I'll watch telly.'

'Couldn't you do something more useful,' he carped.

'Like what! Do you think I like sitting back being waited on.'

He opened his mouth, clearly thought better of releasing the words that had immediately sprung into it, clamped it shut, swallowed, shrugged, rattling the contents of the stacked trays in his hands in the process.

'Don't you think I'm frustrated and bored,' she cried, banging her foot down then screeching with pain. She made to stand up, thought better of it, and flopped back again, knowing she needed to save all her hopping strength for getting to and from the bathroom.

'Yes of course, of course,' he said gently, his true soft nature bursting out like a beautiful rose overriding its thorny stem. 'I'm just used to caring for someone. It's been years since my dear Nellie was poorly.' He placed the quivering tray down, dutifully readjusted the position of her back-supporting pillow, then suddenly exclaimed: 'I tell you WHAT you should do ... why not carry on with your NOVEL!'

'I'd *love* to but the computer's down in Wood Hill,' she said, a sudden spear of yearning impaling her heart, inflicting yet more pain. How she longed to get typing.

'I'll get you a pen and paper,' he said eagerly. 'You can write out the next bit, then, if you stay on, I'll buy a computer.'

And, from the intensity of his gaze as he stared down at her, she knew that despite the obviously unwelcome extra work she was giving him, he wanted her there and what he meant was: If you stay on, maybe you'll stay here for good. And probably, deep inside his mind a voice was saying: *because she won't always be lazing around with a bad back and a swollen ankle, in a week she'll be up and running, and then I can snooze after lunch while she goes out to do the shopping.*

'I thought you must have a computer already - you once said you could get me going,' she remarked as he handed her a lined pad. She remembered at the time wondering if he really could get her going. Now she stared at his kind anxious face and wondered again.

'Justin lets me use his. He's very good at explaining, so I do know the basics. If you write the next episode down, I'm sure he'd set up a file and let you type it in later.'

'Give us a pen then, but I probably won't be able to think of a thing.'

But, as soon as he left the house, the ball point started flying.

Each morning after breakfast, she thought about the story, scrawling down new thoughts on the characters, new twists in the plot. Each lunchtime they'd do the cryptic crossword together as they ate, before he dashed off stating he had to tackle some chore or other. Each afternoon she'd scribble out more of the story. And at some time during most evenings he'd get her to read it out loud to him.

'You say that Tron, the sandy-haired so-called Black-sail-man, is back on Sydney Harbour wind-surfing each day,' he observed, 'so he doesn't spend much time with his wife and new baby then?'

'No, he's very single-minded about his hobby. They all are. All his friends in the flotilla. They've adapted the boards to practically fly and are practising flipping over in great high loops.'

'Isn't that a bit selfish of him?'

'If it's to the exclusion of everything else, I suppose it is,' she agreed, wondering if bird-watching every spare second was in the same category as wind-surfing every spare second, deciding it possibly was.

'So Venus is attracted to Tron's looks, and that's all there is to it?' he said, his hands gripping tightly at the arms of the recliner.

And she wasn't sure if it was to control the chair from flopping back, or to control his feelings.

'Suppose so.'

'And as she gets to know what lies beneath Jupe's skin, will she fall in love with him?'

Did she imagine the awareness in his penetrating look? Did he realise he was that big black, kind Negro Jupe, and she was that shallow Venus? *Does he hope that I'll fall in love with him - and am I falling?* she wondered, startling herself.

'Maybe, haven't decided yet,' she mumbled. 'Though I doubt it.'

'You haven't explained why Tron is the only one wind-surfing with a black sail,' he observed, releasing and reclamping the arms of the chair in a finely calculated movement allowing enough flop to tilt him into a semi-reclining position.

'I've still got to work that out,' she admitted.

Six days later and, though her back was completely okay, she still couldn't put full weight down on her foot without it hurting - so driving the car was still impossible. Wally continued to go out every afternoon to rev up her engine, though if he'd really wanted her to stay he'd surely have left it to seize up. But, maybe a man's mind didn't work in such devious ways - especially the mind of an ex-engineer.

'When does your Novel Group meet again?' he asked as she limped into the kitchen. 'It would be good for you to get feedback more expert than mine - I could run you there and pick you up if you liked.'

For some reason her heart really lurched, she truly felt it bang into her ribs, though whether it was due to the idea of reading out to the Group again, or heartfelt emotion at his thoughtfulness, she couldn't fathom.

'It's usually the first Tuesday in the month, but they said it sometimes changed in the summer. I'll give Hugos Thayre a ring, but first things first,' she said, wresting the potato peeler from him.

'What're you doing!'

'Taking over. You've done enough and I can stand now.'

His face brightened, then he said anxiously: 'There's broccoli and sausages to cook and I was going to mash the potatoes.'

'I know how to cook a dinner!' she laughed, 'and thanks to your care, I'm practically back to normal. So, go on, relax, watch the news, or finish our crossword.'

He cast her a tired appreciative smile and, after he'd tottered off, she searched for some rubber gloves but could find none. Luckily though, she did spot the sunflower oil hidden behind a hexagonal tube of J-cloths inside the sink cupboard. Quite glad to be cooking again, she poured a little oil into a frying pan, heated it up, spread out the sausages, then hobbled out to get her flip-top telephone/address book from her bedroom. She hurried back and, with one eye on the sizzling bangers, dialled Hugos' number.

'We're meeting tonight,' he said in answer to her question. 'Tried to let you know, but your phone just kept on ringing.'

'I've let my house out, maybe they're away, but I'm with a friend in Tooting Bec at the moment, so I can come.' Excitement and fear surged through her. 'Why did you change the date?' she asked, reaching across to shake the pan.

'I always go to Wales at the start of August. I like walking in the rain amongst the sheep, they're a friendly lot.'

'Who, the Welsh?'

'No, the sheep. The Welsh mostly stay inside when there's a downpour, that's another bonus. Not that I dislike the Welsh. I just don't like people around'

Weird pictures of Hugos communing with soggy agreeable sheep popped into her mind as she replaced the phone. But as she recklessly delved her bare hands into the muddy water in the bowl, risking dry wrinkled skin, she wondered what the Group would think about the way her novel was panning out, knowing it could hardly perplex them more than it was perplexing her. She lifted a potato and, as she started to peel it, she gazed through the window to the paved patio garden that was dotted with colourful tubs of geraniums and trailing lobelia. It had been a treat lazing out in deck chairs yesterday when the afternoon sun had come round. No grass to cut either, so no danger on that score.

She plopped the potato into a saucepan and hoiked out another, absently watching a bird flitting in and out of the honeysuckle, her gaze sharpening as she spotted its rusty coloured cap. Surely a female blackcap. She'd never seen one before but recognised it from a photo she'd seen in Buzz's *Guide to Birds*. Inexplicable excitement flooded over her. Bird watching was more fascinating than she'd first thought. It wasn't a selfish hob ...

The smell of burning hit her nostrils at the same instant as the shrill bips of a smoke alarm hit her ears. She whipped round, seeing clouds of smoke rising up from the stove.

'All right, all right, I *know*,' she yelled up at the white box still boisterously bipping. She dived at the frying pan, scooped it up off the gas, shook it vigorously, but not one blackened sausage moved.

'What's going on?' Wally's faint voice called from the sitting room.

'Nothing,' she shouted, banging the pan back down and skittering round the kitchen to find a broom to poke up at the high alarm to dislodge its casing. But all she found was rejuvenated black smog billowing up from the pan she'd mistakenly replaced on the lighted hob.

As she wrenched the gas tap round and lifted the pan, Wally crashed in.

'What do you *mean* by this,' he bawled, flacking his hands, dispersing the pollution in her direction, making her cough.

'Stop ... stop doing that,' she croaked.

'What do you *mean* by this,' he said again, now flacking his hands so energetically the smoke spiralled round like mad whirling dervishes.

'Well-cooked sausages ... I like them like that,' she blustered.

'What do you *mean* by ...' he started again.

'For Pete's sake shut *up*,' she cried above the insistent bip that was driving her crazy. His lips clamped shut and, despite the deepset hurt that she saw in his extra damp eyes, she bawled: 'The smoke alarm is over-reacting. For God's sake turn the bloody thing off.'

'Over-reacting! OVER-REACTING!' he exploded in an over-reactive bellow, lips quickly back to full mobility, eyes quickly back to full flashing anger. 'That smoke alarm has just saved our LIVES.'

He dashed one hand across his eyes, flicking a teardrop out sideways, though whether it was a tear of rage, or emotion, or just its normal rheuminess, Maeve wasn't certain.

Suddenly, he propelled himself upwards in a flurry of jumps, arms stretched, reaching higher and higher, until, with a shout of triumph, his fingers made contact with the bipping torturer and he flipped its front flap down.

'It's still going,' she needlessly said as he shot up in a final stupendous leap, clawing the wires and battery out all at the same time.

'I *like* my bangers well done,' she shouted into the blissful silence.

'So I see,' he panted, his eyes on the contents of the frying pan which she was shaking fiercely.

'It's a skill, getting it just right,' she muttered, giving another shake, desperate for some movement.

He cast her a grim look. 'Have you ever thought of working in a crematorium?' he asked, snatching the pan from her, poking one sausage with his digit finger, forcing it over like a dead animal, revealing its charred underbelly.

'I'll scrape off the surface - it works with burnt toast,' she reassured him.

'Hmm. Might work. But remember, pork's a lot different from bread.'

'I'll try.'

'Try what?'

'To remember.'

'Remember what?'

'Pork's a lot different from bread. I'll tell Freda too.'

'Very funny.'

'Well at least the kitchen hasn't burnt down,' she said, having glanced around during their exchange of words and seen that the wooden wall units around the stove weren't even scorched.

He glared around. 'Not burnt down maybe, but look, there's sooty black on the sides of those cupboards - and the tiles should be white, not that smudgy grey.'

'I'll sponge them down. You go back to the other room and relax while I clean up and prepare the meal.

'Relax! Fat chance!' he scoffed, though in a kindly manner, considering.

During the meal, the burnt bangers were consumed with totally unconvincing 'yummy' murmurs from Wally and she was consumed with totally realistic fear about what was coming next.

'Okay. Get your four pages out ready for the Novel Group and we'll be off,' he stated, patting his lips, transferring black charcoal bits to his mauve-stained handkerchief.

More humiliation on two fronts, she brooded. One on a sheet of white cotton. The other on four sheets of white paper.

Thirty five

She limped into Hugos' sitting room, the last one to arrive, having directed Wally, against his better judgement, into a one-way system which he wilfully drove round twice - just to show her - before heading off for Dickens Road.

'Glad to see you,' said Dora Dome, with no sign of malice.

How would she feel if she knew she was staying at Wally's, she thought, as she took a vacant chair.

'I'm sorry I've missed a few meetings ...' she started.

'You haven't missed one,' Dora said, checking her notebook. 'You were present for the last one at the beginning of July. It's almost two months since any of us met up.'

She could scarcely believe it. All that had been happening in her life and she hadn't missed a single meeting!

'Hope you've been persevering with your promising novel,' James Joist said.

'Me too,' said Shirley Shakespeare, roundly smiling, 'Can't wait to hear what happens next.'

'It's so good for us all to be back together,' beamed comely Abigail, flexing her upper arms, forcing her breasts together forming spectacular cleavage.

And contentment settled on her like a favourite old cardi. It *was* good for them all to be back together. This shabby room in Tooting with all this literary talent was where she belonged.

'Let's start with you then Shirley,' said Dora, red pen poised.

In a breathy dramatic voice, Shirley explained that the title *Two into One Will Go* has been renamed *Two into One Won't Go*. Then, when asked, she refused to say why, but Maeve guessed it must be something to do with her personal life because she'd heard Conan, who sat beside her, whisper to Abigail that Parsnip had left her.

After Shirley had read her four pages and they'd all had their say it was Hugos' turn and the main drama in his four pages was that the man in love with his postman discovers that his wife is in love with him too.

'That's pretty neat,' observed Shirley.

'Yes, brilliant,' said Conan Coconut. 'Has this happened to you?'

'What do you mean,' said Hugos, looking shifty.

'Well, you being our postman - there's this odd couple down our road ...'

'We haven't got time for chitchat,' said spoil-sport Dora just as it was getting interesting.

Civil Roar came next, read with precise diction by James.

'Did you say neither ... or,' ventured Abigail.

'I certainly did *not*,' thundered James, with more vehemence than if she'd accused him of raping her.

That little spat over, and James' deep furrows easing back into the normal network of shallow creases, Dora turned to her.

'Now Maeve, let's hear your excerpt, it'll be the last reading of the evening.'

'What about you?' she asked. 'Aren't you going to read?'

'Next time. I've only just started.'

'Oh do tell us,' gushed Shirley, 'what is it called?'

'Bridge over Troubled Daughter - it's semi-autobiographical.' She cast Maeve an enigmatic glance which made her worry about the bridge part.

Expectant eyes were now fixed on her so she took out her hand-written pages and, all fear banished by the bonhomie of the Group and the knowledge that her writing was good, if not superb, she started to read:

'Not going out to play cards with Geranium tonight then?' Venus asks.

'No, I'd prefer to be in with you,' Jupe replies.

She looks up, grateful for the devotion shining in his dark eyes, wondering if he, after all, is the one she truly cares for. Ironic really. All that time wasted longing for the handsome stranger, a man who already had a wife and son.

As she read, she realised that Dora could have no inkling that Venus and she, the author, had become one, and that Geranium was her, and Jupe was Wally, their mutual friend.

At last she had reached the last page:-

Later, as they eat, Venus appreciates, probably for the first time, how good it feels to share her life with a trusted friend who loves her and knows who she is. Someone who loves her DESPITE knowing who she is, she muses, smiling to herself. A man who, rather belatedly, she is learning to truly appreciate.

She held her breath, waiting for the acclaim. But there was an off-putting silence, broken at last by James Joist who said in that clipped perfect way of his: 'It's still fascinating and has masses of potential, but you've more or less spelt out what the outcome will be and it's too predictable.'

'Yes,' said Dora, 'it'll turn into a Mills and Boon, or one of the trashy love stories you read in some magazines. She'll live happily ever after with a good man. The end.'

Wally was waiting outside in his car as she mooch-limped out.

'Thanks for collecting me,' she said flatly.

'Did they like it?' he asked eagerly, turning the ignition key.

'They thought the outcome was becoming too predictable.'

'That's what I was beginning to think,' he said.

And he wondered why she thumped him. Though she was sorry that it caused him to break his wing mirror on the telegraph pole as they veered left.

Neither of them spoke as they drove back and, as she listened to the constant sound of the engine labouring in too high a gear, she gazed sightlessly out of the window. Okay, she thought at last, okay, if that's how you all want it, Venus will leave Jupe, which means I will leave Wally.

But as he carefully helped her out, murmuring that it was only a wing mirror and he understood her disappointment because her writing meant so much to her and that maybe everyone was wrong and the predicable ending was the best and that she had to mind her ankle because she didn't want to twist it again, she was so overcome by his sympathetic understanding that she changed her mind.

The next evening they went to the bridge club where she was greeted like a long lost friend by a host of people. She hadn't realised how much she'd missed them, or how important it was to belong to groups of like-minded people. Even during the inquests after each hand, with Wally going on about her *outrageous bidding* and *appalling defence*, she found she enjoyed the cut and thrust of the arguments almost as much as the playing of the cards.

Early next morning, still stimulated by the lively spats and mental challenges, she leapt out of bed, bounded to the bathroom, then realised with a shock that there was no pain. As she squeezed out the Sensodyne, her hand shook. Now there was nothing to stop her driving back to her fiancé. She scrubbed at her teeth, knowing that she didn't want to leave this warm haven, but that she had to go back to tell Buzz their engagement was off. But, as she spat foam into the basin, she worried that Wally would then expect her to marry him. *I've become fond of him*, she thought. *He's such a kind, lovely man. Maybe I'm even in love with him!* Again, the thought stunned her. Confused, she decided to do and say nothing for a day.

'Maeve,' Wally said tentatively as, with a forced limp, she joined him in the sitting room that evening. 'Do you ever have cravings for sex?'

'Mmm,' she admitted with an air of deliberate vagueness, wondering where this line of talk was leading.

'So, do I,' he mumbled, looking down at his slippers. 'My father was lucky,' he continued, as if talking to the chequered fawn uppers. 'He was at it till the day he died.

'What, the very day?'

'The very second actually. He always said that was how he wanted to go.'

She thought about how terrible that would have been if Hector had died upon her. 'Bad luck for your mother,' she said.

'The woman next door actually.'

'Oh. How old was he?'

'Eighty-nine. It was fortunate he died before my mother *and* the woman next door, it meant he never had to, you know, fend for himself in that direction.'

'Wank, do you mean?'

'Yes,' he muttered to his slippers, the toes of which wiggled.

'Well, no problem then.'

'But it's not the same,' he told his slippers. 'The uncontrollable urge goes, but you haven't had the tenderness and love of a good woman. No, it's not the same by a long shot.'

He dragged his gaze up to her, his brown satin eyes conveying covert emotions and overt messages in their profound depths.

Amazingly, his timing was perfect for it was one of those occasions when, for no apparent reason, she was switched on.

'Do you want to go to bed then?' she asked boldly. 'Is that what you're saying?'

'Would you?' he gasped.

'I'm out of practice, but yes.'

'As out of practice as you are at bridge,' he tittered nervously.

'More so.'

'Oh my God!' Theatrically, he passed the back of his hand across his brow, then dived over, pulling her up to her feet. Awkwardly, they stood facing each other, then, gently, he kissed her full on the mouth.

'You know I do love you,' he whispered when, at last, their lips had parted.

'So you've said,' she quavered, now struck by nerves as he took hold of her hand and started to lead her. 'But before, you know, before we ... I must ...'

She shook his hand off and dashed to the bathroom, ostensibly to spend a penny but in reality to get to her toilet bag and the tube of KY.

'Are you on HRT?' he asked later as, giddy with the joyous fulfilment of satisfied sex, they lay snuggled together.

'No need ... I'm still ... choc-o-bloc with hormones,' she yawned, immediately zonking out.

A gentle shaking of her shoulders woke her.

'I've had my breakfast and it's nearly nine o'clock,' Wally informed her.

'Sex seems to make you need more sleep when you're older,' she murmured.

'Perhaps not quite so choc-o-bloc with hormones,' he said with a kindly laugh, kissing the tip of her nose. 'Why not take a shower to wake yourself up,' he suggested, handing her her dressing gown as she staggered out of his bed. 'Have you thought about Buzz?' he asked anxiously, following her into the bathroom.

'Yes,' she said, stretching over the bath and turning the shower on to heat up.

'Are you going to ring him - tell him the engagement's off,' he asked, slipping his arms around her waist and hugging her to him.

'No. I'm not going to ring, I ...'

'But, you must! It's only fair on him - and me.'

'I'm not going to ring because I'm going back to Buzz ...'

'Going back to Buzz! You *Jezebel*!' And, before she could

explain that she needed to tell him face to face, he'd snatched the shower head off the wall and aimed it full at her.

'You PIG!' she cried, as the torrent hit her.

'Well, I was devastated,' he said later, miserably watching her pack.

'I've had enough of your devastations,' she bawled, 'they do nothing for me except soak me through.'

Deliberately, she didn't tell him that she was going to Buzz to break off their engagement and collect her belongings. Two of his drenchings were all one woman could take in one lifetime. She really did care for him, but, let him stew for a while. Serve him bloody well right

Without looking back, she drove off. But, in her wing mirror she could see his forlorn figure, one hand waving feebly, the other dabbing his eyes. When she'd rounded the corner she stopped the car. *Is this any way to treat the man I love?* she asked herself. And the unanticipated question appalled, yet, at the same time, excited her. *Is Wally truly the man that I love?* she asked herself. *Was my erstwhile passion for Buzz merely physical? Just like Venus's lust for the Black-sail-man. And at my age too!* The thought amused her. She pictured Buzz when she'd first met him. So shy and unassuming. The attraction had been instant. *But I quickly learnt we had nothing in common, not intellectually at any rate. Whereas Wally and I, we share the same interests.* And *he is more my age!* Maeve smiled to herself. Then a thorn of guilt unexpectedly pricked her.

What about Hector? How could she be ignoring his existence barely nine months since he had died. Enough time for a human baby to grow from scratch - she smiled once more, reminded of the zany conversation she'd had with Georgie about the gestation period of piglets - but not enough time to get over the loss of a husband, she reflected, quickly serious again. Maeve closed her eyes, her thoughts in turmoil. In that relatively short time she'd become engaged to one man, now fallen for another. But, who was to say how long grieving should take - there weren't rules laid down - and mustn't it depend on the relationship?

Even when I was married to Hector, I didn't feel the deep contentment I feel when I'm with Wally. Hector seemed to think that being a husband meant browbeating ...

She halted the disloyal flow of thoughts, waited to hear his wail of protest, but nothing came. She'd reasoned before that the words she'd had with him since his death were all in her own mind. Now, she hoped, her mind and his spirit could both be free, both resting in peace.

Slowly, she put the car into gear. *Should I put Wally out of his misery - turn back to explain?* she wondered, glancing around the narrow street lined with parked cars. She'd never been much good at three point turns, or even five point ones, come to that. And to go back by driving round the block was nigh impossible because of the one-way system. *No, he'd know soon enough*, she reasoned, firmly releasing the hand brake then pressing down on the accelerator. She'd made up her mind.

As she sped along the motorway, she wondered if Buzz would be as equally devastated as Wally had been when she told him she was going. Somehow, she thought not.

Thirty six

Flashing lights from the car behind forced Maeve into the left lane. You go over seventy, she thought vindictively, there's a camera on the next gantry and you'll be caught.

As she took the slip road off the M3, turning left at the top, the sun burst out, lighting up the beautiful Hampshire countryside and, despite her worries, her spirits lifted. Twenty minutes later she pulled up behind the green Jag outside *The Bungalow*. With a strange kind of ache deep inside her, she walked slowly down the path and, guessing that he'd be round the back on such a fine day, she went round the side. But, the shock that greeted her eyes when she reached the end of *The Bungalow* wall halted her dead in her tracks.

Buzz and Sophia sat at the wrought iron table talking together, their backs to her. His hands cradled the back of his head, his elbows raised high. She absently stroked his wispy underarm hair with the back of her fingers as she murmured to him. It was a scene of such natural intimacy, more revealing than if they'd been having full-blown sex.

Maeve cleared her throat.

They both turned. 'Oh hi Maeve, we were just making plans,' he said, his face flushing pink.

'Plans for Georgio,' Sophia expanded, smiling with her mouth - but not with her eyes.

'Come and join us,' said Buzz. Then, 'No, you stay there, don't move an inch.' He pushed himself up, looked down at his feet, saying: 'Will you note the new shoes.'

Soft lace-ups in pale blue linen or canvas material clad his feet. Tentatively, arms stretched sideways to balance, he slid one foot forward, and she shivered, noticing the slight bulge in the big toe area, and the tell-tale dent alongside. Gingerly he transferred his weight, sliding the intact one to its mutilated partner's side. He glanced up, grinning triumphantly, before returning his attention to his feet.

'So you don't need your crutches any more,' she cried joyously. 'No, look, I can walk!'

He laughed, progressing towards her step by tentative step, his body rolling slightly like a sailor traversing a heaving deck. And the memory of his rolling gate chortles with his wife on the phone flooded back to her.

She glanced across at Sophia, but she wasn't looking.

'Honest to God, it's good that we're each back on our two feet again,' he sighed, finally reaching her. They kissed in a transient meeting of lips that conveyed no passion. 'And how is your ankle?' he asked, as they set off back to the table.

'That's fine now thanks.'

He took his seat next to Sophia, and Maeve sat down opposite her.

'I thought you were going,' Maeve ventured, holding the hard-faced woman's stony stare.

'She is, tomorrow, aren't you Sophia,' Buzz answered.

'Aye, I'm leaving for Italy, but my Georgio, he issa staying.'

Maeve looked deep into her eyes seeing a turmoil of emotion swirling in their murky depths. Maybe Sophia did care for Buzz. Maybe she still loved him, and not just for his money. Her armpit hair caressing had been so natural. She would never have chanced that herself in case he'd been sweating.

'Georgie has said he wants to live here with me,' beamed Buzz.

She noted he said with *me*, not with us. Was he expecting the news she was soon to impart?

'Honest to God, he loves working at Freda's, says it's the kind of life he's always dreamed ...'

'So, woulda your daughter gie the wee chappie a permanent job?' Sophia cut in, flicking the air around her, as if bothered by gnats.

The wee chappie. He was six foot at least!

Their eyes locked and she wondered if Sophia was really saying: *And me, can I live here in this demi-Paradise with my husband and son.*

'Anda maybe I could stay here too,' she said swivelling her eyes to Buzz and smiling coquettishly.

Maeve knew it!

'Hardly,' he said, glancing awkwardly towards her, his fiancée.

'Sure and we don't know there's a job going at FAB CAZ yet anyhow.'

It was then that a plan to test Sophia's sincerity flared into Maeve's mind.

'I'll ask Freda,' she volunteered, adding: 'Sophia, I need to talk to Buzz alone for a minute, so would you mind ...'

'I'll go inside and pack,' she said tersely.

And if looks could kill, Maeve knew she'd be up there with Hector.

After their discussion, Maeve drove round to see Freda.

'Did Wally look after you well?' her daughter asked meaningfully.

'Very well. He's a nice man. I liked being there.'

'So?' Freda raised her palms and her shoulders, Jewish fashion.

And Maeve couldn't tell by the gesture or the look on her daughter's face if she was exhibiting gladness or displeasure in anticipation of what she thought was to come.

'So what?' Maeve asked, deciding she wouldn't say a thing until all was settled, which it certainly wasn't yet.

Freda pushed a wayward corkscrew curl back off her forehead. She must have been to Raymond's during the week Maeve deduced, thinking how fetching her fifty-two year old daughter looked with her hair re-permed and back to the vibrant titian colour of her youth.

'You look lovely,' Maeve exclaimed, an unexpected ache taking over her heart at the thought that maybe she'd soon be leaving her.

'Why thanks mother,' Freda said, visibly glowing.

And Maeve wondered why she hadn't praised her daughter more over the years.

'We're eating soon, stay and have dinner,' Freda urged. 'Georgie's been helping us out, he's upstairs now cleaning himself up. He'll be with us too.'

'Thanks. I'd really like that.'

'Is your ankle okay to come out and see the piglets first?'

'Yes, it's fine now.'

'You must see them, they're so cute, and after all you are their great-great-grandmother.'

'I'd *love* to see them,' she said, suddenly overcome by a feeling she couldn't put a name to but was significant and something to do with being part of a family, albeit pigs.

As Freda opened the back door to go out into the garden, Hermione ambled in and Freda bent down, patting her snout and making soft crooning noises.

'Poor darling, she's getting old,' she said, casting a worried look at her cherished porker. Then the sad look of concern slid on to her mother, but she didn't say anything though Maeve guessed what she was thinking. She wondered whether to put her mind at rest by describing the satisfying afternoon she'd spent in bed with Wally, but decided against it, knowing there were some special moments one couldn't divulge to a daughter.

The raucous snorts and squeals of the latest generation filled the air as they drew near.

'Just listen to them,' Freda laughed, bounding up the ramp and through the swing doors into the mobile home.

Grinning, Freda stood back for her mother to enter the hot atmosphere, filled with the pungent smells of straw and pig, and the din of eight piglets vying for the juiciest dugs at the milk bar. And, even though she wasn't usually that way inclined, the sight of those babies swarming all over the sleeping Princess really did touch Maeve, though, at the same time, it also made her profoundly thankful she'd only ever produced one.

'Haven't they grown and aren't they adorable,' Freda crowed, leaning over the make-shift partition and lifting a plump smooth wriggling piglet from the seething mass, shoving it snout-first at her.

Truly adorable,' Maeve agreed, deciding not to upset Freda by mentioning that its extra long nose gave it a peculiar horsy look.

'Take it, it won't bite you,' she said, pushing the wild-eyed, squirming creature at her.

Reluctantly, she clasped its body. Immediately, it emitted a stream of high-pitched squeals and a torrent of hot pee.

'You know I'm no good with bodily secretions,' Maeve shrieked, shoving it back at her.

'You naughty Royal,' chuckled Freda, tapping the piglet's long nose, placing it back down with the others.

'Royal?' Maeve queried, momentarily distracted from the repugnance of her urine-splashed feet.

'Being Princess's babies, we've called all six females after Princesses,' she explained. 'This is the Princess Royal - because of the horsy look. See that perfect beauty over there, that's Grace. That one drinking a lot is Margaret. That one with its legs in the air is Stephanie.'

'What about the males?' Maeve asked, cutting short the list, anxious to get back to the bathroom to wash her feet.

'There's one there. See his testicles. That's Norton. And there's the other, he's called Clarey. I know they're both queens but it's the nearest we could get.'

As, cracking up at the warped wit, and arm in arm, they retraced their steps, she again realised how much she was going to miss being close to Freda. That's if it came to it. She wasn't so sure now.

Clean of foot and hands, Maeve sat at their kitchen table.

Georgie came bounding in and crashed noisily down opposite her.

'They've said I can work here permanently, yesssss!' he whooped, raising his shoulders, scooping both fists in the air, looking about to punch his own face.

'Congratulations,' Maeve said, delighted it had been organised between them and not as a favour to her.

'He's a great help,' said Freda fondly, handing out baked potatoes piled high with tuna. 'Help yourselves to salad.'

'What's it like living in Italy?' Bernard asked, knifing mayonnaise out from a jar.

Contentedly, Maeve listened to the conversation only half taking it in, her mind always drifting back to Buzz. *He hadn't seemed to really mind when she'd told him she wasn't staying. He wasn't devastated. Not like Wally.* Georgie was enthusing about the beautiful Umbrian scenery; the exuberant warmth of the Italians, though not Giuseppe, who merely put up with him while he recuperated after being gored. *Buzz had pretended to be upset that their engagement was off. Yes, she was sure it was pretence, though he'd said all the right things.* Freda asked if Georgie had missed London. Just his friends, he said, not the dirty streets, not the ugly buildings. Maeve thought about defending city life but then decided against it, after all where he'd been brought up, on a council estate in Kilburn, might not have been the most attractive of places. *Buzz had protested when she'd returned his ring, but in the end he'd taken it saying she must have the computer in its place. My finger's not big enough she'd joked, kissing him, overwhelmed by his kindness. With that computer she could finish off the thing that meant most to her. He had taken her hands in his, thanking her for being there with him when he needed support. He said they'd always be best friends.*

'You're not saying much,' said Freda.

Maeve fluttered her right hand about for her to see that the ring that had so upset her had gone, but she didn't notice. 'Sorry I'm not much company - just a bit tired after the journey,' she justified, which was mainly true.

'No wonder, it's a long drive,' Freda said, turning to Georgie adding, 'because she's not getting any younger.'

And to her surprise, she didn't feel riled, either by the content or the cliché. Maybe she was mellowing, she thought sleepily, mellowing with age and just happy to be sharing precious time with three lovely people in the warm atmosphere of her daughter and son-in-law's home.

'I hear your parents met up in Scotland, though you were brought up in London,' said Bernard. 'Have you ever been there?'

Maeve was still only half-listening, as Georgie started telling about a holiday up in the Highlands with Buzz. *How would Sophia be responding to the test they'd devised, she wondered, wishing she could invisibly flit there to see.* 'I was fifteen,' said Georgie, 'and we met up with a couple of dad's old roustabout friends and went shooting with dogs.' *What was that he said? Buzz shooting! The Buzz she knew and once fancied wouldn't go shooting. Would he? Did she really know him? Hardly, she realised. To marry him would have been foolhardy. And maybe fun. She almost wished they had made it together on the bed that time. But not quite. Two men in quick succession at any age, let alone ...*

'My dad had a shot gun,' continued Georgie, abruptly re-focusing her drifting thoughts. 'I had an air rifle. The other two shot dozens of pigeons and rabbits, but dad and I had shot nothing all day. A raven appeared, high up, directly overhead, its wings outstretched, lazily gliding on thermals. They take young birds and eggs, dad had said, taking aim, so I suppose if I have to shoot anything it had better be this one. I remember the gun exploding and the bird crashing down through branches, landing almost at our feet. Dad picked it up before the dogs got to it. He looked so sad, but all he said was: Just look how black it is.'

It was then that Maeve knew she had the ending to *Twenty Ninety-Five*.

Georgie stayed at Freda's. Maeve drove back alone. The hall light had been left on, but the rest of *The Bungalow* was in darkness. She let herself in, smelling the faint rotten-apple sweetness of Sophia's perfume still polluting the air. She crept down the passage, seeing in the dim light that his door at the end was firmly shut. She passed her old bedroom, wondering if its door was shut to make her think Sophia was in there. Maybe she wasn't a gold digger. Maybe she'd proved that she loved him and was snuggled up with him in bed. For Buzz's sake, she hoped that she was.

Maeve undressed, lowered herself down to the mattress still made up on the study floor, thrilling as she saw the clock showed 11.11. When next she looked, her heart quickened. It was 5.55. The fates were with her. Now was the time. She threw on her dressing gown, punched on the computer, tip-toed to the bathroom, then hurried back, sat down at the desk, tried to remember the stage she'd reached in her hand-written notes, then, when it was clear in her mind, started typing:

Satty's face looms up on the vid-phone screen set in Venus's kitchen wall. Her violet eyes stare coldly at Venus. 'Hi,' she says without smiling, 'I wasn't expecting you to contact me so soon - last time I had to wait five years.'

'I have to know something,' Venus states bluntly.

'About Tron and Bria?'

'About Tron.'

'Are you still spying on him from your garden - still yearning for him?' The tone in her voice is jeering.

'Not now I know him ...'

'Know he's married with a son you mean.'

'Not only that,' Venus says defensively.

'Isn't he good looking enough for you then, in the flesh?'

'He is very good looking, but I need to know something.'

'What?' she asks, heaving a deep sigh, glancing over her shoulder, obviously wanting to go.

'Why is he the only one windsurfing with a plain black sail?'

'How should I know,' Satty laughs.

'But I have to know,' insists Venus. 'You're on the World Government Committee, won't you make enquiries for me. Please.'

'Don't know why I should,' Satty says sullenly, 'but I suppose I could ask.'

Thirty seven

Maeve stopped typing, hearing the faint sound of the toilet flushing in Buzz's en suite next door. Was that him - or could it be Sophia? What did it matter anyway.

She picked through a pile of her clothes folded neatly in the corner - obviously tidied by Mrs Norris after she'd left - extracting the silver satin bra and panties bought at Lovely Lynda's and her loose navy T-shirt and comfortable jeans.

In the kitchen she set the percolator going and as the pops and fizzes started up, and the inviting aroma filled the air, Buzz entered, rolling a little, arms stretched out sideways.

'Good morning Mauve,' he said, taking her right hand, kissing the bare third finger.

'Is she still here?'

'Indeed she is.'

She poured the coffee, handed his mug over.

'Don't keep me in suspense then. What happened? Did you keep to the plan?'

She glimpsed the wide open door and went over, pulling it almost shut.

He twisted a chair round, sat astride it, tugged on his pony tail.

'Exactly as we'd said. First, I told her our engagement was off and you were going back to London, and she went trilling on about how grand it was going to be, just the three of us together again. Then I said I'd lost nearly all my money on bad stocks and shares investments.'

'What did she say?'

'She went deathly silent. But, when I said I was having to sell *The Bungalow* and was going to buy a small two up, two down, in the village, she exploded, telling me I'd always been a stupid eejit.' He looked upset.

'Is she going back to Giuseppe then?'

'After a load more ranting on about me always being a loser, she stomped off to bed without saying.'

'Would you like her to stay?'

'Aye, woulda you like me to stay?' said Sophia, flinging the door open and stalking in. She stood, arms folded, glowering at Buzz and then at Maeve. 'Woulda Mr No-Money like me to stay?' Her lips were twisted into thin red sneering threads.

Buzz gazed at her with sorrowful eyes. 'No I wouldn't,' he said softly. 'Once upon a time, yes, but now I know what you're really like, no, I wouldn't like you to stay.'

'And I wouldna stay if you paid me,' she screamed.

'I can see Georgie outside in the lane, he'll soon be with us,' Maeve warned.

'Are you packed and ready for the airport?'

'Packed and justa *dying* to go. Nae doot you told *her* you'd lost your money afore me and that's why she's dumped you too,' she jeered.

Just then the bell rang.

'You're wrong Sophia,' Buzz said. 'Maeve is leaving for personal reasons. I haven't lost my money, it was a ploy to test you. And I'm sorry to say that you passed with flying colours. Honest to God, I kind of hoped that you wouldn't.'

The taxi had taken Sophia off and, whilst Georgie was in the office packing up her computer, Maeve telephoned the S. State Estate Agency. Then she rang Jatinder.

'Sure you know you can stay as long as you want Mauve,' said Buzz a while later as she collected all her things together from the bedroom that had been hers before Sophia came. 'I like you being here,' he said, sitting down on the bed. 'It's a pity it didn't work out'

'I'm sorry too, but, well, as I said, there's the age difference. And also there's Wally. I really do care for him.'

'I still can't believe you're as old as you say you are, but it would have made no difference to me, honest to God.'

'It would in a few years.'

'Well, maybe.'

'You've changed you know,' she said, opening a drawer and finding all her old hair pins, combs, elasticised bands and sprung clips she'd almost forgotten about. 'You were so shy when I first met you.'

'It's what money does I suppose,' he said, self-consciously laughing. 'Gives you the whip hand.'

'Maybe the shyness was what appealed to me most,' she said, taking out a handful of combs, placing them with loving care into a plastic bag.

'You mean you wanted to mother me.'

'Not what I'd had in mind,' she giggled, 'You made me feel like a teenager not a mum.'

Thrilling to the feel of fine metal pins, she gathered them up, placed them in with the combs. Soon she'd be back to her old self. Soon these would again be part of her. She placed the bag in with the rest of her stuff and zipped up the grip.

'Well, that's that,' she said.

Buzz stood, taking her loosely in his arms. 'Come down and spend holidays with us - it's a nice quiet spot for an OAP,' he whispered.

'You blighter!' she shrieked as he burst into laughter.

And, just as they used to, they both fell about.

'What's so funny?' grinned Georgie, coming in.

'Just an old people's joke,' he spluttered.

'I've wedged everything into your boot, bolstered with masses of old newspapers, so they shouldn't shift,' Georgie said.

'Unless you start driving like Schumacher now that your parachute jumping days have been knocked on the ankle by your table leaping!' said Buzz.

'*I'll* be driving like Schumacher when you next come down,' Georgie said, his dark eyes sparkling.

'What do you mean?'

'Dad's going to teach me to drive in his Jag, *yesssss*.' He jiggled his fists in the air, doing a kind of war dance.

'I'd better be off while the streets are still safe then,' she said, wiping her eyes to get rid of the blurring.

'Are you absolutely sure your tenants have moved out?' said Buzz.

'Yes, when I rang the Agency this morning to find out if there was a chance I could get back into my house early, I was told that the tenants had unexpectedly just gone. Steven State Junior was about to let me know.'

'And you're sure that Jatinder will be there to help you out with the PC,' checked Georgie, as kindly considerate as his dad.

'Positive. And I can't wait to finish my novel and send it off to a publisher.'

'Let us know when the launch party is,' said Buzz, opening the car door for her.

'There it is Mrs S, no prob, all set up looking just like it used ta look before your old one got nicked.' Jatinder stood back surveying his work.

She looked around the familiar room. Her room. Nobody else's. Like the rest of the house which was just as she'd left it, though definitely cleaner. As S. State Junior had said, she'd been lucky with her tenants, especially as they'd paid for the whole six months and stayed there for just under three.

'Here, take fifty pounds for all your trouble,' she said, sharing her good fortune with her kind-hearted young friend.

'Wow! Gimme five,' he cried jubilantly, raising his palms.

'No. You take the fifty,' she said, touched.

'Mega wicked!' Jatinder took the notes from her, his eyes sparkling. 'Now I can take Cherie to Saturday's Day/Night game at The Oval to see India beat England.'

'What, Cherie Blair?'

'Naw, don't be daft, she's much too old for me. Cherie Patel, she's me new girlfriend, in't she.'

'Just enjoy it,' Maeve advised, 'even if India lose.'

'No way,' he said, grinning, kissing her cheek then bounding out, leaving her alone in her old house.

Hector, please tell me - am I being stupid? But he didn't answer, and she didn't blame him after all the things that she'd said. Slowly, she walked to the phone.

'Hello Wally ...'

Thirty eight

Wally brought round fish and chips which they ate at the small table in her kitchen.

They cleared up then took the champagne he'd also brought into the sitting room.

'Here's to us,' he said, handing Maeve hers as they sat on the sofa.

'Here's to us. You in your place and me in mine.'

'So what you're saying is that you'll live here and I'll live in my house, but when we get lonely or need, you know, a bit of a cuddle and that ...'

'*Then* we can spend a night together,' she spelt out.

'Or an *afternoon* together. Or, if one of us gets very lonely, several days together.' His deepset eyes glistened beneath their bushy white brows.

'Several days! I don't think I'd be up to that,' she giggled.

'I didn't mean, you know, *that*, I meant just being together.'

They each took a slurp.

'That way you can have the love without all the hassle of me living with you,' she pointed out.

'*And* I could have my snooze after lunch too,' he said brightly, obviously warming to the advantages. 'I do love you, you know,' he added, stroking her knee.

'You're just glad to be with someone who remembers the old days!' she teased, feeling his hand drifting round to her inner thigh which amazingly did start to tingle.

'*And* who can bid and get a slam.'

'Okay, yes, all right, *and* who can bid and get a slam,' she retorted, slightly miffed at his ready agreement and the sudden withdrawal of his hand.

There was silence for a while, then he took her right hand in his and caressed the newly released finger, gazing in apparent rapture at its bare state.

'I *am* in love with you,' he reiterated. 'You couldn't have married that Buzz ... he was too ...'

'Too what!'

'Too ... too ...' He looked at her '... too rich,' he said gallantly. 'And, besides, it would never have been right for a Salmon to marry a Pike, he'd eat you for dinner.'

'Yes, far too fishy. All in all this has worked out well.'

'Maeve, there's one thing that worries me in these arrangements,' he said slowly.

'What's that then?'

'I couldn't just blatantly ring you up and, you know, ask to go to bed with you. It wouldn't be gentlemanly.'

'Well how about thinking up a code word to bring into the conversation?'

'Good idea. How about ...' He glanced around '... how about *book*. If I say something like: do you fancy a good book tonight, then you can say yes or no without embarrassment.' He nodded encouragingly, beaming at her.

'Okay, agreed. Anything to do with a book then.'

'So, how d'you fancy reading a book with me tonight?' he asked, squeezing her hand so tightly she winced. She pulled away, knowing she'd be needing those fingers in good working order tonight.

'Sorry, not tonight Wally. I do have an urge. But it's my creative juices that are flowing, not the other sort. Tonight I shall start on the final chapter of *Twenty Ninety-Five*.'

As she sat down and switched on the computer, she knew that at last she was making the final break between her life and Venus's, for the sandy-haired man she'd once fancied would always remain gentle and kind, of that she was sure, whereas her sandy-haired protagonist ...

Venus activates the vid-phone screen incorporated in her bedroom wall.

'Satty Kemp, Kensington,' she states urgently.

After a while, the beautiful face of her friend appears. 'Thanks for getting back to me,' Satty says. 'I've been sworn to secrecy - didn't want either of our partners to overhear.' Her eyes are round and scared looking. Her face is frost white. 'Jupe isn't there is he?'

'No, so tell me what you found out from the World Government Committee.'

'It wasn't them who told me - they didn't know.'

'Well, whoever, so long as I know. Why is he the only one on Sydney Harbour with a pitch black sail.'

Satty shakes her head in agitation, sending her silky hair swirling.

'They say it's a symbol only recognised by members of a secret cult,' she whispers, 'a trophy for carrying out an act that is ...' Satty gulps, 'that is, to decent citizens ... despicable.'

Venus plumps down on the bed. She's never seen Satty shaken like this. She's always been the ice cool one.

'And when the next vile person repeats the crime, Tron will have to give that sail up. Only he's held it for five years now. No-one else has been that evil.'

'What did he do?' Venus asks, her heart thumping. 'What is it that is so dreadful?'

'The cult's aim is to annihilate the few pure-bred native Australians still in existence.'

'Genocide!' Venus gasps.

'Yes. That is their aim. So Tron slaughtered an innocent young Aborigine boy, shooting him twice in the back. It's reported he showed no emotion as the child fell, merely saying: Just look how black it is.'

The phone rang.

'Sorry it's late,' said Wally. 'I've just rung to ask about your novel.'

'I've practically finished, just got to write the final scene where Venus and Jupe scrap their contract partnership and get truly married.'

She waited for him to say: not like us then. But, either he'd not made the connection or else he wasn't talking about it. But then she realised what he meant! A novel was a book. It was his gentlemanly way of asking to go the whole hog! And she was on a high and too excited to sleep.

'Yes. Yes. Wally darling,' she cried, 'come round straight away.'

And, as she stripped off and slipped into her black satin dressing gown, she reflected on how impossible it was to tell the contents of a book by its cover, because last time he'd opened up he'd turned out to be a surprisingly good read.

Two hours later, satisfied beyond belief, they lay snuggled up together.

'You know when I asked about your novel,' he said softly. 'I actually did mean *Twenty Ninety-Five!*'

'What! I thought you said novel because you were too embarrassed to say book.'

'Book again! You're insatiable, but I'm too old for it twice on the trot, give me a day or two.'